The Traveler

>> >> >> >> >> >> >> >>

DON COLDSMITH

BANTAM BOOKS

NEW YORK • TORONTO • LONDON • SYDNEY • AUCKLAND

THE TRAVELER
A Bantam Domain Book / March 1991

DOMAIN *and the portrayal of a boxed "d" are trademarks of Bantam Books,
a division of Bantam Doubleday Dell Publishing Group, Inc.*

ISBN 0-553-28868-7

Published simultaneously in the United States and Canada

---

*Bantam Books are published by Bantam Books, a division of Bantam Doubleday Dell
Publishing Group, Inc. Its trademark, consisting of the words "Bantam Books" and the
portrayal of a rooster, is Registered in U.S. Patent and Trademark Office and in other
countries. Marca Registrada. Bantam Books, 1540 Broadway, New York, New York 10036.*

PRINTED IN THE UNITED STATES OF AMERICA

RAD   0 9 8 7 6

THE STORY FIRES BURNED BRIGHT . . .

"Star," suggested Traveler, "would you tell us of your people's beginnings?" He did not know her Creation story, and had no idea what she might tell, but he recognized a natural storyteller. She had already captivated her audience. And in sign-talk!

Star shrugged, still embarrassed by all the attention. "This story, too, tells of the Old Man," she began. "He brought my people from inside the earth. It was soon after Creation . . ."

She went on, describing the cold, the darkness, and the hunger in the depths of the cavernous nether world. Her audience was completely absorbed. "Then Old Man sat on a hollow cottonwood log, and tapped it with a stick. First Man and First Woman crawled through to the outside."

She paused, and seemed to be waiting for something. The crowd sat quietly, and finally a young man rose. "Are they still coming through?"

Ah, Traveler understood now. This was part of the game. The listeners try to catch the storyteller in a contradiction. Why is not the whole world filled with Star's people? This must be a trap, to let the storyteller catch the listener. He watched as the girl turned an indignant frown on the innocent questioner.

"Of course not," she signed. "The third person was a fat woman. She got stuck in the log, and no one has been through since!"

Part I

The Storyteller

Woodpecker lay on his belly in the sunlit meadow and watched the rabbit as it came toward him. Surely now, at any time, it would sense his presence and flee. But it came closer, nibbling eagerly at the succulent grass of springtime. Never in his nine summers had he seen such a thing.

He flattened his body to the ground and held his breath —waiting, waiting. It seemed a long time as the rabbit nibbled, hopped a step or two, nibbled again. Twice he emptied his lungs, slowly, not to disturb the long-ears. Then, just as carefully, he refilled his chest with a long, slow inhalation. Finally, against all reason, the creature hopped, unafraid, within an arm's length of his face. Then it seemed to notice him for the first time, and froze, motionless. He was looking directly into the eye—large and brown and shining. It reminded him of the shiny seeds of the bur chestnut. They were not good to eat like other nuts, but marvelous to play with. The rabbit's eye was like that . . . shiny and glistening as it stared into his. It had one other characteristic that the shiny nut-seed did not have—life, recognition, and awareness of the world. And, of course, fear. He was not certain whether he *saw* the fear in the unblinking eye of the rabbit or *felt* it in the animal's spirit.

It made him think, somehow, of the tales around the

story-fires, of long-ago times when the animals could talk. He wondered when they had lost that ability. It was always there in the Creation stories. *Maybe,* he thought, looking into the depths of the rabbit's eye, *maybe they never lost it at all. What if, for instance,* men *had lost the ability, or the wish, to listen*?

Softly, he began to whisper. "It is well, Little Brother," he said. "Talk to me . . . I will listen . . . I mean no harm to you."

There was no sign that the rabbit heard unless the slight twitch of its whiskers indicated it. Woodpecker took this motion seriously, however. The creature was so close that he could count every hair on its nose. He watched the nervous quiver of the whiskers, and for a moment, *there,* it seemed that the rabbit *was* ready to speak. Woodpecker waited, and finally, when nothing happened, he whispered again. "Go on, Little Brother . . . speak! I will tell no one."

The rabbit jumped convulsively, startling the watching boy as it fled. It had been so close. The dirt and dry grass kicked up by the rabbit's long hind feet struck him across the face, and he jumped uncontrollably. Then he laughed at himself for his response and sat up to watch the bobbing fluff of white tail bounce out of sight in the bushes along the stream.

He was pleased with the day. This was closer to the rabbit than he had ever been. More important, his medicine had been good. He would long remember this as the day he had *almost* persuaded the rabbit to speak, as it had done in long-ago times. Maybe next time . . .

Woodpecker rose and started along the stream toward the village. Then he remembered his original mission and retraced his steps to the meadow. He picked up the sticks he had laid aside when he first saw the rabbit and hurried on, gathering sticks for the cooking fire as he went. In his excitement over the rabbit, he had almost forgotten. Today he wished to finish quickly because it was an exciting time. The Storyteller was here.

Of course, there were always stories. In the moons of winter or in bad weather, the elders of the tribe gathered in the longhouse and told and retold the stories. Stories of the People, of long-ago times. The boy thrilled at these tales, stories of how the Redbird became red, how Bobcat lost his tail, and why the moon is red when it rises.

There were stories of Creation, and Woodpecker loved these most of all. There were tales of the Trickster, who had been present at Creation and could speak all languages—not only all human tongues but those of all animals and birds. Even the song of the stream murmuring over the rocks was language to the Trickster, it was said. When the wind sighed among the tall treetops, it was talking to the Trickster.

"Good day to you, Uncle," it said.

At least, that was according to the Storyteller. The one that had created the greatest impression on young Woodpecker was not of the People but an outsider. Once or twice each season, a Trader would come to their village on the river. Travelers came oftener than that, of course, but the ones who entranced the imagination of Woodpecker were those who told stories well. Some people could not tell a story at all. And the Trader could tell one to perfection. He and two or three of the old storytellers of the tribe would sit and trade stories as long as anyone would listen. Longer, probably. More than once, Woodpecker had fallen asleep while the stories still flowed freely and had been carried home in his father's arms.

Of course, that was when he was merely a child. Now he could probably stay up all night if necessary. He was prepared to do so tonight, for a number of reasons.

One was the Storyteller, of course. Some knew him as "the Trader," but to Woodpecker, he was the Storyteller and a master at his craft. If anyone knew where the man came from originally, they had forgotten. Even his tribe was a question. For the past ten, maybe twenty seasons, he had traded up and down the rivers of the region. He traded with all and seemed to have no enemies. He was welcomed for his stories as well as for the fascinating assortment of items he carried.

The Trader would enter a village or camp, attract attention with the stories, and spend the next day in trading from his packs. There was some limit to what could be exchanged because items taken in trade must be small enough to transport on the back of the Trader. All of the reasons for this were not well understood by Woodpecker. He only knew that when this man came to the village, a wonderful evening was in store.

Also, it was the Moon of Roses, and the weather was exceptionally fine. The story-fires would not be confined to the longhouse but outside in the night. All stories, of course, were best when told by firelight. For some stories, it was a requirement. Stories of the Trickster must never be told until after dark. He had decreed it himself long ago, shortly after Creation.

There was always more excitement to stories after dark. One could see strange little movements in the dusky corners of the longhouse. During the more frightening stories, children would edge quietly closer to a parent or older friend, casting fearful glances behind. The circle of firelight seemed safer somehow; some racial memory suggested that it was so. The flicker and crackle of the flames pushed back the demons of darkness and made the world seem a safer place.

While this was evident in the longhouse, it was much more so outside. It was deliciously fearsome to hear the scare-stories of long-ago times retold in the darkness under the starry black dome of night. There was a fire, of course. Any story, properly told, must have a fire. But in the longhouse, fearsome story-creatures were confined to the dark corners and along poorly lit walls away from the fire. Outdoors, with the whispered night-sounds out beyond the fire's reach, the whole world might be filled with such terrors. Woodpecker found it a delicious fright, fearful yet relatively safe. At least, it had never been known for a story-creature to come out of the dark to assault cringing children. Still, they cowered and squealed and giggled, and the story was a success.

Woodpecker arrived at the lodge and deposited his firewood where it would be convenient to the cooking fire. His mother glanced up and smiled at him. It had been hard for her, he knew, since his father's death two winters past. He had all but forgotten what his father looked like now, but he remembered the incident.

One of the other men had come to report that Red Squirrel was dead. A freak accident: He had climbed upon a fallen tree to watch a band of deer some distance away. He had slipped and tumbled into the tangle of brush below. That might not have been serious, but unknown to any of the hunters, the brush pile was the winter lodge of a bear. A sleeping bear was slow to waken in the Moon of Snows but quick to anger. The end for Red Squirrel was quick but unpleasant. It was some time before the others could recover the mangled remains.

There was the traditional period of mourning, and soon after that, Owl Woman and her son moved into the lodge of her mother. Woodpecker wondered sometimes if his mother might marry again. There were men who looked upon her with favor, but she did not seem interested. It seemed quite satisfactory to her to remain in the lodge of her parents.

The boy had mixed feelings. It would be good to have a father again, like other children. Bent Arrow, perhaps, or Lame Fox. Fox had demonstrated some interest. He had only one wife and was considered a good provider.

Meanwhile, Woodpecker felt uneasy and out of place because his family was different. He had withdrawn into the story-world of long-ago tales. These, at least, seemed predictable, unchanging, and timeless. Woodpecker could imagine himself as a skilled and respected storyteller, his calling above and beyond that of most of the People.

With this in mind, he would build a tiny fire of sticks— a pretend fire, not lighted of course—in some hidden retreat. A circle of stones and sticks would represent his audience, and he would spend long times telling stories aloud. Not stories of the Trickster. Those could only be told after dark. Woodpecker could not easily be alone in his secret places after Sun had gone over to the other side of Earth's rim.

The boy was not completely isolated of course. He took part in instruction with the other children. He had long ago mastered and enjoyed the simple hopping steps of the Rabbit Dance. Now, he was relatively proficient with the bow and could *almost* make fire with the firesticks; at least he could make much smoke. With a little more coordination—well, maybe someday.

He had helped plant the corn this season, and the beans and pumpkins. There was a great sense of satisfaction that he could do this work, but it was tiresome. His mind would wander, and he would tell himself the stories, silently. Then one of the adults would notice and speak to him harshly.

"Not so deep, boy!"

And he would return to the present, carefully placing the seeds in the furrow, covering them and pressing the dirt down firmly.

Today, he could hardly wait for dark, and the story-fire. His mother, who had some idea of Woodpecker's restlessness, smiled to herself.

"Come, eat," she called to him. "You will want to be there early, at the stories."

"Are you coming too?"

"Maybe." Owl Woman smiled. "I will be along later. You eat and go ahead. You will want a good place in the circle."

"Yes, Mother," Woodpecker agreed breathlessly.

He had not been aware that she understood him so deeply. He finished his stewed corn and beans, and rose. "I will meet you later, Mother," he called as he trotted away.

His grandmother watched him go, somewhat disapprovingly. "He is a little bit lazy, that one," she suggested.

Owl Woman smiled sadly. "No, Mother. He is busy thinking of other things. He is much like his father."

The older woman's face softened, and she patted her daughter's shoulder. "Maybe so," she said gently. "He is a good boy."

"Yes. He will make us proud."

Maybe, admitted the grandmother to herself. *In a different way. This is an unusual child. He spends much time in thought, but he also talks well. We will see.*

2

The shadows were growing long as the Storyteller prepared for an evening of entertainment. He remembered this village as a good one. For stories, at least. There were a couple of old men here, he recalled, who could match story for story until far into the night. A tale would remind one of the other storytellers of another, and that tale in turn of yet more as the stories went on and on.

Maybe, he thought, he could use some of the Creation stories tonight. Stories from various tribes, their own stories of their origins. The tribe he visited last season—how did that tale begin? Four brothers, who came up out of a lake to create the four bands of the tribe. Or the tribe to the southeast. Their first people, it was said, came from the sky. Slid down the dome to reach Earth. Yes, a good story.

This tribe had already heard the tale of the grapevine, and the people who climbed out of Earth on its roots. Their own story was similar, was it not? Ah, well, no matter. A good story was always worth retelling.

He rose and walked from the place he would sleep to see where the fire would be. Yes, near the longhouse at the center of the village. A couple of young men were bringing sticks for the fire. Then he noticed a much younger boy, enthusiastically engaged in fuelgathering. The youngster looked familiar. Yes, he remembered now, from last season. This was the boy who had become so entranced by the stories. When other children had become distracted or bored and wandered off, this boy was still listening, fascinated. It was good to see young people who understood the importance of the story-fire and the Storyteller.

"Good day, young man," he said to the child.

The boy smiled a little shyly and nodded a wordless answer.

"You will come for the stories?"

"Yes, Uncle."

"I remember you from last year. You liked the storytelling."

The boy nodded. It was plain, the excitement in this child at the prospect of the story-fire. It was to be hoped that someone would encourage the boy in this interest.

"Is your father a storyteller?" he asked.

"No, my father is dead," the boy answered. "A bear . . ."

"*Aiee*, too bad. Your mother?"

"We live in her mother's lodge. How is it you speak my tongue, Uncle?"

The Storyteller smiled. "Ah, a trader must speak many tongues. And hand-signs, of course. Some tongues are easier than others. Do you know any others?"

"No, only a little sign-talk."

It was apparent that the boy was interested and intelligent, and could communicate well. The Trader suspected that the boy was overly modest in his mention of "a little" sign-talk. An idea began to form in his mind. The boy's mother was a widow, living in her parents' lodge. She might welcome an opportunity such as he had in mind. A season's travel for the boy, then home for the winter. An extra pair of hands would be useful on the trail or the river.

It had been a lonely trail since the loss of his wife a few seasons ago. The two had approached the world with happiness in all Earth's glory and in each other. They had only a few seasons together, wandering the trails, trading with distant tribes for exotic foods, furs, and other objects of value, such as stone for making pipes, implements, and weapons. Lark had succumbed to an illness of a strange sort during a visit to a tribe that had the illness. Their holy men had been of no help, going through the ceremonies but privately shaking their heads in despair. Their medicine was ineffective, one explained to the distraught husband, because the spirit of the disease was foreign.

"Foreign?" asked the Trader through his tears.

"Yes. Our people first fell sick with it from the *French.*"

"I know little of them."

"Of course. They are one of the tribes from beyond the Big Water."

"Mishi-ghan?"

"No, no, the Big Salt Water. They have pale skins and sometimes grow fur upon their faces. Their eyes are light-colored, sometimes."

"Aiee! They are blind?"

"No, they can see, even with light eyes. But no matter. They bring good things—blankets, knives—but also some bad spirits sometimes. Like that which oppresses your wife. Many die."

It was painful, watching Lark weaken and suffer. When the end finally came, with the sores covering her once beautiful body, he had welcomed the relief for her.

That had been a lost season for the Trader. He had very little memory of it. The period of mourning helped, but he still felt lost, abandoned. In the seasons since, he had immersed himself in the storytelling, using the ever-lasting stories as a sign of permanence that seemed to escape him otherwise. He missed Lark deeply and had found no one who could take her place. Maybe he never would.

However, the conversation with the boy was bringing a new idea to his mind. It was not possible to replace Lark, but companionship—that could be quite pleasant on the trail. If the boy's widowed mother would consent to the season's apprenticeship . . .

"How are you called?" he asked.

"I am Woodpecker, Uncle."

"It is good. Will your mother come for the story-fire, Woodpecker?"

"Maybe so. Why do you ask?"

"I only wondered. We will see."

It was nearly full dark now, and people were gathering. It was time to light the fire. Someone brought a brand from one of the cooking fires, and orange tongues of flame licked at the tinder and crept upward, flickering through the jumbled pile of fuel. Firelight pushed back the circle of darkness, enlarging the lighted area. There was something about a fire, a declaration of human existence, that was exciting and thrilling. It prepared the scene, stimulated the imagination, and readied the spirit for the coming entertainment.

The elders of the village were ceremoniously making their way to the front rows now. Yes, the Storyteller remembered these men. That one-eyed man; he had been a good storyteller last season. A dry sense of humor. Well, young Woodpecker had had an advantage in his childhood. He had listened to this man and, yes, the portly man next to him. The visitor remembered that one as a powerful orator.

One of the chiefs spoke a few words of welcome and sat down again, relinquishing the council to the visiting trader. The Storyteller stood, having carefully positioned himself against a background of dark trees for maximum effect. The crowd was still waiting expectantly. The only sounds were those of the crackling fire and the cries of the distant night-creatures beyond the reach of its light. It was warm, but in such a setting, there was always a chill of excitement that sent icy fingers up one's spine and caused the hairs to prickle on the back of the neck.

The Storyteller was about to speak when he caught a glimpse of a face in the back rows of the listeners. It was such a striking face, one of the most beautiful women he had ever seen. The large dark eyes were well spaced and the other features exquisite. It was a face that showed, even at this distance and by firelight, intelligence, humor, and a hint of sadness, all at once. So striking—the thought crossed his mind that it was an apparition, a trick of the flickering light and shadows. Maybe the woman was not real at all and existed only as an ideal in his own mind.

He tore his attention away, and began his story a little shakily. "In the long-ago times, when Earth was young, Bobcat had a long, long tail. . . ."

That was always a good starter. There were many versions of it. He would tell one, giving one of the local storytellers the opportunity to counter with his own, always a good way to ensure popularity with the host village, make their own storyteller look good.

It was hard work tonight, resisting the temptation to stare again at the beautiful face in the back row. A time or two he risked a quick glance while other storytellers were talking. She was still there, smiling in absorbed amusement.

As the crowd began to tire and thin out, the pretty woman disappeared, and he was sad. The stories ceased earlier than they sometimes did because his heart was not in it. He was distracted. This was the first time since the loss of Lark that any woman had impressed him, beyond the bounds of a temporary diversion to relieve the call of nature, of course. This feeling was different.

Ridiculous, he told himself. A woman like that has a husband. Probably a jealous one. He would put her out of his mind.

He slept poorly and awoke with his senses dulled. It was not good to trade when he was not at his best. But there was no help for it. He must finish here and move on. Maybe that would help to rid his mind of the face in the firelight and its sad-sweet smile.

He spread his goods on a robe and began the day's trading. Some things he kept hidden, to bring forth as a dramatic surprise those items he considered best. He was engrossed in haggling over a trade involving an exceptionally fine otter skin and a black obsidian knife when he noticed the approach of the boy. Ah, yes, Woodpecker. He had suggested that the boy bring his mother. He had almost forgotten.

"In a moment," he said aside to Woodpecker.

"Yes, Uncle."

Finally the deal was completed, and the customer turned to leave, pleased with his new knife. The Trader looked up. "Now, my young friend!"

He almost choked on the last words. He had not really looked at the boy's companion until now. *"You* are his mother?" he blurted, feeling completely stupid.

"Yes, of course." Owl Woman smiled, looking a trifle confused. "Woodpecker said you wished to talk with me."

She was even more beautiful in daylight, he thought. The dim light of the fire could not do justice to her fine features and the texture of her skin. He could now see that she was tall and willowy, and the soft curves of her body pressed suggestively against the restraining buckskin of her dress.

"How are you called?" the woman asked, bringing him back to reality.

"Ah . . . I am c-called many things," he stammered. "Mostly good, I think. My first name was Turtle. Now, I am the Storyteller, or the Trader." *Or whatever you would like to call me,* he thought. *Anything.* Then he made an attempt to recover his composure. "And how are *you* called, Mother of Woodpecker?"

She laughed, and he was pleased at the little wrinkles at the corners of her eyes. It was far better than the hint of sadness he had seen earlier.

"I am Owl Woman," she said. "As you have mentioned, the mother of this one."

She paused, waiting. Now was the time, the Trader thought, to ask about the apprenticeship for the season. He could not bring himself to do so. What if she said no? Or, worse, became angry? It would destroy any possibility of seeing her again, and he was not willing to take that chance. As things now stood, Woodpecker did not know of the plan, so talk of it could be postponed. He could perhaps stay here an extra day or two, become better acquainted.

Owl Woman's look of puzzlement was changing to one of impatience. He must do something very quickly. "I wished to tell you," he blurted clumsily, "you have a fine boy. He understands the stories well. I can tell that he has a talent."

He felt like an idiot. What a stupid thing, to ask the woman to come here, but of course he had not known who she was. *Aiee,* he felt like a child. But Owl Woman was smiling.

"Thank you!" she said. "He is much like his father, who was killed . . ." The sadness returned for a moment.

"Yes, Woodpecker told me."

She smiled again. "You two have become friends," she observed. "Will you be here long?"

He had planned to depart no later than the next morning, but he now experienced a sudden change in plans. "A few days, maybe," he answered, trying to sound casual. "Maybe I will see you again."

"Maybe so," she said with a smile that was almost an invitation. She turned away.

"Mother, may I stay and watch the trading?" Woodpecker asked.

Owl Woman paused for a moment and looked questioningly at the Trader. "Maybe so," she agreed, "but do not be a bother."

"It is good," the Trader said quickly. "He will be no trouble."

3

» » »

Owl Woman sat bolt upright in her sleeping robes. It must be nearly dawn, she thought. Yes, the doorway opening was clearly showing the gray light of coming day. Her parents were stirring in their pallet of robes.

"What is that noise?" she asked.

A plaintive hollow call, like the *coo* of a dove, wavered outside, rising and falling, continuing on and on. It was not unpleasant but was unlike anything she had heard before.

Suddenly her mother chuckled somewhat nervously. "Someone is playing a flute."

"What?"

"A sort of whistle, but with holes. They are used by some of the prairie people."

"For what purpose?" Owl Woman asked.

Suddenly Yellow Bowl gasped in realization, then laughed aloud. "For *courting*!" She chortled. "Owl Woman, maybe someone is courting you!"

"Nonsense!" Owl Woman snapped irritably. "I know no one who—" She paused. The Trader! Could it be? He had acted very strangely when they met.

"Ah, you *do* know!" teased her mother. "The Trader? Of course! He travels everywhere. He would know of the flute; maybe his tribe uses it. What *is* his tribe?"

"I do not know, Mother. Why would he . . ." Owl

Woman was confused but excited. She had been quite impressed by this young man, even in his embarrassment. She had been at a loss to explain that, but now . . . She had wondered whether he had a wife and finally mustered courage to ask whether Woodpecker knew. No, the boy said, he believed that the Trader had no one.

"I will go and see about this," Yellow Bowl was saying as she shrugged into her dress.

"But, Mother, I—"

The older woman waved her objections aside and stooped to pass out the doorway. Owl Woman waited nervously.

The song of the flute stopped, and there was a long pause before it resumed. It was rapidly growing light when Yellow Bowl returned, chuckling to herself. She stooped to reenter the lodge and straightened inside.

"Well?" asked Owl Woman expectantly.

"It is as we thought," stated Yellow Bowl. "He plays a courting song. And he has no wife."

"This is his tribe's way?" asked Owl Woman.

"No," answered her mother. "This is a custom that he learned from a plains tribe where he visited. It is nice, no?"

"But why does he play it for me?"

"That is the best part! He says that you are a special woman who deserves a special courtship!"

Owl Woman frowned. "No, he has traded for this whistle thing somewhere and wants to play it."

But though her words were sarcastic, her heart was very good. It was exciting to have a man like this interested in her. "What does he expect to happen now?" she asked her mother.

"I do not know. Maybe you should ask him."

Owl Woman was slipping her dress over her head. She did not want to take time to replait her hair but attempted to pat it into shape as quickly as possible. *This is silly,* she told herself. But her heart beat rapidly, and her palms were damp. A bit angry at herself, she ducked through the doorway and straightened to full height outside.

She did not see him at first and followed the hollow flute tones until she located his position. He was seated, his back leaning against the trunk of a giant old sycamore. His eyes were half closed, and the warbling notes from the flute rose and fell, rhythmic and clear, in the still morning air.

Embarrassed a little at what their neighbors might think, Owl Woman paused before the seated musician. "What are you doing?" she demanded in a half-whisper. "You will wake the whole village!"

He lowered the flute and looked at her with a placid smile. Even in her state of tension and embarrassment, she did not fail to notice that it was a nice smile. It showed even white teeth and crinkled the corners of his eyes in a way that suggested a sense of humor.

"Then they will know that I feel much for you," he said calmly.

"Is this the way of your people?" she asked, trying to regain her composure.

"No, no. I learned it from others. People of the plains, to the west. It is a pleasant custom, no?"

She did not answer but stood fighting a mixture of emotions. It was pleasing, flattering, to have such a man courting her—at the same time, embarrassing. She could see that people were sleepily looking out of lodge doors to see what was going on. She saw Bent Arrow, who had shown considerable interest in her, poke his head out, then quickly withdraw it. Ah, how the other women would tease her over this! Her mother had already started.

Her greatest concern was that she was far from certain that she was ready to be courted at all. The loss of her husband, even though it was a constant threat to young wives, had been a crushing blow. Such things always happen to someone else, she had told herself repeatedly, not to us, not to Red Squirrel. And such an ignoble way to cross over. No chance to fight for life or even to die heroically.

Her heart still hurt for her husband. She hoped that on the Other Side, he knew that she would always consider him brave and noble. She was not ready to let go of his memory. Yet here she stood, more excited over the interest of a man than she had been for years. Her heart quickened. She was amused at herself, and a bit irritated. She wanted to turn and walk away but was afraid that such an action would start the song of the courting flute again, drawing more attention to her predicament. She must know more. "What do you expect to happen now?" Owl Woman demanded.

He shrugged. "Whatever you wish."

His expression was questioning. She realized that whatever the customs of this strange courtship, he was waiting for her to make the next move. The flutesong, it seemed, was his question, and he had now asked it. He expected her to answer.

The entire scene suddenly struck her as outrageously funny. Here was a courtship in progress. It involved two people of two entirely different cultures, and neither of them knew whether it was progressing properly. She wondered whether the Trader knew what was supposed to happen next.

Well, she must do *something*. What if she rejected his courtship? Would he sit forever outside her lodge, playing the flute? The thought caused a moment of panic. She knew of no way to silence this obvious act of his. On the other hand, she was certainly not ready to give him any encouragement, and for that matter, such encouragement might renew the flutesong.

"Look," she began, "I do not understand what is happening." She was distressed at the look on the face of her suitor, a look of pleasure. "No, no," she insisted, *"nothing* is happening."

He moved his arm a little, and she thought he was

preparing to play the flute again. "We must talk," she said quickly. "Later?"

He seemed to think for a moment, and then nodded. "When?"

"Are you not leaving today?"

"Not yet. I must know—"

"Of course," Owl Woman interrupted, unwilling to let him finish that question. "Let us meet . . . just before dark?"

He nodded. It was obvious that he would have preferred it sooner, and for a moment the possibility that he would play the flute all day occurred to her. But she forged ahead. "There is a clearing upstream, near the river . . . an old cottonwood log."

"Yes, I know the place. It is good."

With a sense of relief, she saw him place the flute in a handsome beaded case and tie its thongs. At least that threat was over for the present. He rose with the quick smile that she was beginning to expect and, yes, enjoy.

"Until sunset, then." He turned and was gone.

Owl Woman stood, looking after him. What had she done? She was to meet a man who was practically a stranger to talk of romance. And neither knew the courtship customs of the other. The whole thing was sheer idiocy. How had she become entangled in such a situation?

She turned away, disturbed at her behavior, at the same time beginning to plan her tasks for the day. She must wash her hair, see that her buckskin dress was presentable. Maybe her new moccasins . . .

Shadows were growing long when she stepped into the clearing. The Trader was seated on the big trunk of the fallen cottonwood. She had thought that he might be playing his flute when she arrived and was somewhat relieved that he was not. Still, it would have been nice. . . .

She shook her head to free it of such thoughts. This

must be a calm conversation. She must find out from the man what he expected and how seriously *he* considered this courtship.

He rose as she approached with his quick gentle smile. "I am pleased that you came," he said.

"Only to talk."

"Of course. I made you uncomfortable this morning. I am sorry for that."

"It is nothing."

There was a clumsy pause. Then both started to speak at once, and both stopped again. They laughed.

"You first," he said.

"How many wives have you?" she asked. Instantly, she was sorry. She had intended to ask that as a challenge, to put him off guard. She had not expected the hurt that she now saw in his face. He looked so vulnerable that she not only regretted the rude question but wished for a moment that she could comfort him in her arms. *What an odd thought!*

"I have no wife," he was saying sadly. "She died, from the pox, two seasons ago." The enormity of the loss he had suffered was apparent.

"I too," she blurted. "My husband was killed . . . but you know of that."

"Yes."

It was quiet for a moment. *We have much in common,* she thought. *I can see it in his face.* "Do you have children?"

"No. We never had . . . you have only Woodpecker?"

"Yes."

"He is a fine boy."

This was not going well. A clumsy silence, punctuated by small talk. But maybe there was progress after all. She did know much more about him now. They had both suffered a great loss. He had no children, while she had had young Woodpecker, so like his father, to comfort her. But . . .

"I do not know if I am ready to think of courtship," she said shyly, amazed at herself.

He looked at her in the twilight, serious yet pleased at her statement. "I am not sure of myself either," he said. "But I am ready to try if you are."

"I may need some time. How long will you stay?"

"Who knows? Tomorrow is tomorrow. We will see."

4

» » »

"**W**hat is your tribe, Uncle?" Woodpecker asked respectfully.

Things had happened so quickly that the boy was still somewhat confused. His mother and the Storyteller had quickly become interested in each other. To the amusement of the People, they started almost immediately to make plans for marriage. Owl Woman's other suitors were disappointed, of course, and suffered the friendly jibes and ribald jokes of the villagers.

The marriage ceremony was a strange mixture of customs. The ceremony of Owl Woman's tribe was included but also bits and pieces of other tribal ways. The Trader, now known to her as "Turtle," had picked up interesting and meaningful ideas from many tribes in his travels. It was like the song of the courting flute in a way. That had been embarrassing at first, but as Owl Woman quickly accepted her own feelings, she became almost defiant about it. She was proud to be pointed out as the woman who was to become the wife of the traveling Storyteller, the most exciting man she had ever known.

So on the day of their marriage, the happy couple had come to the point where it did not matter to them. The good-natured jokes and jibes were accepted as they were intended, as expressions of well-wishing. There were, of course, those oldsters who shook their heads, clucked their tongues, and predicted that no good could come of this.

"Does the jay nest with the robin?" someone asked.

But all in all, the People were happy for their daughter to find a husband. There was certainly precedent. Many among the People traced their heritage to outsiders who had married into the tribe. It was the usual thing for the husband to join his wife's people, but this was a special circumstance. The whole thing was viewed as an amusing diversion as the new couple prepared to move on down the river, following the call of the Trader's vocation.

Woodpecker had hardly had time to catch his breath. It had been so sudden for him, the acquaintance with the Storyteller. He had held the man in awe, had admired and respected him more than any other person in his young life, anyone since the loss of Woodpecker's father, of course. He had not quite understood why the Traveler had wished to meet his mother, except that somehow it involved Woodpecker.

Then suddenly everything seemed to change. The boy felt almost forgotten in the swift progress of the whirl-wind romance. His mother and the Storyteller had seemed oblivious to the whole world, their attention absorbed in each other. He felt a small pang of jealousy at first. That quickly abated when they included him in their planning. When he finally realized that this magnificent person, the Storyteller, was to be his new father, Woodpecker was overwhelmed. He would be the envy of all the boys his age. It was like the best of dreams, the preparation to depart on an exciting adventure with his mother and his new father.

There was a question of how he should address this important new person in his life. Woodpecker had considered him the Storyteller, though others called him the Trader, depending upon the man's importance in their lives.

"Whatever you wish," was the answer when Woodpecker ventured to inquire of his mother. "Why not ask him?"

Woodpecker went to the little fire where the Storyteller still camped, pending the marriage.

"What would you have me call you, Uncle?" he asked. "Uncle," of course, was a customary term of address for any adult male older than oneself in many tribes.

The Storyteller spread his palms in the gesture of not-knowing that was now becoming familiar. It was a thing of habit, and Woodpecker had already noticed its usefulness in trading. "What would *you* call me, Woodpecker?" The Storyteller skillfully turned the answer into another question.

"I do not know, Uncle. My heart would not be good, to call you Father. Not yet, maybe."

"That is true," observed the other seriously. "What have you called me until now? To others, I mean."

"I have thought of you as the Storyteller."

"Yes, I am called that."

"But it seems distant, Uncle. You will be my mother's husband."

"Yes . . . well, as I told your mother, I was first called Turtle."

Woodpecker thought for a little while. "No," he decided, "it is a good name, but would it show respect to call you that?"

Turtle smiled, inwardly pleased. Many boys would not feel this. "It would depend *how* you used it," he noted. "But as you wish."

Woodpecker pondered a little longer. "Maybe . . . Uncle, maybe I could call you that!"

"What? Turtle?"

"No, 'Uncle'!"

"Why not? It is good! Now, how shall I call *you*?"

" 'Woodpecker,' I suppose. That is my name. Until I earn another, anyway."

Woodpecker did not realize the depth of the question. His new father was asking tentatively to call the boy his son, the child he had never had. But, since Woodpecker had not realized, it was best to drop the subject for now.

"It is good! Woodpecker!" said Turtle proudly.

The three had traveled several sleeps now and were beginning to fall into a pattern. They had stopped at one village to trade, a village much like their own. Woodpecker was proud to be a part of the Storyteller's family. He could see the envy in the eyes of the children, became just a trifle haughty, and behaved as if he considered himself better than they. His mother quickly stopped that trend.

"You must be friendly to everyone," she advised gently. "If we are not well liked, no one will wish to trade!"

It was so obvious that Woodpecker was ashamed. Of course! That was his new father's entire approach. One trades freely with those whom he trusts, and one trusts his friends. Thus, in the first three days on the trail, Woodpecker learned his first lesson in trading.

He brought out his bull-roarer, a toy Turtle had given him. It was a device from the far prairie tribes, Turtle had told him. A flat stick, scraped thin and fastened to a slender thong, it could be whirled rapidly around one's head by the thong to create a roaring noise like the distant bellow of a bull. Woodpecker whirled the noisemaker, which attracted some boys of his own age. He allowed them to try it, then showed the construction so they could make similar devices themselves. The game caught on quickly, and the prestige of the Trader and his family increased. Turtle nodded, pleased.

"He is a good boy," he told Owl Woman. "He can be a great help to us."

She too was pleased.

They traveled on foot, following an ancient trail along the river. Turtle took the lead, followed by young Woodpecker, and Owl Woman brought up the rear. Each carried a pack. Woodpecker was pleased to be allowed to carry some of the important trading goods. Turtle had been careful not to start with too heavy a burden.

At a village a few sleeps downriver, Turtle assured them, he had left a canoe. When they reached there, travel would be easier. Paddling was easier than walking with heavy packs.

It was the second night after they left the first trading stop that the question occurred to Woodpecker: What was the tribe to which Turtle had been born? Everyone had always considered the Trader to be without a tribe. Yet he must have been born somewhere. The boy thought long and hard about this. Finally, after their little camp was established and they had eaten, he ventured to ask.

"What is your tribe, Uncle?"

Turtle did not answer immediately. The fire flickered hazily, sending shimmering patches of light dancing in the leafy cover overhead. "We call ourselves the People," he said finally.

"But that is the same as ours," the boy protested.

"Yes."

"But . . . you are not of *our* People."

"No, no, of course not. But does it matter?"

"Yes! It matters!" gasped the astonished Woodpecker.

"Why?"

"Well . . . well, because . . ."

"Because your tribe is *better*?"

Woodpecker was embarrassed. He had not foreseen that question. But now that he was faced with it, it was hurtful to admit, and he was sorry that he had hurt the feelings of the man he had come to admire so much. He did not notice the twinkle of amusement in the eyes of Turtle or the smile on his mother's face.

"Woodpecker, it is good to take pride in one's tribe," Turtle observed, saving the boy from having to make an embarrassing answer. "But why do we like to hear stories?"

Woodpecker was confused. What did stories have to do

with which tribe was better? "I . . . I do not know," he stammered.

Turtle seemed not to notice. "Because," he went on, "they are *different*. You know how Bobcat lost his tail?"

"Which . . . ?" He began to see the point as Turtle continued.

"Yes. In one story, it was frozen in the ice. In another, an eagle swooped down and snatched it off. All are good stories." He picked up a stick and poked a couple of burned ends into the fire. "Now," he went on, "if I think I am better than anyone, they will say, 'I do not wish to trade with him.' Then the trade would stop."

Woodpecker was still confused. "Then, *no* tribe is best?"

"Well, each must think his own is best. That is why he calls his the People. But even if we think this, we have better trading if we do not *act* like it. It is like the bull-roarer."

"But what . . . ?"

"You were proud to show it to the other boys. It is a good noisemaker, yes?"

"Yes, very good, Uncle."

"But it is not of *your* tribe."

Woodpecker was a little ashamed. He had been proud of the toy, proud to flaunt it at first.

"You did well," Turtle went on. "You showed it, shared it. Every tribe has *something* that can be used by others. That is how there can be traders. The trader sees . . . this tribe can use that which the other has . . . he helps them to get it by trading what *they* have. He does better by not showing his pride in his own tribe. He *has* it, but does not let it interfere."

Woodpecker thought about it a little longer. "Then, this is why you say little of your tribe, Uncle?"

"Yes. I do not wish to boast. It might cause bad feelings."

"How is your tribe called by others, then?"

"Some call us Traders, and use the hand-sign for *trade.* We are allies of the Finger-cutters."

He made the hand-sign for *mourning,* a sawing motion across the left forefinger.

"Why is their sign the one for mourning, Uncle?"

"That is how they mourn . . . cut the finger."

"Ah! Uncle, will you tell me more of hand-signs?"

Turtle laughed. "All in time, Woodpecker. You will learn much as we travel."

Another thought occurred to the boy. "What is your tribe's sign for *itself*?"

Turtle solemnly made the sign for *tribe,* rubbing the back of his left hand with the right forefinger. Then he doubled his right fist and gently thumped his chest over the heart three times.

"Mother?" asked the puzzled boy. *"Mother-Tribe?"*

"Yes. We say, 'Mother-of-All-Tribes.' "

They looked at each other and laughed together.

"But you do not say that to other tribes!" Woodpecker accused.

"No. Not when I am trading!"

They laughed again, and Owl Woman, watching the two, smiled to herself. Her heart was good.

5

» » »

The bond between the two continued to grow stronger. To Turtle, this was the child he had never had. To the boy, it was, in a way, the restoration of his lost father. It was not quite the same, but a good feeling to be a family again. He could see the light in the eyes of his mother, who now laughed again and appeared younger than at any time he could remember.

In some ways, this was even better than before his father's death. He felt guilty about feeling so, but even his father had not been able to make the stories come alive as Turtle could. Woodpecker felt that this life, with its new sights, sounds, and experiences, was the best of all possible worlds. His new father seemed willing to answer his questions—eager almost. He knew much about many things and seemed pleased to have an interested intelligent pupil to share them with.

"Woodpecker is a fine boy," Turtle told his wife after an especially exhaustive conversation. "He has a feel for language . . . the tongues of different tribes."

That was true. There are some, it has always been noted, who never master more than one or two tongues, and even then, with halting and a heavy accent. Others slip easily from one language to another, learning a working use of a new one as easily as changing garments. It is not a learned skill but one a person is born with. If he does not possess it, he will never have it, but if he is born with the gift, it will be his always.

Turtle had always had the gift. Possibly his tribe's status as traders was a help. Because of their location in the Great Plains and their mobility within this area, they came in contact with many cultures and traded with all. The Grower tribes along the streams and fertile valleys, the fishermen of the great rivers, and the hunting nomads of the prairie—all had commodities for potential trade. Turtle had grown up in this atmosphere, exposed to many languages. This had enabled him to perfect the skills that allowed him to become the Storyteller and the Trader.

It was pleasing to him, then, to find that his new son was quick to learn and interested in learning. In no time at all, it seemed, Woodpecker and his new father were chattering in various tongues, to the confused amusement of Owl Woman.

She too was pleased with the relationship that she saw growing between her son and her husband. The rapid use of other tongues, however, was beyond her. Laughing over the impossible task, she threw up her hands in despair and returned to her cooking fire. She did not feel excluded from their shared activity. It was simply a thing in which she had little interest. So she watched with pleasure as the instruction proceeded.

"Show me more of the signtalk, Uncle," Woodpecker pleaded.

Turtle chuckled. It amused him that even though the bonds between them grew stronger each day, Woodpecker still used the term "Uncle." Whatever was comfortable for the boy, of course. Turtle had decided that this usage was out of respect for the lost father. He doubted that under similar circumstances, he could call anyone else Father either. Probably, Woodpecker would never do so. Yet, the use of "Uncle" was a mark of respect, and Turtle understood.

"Hand-signs are of little use here," Turtle observed.

Camped on the middle Ohio River between two villages, they were traveling by canoe now. Turtle seemed to have contacts everywhere, friends and acquaintances from whom they could borrow needed transportation or would keep Turtle's possessions until his return.

"But, I would be ready for later," Woodpecker argued.

"Yes, that is true. In the western areas it is necessary," he agreed.

"In the region of your home?"

"Yes. Our people trade with many tribes, and most use the hand-signs. Mostly, those west of the Big River, the Mississippi. This side, there is little use."

Woodpecker nodded eagerly. "So, teach me more, Uncle."

"Well, you know some already. Let us start with signs for different tribes."

He made the sign for *people,* then one with both hands, like the flapping of wings.

"What do you think this tribe is called?"

"Bird . . . Bird People?"

"Yes, almost. These are the Crows."

"Crows? I do not know them, Uncle."

"Of course not. They live to the west. They were Growers until the horse came."

"Then they became hunters?"

"Only part of them. Some stayed with farming. Others hunt buffalo."

"Ah! Their tribe split in two?"

"Yes, but they meet together each summer."

"And the sign . . . for both halves is the same? The birdsign?"

"Yes. They also are called sometimes by another sign, Like this." He doubled a fist and placed it on his forehead, fingers outward. "That is like a Crow warrior's hair-knot," he explained. "Now, they have enemies, the Lakota. Here is their sign." With a forefinger, Turtle made a slicing motion across his throat.

"The Cut-throats?" Woodpecker gasped.

"Yes. Some call them the Enemies."

"*Your* enemies, Uncle?"

"No, no." Turtle laughed. "I have no enemies. But these are very jealous of their hunting grounds. When the Growers began to hunt, you see . . ."

"Yes . . . but the Cut-throat sign?"

"That is their mark . . . to tell who did the kill. Even a kill with an arrow might be marked that way, to claim credit."

"It is a boast?"

"Yes, maybe."

"What are other signs for tribes, Uncle?"

"*Aiee,* boy, you never tire of learning. Well, so be it. Now here is a tribe to the south of my home. Oh, you remember Finger-cutters, my tribe's allies?"

"Yes."

"They have a southern tribe. They are still one, but yet two."

"So, one could sign South Finger-cutters?"

"Yes, maybe so. Now, in their area is another, with a sign like this." He made a wavy line.

"A snake?"

"Good! Yes, the sign of a snake! Now, there are others, many of them. Their tongues are different, but all use some of the sign-talk. Here is one . . . what is their name?" He made the sign for a man on a horse, the right forefinger and middle finger straddling the edge of the left hand.

"The Horse People?" guessed Woodpecker.

"Yes! A small tribe, in the Tallgrass country. Here is another." He made a sign with two fingers upright, near his face.

"I do not know that sign, Uncle."

"That is *wolf.*"

"Wolf People?"

"Yes . . . Pawnee. Now, one more . . . too many will confuse you." With both hands, he pushed his hair backward over the top of his head, from the forehead.

"I do not understand."

"This means *haircutting* . . . they cut the hair short. Osage is their name."

"Where are they, Uncle?"

"Across the Big River. They are more woods dwellers than some of the others. And farther south. Now, enough! Let us sleep. Tomorrow, we must travel."

Woodpecker lay in his sleeping robe, still excited over all he was learning. Too excited to fall asleep quickly, he listened to the sounds of the night-creatures. Deep in the trees sounded the hunting cry of the great cat-owl. Nearer at hand, a small green heron gave his raucous squall, and on the ridge, a fox barked. Farther away, the chuckling call of a coyote rippled across the distance. A fish splashed in the river. The boy listened to these sounds as a comforting nightsong. He would dream of faraway places, new people, new creatures, new stories to tell.

The world is full of stories, his stepfather had once said. From time to time, they allow themselves to be told. Turtle was surely a master at storytelling. Woodpecker had already heard most of them many times, sometimes in different tongues. Still, each time was exciting.

Sometimes, when he used a tongue not quite familiar to him, Turtle also used hand-signs. This, Woodpecker saw, would be a valuable thing, hence his interest in the sign-talk. Even when a storyteller knew well the tongue of his listeners, would it not be effective to insert a hand-sign here and there for dramatic effect?

He fell asleep, thinking of how one could use the signs. When Bobcat, for instance, froze his long tail in the ice, and lost it as he leaped . . .

6

» » »

"**A**nd when Bobcat leaped, he was jerked up short by his long tail, frozen in the ice, and Rabbit jumped away to escape. . . ."

The children around the story-fire squealed with delight, and Owl Woman smiled proudly. She turned to look at her husband and to enjoy the light in his eyes. Both were proud of young Woodpecker. In the five years since they had been together, he had grown almost to a young man.

In their second season of travel, Turtle had suggested that the boy start to tell stories to the children before the serious storytelling began. Woodpecker had jumped at the chance. Turtle's motives were not completely charitable. He was well aware that the stories he told were to engender trust for the coming day of trading. Not entirely, of course. It was a pleasure to himself and the other participants as well as the listeners. But it did establish credibility and friendship, fostering better trade. Likewise, with Woodpecker telling stories to the children —how could anyone distrust people whose son tells stories to little children?

And the boy was good at it. He had taken to the storytelling with even more success than Turtle had imagined. He made clever modifications and jokes, and dramatized with hand-signs. He was mastering several languages and dialects, and when they were in contact with those who used hand-signs, he increased his proficiency in those also.

This season, when they had approached a village a moon ago, children had run out to greet them, shouting happily. "Look! The Storyteller comes!"

It was with some chagrin that Turtle realized that the youngsters were crowding around Woodpecker, not himself. In the eyes of these children at least, Woodpecker was "the Storyteller."

Turtle looked at his wife and smiled.

"I have been replaced!"

Owl Woman shifted the baby on her back and began to loosen the straps of the carrying board. "Not really. To the adults, there is no storyteller like yourself."

"But he is good, Owl. Next season I will ask him to take part in the serious stories."

She smiled. "He helps the trading," she observed.

"Yes, greatly. He is taking more interest. For a while, I thought he only liked the storytelling."

Owl Woman nodded. She unwrapped the baby, loosened her tunic, and put it to the breast. "Turtle, next season can we go home?"

He looked at her sympathetically. He had had some trouble retracing the trading routes he had first explored with Lark. It was uncomfortable challenging the ghost of his first love. They had talked of it. Owl Woman was having no problem. This was all new territory for her, with nothing to remind her of her first marriage, but she could understand.

They had decided, by common consent, to explore territory new to him also. They had pushed farther south and westward along the rivers, finding new people to trade with, and established new contacts, new friendships. It was successful. They had avoided his people and hers, to avoid their ghosts of the past. But now the situation had changed somewhat. A baby girl had been born to them a few moons ago as they wintered with friends among the Sacs. She was a beautiful child, and Owl Woman felt that now her life was complete—except that she would like to show their success to her parents and her friends at home.

"Home?" he asked. "Your village?"

"Yes. I would show my mother." She glanced at the infant.

"Of course. I thought . . . you did not seem . . ."

"I know. But now it is different, somehow. Do you not feel it?"

"Yes. I would like for my people to see our family too. I had hesitated to speak of it."

She laughed happily. "It is good! How shall we plan?"

Turtle thought awhile. "If we start in that direction now," he suggested, "we could winter in your village."

Owl Woman's eyes lighted. "Could we do that?"

"Of course! That is a good thing about trading. We can go wherever we want!"

So it was decided in a few moments. Woodpecker, completely unaware, was laughing and talking with children who looked forward to the story-fires that evening.

"Will you tell us of Bobcat?"

"No, Rabbit's long ears!"

"Wait, wait," he cried in mock alarm. "I will tell them all!"

It was not until they had set up their temporary camp at edge of the village that his parents told Woodpecker of their decision.

". . . so we will winter at home," his mother explained, "and start to make our way west to Turtle's people next spring. The Moon of Greening, maybe."

Woodpecker sat in stunned silence for a moment.

"What is wrong?" asked Owl Woman. "Do you not *want* to go?"

"Yes, yes, of course!"

"Then what is it, my son?"

"I . . . well, when I left, I was 'Woodpecker.' Some of

the others are probably warriors now, with proud names."

"You do not like 'Woodpecker'?"

"Of course, Mother. It is fine for a child, but . . ."

"What?"

"But . . . well, I would like to feel that I have *done* something, something important enough to . . . to change my name . . . take a man's name."

"But, my son, surely there are men called Woodpecker. It is a good name. You only think of it that way because it is *your* childhood name!"

"Wait!" interrupted Turtle. "Owl, if he has outgrown the name, he should have a new one."

"But he has not outgrown it . . . ," began Owl Woman.

"That is for him, to say what he feels," admonished Turtle. "If he thinks it is outgrown, it is so."

"What name would you take?" demanded Owl Woman.

"Well, I do not—"

"See?" she interrupted. "You do not know!"

"Wait, wait, now," Turtle said soothingly. "The children already call him the Storyteller."

"But *you* are the Storyteller," Owl Woman protested.

"I am not the only Storyteller," Turtle pointed out. "Also, I am called the Trader much of the time. He could be 'the Young Storyteller.' Or he 'the Storyteller' and I 'the Trader.' "

Owl Woman looked from one to the other, realizing her defeat. She seemed to see her son for the first time, his face almost on a level with her own. How sudden and unsuspected it had been! She smiled, blinking back a few tears. Her son was grown, almost a man.

"It is good," she said tightly, "but you will always be Woodpecker to me."

"Of course, Mother."

"Just as I am always Small Turtle to *my* mother!" said Turtle.

"Yes," agreed Owl Woman. *"Just* like that. Turtle, I want to meet your mother. Next season!"

"It is good! Next season."

So Woodpecker became "Storyteller," except for his mother. The children in the villages where they traded already called him that. Usage solidified the designation, and they settled comfortably into the shifting pattern.

The infant sister, as she grew, did not remember her brother by any other name. Her earliest memories were of listening to his stories. The child was called Lark, after Turtle's lost first love. He had protested, but Owl Woman was firm. "I owe much to a sister called Lark whom I never met," she explained, cuddling close to her husband in the robes. "I know I would have loved her."

Turtle could not speak because of the lump in his throat, but he managed to nod. Their marriage became even stronger.

There was one other change that occurred that summer before they reached the home village of Owl Woman. It was less than a moon after the decision to go home, and the name changing. They had entered a village to trade, and were preparing their camp when Turtle drew Storyteller aside. "Tonight," he suggested, "I will start the Creation stories, and then we will both answer their storytellers."

"But the children . . ."

"Yes, go ahead with those. But this town has two or three good storytellers. We will answer. I will tell one, then they will answer, then you . . . and so on. But you start with the children. When it is dark and the elders come to the fire, I will start with a Creation story."

"You would let me tell stories with the elders, Uncle?"

"Of course. Why are you called Storyteller?"

It was a glorious evening. Turtle began the formal part of the stories with a Creation story from the plains. This tribe, he related, crawled into the open world from below, First Man and First Woman, through a hollow cottonwood log. One of the locals countered with a similar story of their own, and then Turtle nodded to his assistant.

Young Storyteller rose, a nervously tight tone in his voice and his palms moist. "I have heard," he began carefully, "of a tribe to the south and east, whose world was water. They lived above, on a great blue dome, the sky. But they wished to live on the earth, so tiny Beetle was sent to the bottom of the water, to bring mud and spread it to dry on the surface. Buzzard flew over it, fanning with his wings to dry the mud . . ."

His listeners were enthralled, and by the time the humans slid down the dome to dry ground, Storyteller had earned his new name. He sat down amid a murmur of approval.

"Well told," whispered Turtle proudly.

Storyteller was still intoxicated with the excitement of the moment and his coming of age, but he did not overlook the pride in Turtle's words. "Thank you, Father," he whispered.

It came easily and seemed no disrespect to his first father.

7

» » »

Storyteller the Younger had noticed the girl at the story-fire but did not recognize her. She was tall and slim, with shapely legs and womanly bulges beneath her buckskins that suggested further beauty. Her eager smile at the story-fire had been mildly disconcerting to him. Twice their eyes had met, and his line of thought was interrupted, to the extent that he had to look away, gather himself, and resume the story. He hoped that the listeners would perceive this as only a dramatic pause in his narration. Thereafter, he avoided eye contact with the girl.

In fact, probably no one had noticed except Turtle, who had heard the young storyteller relate this tale many times. Never before had the youngster placed a pause at that point in the story. Curious, Turtle watched closely, and when it happened again, looked quickly in the direction of Storyteller's gaze.

There was no longer any question. Well, some questions, perhaps. Turtle did not know who this girl might be and what she might mean to Storyteller. Had the boy known her before, or was this their first meeting? But the main question had been answered: Yes, this was the cause of the awkward pause in the flow of the story.

Now Turtle watched the girl instead of Storyteller. She was remarkably pretty and seemed unaware of her beauty, with the innocent charm of youth. He could understand how this creature, on the verge of flowering into the fullness of womanhood, could distract Woodpecker . . . no, Storyteller. It was amusing now to watch the two. It was plain that the young woman was entranced with Storyteller's art, just as he was with her beauty.

To Turtle's amusement, the young man dared not look at her again, for fear of interrupting the flow of his story. It would be enjoyable later to discuss this with Owl Woman. He looked around to see if his wife noticed this interplay. Owl was seated some distance away. Turtle felt it necessary to be near the story-fire so that he could rise to speak. Owl Woman usually sat well back to see how the stories were coming across to the other listeners.

He tried to catch her eye for some time. Finally she looked around, and their eyes met. Owl nodded and smiled. So the scene had been so subtle that even the young man's mother had missed it. It had taken the expertise of another storyteller to pick up the slight hesitancy, the break in the smooth rhythmic flow of the narrative. Turtle chuckled to himself and waited for the coming of darkness and the transition to stories that would please not only the children but everyone.

They had been welcomed here before and had planned to return here for the winter two seasons later. Young Storyteller was welcomed enthusiastically. He was now an important part of the routine. There were, of course, a few boys his own age who had a tendency to jeer or sulk in jealousy, but that was to be expected. The girls seemed enthralled, especially the one whose eager smile and bright gaze had so disconcerted the young man.

The story-fires burned far into the night, the local storytellers trading tales with the visitors to the enjoyment of the crowd. Finally, it was Turtle who brought the festivities to an end. "Ah," he exclaimed, "I must seek my bed. We will be trading in the morning, and I will be an easy mark unless I have some sleep!"

The crowd laughed and began to disperse, greatly pleased at the evening's entertainment.

Storyteller looked for the girl as the people separated to go their own ways, but she had disappeared in the darkness. He spent a restless night dreaming of that smiling face in the crowd, so alluring yet so unattainable. Then he would wake and lie staring at the leafy vault overhead. The whisper of the river and the soft sigh of the breeze in the treetops made a background for the voices of the night-creatures. It was a night of great medicine, frustrated by the one question that dominated his thoughts: Who was the exciting girl at the story-fire?

He rose early to walk along the stream, absently gathering sticks for the morning fire, still preoccupied with the excitement of the previous evening. Ahead was a little clearing, much like that where he had played as a child, the place of mystical charm where the rabbit once came close and almost spoke to him. He smiled to himself. That was another world and seemed long ago now.

The clearing that had seemed so remote, he now realized, had been no more than a bow shot from the village. The clearing had probably shrunk appreciably since his early years. He wondered if any other child ever felt that way about this place, that it was a place of enchantment. Lost in thought, he sat on a log at the edge of the glade, watching a rabbit. The creature came cautiously into the open, pausing to nibble, sitting erect to stare around for any danger. In his mind, it was the same rabbit. This was a place of exceptions where anything might happen, and probably would if he could allow his mind to accept the strong medicine of the mystic.

His eyes were half closed as he watched the daylight brighten, the warm rays of the rising sun probing into the clearing. He could imagine that this was the first morning of Creation and that the magic was still strong. "Speak to me, Little Brother," he said softly to the rabbit. "I will do you no harm."

Someone giggled, and he was jolted rudely back to reality. He was somewhat embarrassed, resentful of the intrusion. He glanced around, ready to react defensively, but when he saw the intruder, his mood softened instantly. It was the girl from the story-fire, she of the bright eyes and eager smile. She was even more alluring in the morning sunlight.

"I am sorry," she said, stepping into the open. "I did not mean to intrude."

"It is nothing," he blurted clumsily. "I was . . ." He looked around for the rabbit, but it was gone. "I was just enjoying the morning," he mumbled, hoping that he would not appear too foolish.

"I too." She smiled. "It will be a beautiful day, yes?"

"Yes . . ." There was a long and clumsy pause. "I . . . do I know you?" he asked. "You were at the fire last night."

She laughed, a rippling musical sound like none he had heard before, yet familiar somehow. "I am Plum Leaf," she said. "We played together as children."

Of course! Two, three seasons ago, when they stopped here, they had played—yes, in this very clearing. Both were a trifle shy, and when the other children began more boisterous games, these two drew aside to play more quietly. How could he have forgotten? But then, he had left immediately and had not seen her since.

"Forgive me," he said clumsily. "You have changed!"

She laughed again, the little musical trickle that he found so delightful. She turned slowly, a complete turn to face him again. "You like the changes?" she asked provocatively. "You have changed much yourself, Woodpecker."

He was dumbfounded. This was not the shy, retiring child he had known, but a capable-looking young woman, confident in her womanhood and her beauty.

Then he realized how much he had changed. From a shy and retiring boy, he had become the confident Storyteller, proud of his expertise. "We have both changed," he laughed.

"Yes. I liked your stories last night. I was proud." Then she became embarrassed. Her statement of pride implied a relationship that was not there. It might have been once, but no longer. There was a clumsy moment as both pondered that implication.

"Has it been well with you?" he asked, seeking safer ground.

"Yes . . . my brother, Tall Pine, . . . you remember? He is married. Big-Eared Man—he was older than we—he drowned last year."

"But what of you?" he asked.

Her eyes dropped shyly. "There is nothing to tell. I grew up, like you. Is it exciting, to travel and trade?"

"Yes, mostly. Sometimes hard work."

"Dangerous?"

"Maybe, a little." He could not resist a little boasting.

"I think that would be an exciting life," Plum Leaf said, her eyes dancing. "Your mother seems very happy."

"Yes. She and my—her husband—are well suited to each other."

"You told me that he courted her with the flute." Plum Leaf chuckled happily. "I thought it was very romantic. He is an exciting man."

There was a strange pang for a moment as the young man wished silently that Plum Leaf might feel that way about *him.* Maybe she did. After all, she was here with him, at this odd hour and place. Did that signify something?

"When will you travel on?" she asked.

"Soon . . . no more than a day or two. My grandfather is old. My mother wishes to be with them. We will winter there."

"Yes, that is good." Her tone was a bit sad, befitting the conversation about the ailing grandfather, but her face was radiant. "Then, we will have no chance to become reacquainted," she suggested cautiously.

"No . . ." This was moving almost too rapidly for Young Storyteller, yet the excitement drew him like a moth to the flame. "I . . . I should go back to the camp," he said. "They will wonder where . . ."

"Yes, of course!" she agreed. She turned and led the way back toward the village, her stride long and confident. He liked the way she moved and hurried to walk with her. She matched stride for stride, and it occurred to him that they walked well together. For a moment he wondered what others would think when the two returned together.

An old woman peered sleepily out of her doorway and smiled at the two. They waved self-consciously and hurried on.

Young Storyteller's heart was very good.

8

》 》 》

"Things are very bad here," said Yellow Bowl, shaking her head and clucking her tongue.

"How so, Mother?" asked Owl Woman. "My father's health?"

She had been startled at how feeble her father appeared. Once a proud warrior, Bear Sits now shuffled weakly, his aging joints stiffened by the years and old injuries. It hurt Owl Woman to see him so. She remembered his active years when she was a child growing into womanhood.

"No, no, not that. It is the way of things that one grows old. Bear is well respected and proud. He is older than I, you remember," said Yellow Bowl.

"Yes, but he has changed so . . ."

"Of course, Owl. The years have passed. But oh, they are good to you! You have never looked prettier! And how Woodpecker has grown, and this lovely child . . . Lark, you call her?"

"Yes, Mother. But, you said things are bad? How so?"

"Ah, yes! I am sorry . . . there is much to tell. You remember the stories of tribes from beyond the Big Salt Water, men whose eyes are bluish, yet they still see?"

"Yes, Mother, but there have been such stories for a long time."

"No, it is real! They are here."

"Ah! *Here,* in the village?"

"No . . . well, yes sometimes. They have built a town downriver, only a sleep away."

"You have seen them, Mother?"

"Of course. Everyone has seen them."

"But what do they do?"

The older woman shrugged. "Hunt a little. Trade for some furs. Mostly, they fight. They are warriors."

"Fight who, Mother? Our people?"

"No, no. Not now, anyway. One wonders, of course. But they fight each other."

"I do not understand."

"Nor do I," Yellow Bowl stated, shaking her head sadly. "There are two kinds of them."

"Two *tribes* of these outsiders?"

"Yes . . . maybe so. They speak different tongues, anyway."

"How are they called?"

"Well, the nearest town is of *Yen-glees.* The others are farther north. They are *Fran-cois.*"

"And they fight?"

"Yes. To see who will stay here."

"But why?"

"To trade! For furs, robes."

"What do they offer?"

"Oh, knives, beads, cloth." Yellow Bowl was preparing food and turned to hold up a small knife. "See?"

Owl Woman examined the knife closely. Its blade was smooth and shiny, and its edge straight rather than chipped in serrations. "What sort of stone . . ."

Her mother laughed. "Not stone . . . it is called metal. Very useful! It can be resharpened."

"Mother, this is strong medicine! I must tell Turtle. Knives such as this would be good for trading."

"Yes, that is true. They have axes too, made of this."

"Axes?"

"Yes. They can be thrown, as a weapon. A small ax."

"Mother, these are useful things. Why do you say that times are bad?"

Yellow Bowl's face fell, losing the cheerful good humor that it had shown a moment ago. "Ah, my child, that is the bad part. Each of the outsider tribes has tribes here for friends."

Now Owl Woman was completely puzzled. "But how is this bad?"

Yellow Bowl clucked her tongue. "Well, you know how tribes have others who are enemies? Some have always fought. Now, if your enemy joins the Yen-glees, then you join the Fran-cois."

"But why? For what purpose?"

"To kill the other. One tribe is paid to kill Yen-glees, another to kill Fran-cois."

Owl Woman was beginning to understand. It was horrible, this thing of hiring to kill. It was one thing to kill in a battle over territory or political unrest, quite another to kill for payment, to kill someone with whom you have no quarrel.

"How . . . how are they paid?"

"In trade goods."

"No, Mother. Paid for each kill?"

"Oh. Yes, proof is required. A scalp. They skin the top of the head."

"*Skin?* . . ."

"Yes. Some have become quite wealthy."

For Owl Woman, the enormity of this situation was just starting to sink in. "And our people kill for the Yen-glees?"

"We have tried to be for neither. This is what the chiefs say. But some of the men hunt scalps on their own."

"For which side?"

Yellow Bowl shrugged. "Who knows? Who pays the best?"

"Mother!" Owl gasped in horror. "The hair of men is sold like that of a beaver?"

"Not quite. It is usually worth more."

Owl Woman was silent. Even Yellow Bowl, without realizing it, was thinking of the hair of the slain as an item for trade like a beaver pelt. Times were worse, it seemed, than her mother was aware.

It was difficult to tell how much of all this her father understood. Bear Sits spent most of his time merely staring blankly. He smiled and spoke when spoken to, then lapsed back into his detached haze. It seemed too much effort to concentrate, even to think about the situation that had developed. The old warrior appeared to have simply lost the will to question, perhaps even the will to live. Owl Woman wondered if he could last another winter.

Worst of all, the thing that permeated the village was something that could not be seen or heard. It was an uneasiness, a feeling. At first, when the travelers had arrived, it was not quite so apparent. In the excitement of the homecoming, more subtle things were overlooked. Only gradually it had become apparent, a vague unrest that kept everyone tense and suspicious. Even after learning its source, Owl Woman could hardly believe the change. It was a moody brooding thing that oppressed the very spirit of the place. She was saddened by it and a little fearful. She was glad that Woodpecker had not grown up and come of age in these surroundings. But that saddened her again. How different from the mood of the People in her own childhood.

Childhood—ah, Woodpecker was no longer a child. Even as the two women visited, he and Turtle had gone to make their courtesy calls on the chiefs and prepare for the storytelling. She would be proud tonight, at the fire, when both her husband and her son took prominent places in the festivities.

Yes, it could be a good stay here, she tried to convince herself. Despite the strange mood, it *was* home. Trading could be very good. She must tell Turtle of the medicine-knives made of a new sort of stone. Yes, here was opportunity. They carried a good variety of items for trade.

Red medicine-stone for pipes, from west of the Big Lakes, heavy to carry but valuable since there was only one known source. Turtle had also acquired several shards of shiny black stone from the far western mountains. It was unexcelled, he said, for knives and arrowpoints, flaking cleanly when worked and leaving a very sharp edge. Probably only a skilled stonebreaker would wish to trade for that.

Turtle was fascinated by the odd and unusual, and loved to trade for new and unknown items. Only last season he had obtained a small flat cake of a substance from the far South, "choko-latl." It was used as food, or for flavor, in the region where it was grown, at least so said the trader from whom Turtle obtained it. There were medicinal properties to the choko-latl too, they had been told. A small piece, broken from the slab and stirred in hot water, made a pleasing drink.

They had sampled the choko-latl out of curiosity.

"Its taste is strange," Owl Woman said as she sipped the dark fluid from a horn cup.

"But good," added Storyteller. "What does it do?"

"Everything, the man from the South said." Turtle chuckled. "More strength, bravery. It makes one a better lover."

Owl Woman smiled smugly. "Then you need none," she stated flatly.

Storyteller, in the self-consciousness of newfound puberty, said nothing.

"They use it to flavor meats too," Turtle said. "I cannot think how that would taste."

He had not traded any of the choko-latl, but now, Owl Woman thought, he might wish to do so for some of the new things brought by the outsiders. Yes, it should be good trading.

She had no chance to speak to him of the things she had learned, good and bad, before the time came for storytelling. Turtle, true to his word, boasted of his son's ability and promised the children extra storytime just before dark. It was exciting to come home to such recognition. Storyteller had developed his skills and showed great promise. Owl Woman was eager for her friends and relatives to see how well the boy had grown and matured.

As the crowd gathered, Owl Woman and Yellow Bowl arrived early to choose good places. Bear Sits had stayed at the lodge.

"I will come later," he said vaguely.

"Will he come?" Owl asked her mother.

"Probably, if he remembers." Yellow Bowl sighed. "His spirit wanders."

They settled down in an open space and watched the crowd gather. It was pleasing to hear the remarks about the new Storyteller.

"They say he is very good for one so young."

"Is he not one of the People?"

"Yes! You remember Owl Woman, whose husband was killed? He is her son."

"Son? Ah, yes, there was a child. She married the Trader, no?"

"Yes, that is the one. . . ."

The two woman laughed softly together.

"Is he really good with the stories, Owl?" her mother asked.

"Of course! But, you will soon see."

Shadows were long now, and the assembling crowd was growing. Turtle threaded his way among them, carrying a firebrand toward the stack of fuel. There must be a fire for stories. Even when it was not needed for heat and not yet for light, there must be a fire. The rising of smoke to mingle with the spirits of the place was necessary for the mood, for the stories to come alive. Excitement was in the air as cheery little tongues of orange licked at the dry tinder and began to grow. In a short while, the heavier sticks began to ignite, and the fire assumed a life of its own.

Storyteller stepped forward and selected a place to stand. Turtle had taught him well the showmanship of the storyteller. He must avoid the possibility of a chance shift in the breeze, blowing smoke or sparks in his direction to interrupt the story. He chose a spot where the background would be good, a solid mass of dark foliage that would stir the imagination and improve the imagery of the story. He was especially nervous tonight. Many of his childhood friends would be there, and he must do well.

The young man's palms were damp as he held his hands to the darkening sky in a silent invocation. The murmur of the crowd died, and silence descended.

"In the long-ago times," he began, "animals could speak as we do, and all tribes spoke the same tongue. . . ."

9

» » »

It was late in the autumn of that year that Owl Woman saw the restlessness in her man. Not a restlessness to be free from her, simply the longing to be on the trail again.

The trading season had been cut short by their arrival at her home village. Turtle had cheerfully accepted it and had carried out a brisk trade for a few days. Then it settled down to a sporadic, one-at-a-time trickle that Owl Woman knew was a frustration.

The Moon of Ripening had passed and the Moon of Falling Leaves, and it was now the Moon of Madness. Maybe that was part of Turtle's restlessness. The coming of the Mad Moon always affected people to some extent. Maybe it was a frustrated migration urge, a primordial wish to join the great geese in their long lines of flight across the clear blue of autumn skies.

The deer were rutting, the bucks polishing their new antlers on trees, preparing to establish their right to the strongest and most alluring does. Bull elk were bugling. Many of the birds had gone south already, but of those who would stay, the madness seemed to hold sway. Grouse and quail flew wildly, blindly, and irrationally through the woods, sometimes crashing into trees or rocks in their frantic celebration of the Moon of Madness.

Squirrels scampered fearlessly where they would not

have risked going earlier, gathering and burying nuts, more nuts than they could ever use. The forgotten nuts in the ground would sprout in the Moon of Awakening to begin new trees. This, at least, lent some purpose to the activity of the Moon of Madness. It was part of the way of things.

But Turtle fretted over his own inactivity, and Owl Woman was concerned. "There is a village of our people only one sleep upriver," she observed casually one morning. "Maybe you could take Woodpecker, and the two of you could spend some time trading."

Turtle was silent for a moment. "Are you trying to get rid of me, woman?"

There was a moment of concern, but then she saw that he was teasing her. "Maybe." She giggled. "Old Lame Badger, there, once wanted to marry me."

They discussed the possibility seriously then, and it was decided.

"You are sure you do not want to go with us?"

"No, go ahead. It will be good for me to visit with my mother. She will enjoy her granddaughter, too. You and Woodpecker need some time together. But I will miss you both."

So it happened that the two storytellers traveled upstream to trade. Yellow Bowl had grave doubts about the wisdom of such a trip. "You do not understand the danger," she protested.

"It will be all right, Mother," Owl assured. "He has traveled and traded everywhere, with strange and unknown tribes. He can get along with anyone."

Yellow Bowl, unwilling to prolong the argument, shook her head in despair, clucked her tongue, then closed her lips in a tight determined line. She would not discuss it again.

The first night away from the village the two men spent at a pleasant glade where a spring trickled from the rocks. There were indications that this was a common stopping place; there were ashes of burned-out fires and several spots where travelers had spread their sleeping robes. The spring, they noticed, had been cleaned out and flat stones placed around the rim to form a clear pool of sparkling water.

They saw no other travelers and arrived at their destination the following afternoon. It was a good evening of stories, and the trading was brisk the next day. It was undoubtedly helpful that Storyteller was one of their own and many remembered his father.

Turtle was able to barter for a very fine steel knife, an object he had been unable to acquire so far. Everyone who possessed one wished to keep it, he decided, and the trade value was very dear. The specimen he was able to buy cost him dearly—a medicine pipe, a shard of the finest black obsidian, and half his cake of choko-latl. He hated to part with the choko-latl; there was no telling when he might acquire more. But first and foremost, he was a trader, and the function of a trader is to trade.

The knife was certainly an incentive. It was apparent that its medicine was important, its spirit strong. In the right light, it sparkled like the reflection of sunlight on water, and at times it seemed that blue fire licked along its cutting edge. Turtle spent much time staring at the knife, trying to fathom its spirit. But as with many things of the spirit, its mystery continued to elude him. Meanwhile, it was surely a useful item. Storyteller too was greatly impressed by its mystery. He would never ask to use the knife; it was too important a thing. It was much like the personal quality of one's medicine, which was inappropriate for another to covet. In the back of Storyteller's mind, however, an embryonic idea was forming. *Someday,* he thought, *someday I will have such a medicine-knife.*

They spent another night at the host village and set off for home with plenty of invitations to return for more stories and trades. It was that evening that their world was rudely shaken apart.

Until now, they had rather discounted Yellow Bowl's dire predictions of doom. It is the privilege of the older ones to voice warnings and caution the younger generation. Such warnings are partly taken to heart and partly observed, but after all, the older ones are cautious. Their advice must be tempered with reason.

Shadows were growing long when the travelers approached the camping spot by the spring. They would stay here and travel on to the village tomorrow. Through the trees ahead, they could see a campfire burning and smell its smoke.

"Good!" said Turtle. "We will have company tonight."

They walked in boldly, unthinking of danger, to confront three well-armed men. The strangers were obviously surprised and drew weapons threateningly.

"Greetings, my friends. We come in peace," announced Turtle in his wife's tongue. Simultaneously he extended his right hand, palm forward, in the hand-sign for peace.

"Who are you?" one of the strangers demanded. "You speak our tongue. Why?"

"Wait!" exclaimed another. "Are these not the storytellers?"

"They carry heavy packs," said the third greedily. "We can—"

"Stop!" the second insisted. "You cannot harm them. They are our people."

"Not this one," argued the man who had spoken first. "Look at his hair, his moccasins!"

"But his shirt and leggings," the other man replied. "They are ours."

It was a fearful, chilling thing to realize that the strangers were debating their fate—even worse, as if they did not exist and the ultimate decision did not matter much.

"One scalp is hard to tell from another," said the hardlooking warrior who had looked greedily at their packs. "Who is to know?"

"*We* are to know. These are the storytellers. This

younger one is a relative of mine. His mother was married to an uncle . . ."

Reluctantly, the others lowered their weapons.

Turtle laughed nervously. He had occasionally been robbed in his travels but never threatened this way. "Look, my friends," he ventured, striding boldly past them, "we would like to make camp before dark. We—"

He stopped short. Beyond the fire were two sleeping places with rumpled robes tossed aside. Near each lay the body of a man, sprawled grotesquely in death. The brightness of the blood that still flowed from their wounds told that they had been killed only a short while ago.

"Who . . . who are they?" he mumbled.

"Enemies," one man said.

The other strangers laughed.

"They are nobody, now."

The one who seemed to be their leader sighed impatiently. "Let us get rid of them," he urged. He drew his knife and stepped forward, gripping the hair of one of the prostrate forms.

"Wait!" said one of the others. "That one has good hair. We can get two, maybe three scalps."

"I know how to take a scalp," snapped the other, slashing a circular cut around the top of the head.

"But there are three of us and only two scalps. We can make another. Look, if you cut this way—"

"Where will we take them? Yen-glees?"

"It does not matter. Who pays the best now?"

"I am not sure."

"Well, we can ask. No hurry. Scalps keep well when dried."

They laughed again, finished their ghoulish work, and stripped the bodies of anything useful. Then they dragged them into the darkening woods and returned to the fire.

"Well," said one to Turtle, "where are you heading?"

The casual conversational tone was so bizarre under the circumstances that Turtle could hardly answer. "My wife's village," Turtle mumbled. "It is as you said. We are storytellers and traders, returning home."

"Good! Let us do some trading! What do you have?"

Mildly protesting, Turtle opened the packs and still under duress, tried to carry on trade. The goods offered by the strangers were largely the possessions of the dead men, for which Turtle had no desire at all. However, he felt obliged to keep the others in good humor. They accomplished a few trades, but when one of them offered a still-oozing scalp, it was too much.

"We do not deal in scalps!" he snapped.

The three men laughed.

"You wear one!"

"But it is not for sale," insisted Turtle.

They laughed again.

It was a long, sleepless night, but Turtle and Storyteller were not harmed. At daylight, the strangers left, heading upstream. Turtle urged haste as they broke camp to head downstream. They made one stop, to dispose of the belongings of the dead they had been forced to take in trade. The items were bundled together, weighted with stones, and dropped into a deep hole in the river.

"We will say nothing of this, Storyteller," Turtle advised.

"Not to my mother?"

"Maybe to her, later. Not now. My son, these are bad times."

10

» » »

In most respects, it was an uneventful winter. The two Storytellers, Elder and Younger, would not have believed it could be so after the chilling experience at the camp beside the spring. It was a day or two before they fully realized the narrow margin of their escape. If one of the warriors had not been a distant relative of Owl Woman's, their bones would even now be moldering in the forest with those of the other victims. Their scalps, no doubt, would by this time have become merely a commodity, to be traded for a knife, a mirror, or with other scalps or furs, maybe a blanket.

They decided after much discussion that neither would say anything to Owl Woman about the incident. She would only worry. They would agree that they had been well received and that the trading was good but not great. Some of their trades were ill-advised probably, they would admit. Turtle, who usually shared everything with his wife, would go so far as to say that the People there were quite preoccupied with the rewards of scalping. This, he stated flatly, could do great harm to the trade. Turtle even mentioned that someone had offered them a scalp in trade. He had refused, he related, by implying that among his own people there was a religious taboo.

In this way, everything the returning traders reported

was literally true. They did not relate the entire story yet managed to share their fears and the reasons for them. The women were quite upset with even this superficial description of the events upriver. Yellow Bowl shook her head and clucked her tongue.

"It is as I told you," she said almost triumphantly.

Owl Woman demonstrated a deeper concern. "This is worse than I thought, Turtle," she said as soon as they were alone. "I am worried about Woodpecker."

"You need not worry for him," Turtle stated positively. But he could not tell her why or how he was so certain. "He understands the danger," he finished lamely.

"I do not like it!" Owl insisted. "Turtle, let us go on. Let us winter with your people."

Turtle shook his head. "That would be my choice too," he admitted. "I did not expect this problem. But we are here now, and the days grow shorter. My people are many sleeps away. No one travels the prairie at this season."

"But the good weather holds!" she insisted. "Look, the day is warm, though nights are cool."

"Yes, for now. But, Owl, this is Second Summer, when everyone uses good weather to prepare for winter. Any day now it will be over, and Cold Maker will waken."

She said nothing, and Turtle tried almost desperately to explain. "It is different here, Owl. When it snows, your people go inside by the fire. Even travelers in the woods can make a shelter. A traveler caught in the open prairie is dead!"

"Then how do your people live there?" she demanded.

"You will see, when we go there. They move to a sheltered area . . . before Second Summer . . . and stuff the lower part of the lodges with dry grass, a line of brush, maybe, to break the wind. Right now, they have done these things, and they are ready. We . . . if we left now, we would be in the open, searching for them, in the worst of the Moon of Snows!"

Finally, he managed to convince her. To stay here was the lesser of two dangers. Here, there might be danger. On the open prairie in winter it was certain. For a time, Turtle was afraid he would have to argue the merits of a quiet sleep by freezing to death versus the violence of being killed for one's pelt. It did not quite come to that, however, for which Turtle was thankful.

They settled in for the winter. There was little travel, even in the more sheltered woodlands, as the Moon of Long Nights descended. It was too dangerous because of Cold Maker's unpredictability. In the open country of his home, a storm could be seen approaching for half a day. Here, with trees and hills obstructing one's view, it could descend suddenly and unexpectedly.

Turtle had had to deal with that when he left the wide skies of the open plains to trade in the woodlands. For a season or two, he had experienced a sort of trapped, panicky feeling, like the one a caged bird must feel. He would find himself wanting to run, to escape to some place where he could at least see the horizon. He had never entirely overcome the feeling but had managed to control it. Some of his brothers of the prairie, he knew, could never have wintered in the close confines of such areas.

So while he did not relish the prospect of wintering here, he was prepared to tolerate it. It helped greatly that his bed was shared by Owl Woman. She always tried to understand, usually quite successfully. She did not fully understand his occasional need for the open spaces and the spiritual feel of the big sky, but she was willing to try. And that in itself was important.

The warm days of Second Summer continued that year well into the Moon of Madness before Cold Maker awoke in his ice cave somewhere in the northern mountains to sweep down across the land. In only a few days, people were adapting well. Through the Moon of Long Nights there came a succession of snows, blanketing the woods and freezing the edges of the river. On days when the sun was seen at all, its watery yellow rays seemed barely to warm the day before it began to sink again.

Turtle's stories from the plains perhaps expressed it best. It was the annual struggle since Creation between Cold Maker's onslaught and the waning torch of Sun Boy. Cold Maker pushed his adversary far to the south in the Moon of Long Nights. But each year, Sun Boy managed to renew his torch in time, slowly to battle his way north, driving Cold Maker back to his icy lair in the mountains. At least, it had always been so. Turtle always managed to leave just a little bit of doubt, the slight twinge of fear that *this* season . . . It left a delicious hint of danger hanging in the air.

One of the storytellers of the village who was also a holy man performed a ceremony to assist the sun's return. He chanted and danced, and made symbolic sacrifices over a fire in a clearing near the village. This ceremony was carried out annually, it was said. It was performed late in the Moon of Long Nights and was sure to prevent the dying of the sun. The ceremony was successful once more, and by the middle of the Moon of Snows, it could be seen that the days were growing longer. There was still much winter ahead, of course, but the turning point had been successfully passed.

Turtle congratulated the holy man, agreeing that the ceremony had been impressive as well as effective. "Sun Boy," he stated seriously, "needs the help of all of us to banish Cold Maker again each winter."

The old priest's eyes twinkled in friendship. This was a skill for which Turtle was well known, the ability to see events in terms of the customs of others. It had made him successful both as a storyteller and a trader.

There was much need for storytelling during the Moon of Snows. It was impossible to travel much, not at all without snowshoes. It was better to stay inside, smoking with friends and acquaintances, sometimes gambling, and exchanging stories.

Turtle did not gamble and advised his apprentice against it. "It is a bad habit for a trader," he explained. "Everything can be lost very quickly."

Both men, however, were in demand at the social "smokes" in the longhouse where stories went on and on. Paths in the snow were beaten down by the pressure of many footsteps—from each lodge to the others, to the woods for fuel, to the river for water, and to the longhouse.

It was a fairly heavy winter, said the people of the village. At a time near the end of the Moon of Snows there came a storm that seemed to be the most furious of Cold Maker's attacks yet. For two days, he howled around the lodges and piled snow among the trees. The river froze completely, so that a man could walk to the other side. Those who ventured out suffered frostbite on their faces and fingers. Lame Dog lost part of an ear from not wearing a head covering when he went out for firewood. Even the gatherings at the longhouse were discontinued.

Everyone relaxed when Sun reappeared, but it was apparent that the winter was not over. Still ahead was the Moon of Hunger. There might not be many more of the prolonged severe storms this season. What attacks by Cold Maker did come would be short-lived. His dreaded power was weakening, and he only struck back in retreat.

But the Moon of Hunger was aptly named. Provisions for the winter, no matter how many or how well stored, would run short by the Moon of Awakening when it became possible to hunt again. There could be hunger in the village and even starvation. This year, despite the severity of the winter, supplies had been good, and there was little actual suffering.

There was one tragedy. During one of the brief but furious late snows, Bear Sits had stepped outside to relieve his bladder and had not returned. By the time the others had realized the danger, it was snowing harder and growing dark. They tramped the nearby woods and inquired in other lodges, but the old man could not be found. It was assumed, even when his body was not discovered after the storm, that he was dead. No one could have survived the night in the open. In his senility, he might have wandered off in the wrong direction, into the storm.

The crossing over of Bear Sits was observed with the ritual Songs of Mourning.

Yellow Bowl did not take the loss well. She was convinced that her husband had not merely wandered off, but that it had been a deliberate act. Bear Sits had sacrificed himself, she insisted, to be sure that there was enough food for the children. "But there *was* enough," she cried repeatedly. "There *was!*"

Turtle had a slightly different theory. During Bear Sits's more lucid moments, he thought, the old warrior was depressed at what he had become. He was now virtually helpless, his eyesight fading, his memory for all but his youth nearly gone. The journey through the storm to the Other Side was a last defiant gesture of courage. If it provided more food for the living, so be it. But the gesture itself was for Bear Sits, his last decision as a warrior —to die on his feet, fighting.

After the three days' mourning was ended, there was some concern that Yellow Bowl would not be able to return to the activities of the living. She continued to mourn. Owl Woman and Turtle took her aside. "Mother, it does not matter," Owl insisted. "Of course there was food, but it does not matter now."

"It does!" Yellow Bowl argued. "He knew what he was doing, but he was wrong! We had plenty."

Turtle finally tried a new approach. "Mother," he said, "Bear Sits was a great warrior. For whatever reason, he did this as he wished. He crossed over when he chose to do so."

That idea seemed to help. Gradually, the mourning of Yellow Bowl became more appropriate, and she resumed the life of the village as they looked forward to the coming of spring.

The body of Bear Sits was never found. In body and in spirit, he had crossed over.

11

» » »

The Moon of Awakening brought mixed feelings to Storyteller. The major feature of the previous year had been the renewal of his acquaintance with Plum Leaf. The conversations had been halting at first, but quickly grew more comfortable as the relationship solidified. Storyteller had managed to prolong the trading for several days. At every spare moment, the two young people shared hopes and dreams. He told her of the time when he was a child and felt that the rabbit almost spoke to him. He had never told that to anyone but unashamedly shared it with her, knowing that she would understand. She did, of course, and smiled her knowing smile as she placed a hand on his arm.

They had found that as children, both had loved the little clearing where their reunion had taken place. Both had considered it a special place of enchantment where wonderful things might take place.

"Maybe they still do," he had suggested. "That is where we found each other."

She smiled and snuggled closer.

"Ah, but soon I must leave," he reminded her.

He could hardly bear to part with the beautiful girl who had become a part of his life. They had talked of it. They had talked of many things—of marriage, even, though both wondered if they were too young. If their lives were a little different . . . If their world was a bit more stable . . . If Storyteller was not committed to travel and trade . . .

"But you *must* do that," Plum Leaf insisted. "That is your life."

It was true. At one time, he could have envisioned himself as a resident of this village, a hunter like his grandfather Bear Sits, and a mighty warrior. That had been his aim in life as a very young child. His father too had helped this image. It was after the loss of his father, maybe, that the boy had turned to things of the spirit. Then, the coming of Turtle, who had changed his life and that of his mother so greatly. Now he could think of nothing except to follow this line of endeavor.

The coming of spring would make travel possible, and Turtle would wish to leave. Storyteller too wished to leave the area that had become so threatening. It had been his home as a child, protecting and sheltering. But now its spirit had changed. The dark threat of mercenary violence hovered over the entire region. He could not erase from his mind the memory of the two dead men in the glade by the spring, their sightless eyes staring unseeing at the darkening sky while someone ripped the skin from their heads. Sometimes he dreamed about it, waking in a cold sweat of fear. Yes, it would be good to leave this region of bad medicine.

But travel toward Turtle's people would be to the west, while to the south lay the village of Plum Leaf. They would be moving *away* from her. This was the cause of his mixed feelings.

There came a day, finally, when the village awoke to a new sound. The wind had changed in the night and blew softly with a warm breath. The new sound was the drip of melting snow, forming in crystal drops along the edges of the thatched roofs, to fall to the snow below.

The rising sun sped the process on its way. Soon little rivulets sliced their crooked paths toward lower levels, merging into tinkling streams that rushed toward the river. Cold Maker's power was broken, and he was in full retreat. They would leave soon, and he thought of the parting last season as they had prepared to travel.

He and Plum Leaf had met at the clearing for one last time. They had made small talk for a while to avoid more serious conversation. Finally, Plum Leaf had approached what was on their minds. "When will you leave?"

"I do not know . . . It depends much on the weather."

"I do not wish to see you go."

"I know. My heart is the same, Plum Leaf."

"When will you come back?"

He shrugged. "Who knows? Maybe next year."

"Does your father know about us?"

"Yes. My mother too. I do not know whether they know how serious we are."

"Can you ask them?"

"Yes, maybe."

It was so frustrating—to talk of this but to be unable to make plans.

"I *will* come back for you," he promised.

"I know. And I will wait for you."

"Promise?"

"Of course!"

"I will speak to Turtle," he said. "I know he wishes to visit his people next season. Maybe winter there."

"Then it would be more than a year. . . ."

"Yes. Plum Leaf, I must talk to him. And to my mother, of course . . . see what they plan."

The proper occasion had not seemed to arise, and nothing definite had been asked or promised. But now Storyteller felt that he must know. He approached Turtle about his plans for the coming season.

Turtle was rather noncommittal. His was a day-at-a-time, see-what-happens approach to life.

"Who knows what may happen, Storyteller? The season is young. First, let us leave this area, for reasons you understand well."

"Yes, Uncle. But . . . there is this girl . . ."

"Ah! That is it! Yes, I remember her. Your choice is good." He chuckled.

"But, Uncle, I need to know . . . when will I be able to see her again? I . . . I do not like to think of her so far away!"

"You *are* serious!" Turtle observed. "Well, it could be many moons before we come back. Maybe she should go with us!"

Storyteller gasped. "Father . . . I . . . we . . . I have not courted!"

"But you are sure?"

"Of course."

"And she is, also?"

"Yes, but I . . ."

"Then where is the problem?" It would never be said that Turtle's approach to anything would be commonplace.

"But, Uncle, there must be *some* courting!"

"Yes, of course. We will go south for her, then go on."

"Is there time? Before we go west to your people?"

Turtle laughed. "Who knows how long such things will take? But you said she is ready. We will leave when your courting is finished!"

"Uncle . . . one more thing. Can you teach me to play the courting flute?"

"Aiee!" shouted Turtle happily. "Yes! It worked with your mother!"

"Yes. Plum Leaf spoke of that. She was greatly pleased to hear of when you did that."

"Ah, so was your mother! Yes, it was good. I will teach you. But this may take longer!"

"Or shorter, if I learn quickly!"

Both men laughed.

* * *

So it happened that when the storytelling traders moved on to the west, their number was increased by one. Plum Leaf was now the wife of Storyteller the Younger.

Her mother had at first resisted. "She is so young!"

"That is true," admitted Owl Woman. "I had doubts when they came to me. But think of this: They have decided, and it will be good."

"That is true. But . . ."

"Look! How old were you and I when we married?"

The two women giggled like children.

"Yes. But she . . . my oldest, you know. I am not ready to be a grandmother!"

"Nor am I!" Owl Woman laughed. "But I will look after them. She will not forget the ways of your people. My husband is not of *my* people, you know."

Finally, Acorn, mother of Plum Leaf, consented, and the two were married, to start out into the world together. Owl Woman was pleased, both for her son and for the chance to have another adult woman in the party. Lark, just approaching womanhood, was delighted at the prospect.

"If we travel well," Turtle noted as they loaded the two canoes to start upriver, "we will be in the prairie by the Moon of Roses. That is a beautiful time."

It would be good, he thought, to see again the country of the big sky, the open plain, and the far-off edge of Earth. He had not realized until now how much he missed the prairie, how closed-in he had felt by the winter among the forest trees.

12

"It is so big!" said Owl Woman in awe.

The five stood gazing over a vast expanse of grass. For several days they had seen larger areas of grassland and smaller areas of forest. Now there was almost entirely grass. It was nearly a moon now since they had left the village to travel southwest toward Turtle's home country.

They went by canoe at first, stopping to tell stories and trade as they traveled down the small river to progressively larger streams, as other streams joined the one they rode on. They came to a great river, which Turtle said was the *Missi-ssippi,* the Father of Waters, and floated southward on it for several days. They camped at night or stopped at one of the villages along the shores.

Turtle seemed to be watching for something on the west bank of the Big River. Finally one day he pointed ahead with his paddle. "There!" he said. "The *Missouree!*"

They stopped to trade for a day with the people of a town at the place where the great rivers joined, then moved upstream on the Missouri. It was apparent that the country was changing. While there were trees along the river everywhere, they could see vast open areas from time to time. Storyteller was enthralled by his first sight of a large herd of buffalo; hundreds and hundreds of the animals grazed calmly on open grassland.

It was obvious from Turtle's increasing excitement that, experienced traveler though he might be, coming home was important to him. He spent increasing amounts of time in discussion with the natives at each stop. Usually he seemed familiar with their tongue, but sometimes he resorted to hand-signs. Storyteller noticed increased use of the signs as they moved westward. Turtle was asking, he realized, for information regarding the summer camp of the "Trader People." Usually, he received a negative shrug.

Then came an evening when they stopped as usual, and Turtle's usual question brought a new answer. "Yes! They were here, in the Moon of Falling Leaves, traveling southwest. Our hunters saw them following the herds."

"But you do not know where they are this summer?"

"No, no. We have not seen them this year."

Turtle explained how the great buffalo herds would migrate south in winter and each spring move north again, following the greening of the prairie. "My people sometimes burn the grass to make them come into an area."

"How is that, Uncle?"

"When the old dry grass is burned, it makes tender new grass. Then the buffalo come."

"Do your people follow the buffalo?"

"Sometimes, if we need meat. Usually not. It is easier to let buffalo come to you."

"But, Uncle, why did they go south?"

"Who knows?" Turtle shrugged. "The chiefs did not like the thought of a coming winter, maybe. This is not unusual, Storyteller. A hard winter or two makes people think of warmer places, no?"

After another day or two, and questions at another village, Turtle elected to leave the river and turn southward. He made arrangements to leave the two canoes, trading for horses for each of the adults, and one pack horse. Little Lark would ride the pack horse or ride behind one of the others.

"How will he know where to go?" asked the bewildered Plum Leaf.

"I do not know," answered Storyteller, equally puzzled. "The spirit of this prairie is strange . . . different. Maybe it takes special medicine to understand it."

"The sky is so wide." Owl Woman pointed. "Look, you can see farther than you could travel in a whole day!"

"Maybe that helps to find his people."

Turtle had led the party away from the river with seeming confidence. It took a few days for the inexperienced riders to become accustomed to the swaying rhythm of the horses' gaits. They were stiff and sore after a day's travel. Even Turtle admitted that he was feeling the protest of unused muscles. Before long, however, they became accustomed to the new activity. In his eagerness, Turtle continued to set a demanding pace.

On the third day after they left the river, the travelers came to a smaller stream. A haze of smoke hung over a fringe of trees far upstream, and Turtle pointed. "That is a village of Growers," he stated flatly.

"You know where we are, Father?" asked Storyteller in astonishment.

"No, but that is where they would be." He nudged his horse in that direction.

It was late afternoon before they approached the town. It was as Turtle had said, a collection of lodges made of logs and mud. Surrounding the village were carefully tended fields of corn, beans, and pumpkins.

"How did you know, Father?"

"Know what?"

"That these were Growers?"

"Ah . . . well, hunters' lodges are different . . . skin tents, you know."

"But you could not see the lodges from a half day's travel away!"

"That is true. Well, maybe. You can see a skin lodge much farther. See, these are dug partly into the ground.

The lodges of my people are tall . . . maybe two, three times the height of a man."

"So they can be seen farther?"

"Yes, of course. But there are other things. These lodges are close together and close to the river. Our lodges are more scattered."

"Why, Uncle?" asked Plum Leaf.

"Well . . . you children ask many questions!" he complained mildly. "Well, my people have many horses. They need more room to ride among their lodges. And the door must face east, of course."

"East? Why?"

"To greet Sun. But come now; we must pay our respects to their chief."

Storyteller and Plum Leaf were still puzzled about Turtle's preoccupation with the doorways' facing east. They only saw that he was excited, eager to be back in his own country. They spoke of it to Owl Woman, who smiled affectionately.

"Yes! He is like a child coming home, is he not? I think . . . maybe . . . there is something about this farseeing land that makes him that way. He has spoken sometimes of how he feels closed in, trapped, if he cannot see far enough. I have never known what he meant, until now. The far distance is beautiful, no?"

They watched the sunset, a blaze of color across the vastness of the rolling hills in the distance.

"See how the nearer hills are green, those beyond bluish?" observed Owl Woman. "Then in the shadows they are purple."

"But the sky!" Plum Leaf pointed. "So many colors."

Turtle returned from his courtesy call to rejoin the others. "Yes, it is good tonight," he agreed, seeing their wonder at the brilliance of the spectacle. "Some tribes say Sun Boy paints himself before he goes to his lodge on the other side of Earth. Tonight, he chooses good colors for his paint. Well, come, we must camp."

"We are welcome, then?" Owl asked.

"Of course. Growers always have crops to trade. They trade with everyone."

"Have they seen your people?"

"Yes! They know where they wintered, south of here."

"And now?"

"This summer, they are not sure, but he told me of a camp of Cut-Fingers, maybe two sleeps, he said. They will know."

"We trade tomorrow?" asked Storyteller.

"Not much. They have only crops to trade, and we cannot carry enough. We will trade a little, to show that our hearts are good. But they will like stories tonight, Storyteller."

"It is good," agreed the young man. "Do they have storytellers?"

"Of course. Everyone does. How good, we will see."

"They use hand-signs?"

"Yes. I know some of their tongue, but you can use the signs. You may hear some new stories!"

No one was more pleased at the prospect of the evening's entertainment than Plum Leaf. She was so proud of her man's skill with the stories that she never tired of listening to him. It had been swift, their courtship and marriage. Sometimes she still could not believe that it had happened. But here she was, far from home, with a husband she adored, experiencing new places, new people. Owl had been very kind to her, teaching her the role of the wife of a storyteller and trader. Plum Leaf, realizing the importance of the hand-signs, had concentrated on learning their use as they traveled. Already she felt that she was more proficient than Owl Woman and nearing the skill of her husband or even Turtle, the master of many tongues.

It was indeed a good evening of stories, the weather pleasant, the listeners' interest apparent, and the two storytellers at their best. Turtle seemed inspired and used stories that even his apprentice had never heard.

In addition, there was an ancient storyteller among the Growers who, as he warmed to the occasion, seemed more skilled than any they had seen. Sensing that he had an appreciative audience, the old man seemed to begin with Creation and follow through the generations toward the present. He had traveled much as a young man, he said.

"Do you know how we got corn?" he asked.

Without even waiting, he launched into the story. It was long, drawn-out, and began once more with Creation. The storytellers were fascinated. Even Turtle had never heard this tale. Owl left to retire. Plum Leaf tried to stay but found herself dozing. Finally she too gave up and made her way to their temporary camp.

Owl Woman and Lark were sleeping soundly as Plum Leaf snuggled down in her sleeping robes. She wished that her husband could soon join her. For a while she managed to stay awake but at last fell asleep, dreaming a confused tale. Her own new experiences on the great prairie became entangled with the stories. She was watching when, at Creation, the gods quarreled. The evil god, whose name she could not remember, was struck down before her eyes. His adversary, a benevolent figure, pried out the dead god's teeth and planted them like seeds in the rich loam of the prairie. In the inconsistency of the dream state, she watched the seeds sprout into cornstalks. By the time Storyteller joined her in their sleeping robes, humans had harvested their first corn crop.

She seemed to realize that she was dreaming, even as she did so. *I must remember this dream-story,* she told herself. *I must tell it to my storyteller.*

13
» » »

Storyteller did not know what he expected in the villages of the nomadic buffalo hunters. He had seen skin tents elsewhere, mostly a makeshift shelter of hides thrown in a haphazard manner over a frame of sticks. Somehow it had not occurred to him that people whose entire life consists of hunting buffalo would have a highly developed portable dwelling. Even Turtle's description, and the statement that such a lodge was often two or three times the height of a man, had not prepared him for this.

The lodges were scattered along the stream for some distance. Now that the camp was in sight, the travelers paused to dismount on the ridge above and allow their horses to blow.

"Someone comes!" pointed Owl Woman.

Two riders swept across the little valley, their horses at a dead run. They were well-armed warriors and appeared to be capable in their duties.

"Dog Soldiers," Turtle said, half to himself.

"What?" asked Owl Woman.

"Dog Soldiers . . . that is a warrior society of the Cut-Fingers. These will be their Wolves."

"Wolves?"

"Yes . . . oh, I forget. You have never been here. The tribes have warriors who circle the camp, or circle the main party when they travel. They are called Wolves after the wolves who circle the buffalo herds."

"And these are not your people?"

"No, but they are allies. Now their Wolves come out to meet us, to see that there is no trickery."

"Ah-koh!" he called out in greeting as the riders swept up the slope and slid their mounts to a stop. "Who is your chief, Dog Soldiers?"

"Who asks?" responded one suspiciously. "How is it that you know our tongue?"

"Ah, yes," said Turtle pleasantly. "I am Turtle, the storyteller and trader. My people are your friends, the People-Who-Trade."

"That much is true. And, you are called Turtle?"

"Yes. I have not been home for several winters. Now I seek my own tribe. You have seen them, no?"

"Maybe. Who are these others?"

"My wife, our son and his wife, our small daughter."

"How is your son called?"

"He is called Storyteller."

"Ah! He trades too?"

"Of course. We have much to trade, my friend."

Finally, the warriors seemed to relax. "It is good," said one. "Come, we will take you in."

The entire party mounted, and turned toward the camp.

"Are you at war?" Turtle asked. "Why such a challenge? And, where are my people camped?"

"Ah, my friend, we were only being careful. You and your party do wear a strange mixture of garments and customs, you know. Your people . . . about a day west of here."

This was more like what Turtle had expected from friends. But he had to admit that his was a strange caravan. He could see how they might arouse suspicion. And these were conscientious young warriors, taking their turn at Wolf.

"It is good!" he said. "Now, who is your chief? I must pay my visit."

"Of course. He is Five Elk."

"Ah, I remember him, from when I was your age," Turtle said. "A great leader . . . a credit to the Cut-Fingers."

"Yes. This is a proud people," one stated.

"And justly so," Turtle said. "We are proud to bring you stories and trade."

They were among the lodges now, and the newcomers, except for Turtle, were absorbed in looking at the dwellings, so unfamiliar in design. Each was made of many buffalo skins, squared and sewn together, maybe twenty or thirty skins in the larger ones it seemed. The doorways faced east to greet the rising sun, as Turtle had said.

A most remarkable thing about the lodges, to Storyteller, was their height. Some of the big lodges were five or six paces across. Since it seemed to be a general rule that the height was about the same as the width, the poles that supported the structure must be at least as long, plus another pace to allow for the protruding portion above. Even in the forests of his childhood, he had never seen so many long, slender poles. He could see them well. The weather was hot, and the people of the village had rolled up the bottom edges of the lodge skins, like lifted skirts, to let the breeze cool the interior. People sitting in the shady lodges watched the riders curiously. Some waved and smiled. There was much to learn about these lodges, the young man realized. He still did not see how they could be made habitable in a hard winter.

The party stopped before one of the largest of the lodges. It was brightly decorated with geometric designs and somehow radiated an aura of affluence. On a post in front hung a decorated shield, a lance, and a stone ax or club with a long handle. They had noticed such displays in front of most of the lodges.

"That shows who lives here," Turtle had explained.

Knowing this, it was possible to see that there was a

design that could be an elk, both on the lodge cover and on the shield by the doorway. This, then, was the home of the chief, Five Elk. A dignified man who could be no one else was sitting comfortably in the shade of the big lodge, leaning against a willow backrest.

The Wolves spoke to the chief briefly in their own tongue and turned their horses away. The travelers dismounted.

"Ah-koh, my chief," Turtle greeted, using both words and hand-signs. "We are honored to stop in your village."

"It is good," grunted Five Elk. "Tell me, trader, you use our tongue well. Why do you also sign?"

"Ah, I grew up using the tongue of the Cut-Fingers as well as my own," Turtle explained. "I have been in your village many times when I walked in a younger man's moccasins."

"Ah, yes," said the chief thoughtfully. "Do I remember you? You were called . . ."

"Turtle, my chief. Yes, you might remember me, but I have been away many years."

"But why the hand-signs?"

"These others—my wife, my son, and his wife—they come from tribes far away. They do not know your tongue, so I used signs also."

"It is good. Welcome again."

Chuckling, Five Elk also used the hand-signs. It was a very polite thing to do for his guests.

"Now, you wish to trade?" he asked.

"Yes, briefly, my chief, if you wish. It is said that my people, the People-Who-Trade, are only one sleep away."

"That is true."

"I have been away from them for many winters. Now I return with my family."

"It is good. Family is important."

"Yes. May we trade tomorrow, then move on?"

"Of course. Our Wolves said you are also storytellers?"

"Yes. That goes well with the trading."

"True. I will look forward to it."

"It is good!" said Turtle. "Now we will make camp, before dark."

"Yes . . . there should be good places upstream a little way. You can turn your horses out with the herd. Our young men will take care of them."

"Thank you, my chief!"

They found the camping place and settled into their temporary camp, unsaddling and unpacking the horses.

"Shall we picket the horses, Father?" asked Storyteller.

"No, turn them out with the herd. They will find better grass."

The young man swung to the back of one of the animals to drive the others to the grassy meadow where the herd grazed.

"Ah-koh!" someone called. A boy trotted toward him, smiling.

"You are the Storyteller?" the herdsman signed. "I was told you might bring horses."

"Yes. We have ridden far, and they need to rest and find grass."

"I will see that they get the best. You will have a story-fire tonight?"

"Of course! I will look for you!"

He thought of himself a few seasons ago and his own eagerness at the coming of the storyteller. He swung a leg over and jumped to the ground, untying the rawhide war bridle to free his mount.

"I will be there!" called the youngster after him as he turned away.

Probably, in all his storytelling and story-listening experience, that evening was the most remarkable. Not only did the Cut-Fingers have an excellent storyteller, but Storyteller began to have a better understanding of the stories of Turtle. Some of the tales he had heard many times now took on new meaning. The great bowl of the sky, sprinkled with as many stars as there are grains of sand, it seemed, was a fitting background to dramatize some of the stories. In addition, he could feel the vastness of the great buffalo herds that reached from one horizon to the other. Before, he could only imagine; now he had *seen*.

"Once there was a season," Turtle was saying, "when hunting was very poor. This was in the old, old, long-ago times, not long after Creation. Seldom could the hunters find even a deer, and the people were starving."

Storyteller loved this tale, the coming of the buffalo.

"But there was one hunter who always hunted alone. His family remained fat, and the children happy. One day when all of his family had gone to the river to bathe, three of the other hunters crept into his lodge."

There was the usual expression of dismay. Such a thing was not done.

"They were starving, you see," Turtle went on apologetically. The crowd nodded understandingly.

Ah, thought Storyteller, *he really has caught them tonight. It is good.*

"Inside the lodge, they found a big flat rock," Turtle went on, with appropriate gestures. "It took two of them to lift it. Now, underneath was a large hole, and a buffalo ran out! The hunters quickly ran after it, so intent on the hunt that they did not replace the stone. When they looked back, more buffalo were coming out, one after another, more and more, until the whole prairie was covered with them."

The crowd gasped in pleasure, and for the first time Storyteller fully appreciated the description of the prairie and the great herds. A person bred to the woodland simply could not understand the numbers or the distances involved unless he had seen them.

"The hunter whose lodge had been violated," Turtle continued, "was a great medicine man, of course. A god, maybe. But he saw the great herds and realized that something was wrong. He hurried to the lodge and slammed the rock back over the hole.

"It was nearly too late. The whole plain was covered.

The herds trampled the grass and fouled the water, and there were too many. But it was good too. Ever since, people have had buffalo to eat. And, when the great herds come through, trampling and fouling until the river runs dung, we remember how it happened."

There was applause and much laughter about rivers of dung, and finally the Cut-Fingers' storyteller rose.

"That is very good," he said approvingly. "Now, my story, too, is about the hunting of buffalo. Did you ever wonder why some horses, when chasing buffalo, always approach from the left, while others do so from the *right* side of the animal?"

The general murmur from the listeners told that there were some who knew and appreciated the story. Others did not know why. Still others did not care, probably.

And Storyteller had thought until now that he had heard nearly every story in the world. This was an eye-opener. Not only was it a new story, but he had not even realized until now that some horses *do* approach the buffalo from the left and some from the right. He felt like a child, just beginning to learn.

At the time of Creation, the storyteller related, it was seen that Man could not catch many Buffalo on foot. The People asked Sun Boy to give them a way to run faster than their quarry. Their wish was granted, but deferred for many lifetimes, until they were well established. Then, they would be given the Horse, to ride upon like the wind, faster than a Buffalo.

"But it must pass on the right," insisted a hunter, "so we may use the bow. One cannot sit astride and shoot to his own right."

"No, the *left*," argued another, who wished to use a spear, held in the right hand.

The council dissolved in angry shouts, and Sun Boy stopped them.

"Let the decision be with the Horse," he decided, "your Elk-dog who runs like the wind. Some will run to the right, some left, so each horse will pick his own hunter."

The storyteller spread his hands as if in explanation. "And so it has been ever since. Some right, some left."

Most of the listeners enjoyed the story, and laughed long about horses choosing their riders. Storyteller laughed too, though he did not fully understand. Full insight came a few days later, after they reached the camp of Turtle's people.

14

» » »

He soon had friends among Turtle's people. He was, by nature, an outgoing and friendly young man, and in addition, carried a degree of prestige as Storyteller. He was invited to join some of these new friends in an upcoming hunt. Only then did the humor and the full meaning of the Cut-Fingers' story become clear to him.

From the way everyone in the camp spoke and acted, it was apparent that this would be an exciting time. The weather had broken, with a change in the wind and a refreshing coolness to the breeze. Through the Moon of Thunder and the Red Moon, the prevailing wind had been from the south, cooling only a little at night. Rain-Maker occasionally charged across the prairie, throwing his spears of real-fire and thumping ponderously on his drums to give the Moon of Thunder its name. Between storms, the weather was hot, muggy, and oppressive. So it was with great relief that the people of the camp saw a change in the wind late in the Red Moon. They awoke one morning to find the grasses stirring with a breeze from the northwest, a slight chill in the air. Immediately, people began to talk of two coming events, the impending move to winter quarters and the great fall hunt.

"Which will come first?" Storyteller asked.

"Who knows?" Turtle shrugged. "It depends much on

the buffalo. But it is time to decide now whether we winter here. We will need to prepare."

Thus far, they had camped in a temporary arbor, retreating to the lodges of friends or relatives only in the event of heavy storms.

"Where else would we winter?" asked Owl Woman.

"We could go many places," said Turtle. "We have before. But this is good." It was obvious that it would please him to stay with his people. "We must have a lodge," Turtle explained. "Five of us . . . we cannot move in with relatives."

So plans were begun. They would not need a pretentious lodge but must begin to assemble and prepare skins. Turtle's mother, aged and wrinkled but bright-eyed, was considered an expert in cutting lodge covers. She would advise, as well as assist in collecting skins. It was common for people to give her a skin or two in return for her expertise. Lodge-Cutter the old woman was called appropriately. She dragged out several skins.

"We will begin to sew these," she told Owl and Plum Leaf. "You will need more, maybe ten, but the fall hunt is coming."

Storyteller was beginning to see how the entire being of these people revolved around the migrations of the buffalo. They spoke of the fall hunt with a reverence that was almost a religion. Almost anything to be deferred was mentioned in terms of "before the fall hunt" or "after the hunt."

"It *is* a thing of the spirit," Turtle explained in answer to Storyteller's question. "I have told you of the Sun Dance in early summer, which the plains people celebrate. It honors the return of Sun, which causes grass to grow, which brings back the buffalo. The world starts over . . . a new Creation almost. Maybe next year we will be here for that."

Gray Otter, one of the young men of the village, had befriended Storyteller almost from the day of their arrival. He seemed intrigued by the stories and the young man who practiced the art.

"You will join us for the hunt?"

"Yes, it is good," Storyteller answered.

He was rapidly learning the tongue of Turtle's people. There is no better way than to spend time with a friend who speaks the tongue you wish to learn. Sometimes they would reach an impasse and were forced to augment the conversation with hand-signs, but these times were becoming less frequent.

"Will you use the bow or the lance?" Gray Otter asked.

Storyteller was unsure. He had never hunted buffalo. "Which would be best?"

"*Aiee*! I forget . . . wait! Have you hunted with a lance?"

"Well . . . no."

"Ah, then you use the bow? Does your horse run that way?"

"Otter," his friend blurted, "I have never hunted from a horse."

Gray Otter's mouth dropped open. "But you *have* horses!"

"Yes, to travel, but . . ."

"No matter, my friend. We will supply a horse. Now, you are familiar with a bow . . . that is good. I will find you a horse that runs to the right."

"I do not understand, Otter. Turtle also spoke of this. Why is that important?"

"Think about it," urged Otter. "You are sitting on a horse with a bow in your left hand. How could you shoot to your right?"

Of course. Once it was explained, the point was obvious. The hunter *must* shoot to the left side of his mount because he cannot turn far enough to the right. "What of the lance, then?" he asked.

"The same. A lance is braced under the right arm. The

horse must approach from the *left,* because you cannot reach across the horse with the lance, no?"

Storyteller began to understand the story he had heard back in the camp of the Cut-Fingers.

"Otter," he asked, "how do you make a horse run right or left?"

Otter laughed. "Ah, you begin to see! You guide the horse with the reins, but in the hunt, both hands are busy. The horse must know what to do."

"Yes . . . I do not see . . ."

"Well, partly with the knees, but a good buffalo-horse does much of it himself. He enjoys the chase."

"Then the *horse* chooses which side?"

"Yes, mostly, but . . . when his training begins, we look to see which way he likes best. Then he may be traded to someone who hunts that way. Now . . . let us go and talk to my uncle. He has many good buffalo-horses. One that runs to the right . . ."

Otter's uncle did have many horses. He seemed pleased to be asked for help. "You use the bow?" he asked.

"Yes . . . I have little knowledge of the horse."

The horseman nodded. "Otter, bring the blue gelding!" he called. "Now, this horse is steady . . . he runs well, but is careful. Try him!"

Inexperienced as he was, Storyteller found that he rapidly gained confidence with the horse. It was a lanky, rawboned animal, sleepy in disposition. Under the tutelage of Otter, Storyteller simply sat on the horse at first, shooting arrows at an old buffalo skin stuffed with grass. The gelding stood quietly, eyes half closed, lazily switching flies with his sparse tail.

The next step involved becoming confident on the running animal. Gray Otter brought his own horse, and the two rode quietly into the open prairie. The gray shuffled along, disinterested. It was a comfortable rocking motion, and Storyteller began to relax. Suddenly, Otter kicked heels into his mare's flanks, and she leaped forward to a run. In a heartbeat, the gelding was transformed from a lazy, shuffling creature to an efficient hunter. He leaped forward like a cat, almost unseating his rider. Storyteller clutched at the saddle, trying to regain balance, while his mount pounded after Otter's mare.

Then, somehow, the young man realized that he was adjusting to the rhythm of the horse's gait. He began to relax, swaying with the smooth swinging flow of the animal's long stride. He had never ridden such a horse, or at such a speed. It was like flying! He drew abreast of Otter's horse, passing on the right side, and the significance of that approach flashed through his mind. Yes, if the running mare were a fleeing buffalo . . . He was not quite ready to release the reins to let the animal run, but he could see that it would work. Yes, he could draw the arrow to its head and release it as they swept past!

Now Otter drew his horse to a slower pace as they reached the top of the low ridge. The gray gelding protested, still wanting to race, but responded to the pressure on the rawhide. Both horses slowed to an easy lope, then a trot, and finally a walk.

"Aiee!" Storyteller shouted with delight. "It is like flying!"

Otter laughed, his eyes dancing with pleasure. "You did well, my friend! We will run a few more times, and then get the bow."

In another day or two, with gaining confidence, Storyteller could sweep past at a dead run and plant arrows in the target skin more often than not.

"It is good!" called his instructor. "You are almost ready."

The only exercise that remained was the pretended shot at the flank of Otter's mare. With confidence growing, he could now drop the looped rein across the gelding's neck, freeing both hands to use the bow.

Beyond that, there was only the waiting for the herds to come.

* * *

In the Moon of Hunting, called by the Growers the Moon of Ripening, all of the creatures of the prairie seemed to become aware of the coming autumn. The prairie flowers told of the change. Storyteller had noticed them when they first came into the grasslands. The roses had been blooming, toward the end of their season, and he had been impressed with the variety of colors. There were roses nearly white but also deep pinks and reds, with all the subtle shades between. The other flowers too showed a remarkable range of color, from white to blue to pink. One plant he especially admired showed clusters of bright orange blossoms. It seemed greatly favored by insects. Bees worked busily at the bright flowers, and butterflies hovered. He had asked Turtle its name.

"Butterfly plant, my people call it," Turtle answered.

All the spring and summer flowers were gone now, to be replaced by others. These were of different hues. There seemed to be two main colors, golden yellow and bright purple. At least six entirely different plants of different heights and shapes produced blossoms of precisely the same color. It was much the same with the purple flowers, though without such wide variation.

Most unusual of all were the grasses. At the Moon of Ripening, all of the prairie grasses suddenly began to thrust seed-stalks upward. To young Storyteller, in the woodlands of his childhood, grass had merely been grass. He had done little to try to distinguish between different types. Now it became apparent that grasses that had looked much the same through the summer behaved much differently. He could distinguish at least six or seven. There seemed to be two "big" grasses. One was called real-grass, which suggested that it would be the largest. In fact, when the seed-heads formed, they were taller than a man. In occasional areas favorable to this growth, it was very difficult to find one's way on foot. It was necessary to mount a horse to see the way. Almost as tall was the feathery seed-head that Otter called feather-grass or plume-grass. Large and fluffy, these stalks were spectacular as they nodded and bobbed in the breeze. But again, one could become lost among the tall stems if one was on foot.

Otter laughed at Storyteller's amazement. "This is why these are called the Tallgrass Hills!"

The growth seemed more spectacular each day. At the same time, though days were warm, the nights brought an uncomfortable chill to the air. Squirrels were busy in the timbered areas along the streams. Turkeys and deer grew fat and sleek, and the first long lines of geese began to trumpet their way southward.

Then came the awaited news. A Wolf came loping into the village, to pull his horse to a sliding stop before the lodge of the chief who would organize the hunt.

"The buffalo are coming!" he announced.

15

» » »

Storyteller sat astride the blue roan gelding, waiting. He was excited. His heart was pounding so loudly in his ears that he feared it would disturb the herd. At very least, he thought, the other hunters must hear the thumping. He looked to his left and met the glance of Gray Otter a few paces away. Otter smiled reassuringly. A deer-fly bit his ankle, a sharp stab, and he flinched, swatting at the creature as it escaped his reach.

The hunters had been concealed in the tall grass of a little swale, waiting for the herd to move into position. He could see very little beyond a few paces in front of the horse. This was partly a result of the uneven lay of the land, but mostly his vision was obscured by the heavy seed-heads of the tall grasses—mostly real-grass, he noted. Directly in front of him, a large clump of real-grass had sent up perhaps ten or more stalks. Each was tipped with a three-fingered seed-head, just at eye level, and several similar growths along the stalk. Turkey-foot, Otter had called it.

"I thought it was real-grass," protested Storyteller.

"Yes, but sometimes this too," Otter explained. "See, the seed-head is shaped like the foot of a bird."

That had been a bit earlier in the season. Now it was more obvious, this local name for the plant. Yes, he thought absently, each stalk does end in a turkey-foot.

His horse was dozing in the sun, knowing from experience that it was not yet time to get excited. The animal shifted its weight from one hip to the other with a deep breath, much like a human sigh. Absently, it nibbled at a grass stem near its nose.

The young man felt a tickle against his right knee, and glanced down to see if the deer-fly had returned. It was one of the fluffy yellow heads of feather-grass, heavy and ripening, nodding gently in the breeze to tap ever so lightly at his bare leg. It was a beautiful day, clear and cool, but warm where the sun's rays struck.

Somewhere out of sight, one of the Wolves returned to report that all was ready. The herd was in position. The chief of the hunt gave a silent hand-signal that was passed along to the other hunters, and the long line of riders began to move slowly forward. Instantly, the roan gelding became alert. Head up, ears pricked forward, he knew what this activity meant. Storyteller had to restrain him slightly, but the animal responded to the tug on the rein, giving only a slight impatient toss of his head as he walked through the tall growth.

Now Storyteller could see ahead to greater advantage. The line of hunters was topping a low rise, and in the more level plain beyond he could see thousands of shaggy dark forms, grazing or standing calmly. Nervously, he looked toward Otter, who smiled and nodded reassuringly.

The hunters kept their horses at a walk, and the advance of the line did not seem to alarm the grazing buffalo in the least. The slight breeze, little more than a stirring of the air, was from the buffalo toward the advancing hunters.

"Their eyesight is poor," Otter had explained, "but their nose is keen."

They were almost within bowshot of the nearest animals before there was any reaction in the herd. It may have been a slight shift of the breeze, a chance scent.

Possibly it was only that the hunters came within the limited range of the buffalo's vision.

The first indication was the reaction of a wary old cow. She raised her head suddenly, sniffing the air, not even chewing the wisp of grass already in her mouth. She took a step forward, started to lower her muzzle again, and then swung her massive head to face the hunters. A low warning rumbled from her throat, and other animals too turned inquisitively. The hunters were moving at an easy trot now.

Everything seemed to happen at once. The first buffalo wheeled and broke into a run. Then they were all running. Storyteller felt the roan leap forward under him, almost unseating him as they joined the pursuit. He did not remember consciously dropping the rein, but he found himself using both hands to fit an arrow to the bowstring.

He had wondered how to choose which animal to pursue but found that he had no choice in the matter. The horse had already chosen his quarry and was rapidly closing in for the kill. It was a fat yearling, and they swept into position so quickly that he was almost caught unprepared. He managed to loose the arrow and saw his feathered shaft disappear into the soft flank.

The running animal jerked convulsively and seemed to stumble. It was falling as the roan swept on past, already pressing toward the next victim.

Storyteller saw other animals falling, heard the shouts of the other hunters, and found himself yelling too. It was wild, exciting, like no other experience. He managed to fit another arrow, and in the tumult of exuberance, missed his target completely. He could have sworn that the horse tossed his head in disgust as he selected another animal. The one that had escaped was already lost in the dusty melee.

His next arrow struck poorly, perhaps glancing off a rib. He knew when he loosed the shaft that it was too far forward; he had waited a heartbeat too long. The stricken animal was running wildly, and he tried to fit another arrow. Otter closed in from the left and thrust home with his lance. The cow fell. Otter waved and quickly moved on, lost to sight in the swirl of dust, horses, horns, and shaggy hides.

A large bull loomed out of the dust, and the roan gelding shied away. Experience told him that this was something to avoid whenever possible. Storyteller, as an inexperienced horseman, did not anticipate the catlike sideways leap. He felt himself lose balance, but there seemed no time between the moment he left the saddle and the sensation of slamming into the ground.

He rolled and kicked, knowing that it was better to lie still but unable to do so. He was unable even to catch his breath and wondered if he was dying. There was thunder in his ears, the thunder of a thousand hooves. Dark forms swept past him right and left, and one young cow jumped directly over him. He could clearly see the animal's udder above him as she passed, immature nipples plainly outlined only a handspan or two before his eyes.

Then they were gone, the thunder and the shouts receding. He lay still, wondering if he dared move. There was little pain, only a feeling of being battered from head to foot. Oddly, the sensation he would remember was the rough texture of the grass against his skin.

Gingerly, as his breathing reverted to normal, he began to move a little. His hands, cautiously at first. It was gratifying to find that the fingers moved. The right wrist was painful to move, but it did move. Now he tried the arms; then feet and legs. It took great courage to try to sit up. He took a deep breath and rolled over. There was a sharp pain in his chest, and he felt for an injured rib—he could not tell. He was stiff and sore all over but felt that he must do something. He sat up carefully, holding the sore rib with his left hand.

Now he could hear the hunters returning, laughing and joking. Soon he could see them through the haze of dust. He could also see dark forms lying scattered across the prairie, some partly obscured among the grasses.

He crawled to the nearest of these and pulled himself up to a sitting position. Dust was settling now, and he was breathing much more easily—unless he took too deep a breath. That produced an unpleasant jab in the ribs.

A couple of hunters rode up.

"Aiee!" exclaimed one, "are you hurt?"

"Only a little, I think."

"It is better to hunt on a horse," the other man said seriously.

Storyteller started to explain but quickly realized that they were teasing him. There were dangers to the hunt, risks that these men considered a part of life. That some-one might fall from his horse was expected and mildly amusing, though potentially serious.

"I will try that sometime," he said, and the others laughed.

"Can we help you?" one asked sympathetically.

"Maybe not. I will rest here a little while . . . my horse?"

"Yes, we saw it. Otter was catching it. That is how we knew."

Storyteller felt considerably better. There had been a moment when he felt that these men were unfeeling, un-caring, but now he understood. The hunting party had been quite aware of the beginner in their midst. Someone might have seen him fall, or they may have recognized the loose horse. These two had come back to see about him and the extent of his injuries, and to reassure him about the horse.

"You did well for a first hunt," one said conversation-ally. "One clean kill. Another with Otter's help."

He had been watched closely all along.

"It was a good hunt," the other added. "Many kills."

"It is good!" Storyteller managed to say. He was begin-ning to hurt now.

"Wait here," one of the men said. "Someone will be here to help you."

It was not long before Otter returned, leading the roan. "Can you mount?" he asked.

"I do not want to try," Storyteller admitted. "My rib, maybe. It hurts some."

Otter nodded, understanding. "We will bring a pole-drag to take you to camp," he suggested. He started to turn away, but turned back. *"Aiee,* your first kill was a good one!"

Storyteller did not particularly care. It had been a strange morning. The thrill of the hunt, the excitement, the wild abandon—then the fall, the injury. At this point, it did not seem a very good trade.

The butchering parties were moving out from camp now, looking for the kills of various hunters. They would be identified by the arrows, painted with the owner's individual colors, or by the lance wounds. He would have to tell them, Storyteller recalled, that his first arrow might have gone completely inside, or even clear through.

For now, though, he hurt in every fiber of his body. He would be glad to see Plum Leaf. She could always make him feel better. Maybe, even, about this.

16

» » »

There were times that winter when Storyteller thought he could be completely happy with Turtle's people forever. He would never have imagined that a lodge of skins could be so comfortable in winter. And the winter was fierce. Cold Maker's thrust was much more severe in the open plains.

They had finished a modest lodge before snow fell and equipped it with a lodge lining hanging straight down all around from about waist-high. The angular space between the lodge cover and its lining was used for storage and insulation against the cold. Unused space was stuffed with dried grasses, effectively stopping Cold Maker's blasts.

It would have been better, of course, if they had had their own lodge. There was little chance for privacy. Actually, there had not been since their marriage. This was accepted as the way of things, and the two couples and young Lark, now eight and growing rapidly, settled in for the winter.

There were long winter evenings of visiting, gambling, smoking, and telling stories. Since the people had no central meeting place comparable to the longhouse, these sessions were held in one or another of the private lodges, usually, of course, the larger dwellings.

Someone would step outside the door of his lodge as

Sun Boy neared the edge and shout into the crisp winter air. *"Ah-koh,* my friends, come and smoke!" People would straggle toward that lodge, and the socializing would begin.

Both Turtle and Storyteller were always in demand because of their skills. Storyteller was held in high regard, especially by people his own age. Everyone knew of his adventure in the fall hunt. It had made a great impression that one of such a calling, a storyteller, would take the time and effort to learn the skills required to participate in the hunt. In addition, it was widely told, his first kill was worthy of an experienced hunter. The fact that the hunt had ended in an accident for Storyteller did not detract in the least. In fact, his willingness to take the risks, to share the dangers with the rest, made him more popular.

He felt the pleasure of approval, that he and his family were accepted, partly, of course, because Turtle was one of them, but there was personal acceptance too. There is approval that goes only to an outsider who tries to understand and respect customs not his own.

His ribs healed slowly. The second and third days were the worst, every bone and muscle aching. To have the unexpected jab of pain when he moved just so—that was the final indignity. Gradually he could get up or lie down without stopping to plan every motion for the least pain.

He came to appreciate the usefulness of the plains people's willow backrest. It was made of slender willow branches as thick as a man's finger laced across a frame of heavier wood. The flexible sticks bent slightly when a person leaned back, conforming to his weight, while the entire device was held steady by the part on which he sat. There was nothing more comfortable to his tender ribs than to loosen every muscle and sink back upon the rest.

The Moon of Snows was aptly named that winter. One attack after another Cold Maker threw across the prairie, but the People had chosen well the site for winter camp. It was a sheltered canyon with enough trees to break the force of the wind. The drifts became deep, but at times even that was an advantage. Many families banked snow around their lodges for added warmth.

The Moon of Hunger, once a dreaded time for these people, was now little more than a joke in good season. Since the coming of the horse a few generations ago, living had become much easier. There were jokes that the Moon of Hunger needed a new name, for there was seldom any hunger. The old expression, "Moon of Starvation," was practically forgotten. True, some of the elders and some of the more thoughtful realized that if ever the fall hunt failed completely, as it could—well, the results would be tragic.

But this winter there was no concern. The fall hunt had been good, better than average, and every lodge was well supplied. They had paused for a few days as they traveled south to winter camp, to trade with a village of Growers. Now, in addition to their supplies of dried meat and pemmican, most lodges had vegetables. Extra meat and buffalo robes had been bartered for corn, beans, squash, and pumpkins. Nearly every lodge had strings of corn and dried pumpkin hanging from the lodgepoles.

But even in a winter with plenty, the time of immobility is hard, especially hard, perhaps, on the people of the prairie whose world is wider from one horizon to the other. This wideness makes human companionship more important in the smallness of man in the vastness of the universe. Yet it also gives the dweller of the plains a sense of entrapment, a closed-in uneasiness when he is deprived of his far horizons. Under these conditions, he becomes irritable and quarrelsome.

In the closeness of the shared lodge, it became increasingly difficult to maintain good humor. Even with the knowledge of its cause, it was difficult. Turtle, the only one whose heritage was the prairie, was first to show the malady. He was short-tempered and gruff, sometimes going all day without a word. Owl Woman did her best to distract him, but in a lodge full of other people—*aiee!*

And the sour spirit seemed to jump quickly from one to another.

It was with a great sense of relief that they welcomed the return of warm breezes. The petty squabbles of yesterday seemed absurd in the warming sunlight of the Moon of Awakening. A different sort of restlessness began to make itself felt. One evening, as a flock of geese honked overhead, heading north, Turtle voiced his new restlessness. "Where shall we go this season?"

Apparently no one but Turtle had given the decision much thought. Perhaps he had not either. There was a rather meandering conversation, largely based on reminiscences of past seasons, with little direction.

"Well, we must think of it," Turtle observed as they prepared for sleep.

Next morning, Storyteller arose to tend the horses. After the custom of their hosts, he had learned to provide food for the animals during snow time by chopping cottonwoods and feeding the smaller twigs and the bark. Horses could subsist, even when the scant winter forage of dried grasses was covered by the drifts.

"I will go with you," Plum Leaf said, jumping to her feet.

He started to say that she was not needed but paused. It would be good, he thought, to have her with him in the brightness of the sunny day, snow still covering the ground. There was no wind, and it was comfortably warm in the sun. The bright reflection of sun on snow was painful to the eyes after a little while. It was best, he had found, to avoid looking at the great expanse of white. There were, in fact, warnings of people who had been stricken snow-blind. It was a temporary condition, but painful and to be avoided if possible.

The two young people reached the sheltered area where the horses were wintering and began to cut cottonwoods. The animals came crowding forward, reaching eagerly for the strips of bark from larger branches. It would be good when they could graze again.

"It is good to be together," said Plum Leaf.

He knew that there was much more to this statement than appeared. It was filled with all the frustration of the winter—the sameness of close quarters in the lodge with no possibility of escape, the being together yet not together because of the absence of privacy. He had felt it too. Perhaps most frustrating of all was that it had been impossible even to speak of it. He knew it could not have been helped, but it was like, well, like the resignation to hunger when one knows there is no food.

"What are we going to do, my husband?" the girl asked.

"What do you mean?" He wanted her to express *her* frustration first, knowing even as he spoke that it was unfair. He attempted to modify his approach. "We will finish this and go back to the lodge," he said, feeling like an idiot.

"No, no, after that. This summer. After that."

Ah, now it was out in the open.

"We must talk of this," he said. "What would you wish?"

"I . . . do not take it wrong, Woodpecker. You know we both love your parents and little Lark, but . . ."

She paused, unsure of herself. He had felt much the same at times. He had noticed on their travels last season that sometimes there was very little trade. They would come to a village or camp, have a wonderful evening of stories, but there would be practically no activity the next day. As a youth, he had not even noticed. When they were three, living was easier, and he was reveling in the joy and prestige of being a storyteller.

Now they were five. It took more to supply their needs. The fall hunt had helped, but still they had benefited greatly from the generosity of friends and relatives. What now? It was apparent that they needed a lodge of their own. But where? It was equally apparent that neither he nor Plum Leaf wished to return to the political turmoil of his people. Hers, in a few years maybe.

Meanwhile, Turtle was already showing signs of restlessness to be on the trail, the life of the trader. In reality, Storyteller too felt the urge. But maybe he and Plum Leaf could stay a season with this new tribe, the people of Turtle. They had friends, yet Storyteller had grave doubts. Did he actually have the skill as a hunter to support a lodge and a family? He had been lucky at his first buffalo hunt, but suppose he had been killed, leaving Plum Leaf a widow among strangers? This was not his gift. His was the telling of stories, the use of words, learning other tongues and customs, trading.

It must finally come down to the thing that Plum Leaf had suggested but not said openly. They must separate from his parents, take different trails.

"It is as you say," he told her. "We must go our own way. But how shall we tell them?"

She smiled. The sparkle was back in her eye, the look of mischief that he loved. "That is your problem," she teased. "They are your parents!"

As it happened, it was not as great a problem as they feared. It was not many days before Turtle took him aside and self-consciously began a serious conversation. "My son, it is nearly time to go on the trail."

"Yes?"

He knew Turtle was serious when he used the term "my son." What could this be?

"Did you notice, last season, a village or two . . . Growers who had very little to trade?"

"Yes . . . we moved on quickly."

"True . . . . because there was no trading to be done."

Storyteller did not see where this conversation was going. "Father—" he began, but Turtle waved him to silence.

"Let me go on. You are experienced in trading . . . enough to see that it is harder to support two families."

That was it, the point that he had not quite been able

to grasp. They were *two* families now. They must take two paths.

"Now," Turtle continued, "it would seem wise if you and Plum Leaf would trade in one area, your mother and I in another."

"She knows of this?"

"Of course. She suggested it."

The thought flashed through Storyteller's mind that the two women may have planned the entire scheme.

"Suppose," Turtle continued, "that you go south and east. There are good tribes for trading, from here to the Big River. Or, across it, even. Owl and I will stay farther north. The Miss-ouri, O-hio, Illi-noy. Then we can winter here sometimes. Maybe each two or three years?"

It was a plan of such magnitude, yet so beautifully simple. Yes, it would work perfectly. They could divide . . .

"We can divide the goods we have now," Turtle was saying, "and start as soon as the weather opens up for travel."

17

"**B**ut she is such a beautiful child!" Storyteller protested.

"Yes," Plum Leaf agreed sadly.

The child appeared well formed in every respect—legs long and strong, chest full and robust, features well placed. But the infant had never taken her first breath. The woman who had assisted Plum Leaf in her labor—it had even been an easy delivery—had breathed her own breath into the tiny lungs and massaged the chest, but there had been no response.

Plum Leaf cradled the baby to her breast, crying quietly. Storyteller wondered—if they had been somewhere else, among his own people, maybe, or on the plains with Turtle's tribe? Would there have been those with medicine powerful enough to bring the tiny spirit into the world of the living? Well, it was no matter now.

The old woman lifted a keening wail, the Song of Mourning of her people, for the dead child. The parents would mourn too with ceremonial purging of the grief through songs and chants, each in the custom of home, of their own people.

It had been Plum Leaf's first pregnancy, a time of great joy for the couple. It was now nearly two years since their marriage. For most of the first year, they had been traveling or living in close quarters with Storyteller's parents. When the couples decided to separate, it became an especially happy time. There was no need for some of the concerns that had been a necessary part of their first year. Not that there had been friction between them, for there had not—at least, less than average, they had all agreed.

But there had been the concern for traveling with a small child. At each stop, each village where they had traded, they had had to seek shelter and food for five people. Transportation too when they traveled by water. There was much difference in the size of the vessels required to carry one couple and baggage, and to carry five people and baggage.

In addition, decisions concerning where to go and how long to stay were simpler. It now concerned only the two of them, and they were a couple in love. They wandered where they chose, sometimes aimlessly, sometimes on a whim. They made good trades and poor ones, camped in good places and bad. They made love, and that was good. And when they discovered that Plum Leaf was pregnant, it was all that their world had lacked. They began to talk of two seasons hence, when they had agreed to meet Turtle and Owl Woman at the winter camp of Turtle's people.

"Ah, they will be so pleased!" Plum Leaf giggled. "But think, Woodpecker! This child who now kicks me will be in his second summer when they see him!"

And now it was over.

"You are young—you can try again," said the woman who had helped.

The young people nodded, but both knew. It would never be the same with another. This was their first, the child that had been welcomed as the fruit of their happy union and for some unknown reason had never taken breath. There might be others but never *this one*.

Plum Leaf recovered her strength slowly, partly because of her grief perhaps. They stayed for half a moon at the village where the labor had taken place and then moved on.

They experienced new sights, sounds, tastes, and smells, and it was a happy time but with a sober overtone. They were more mature, more aware that the world was filled with troubles. There were times when in the warmth of the sleeping robes they shared, they talked of the possibility of another pregnancy.

"Do you wish a child?" she asked him.

"Of course, if you do."

"Oh, yes . . . but, Woodpecker, what if . . . maybe it too would be dead."

Both were a little fearful but agreed that it would be good, even with the risk of another such loss. Several times that next season, Plum Leaf believed that she was pregnant. But each time it proved untrue. They moved on, still enjoying the life of the trader.

They wintered, the second winter of their marriage, with Plum Leaf's people. Her mother, though she had not been ready to become a grandmother, was visibly saddened by the loss and mourned the dead child. Then she recovered and gave the same advice they had heard before.

"You are young . . . you can try again."

Plum Leaf took the remark rather badly, though she said nothing until later when she spoke to Storyteller. "Should it hurt less because we are young?"

"No, no," he crooned gently. "They only try to help."

They wintered there, and Plum Leaf thought that surely in these familiar surroundings, their medicine would be good, and she would conceive. But it did not happen. They even made love, one early morning in the Moon of Falling Leaves, in their enchanted clearing, certain of its powers. It was an inspiring interlude and startled a pair of rabbits bent on similar activities, but no pregnancy resulted, at least for Plum Leaf.

When spring came, they moved on to new areas. By previous agreement, they would seek out Turtle's people this fall for a reunion with Turtle and Owl, and to spend the winter.

"Just ask the Growers," Turtle had suggested as a means to find the camp of his people.

With some difficulty, they did so and at length encountered one of the Wolves, who proved to be none other than Gray Otter.

"Aiee!" he greeted warmly. "It has been too long, my friend! Will you go on the fall hunt with us?"

"We will see," said Storyteller, placing a hand on his chest. "I have none too many ribs left!"

"Come," urged the excited Otter. "The others will be glad to see you!"

"Are my parents here?"

"No, not yet. They are coming too?"

"Yes. I think so. We agreed to meet with you this year."

"Well, the season is still early. They will be along. But come, tell us of your travels! You have new stories, things to trade?"

"Of course!"

Turtle and Owl Woman arrived two suns later, and there was a happy reunion.

"Ah, how Lark has grown!" Plum Leaf exclaimed.

Most heartbreaking, however, was a new babe at Owl Woman's breast. It was a boy of seven moons, with a thoughtful gaze and large dark eyes. The tears came as Plum Leaf cradled the infant and rocked him in her arms. She had almost forgotten her grief but found it just below the surface, ready to bubble up again.

"That must have been difficult," Owl Woman said sympathetically after hearing their sad tale.

Plum Leaf was grateful that Owl did not repeat the now offensive remark about their youth and trying again.

"At my age, I did not really need this one," Owl Woman said, "but ah, he has been a joy. May you have such a one, Plum Leaf."

"I hope so, Mother. Thank you!"

The two embraced, feeling closer now than when they last parted.

"We have much talking to do this winter," said Owl. "You must tell me all the places you have been."

"Yes, you also!"

Storyteller found that he was reluctant to throw himself wholeheartedly into the hunt. It was not fear, exactly, but caution. He was not ready for the risks involved in such dangerous activity. There was a sense of responsibility, a slight shift from the carefree time of youth with its wild escapades. His was the responsibility of a husband now.

He noticed the same change in Otter and in others of their age. These men now had their own lodges, wives, and children. He felt a pang of regret over that as he saw the little ones at play and heard their laughter. He knew that it must be worse for Plum Leaf.

He did enjoy the hunt, the sense of flying that he remembered from his first wild ride on the buffalo-horse of Otter's uncle. But he was more cautious, as well as more experienced. He did make two kills and assisted with a third.

Gray Otter's new wife, Heron, seemed to relate quickly and well to Plum Leaf. It was not long before the young women became best friends. Heron approached her husband with a suggestion. Could Storyteller and Plum Leaf share their lodge for the winter?

So they wintered together, a more satisfactory arrangement than living with Storyteller's parents and their small children. However, it was a bittersweet season. Toward autumn, Heron realized that she was pregnant. Once more, there was the hurt for Plum Leaf, who was not. She managed to be happy for her friend through the early moons of the pregnancy, rejoicing with Heron at the quickening.

But when the Moon of Awakening came, both Plum

Leaf and her husband realized the increasing stress that their friends' happiness was placing on them. It was a great relief when they were able to assemble their packs and take to the trail of the trader again.

Part II

The Trader

18

》 》 》

The Traveler moved along the trail, his heavy pack balanced high on his shoulders. He paused a moment to shift the load and readjust the rawhide straps that cut into the muscles across his chest and shoulders. Ah well, another day would soon be gone, and they would camp at a place they knew, up ahead. Good water—a spring that bubbled up from the rocks.

He licked dry lips and turned to look back at the woman who followed him. She carried a smaller pack, one that would have seemed massive to one unaccustomed to such travel. She never complained. Plum Leaf was still beautiful, he thought, after all the years. It seemed only a short while ago that they had married. But his bones and joints reminded him, after a long day's travel or on a cold morning as they rolled sleepily from the robes.

His wife drew closer, lifted her face, and smiled at him. Sweat beaded her brow. This type of travel was not his favorite, or hers, he knew, but there was no alternative just now. They had decided to winter among her people this season, the Forest People, and her village was accessible only by foot trails.

Plum Leaf's favorite mode of travel was by canoe after she overcame the initial fear of water that is common to the landsman. Her face would reflect the pleasure, and her eyes would sparkle as their craft slid smoothly along one of the great rivers, taking them to new places to trade.

His own preference was to travel by horse. Though his own background was not that of the prairie, he had come to love it. It was the land of his stepfather, Turtle, who had taught him the skills of the trader. There was something about the vastness of the far horizons that always drew him back, no matter where else they had traveled and traded. He still remembered with a thrill the wild abandon of his first buffalo hunt—his broken ribs. *Aiee,* he would hate to take such a fall at this stage of life!

It was a good life though. They both enjoyed the life of the traveling trader. There was only the one thing, the sadness never quite out of mind. They no longer talked of it, but he could tell. He had seen the tears that welled up in her eyes when she watched children at play. In all the years, Plum Leaf had never succeeded in carrying another child. They had wondered if the very active life they led had affected her childbearing, but it seemed not. A season or two, when they had believed her to be pregnant, they had ceased travel, just to be sure. But it seemed to make no difference.

So, they had ceased talking of it. They had thrown themselves wholeheartedly into the life they had chosen. Looking back, he thought perhaps their personal loss had pushed them on. The years had passed so swiftly. It must be fourteen, maybe fifteen winters now since their tiny beautiful girl-child had failed to take breath. His own tears welled up.

They had returned once or twice to that place of sorrow but had hurried on. He knew that their tendency to travel on, to be always on the move, had affected his reputation as a trader. Not unfavorably, for he was known to be honest and fair. But, their far-ranging ways had added a name to those he used. To some, he was still the Storyteller. To most, he was the Trader. But as one with whom they bartered had once asked, was there anyone who had ever traveled so much? He had become known not only as the Trader but the Traveler.

He took a certain pride in this reputation because it was linked to a reputation as one who carried and traded exotic items. Their far-ranging travel and trade gave access to items not usually seen. The red medicine-stone, of course, for which there was only one source, to the far west of his own home country. He often carried the red stone, or medicine-pipes made of it, because its medicine was strong. But it was heavy.

There were other things, easier to pack and lighter in weight. Chokolatl was quite popular among some of the southern tribes, its value increasing as they moved north. There was a variety of vegetable that tasted like fire— "chile." Some of the Caddos with whom they traded used it occasionally, but it was not destined to be a popular item farther north.

More useful, and easy to carry, were the seeds of various types of corn. They had found at least five or six varieties in use in various places along the River of Swans and the River of the Kenzas. Growers in other areas were eager to try new types—some for grinding, for eating fresh, or for popping.

They had wintered with several tribes through the years. Some had emerged as favorites, those whose winter social customs were those they enjoyed. The stories, of course, continued to be a rewarding part of winter activities and replenished his supply for the coming season.

Twice, they had wintered with the people of Plum Leaf's village and intended to do so again. They had not returned to the region of Storyteller's home. Plum Leaf had never seen it. He was not sure he wanted her to, certainly not if the political instability was still there. He had not inquired, and he finally realized that he preferred to avoid it. He could not forget the sightless eyes staring at the sun, the freshly-skinned heads. Maybe next season they could go in that direction and inquire at least.

He stopped at a little rise and waited for Plum Leaf to

join him. He knew she was tired, for he was. She took the last few steps and paused beside him.

"Shall we rest a little?" he suggested.

"No, let us go on, Woodpecker. It is only a little way to the camping place."

"No one calls me Woodpecker anymore except you."

She smiled. Most of the people they contacted knew her husband as the Traveler now, though many still called him Trader. Occasionally, one would remember the seasons when, traveling with his stepfather, he was the Storyteller. But, she loved to call him by his childhood name, the one his mother had preferred, Woodpecker. Many men, she had noticed, were still called by their childhood names where their mothers were concerned.

"You are still the charming boy I met as a child," she explained simply. "Shall we move on? We should be able to camp well before dark."

The camping place they sought was located at the crossing of two trails. It had been a place of reference for many generations. It was easy to describe: "I will meet you where the trails cross." People traveling in the area would necessarily pass this spot.

Its other feature was the unfailing water supply. Even in a dry year, the water seemed always plentiful, sweet, and good. Sometime long ago, some traveler had begun to improve the spring by cleaning out debris and removing stones to make the pool a little deeper. Through the generations, others had continued the upkeep. At the present time, or at least on their last trip, the pool itself, though no larger than a pace across, was deep and crystal clear. It was surrounded by ferns and grasses, worn away only at the side next to the trail where thirsty travelers approached. It was good to think of the cool water and the comfort of a fire in the coming evening chill. The couple moved on.

Idly, he wondered whether they would share their camp with other travelers. He rather hoped so. He enjoyed the companionship, the conversation, and news of other places. Plum Leaf had always said that he could always talk with anyone, even though they did not know each other's tongues. It was true, he had to admit. Such a problem was merely an obstacle to be overcome.

On the other hand, if they were alone at the spring, that was good too. They had never ceased to enjoy being alone together—to talk, laugh, and make the little personal jokes that a devoted couple shares alone. Tonight, either way would be good. They would camp early and enjoy the long twilight of the Moon of Falling Leaves, alone or with others.

It was now only a little farther, and they made a brief stop to rest. A slight south breeze stirred the leaves in a lazy fashion, though it could hardly be felt here. The timbered hills, though shady to travel on a warm autumn day, allowed little breeze.

This thought was interrupted by a slight but unmistakable smell carried on the stirring air. Smoke. There was no village in this area, and the only good campsite was the one they intended to use. Therefore . . .

"We will have company tonight." Plum Leaf voiced his thought.

They moved on, more cautiously now. It would not do to blunder into an unknown situation. It was still some time before they came within hailing distance. Storyteller remembered a landmark now, a large gray boulder on the west side of the trail. Through the trees ahead, a thin layer of smoke drifted. Good. Anyone who wished to conceal his presence or motives would not be so obvious about it.

Still, it was wise to be cautious. And it was only polite to announce one's approach. Travelers had been killed through misunderstanding, by approaching silently. To people who feared attack, such an approach was a threat.

He selected one of the tongues that was probably used in this area. "Ho, the camp!" he shouted through cupped hands.

There was a flurry of activity ahead, and he thought he detected sounds of people slipping into the woods. There was a long pause before an answering shout came. This told him much. It was a party large enough to be confident but still cautious enough not to be caught off guard.

"We are coming in," he called.

He had found that a bold, confident approach was always best. But there was something here that was not quite right. There seemed no danger but . . . something. Plum Leaf seemed to feel it too. The party ahead was cautious, almost too careful. Were they afraid of something? Could it be that the political situation here was uneasy? Carefully, they approached the camp, making certain that none of their moves could be taken as aggressive.

With a practiced eye, he looked around the clearing where the trails crossed: Several men, judging from the robes and supplies strewn around. A hunting party, it seemed, but—ah, there was the cause of their uneasiness! Three children, who appeared to be prisoners. They must not pay too much attention to that.

"Greetings, my brothers," he announced broadly in his wife's tongue, at the same time using hand-signs.

The others nodded, but said nothing.

Storyteller strode boldly toward the spring, Plum Leaf at his side. He flopped to his belly to drink, trying to show a lack of the fear that gnawed at his stomach. He rose and wiped his mouth.

"Ah, that is good," he signed. "It is very dry to the north."

Men were coming out of the woods, back into the clearing. Seven in all, he counted, unless there were some still hiding.

"Who is your chief?" he asked in hand-signs, hoping to establish better communication.

Several of the party looked toward a burly man who now stepped forward.

"I am White Bear, chief of the People," he signed. "How are you called?"

Storyteller was accustomed to the sign for *human* or *people.* It was used by all to indicate their own tribe. Well, he could inquire about that later.

"I have been called many things," he signed, with what he hoped would be taken as a friendly smile. "Just now, I am called Traveler."

There was a slight rippling chuckle of humor, and the group began to relax a bit. Traveler rummaged for a bag of tobacco and signed to White Bear again.

"Join me in a smoke?" he invited.

The captive children watched, wide-eyed. Traveler tried not to look at them. This situation promised to be difficult for Plum Leaf.

19

» » »

The hunting party, it became apparent as the "smoke" progressed, was closely allied to the tribe of Plum Leaf's people but spoke a different tongue. Traveler had found that in such a case, it was prudent to continue hand-signs, even if some conversation was possible. He explained their presence here, their intention to winter in Plum Leaf's village, and their trading customs.

"You have things to trade?" inquired White Bear, looking curiously at the packs of the newcomers.

"In the morning," assured Traveler. "The light will be better."

It was true that shadows were lengthening, and the chief of the party nodded in understanding. Yet it was sometime later before the subject of the captive children came up. White Bear was almost casual about it. "Yes, they are from one of the tribes from the west. Plains people. They came into our region, and we have watched them. It was a dry season for them, I suppose. Usually they do not come this far."

"But the children?"

"Oh, yes . . . we caught them in the woods."

"What will you do with them?"

"Who knows? Sell them, maybe."

Traveler was still fishing for information. Every fiber of his being cried out in sympathy for the captives, and he knew it must be worse for Plum Leaf. The oldest of the girls was about the age that her child would have been. He tried to seem nonchalant. "They look strong," he said. "A little thin, perhaps."

"You wish them?"

"No, my chief! I have no wish for burdens of this sort."

He watched the children closely for the rest of the evening. The youngest, a boy of perhaps six, was not handling his captivity well at all. He alternately cried and smiled. The man who seemed to be his captor teased and played with him, and the boy would respond a little, only to cry again when let alone.

One of the girls was sullen and despondent, but the eldest was defiant. She kept calling out words of encouragement to the others. She was a proud, mature young woman. She could not be more than fifteen, just beginning to fill her buckskins with the soft curves of womanhood. And although she was a captive, she was undaunted. In her eyes was the expression that he had heard called the "look of eagles." It was that of a captive bird of prey, ready to slip from its fetters and escape at any opportunity.

During the course of the evening, he noticed that the older girl talked quietly to the others a great deal. Something was brewing there. Their captors seemed not to notice, but Traveler gained the strong impression that an escape of some sort was in the making. He hoped not. The children had very little chance of success and might be killed or maimed just for trying. At best, their captors seemed quite unsympathetic. He had seen White Bear cuff the older girl, whom he appeared to claim, merely for talking too much. It was possible that such a man could kill a prisoner in a rage if she displeased him.

Even if an escape was successful, the children would have little hope of returning to their own people. They would be in strange and unfamiliar country, and any peo-

ple they might encounter were more likely to recapture
than help them.

He tried repeatedly to think of some way that he might
help the children. Through the years he had seen many
captives. It was not unusual. Most of them were treated
fairly well and eventually adopted into the tribe of their
captors. He was not certain why this situation bothered
him so much. Maybe middle age was affecting his emotions. Or maybe it was merely the age of these captives.
He kept thinking of the proud older girl in terms of their
lost child. If she had lived, this was how he would have
wished her to be.

And what would the future hold for this one? Some
tribes made a point of stealing young women for wives or
to barter to someone else. This girl was certainly pretty
enough to attract attention.

He did not speak of any of this to Plum Leaf, but he
was certain that her heart was heavy too. They prepared
for sleep, and he made certain that he had a clear view of
White Bear and his captive as they all settled in for the
night. White Bear tied a rawhide thong around the girl's
ankle and his own. Any movement beyond the length of
the fetter would rouse him from sleep. This gave the girl
an arm's length of motion but no more. The other children were similarly tied.

Traveler had intended to stay awake and watch, but he
was tired and drifted off. It was much later that he
awoke, dimly aware of quiet activity near by. The girl
seemed to be picking at the thong around her ankle.
White Bear, flat on his back, snored regularly. Traveler
could see quite well by the light of the three-quarter
moon that had now risen, and continued to watch. The
girl had freed her ankle and paused to rub it for only a
moment. She now produced another thong from somewhere in her dress and appeared to tie it to the one on the
chief's ankle. What could she have in mind?

He almost chuckled aloud when he realized what she
was doing. Very cautiously, she unwound the new thong

and extended it to a small sapling a short distance away. The chief was certainly in for a surprise when he jumped up to pursue the escaping prisoners.

Now what to do? He hated to interfere, but these children were about to cause themselves more trouble. His head said that he must help prevent the escape. According to the customs of this tribe, the children were the property of their captors. It would be a breach of his hosts' customs to interfere. Still, his heart refuted the whole situation. He glanced at Plum Leaf, who appeared to be sleeping soundly.

There was a flicker of motion to his left, and he glanced that way. A large owl silently glided across the open patch of sky on fixed silent wings, rising to land on the stub of a dead tree at the edge of the clearing. It was a wondrous thing, *Kookooskoos,* the creature of the night, a silent and efficient hunter. He was distracted for a moment, watching the bird as it looked down into the camp. What did it see? Were there scraps of fur or feather among the belongings of the sleeping party that resembled a mouse or a bird, something for the hunter to strike?

Suddenly the owl stretched its neck and gave its hunting cry, a hollow rendition of its name. "Kookooskoos!"

The cry seemed very loud at this close proximity. There was a stirring in the clearing as sleepers awoke, and then everything happened at once.

All three of the captive children jumped to their feet and ran toward the woods, in different directions. Men sprinted in pursuit. White Bear took one long step, and was jerked from his feet by the thong that tied him to the tree. He landed heavily, partly in the coals of the dying fire. The impact forced a grunt of pain from the big man, followed immediately by a roar of rage. He rolled frantically away from the hot coals, brushing at his smoking buckskins and still roaring.

Afterward, Traveler thought that he might have done well to let the girl escape, but there was no time to think.

She dashed toward him and tripped over some irregularity of the ground as she passed. Almost by reflex, he grabbed her, trying to pinion her arms. She was a fighter —she bit, clawed, and scratched, tried to trip him, even butted his face with her head.

Finally she relaxed into submission. He waited a moment to make sure that it was not merely a ploy and then began to relax. White Bear came over, still cursing, and jerked her hands roughly behind her to tie them. Then he shoved the bound prisoner to the ground near his sleeping robes. The cut end of a rawhide thong still trailed behind his left foot.

Traveler could hardly keep from laughing after the excitement. Though it was a serious situation, it was incredible that this slip of a girl had nearly done it, nearly accomplished an escape. And it had been such an amusing sight, the burly chief rolling in the fire, roaring in pain and rage.

White Bear turned and grudgingly gave the *thank* sign. Men were building up the other fires, and light now flooded the clearing. Others were returning to the firelight, dragging the other captives. Nearly everyone considered the entire episode uproariously funny. There were many jokes at the expense of White Bear, who did not seem amused.

"What is it?" asked Plum Leaf, rousing sleepily.

"The children tried to escape," he told her.

"Did they get away?"

"No."

She did not answer but lay back on the robes, staring at the sky. There would be no more sleep tonight. Still, they did not talk.

Traveler was pondering the situation, trying to make a decision. Normally, he would discuss the problem with Plum Leaf, but on this, he could not. Of one thing he was sure. He could not go on down the trail wondering what was to become of these children, especially the proud one.

If he had his choice in the matter, he would have bought all three captives to protect and care for them. That was impossible. At most, he might be able to trade for one. The defiant older girl, of course. He could not say why, but his heart reached out to her. And he did not know how Plum Leaf would react. He believed that she would approve. But if he was unsuccessful in trading, would she be angry or sad? It was a situation that gave him no guarantee of success either way. And any outcome might trouble Plum Leaf. Well, he must try.

At first light, he approached the chief. "This one gives you trouble," he signed. "Trade her to me and be rid of her."

"Why do you want her?" White Bear asked suspiciously. "I have no wish to trade."

"She is not worth much," Traveler agreed, "but I like her spirit. I might find some small thing to trade."

"She *is* worth much," signed the chief indignantly. "You have nothing that I want, but what would you offer?"

"I have some things in my pack."

"I will look. You want all three?"

"No, only the scrawny one. I could not afford the better ones," Traveler joked.

It was part of the preparatory manuevering, a preliminary to serious trade. Both knew it and enjoyed the sparring. At least Traveler did. The prospective buyer tried to emphasize any faults, while the seller just as strenuously emphasized quality.

"She is strong," White Bear was saying in hand-signs. "Here, feel her." He squeezed her arms and legs, and invited Traveler to do so. "She can work hard. Besides, she is nearly a woman. She is pretty. She will make a man's bed warm in the winter. Maybe I will keep her."

"This is only a child," protested Traveler.

The girl's facial expression indicated pure revulsion. In keeping with the spirit of the trade, Traveler ran his hands over her body, arms, legs, buttocks, and the small budding breasts. "No," he signed, "there is not enough meat here to warm a bed. But I will offer some small things anyway."

White Bear nodded. "Well, let us look."

Now the trading began in earnest. The trader placed a variety of small items on a skin spread between the two seated men. A stone knife, some arrowpoints. White Bear dismissed the objects with an indignant wave of his hand. That was the expected reaction. If the chief had not ridiculed the first offer, something would have been wrong.

Traveler cleared the skin and tried again. He placed a knife of some quality on the skin. It was a desirable item of black volcanic glass from the far western mountains. "This stone is made in fires below the earth," Traveler stated importantly.

White Bear picked up the knife, tested its edge, and grunted. "I have a knife. You have nothing else?"

There was a murmur around the watching circle. White Bear had turned down a very good offer. The black obsidian blade, with its superb workmanship, was a great prize. Bear was driving a hard bargain.

Traveler was not surprised, but he spread his hands as if in consternation. "I have a medicine-pipe," he offered.

"Let me see it."

This was the trade that Traveler had intended. He drew out the pipe case with its ornate quillwork and buckskin fringes. There was a low mutter at its beauty as he handed it to the chief. "The red stone comes from only one quarry, my chief," Traveler boasted. "A sacred place, far to the north."

"Of course. Do you think I have never seen a medicine-pipe?" White Bear signed indignantly.

He handled the pipe a bit longer, then placed it on the skin. "No," he signed, starting to rise.

Now the onlookers gasped. Why would anyone turn down such a trade?

Traveler was taken completely off guard. This should have completed the trading, and White Bear should have felt that he had a bargain. "Wait, my chief! I have nothing else. What could you wish?"

White Bear turned, a determined look on his face. "Your knife!" He pointed to Traveler's waist.

"My knife? I could not give it up!"

It was the medicine-knife, the precious metal blade that he had obtained from the French long ago. He had thought never to part with it. It was his proudest possession.

White Bear was turning away. "So be it!" he signed.

Traveler drew the knife from its sheath, allowing the sunlight to flash in dazzling beauty from its polished blade. "Wait," he called again, holding the knife aloft. "This—for all three." He pointed at the other children.

"Of course not! This is the one you want!"

Traveler, the experienced trader, now realized that he had been outtraded. "It is good," he signed, handing the knife to White Bear.

At this point Plum Leaf, who had watched glumly without comment, began a tirade. "What are you doing?" she shouted at him. "Your *knife,* which you had before we were married? Your finest possession? Woodpecker, you have gone mad!"

He turned and gestured her to silence. They would speak of it later.

He turned to the girl. "Come on, girl," he signed to her. "I hope you are worth it!"

20

Traveler motioned the girl to him. They must establish some things from the first, and the defiant look said that he might have bought more than he bargained for. He was still smarting a little, angry over having been bested in a trade. White Bear, as the two parties prepared to take their separate ways, had taken every opportunity to show off his new acquisition, the medicine-knife. Once he drew it merely to cut a strip of dried meat, which he could have easily bitten or broken in two. Traveler knew that such blatant show was for his benefit, to remind him of the trade and his loss.

"Come here, girl," he motioned. He tied one end of a thong to the girl's wrist.

"What is this?" she signed in mock surprise. "You have not tied me before!"

"Be still!" He tied the other end of the thong around his own waist. Plum Leaf glowered and said nothing. He turned to White Bear. "Here we part, my chief," he signed. "My wife's people live that way."

He pointed south. Plum Leaf had already shouldered her pack and entered the trail, a tunnel of leafy green through the woods. He marveled, as he often had, how a woman can express anger by the swing of her shoulders and hips as she walks. A trifle angry with himself, he gave a tug on the girl's fetter and pointed down the trail.

The girl turned, calling to the other children, a tirade of rapid speech that he did not understand. It seemed likely that she realized they would never see each other again and was shouting her good-byes. The others were crying.

This was no time to become sentimental, he told himself angrily. The situation was already bad enough, and worsening rapidly. Plum Leaf had not spoken to him since the trade.

He shoved the girl forward, and she stumbled a step or two, then turned to face him. "Do not push me," she signed. "I can walk without help." There was a dangerous glint in the proud eyes.

"Then do it!" he signed.

She turned and hurried down the trail after Plum Leaf. He had wondered if the girl might slow their travel, but it quickly proved otherwise. Her long legs, he noticed, could match his own stride for stride. In fact, the long fetter became a hindrance a time or two over rough parts of the trail when he was slowed by the heavy packs. The thong would tighten and throw them both off balance.

Late in the morning, they paused for a brief rest. The girl pointed to the thong on her wrist. "I can travel better without this," she signed.

Plum Leaf broke her silence for the first time with a resumption of her tirade. "You are mad, Woodpecker! The girl is not worth the effort. She will run away. You are like a rutting bull elk!"

Ah, so that was it! Plum Leaf was jealous of this child just blossoming into womanhood. "We will speak of this later," he said firmly.

He turned back to the girl. "You will promise not to run away?" he asked in hand-signs.

There was a long pause before she answered, as she considered the option. Finally she began to sign. "I cannot promise that, my chief. I am of the People. I will escape when I can."

Traveler threw up his hands in dismay. "Listen, little

one! You are in strange country. Winter is coming. Give your promise for now."

She thought for a moment. "I can change it, later?"

"It is good. You will let me know when?"

She nodded and held out her wrist, and Traveler cut the thong. The girl sat, rubbing the wrist.

Plum Leaf resumed her tirade, but he spoke quickly. "Look, we have made a bargain. She will not run."

"She will! She is not to be trusted!"

He turned back to the girl to verify the terms of the bargain. "You will not run unless you first tell me that the agreement is finished. Agreed?"

The girl nodded. Plum Leaf sat glowering, and another idea occurred to Traveler. He might as well take advantage of the situation. "One more thing!" he signed. "If you break your bargain, Plum Leaf says she will kill you!"

He knew that Plum Leaf would do no such thing, but maybe the thought would serve as a deterrent. But, to his surprise, the captive turned to Plum Leaf and began to sign. "If I am dead, I am of no use to you. I could not even be sold. Still, a woman of my tribe keeps her promises. I agree to the bargain."

Plum Leaf sat speechless, and the whole thing struck Traveler as humorous. He turned to the girl. "It is good!" he signed. "Girl, I like your spirit. How are you called?"

"I am Pale Star."

"We will call you so. Yet I am made to believe that this star is not a pale one! But come, let us go on. Cold Maker comes soon."

As it happened, Cold Maker came the next day, much sooner than he had guessed. They were traveling well, still a few sleeps from Plum Leaf's village, when the sky began to darken. There was a crisp chill in the air. The captive girl became quite anxious, glancing at the darkening sky.

He was amused. Among her people, this could be quite

a dangerous situation. A storm on the prairie at this season—well, it was time to make winter camp and stuff the lodge lining. Pale Star became more anxious, and by the time he called a halt, she seemed nearly frantic. He selected a flat place against an abrupt slope that faced south, and they dropped their packs. Here, he signed to her, they would build a lodge.

"Of what?"

"Brush of course!"

She still seemed puzzled, and he was reminded again that brush shelters among the plains people were only for summer use and had no sides.

"You gather firewood," he signed. "We will build the lodge."

He and Plum Leaf had barely lashed the horizontal pole to two saplings to form the front edge of the roof when the girl came slipping quietly back. Her hands were empty, and Plum Leaf gave a grunt of disgust, but it quickly became apparent that something was urgent.

Pale Star motioned them to quiet and quickly signed her news. "There are deer in the woods!"

He nodded and picked up his bow. "Show me!"

He admired the graceful way she moved ahead of him, threading between the trees and thickets. This was a young woman of some skill. Finally she motioned again for silence, and pointed. "Just ahead! In the oaks."

The two peered carefully through the brush and small trees.

"There are three . . . one lying down."

"I see them."

He drew the arrow to its head, and the string twanged as it sped on its way. All three animals fled, and Pale Star looked at him in disappointment. But he had seen the arrow strike. It had been one of those rare shots that the bowman knows will strike true, predetermined when the missile leaves the string. He had felt it, even before he saw the shaft strike between the ribs of the fat doe.

"We have fresh meat tonight," he signed.

He waited awhile, then crossed the clearing and began tracking—a few drops of blood on a fallen oak leave, a bloody smear. They had gone less than a long bow shot when they came to the fallen doe. The animal was quite dead, the feathered end of his arrow protruding like a strange growth from the chest wall.

"Go and bring Plum Leaf," he signed as he drew his knife to begin butchering.

It was that evening that Plum Leaf first began to accept the girl. Without being told, Pale Star plunged into the work of butchering when she returned with the other woman. It was merely an act of self-preservation, of course. If food is plentiful, no one goes hungry. This girl, he supposed, had helped butcher buffalo all her life.

But the effect on Plum Leaf was apparent. They had not yet talked of the acquisition of the girl, and he was not looking forward to the ordeal. He finished the ceremony of apology to the deer and turned to help carry the first load of meat to the camp. The captive was just lifting a bundle of meat when Plum Leaf spoke. "She may be useful, after all," she conceded.

Traveler's heart leaped for joy. Now maybe things could get back to normal.

The lean-to was finished none too soon. Fat fluffy flakes of snow were falling silently through the trees or hissing softly into the dry oak foliage. The fire was crackling, strips of meat broiling before it on sticks. They all ate their fill, propped more strips of meat to dry and smoke-cure, and Plum Leaf spread their sleeping robes in the shelter.

At first, Pale Star seemed reluctant to share their bed. The previous night she had rolled in a robe they had given her, a little apart from her captors. But tonight—on a snowy night, body warmth is a precious commodity not to be wasted. It was snowing harder now. It was apparent that, reluctant or not, there would be a real need to share the shelter and the robes.

Traveler was concerned. He and Plum Leaf had still

not discussed the captive. He could not comfortably suggest that he take the middle position. His wife had already questioned his motives for buying the girl. And surely Plum Leaf would not want her between them. As for suggesting that Plum Leaf take the middle, and the girl her other side—ah, how could he have created such a dilemma? He avoided the mention of the subject as long as he could.

Finally, just when he was ready to speak, Plum Leaf saved him from the embarrassment. "Here, girl," she signed. "You will be warmer between us."

She could not resist, however, a glance of contempt and warning at her husband. Then her face softened for a moment. "She has little body fat," Plum Leaf explained apologetically. "She would be chilled easily."

Traveler nodded agreeably. He was in no position to argue anything with Plum Leaf.

It was a long time before he fell asleep. Cold Maker howled and drifted the snow against and around the little shelter. Once he felt a cold breath of wind persistently whistling through a hole in the brush wall of the lean-to. He rose, went outside, and kicked the drifting snow deeper against the shelter. There—that would be warmer. He replenished the fire before he crawled back into the robes and stood looking at the two sleeping forms for a moment.

He would have loved to snuggle up to Plum Leaf, as he always had, but it was impossible. He considered attempting to go back to bed on the other side. No, there was not enough room, and she might be angry. Finally he crept back under the robe in the place he had just vacated. It was still warm. Not like snuggling next to Plum Leaf, but at least the blast of Cold Maker's breath no longer came through the wall.

"Mother, I would learn your tongue," Pale Star signed.

They were lacing strips of the meat on green sticks and

propping them over the fire. This produced a combination of drying, cooking, and smoking that was not unfamiliar to Star's people, it seemed. It had been decided to stay in this camp for another day while the wet snow disappeared and travel became easier. Meanwhile, they would salvage as much as possible of the venison in this manner.

Plum Leaf was startled though pleased by the request. "My tongue, or his?" She pointed to her husband.

The girl shrugged. "Both, maybe. Which do you use together?"

"Both. Mine with my people, his for his. When we are alone, both, sometimes."

Pale Star worked with the venison strips for a little while, and then signed a question. "We go to your people now?"

"Yes. Three, four sleeps. We winter there."

Traveler happened to observe this interchange. He was pleased that the two were conversing but was also puzzled. The girl had asked if their goal was the village of Plum Leaf's people, as if she already knew it. *How* did she know?

He thought for some time and finally realized. On the night before he traded for her, Traveler had told White Bear that they were headed for his wife's people. And he had used *hand-signs*. The girl had seen and remembered. What a quick mind! It was also apparent that she was a good worker. The time that it would have taken to prepare and smoke-dry the meat strips was virtually cut in half.

Sometime later, the girl asked a question of Plum Leaf as they worked. "Have you had children?"

Ah, too bad, he thought. But the girl had no way to know.

He watched the tears well up in his wife's eyes as they always did when the subject arose.

"One," she signed. "She is dead."

It was fortunate that at that moment Sun Boy overcame his foe. The rays of his heavenly torch burst through the clouds, and its warmth could be felt.

Plum Leaf's expression relaxed somewhat, and she smiled. "Cold Maker's first war party is always a short one," she signed.

21

It was remarkable to Traveler how rapidly the two women became close. As it happened, the thing that he had feared never occurred—the discussion with Plum Leaf about his motives for the trade. It was no longer necessary. Plum Leaf first accepted the fact that another pair of hands made the tasks lighter. Accepting the girl would take longer.

Still, he was pleased to see them communicating. As he had suspected, Pale Star was extremely intelligent. In addition, she seemed to have the facility of learning languages. In a short while, she was speaking the tongue of Plum Leaf's people well enough to chatter conversationally. Moreover, she seemed to have virtually no accent. Well, he told himself, some have the gift of tongues; some do not.

Plum Leaf was still rather reserved until early in the Moon of Long Nights. It was then that the menstrual flow signaled the arrival of womanhood for the captive girl. The attitude of Plum Leaf seemed to change suddenly. The sisterhood of women everywhere came to the fore, and instantly Plum Leaf was solicitous and helpful. She explained the customs of the menstrual lodge. The menstruating woman would spend a few days each month with others in similar circumstances, in a special lodge at the edge of the village.

"Aiee!" exclaimed the girl. "She is sent away?"

"Of course!" Plum Leaf retorted. "It is not so with your people?"

"That she is dangerous, yes. It is known that a bow touched by a menstruating woman will never shoot straight again. But our women are careful not to endanger anyone! She is not banished from her lodge!"

Ah, that streak of pride again, thought Traveler, shaking his head.

If he had known the rest of the story, there might have been much more shaking of his head. For Plum Leaf took the girl aside in private conversation. "You do not understand," she confided. "This is a good custom."

"To be pushed out of one's home?" Star was still indignant.

"No, look, child . . . this removes one from the duties of the lodge too. You will see the same women each month, who become your friends. And who understands but another woman?"

It was in this way, then, that the two became almost conspirators. Almost without realizing it, Plum Leaf came to regard the welfare of the captive quite personally, and during the long dark days and nights of that winter, the relationship grew and prospered. The girl in many ways came to fill the place of the lost daughter. Plum Leaf felt her frustrated maternal instinct become calm and serene, and her heart reached out to the girl. She was strict, as one is with a first child. Perhaps the response of Pale Star was as astonishing. The captive *responded* like a daughter. She was solicitous of her foster mother, finding little helpful things to make tasks lighter, in the best tradition of a loving child.

Traveler was astonished. He felt excluded from the relationship that he saw forming almost before his eyes. He was not entirely excluded, however. Pale Star showed great interest in his language skills. No sooner was she becoming fluent in the tongue of Plum Leaf's people than she began to inquire into his. He had his doubts about her ability to absorb so much so rapidly, but she did well.

She also showed a great interest in his stories. When during some of the long winter evenings he would be entertaining a group around the story-fires, Pale Star would always be there, listening with rapt attention. He had first noticed this quite early, even before they reached Plum Leaf's village. They had camped at a small town to participate in storytelling and trading. He was using hand-signs as well as oral narration because he knew that there were several in the audience of varied backgrounds. He was certain that the captive girl had little knowledge of any of the languages represented there. Yet when his eyes happened to fall on her, Pale Star sat watching and listening, an expression of absolute delight on her face. It must be that she was following the hand-signs.

Then there came a time, late in the winter, when she seemed to have a complete change in attitude. Suddenly there was no interest in learning more language. She seemed to forget what she already knew. Frequently she asked for a repeat of some comment or question. He wondered if she was losing her hearing. He had almost decided that it must be. It was known to happen, even in the young, in the rigors of winter. She did not appear ill, however. She remained cheerful and helpful . . . *aiee,* it was puzzling!

Then he noticed, at a story-fire late in the Moon of Hunger, a further puzzle. Pale Star hung eagerly on every word, eyes shining with anticipation, completely involved in the narrative. How curious, he thought. He experimented a little, dropping his voice to a whisper. The girl's facial expression and half-smile of pleasure still indicated complete understanding. So it was not a hearing loss. He stopped the hand-signs that accompanied his story, and it seemed to make no difference. She still understood, quite well.

What, then? He pondered a long time as he lay in his sleeping robes that night. There had been no chance to talk to Plum Leaf of his suspicions. Star or other people were always present. That was one of the things about the close social contact of a winter season. There was little opportunity for private conversation.

Then it suddenly struck him, the answer he sought. The girl must be pretending. But why? Ah, yes, of course! He had almost forgotten their bargain—her need to escape and her temporary promise. There had been little reason to think of it through the winter, but soon it would be possible to travel. The time would come when Pale Star would announce that her vow was at an end. He was certain that she would do so, would live up to the agreement. He could not think that she would do otherwise.

But meanwhile it would be to her advantage to appear as ignorant as possible. He chuckled silently to himself, his heart holding a confused mixture of emotions. He found himself feeling pride at her cleverness. At the same time, the threat of her loss was alarming. After all, he had paid dearly—no, that was not it. He was almost ashamed of that thought. It was—how strange—it was the way a parent must feel when a grown daughter prepares to leave the lodge. A sadness . . .

There was no way, he realized, that Pale Star could be prevented from escaping. She was far too resourceful. It would be only a matter of time, it seemed, until she would announce her intention to revoke her vow. Well, when the time came, they would let her go. He could not find it in his heart to consider tying her, as they might have done before she became a part of them.

This status was reinforced one afternoon by a strange incident. An old man approached Traveler with an offer to buy the girl. Traveler flew into a rage, and called the man a number of uncomplimentary things. "Son of a snake!" he shouted. "Get away from my family!"

Bewildered, the old lecher protested. "I only tried to do you a favor," he snapped. "I have offered a good bargain, and—"

"Go!" Traveler cried. "You have nothing I want."

Shaking his head, the man retreated, puzzled at this reaction.

Pale Star had seen the entire event and seemed mildly amused by it. Traveler wanted badly to explain. Surely, there was a difference, he thought, between his own acquisition of the girl and the proposal set forth by this—this rutting animal.

Then he remembered that his wife had called *him* something of the sort. But that was different, he told himself, and besides, it was before she became like a daughter. His original motives—could he have actually thought of Pale Star as?—no, of course not. He was irritated at himself over the very thought.

As spring approached and the Moon of Awakening brought long lines of geese to the sky, Traveler began his usual restlessness. The winged travelers honked their way north to distant breeding grounds, and the frustrated migration urge that remains in all of us began to rise in his breast. He longed to be on the trail. This year, they had decided, would be the season to work their way north and try to learn of the political situation in his home country.

He wandered restlessly out of the village, wishing to be alone to think. There was a hilltop a couple of bow shots away where one could see a long distance, and he found himself turning in that direction. It troubled him that Pale Star would tell him soon that their agreement was at an end. He needed to be alone to think. Maybe he could spend a little while alone on the hill.

He emerged from the trees and looked up the grassy slope. To his disappointment, someone was already there. He started to turn back but recognized Pale Star. The girl was standing at the highest point of the hill's crest, her face uplifted to the sky. Her hair streamed out in the wind as she watched the geese. In that moment, he felt a kinship for her that he had never felt before. He understood the restlessness that had brought her here. It was much like his own.

One thing struck him as odd. He would have expected her yearning to be for home—the wide skies and far horizons of the prairie. But she should have been facing west, or northwest. Instead, she faced north, her gaze following the migration of the great birds that trumpeted their way overhead. So, he thought, it was not one urge, but *two*. Pale Star longed for home, but also to move on, to see new things. Her urges were much like his own! Except, of course, that his urges would lead him in the same direction, north.

He climbed the slope to stand beside her. She nodded to him, but neither spoke for a little while.

"Little one," he said finally, "it is almost time to go home." It was an experiment, a trial statement to see what her reaction would be.

She turned thoughtfully to look at him for a moment. "Yes," she said slowly, "time to go home."

He was not at all certain that they were talking about the same thing.

22

Sometimes he felt as if he had spent all his life on the trail, bent beneath a heavy pack. Usually he enjoyed the travel, the new sights, even this woodland travel overland on a forest trail. But then there were days like this— warm, muggy, not a breath of air stirring in the closeness of the dense woods. Sweat streamed down his face, stinging his eyes, salty on his lips.

He knew that the two women behind him were equally uncomfortable. Star, especially, whose own prairie country was wide and open, felt closed in and trapped by this forest. He remembered that Turtle, his stepfather, had occasionally mentioned such a feeling. Turtle was native to the prairie land of far horizons too.

Plum Leaf, who had grown up in the woods, had no such problems of the spirit. But she too suffered physically from such a day. If tomorrow was not better, maybe they should camp for a day or two, or until there was a break in the weather.

Their season had started well. Actually, it was still going well, except that for a few days, here in the Moon of Growing, it had become oppressively hot and hard to travel. They were headed generally northward, stopping to trade at the villages they encountered. They had fallen into a pattern of travel, with Traveler in the lead, Pale Star next, and Plum Leaf bringing up the rear.

It should be only a few more sleeps now until they reached the village of a good friend, Hunts-in-the-Rain. There they could barter for a canoe, and travel would be easier. Maybe tomorrow they would strike the river and follow it upstream. No more than a day or two, as nearly as he could recall. It had been a few years since they traded this area. He wiped the sweat from his forehead, shifted the pack, and moved on after a glance at the women. Star looked up and smiled. Plum Leaf, farther behind, did not notice the pause.

Pale Star—what a difference the girl had made in their lives since last season. She had been quite useful, helping with the packs and the carrying. It would be difficult now without her. And that time, he was sure, would be soon. She had matured so rapidly. Last season, he had thought he was buying a child, but the person who now followed him on the trail was a woman. She had grown taller, a little—she was already tall when he first saw her. But she had been in that leggy, slightly awkward stage, like a fawn . . . no, more like a colt, just a trifle clumsy, not yet accustomed to the skills of using such long legs.

And in that year, the girl had become a woman. Maybe it was not that she had grown taller but merely appeared taller because of her maturity. Her body had filled out, and she was a woman of great beauty now, in face and form. He had seen the young men look at her and resented their glances. But all this would soon be over, he was afraid. She had said nothing more since the day on the hilltop. Actually, she had said nothing then, beyond the vague remark about going home. Even that had been only a repeat of his own statement.

Still, he felt that there was much understood that day that was unspoken. It had been as if their spirits touched. It was a strange thing. There had been times when they had felt close, as father and daughter, but this was something else, something that was not like family closeness. It was more. Yet not like man and woman . . . no, he did not think of her in that way. It was a communion of the two spirits; there was no other way to understand it. He *felt* her need to go home to the prairie. He was sure, too, that part of the sadness he felt at the prospect was *her* sadness. He was a little surprised that she had not yet spoken of this, voiced her intention to end their bargain.

Traveler was experienced in evaluating their location, direction, and distance. He was aware, as they traveled north, that there would soon be a time for decision. It was time to turn westward if one's goal was the prairie home of the Elk-dog People, Star's people. He was certain that she knew this because he had watched her skill in orientation. He doubted that Pale Star could be "lost," anywhere. So she was aware that the time was at hand to revoke her promise. Why had she not done it? Of this he was unsure. It would have been to her advantage to do so.

Maybe he would never understand that part, but he was certain of one thing. Star knew that the time of parting was at hand, knew it, probably, better than he. Yes, within the next few days, before they reached the river, probably, she would announce the end of their agreement. And, he thought, he would do nothing to stop her. How could he? A few moons ago he would have. But now, what could he do? One cannot prevent the departure of a loved one, or a friend.

He rubbed his right eye, to relieve the sting of a rivulet of sweat, or maybe a swelling of tears. Nonsense, he told himself. This was ridiculous. He and Plum Leaf had enjoyed many years of this life, just the two of them. How could this stranger have become such a part of it in only a few moons?

He wondered whether Plum Leaf felt as he did. Probably not in quite the same way. That was odd too. Plum Leaf, with whom he had always shared his innermost thoughts—they had never really talked about the girl. Maybe because of her suspicions at first . . . She had apparently realized that these fears were groundless long ago. But it is hard to discuss a mistake, even with a loved one. *Especially* with a loved one, maybe.

There was a good stopping place ahead, and a rest would do them good. They could pause a little while by the stream there and go on more comfortably. He shrugged the pack straps from his shoulders and set the burden beside a tree. He looked back down the trail. Pale Star was approaching, an expression of great relief on her face. Maybe they should have stopped earlier.

The girl shed her pack beside his. She straightened, stretched her arms and shoulders, smiling to herself with the ecstasy of relief for tired muscles.

"Where is Plum Leaf?" he asked conversationally.

"Right behind—" Star began, then paused to look down the trail.

The two looked at each other, puzzled for a moment, and then Star was running down the path. Traveler followed a bit more slowly, his body no longer equal to a hard sprint, even in a potential emergency.

Plum Leaf was seated with her back against the bole of a large tree several hundred paces back the trail. She had dropped her pack directly in the trail. Her eyes were closed, her face ashen.

"Mother!" Pale Star cried, dropping to her knees to encircle the woman with her arms.

"I am all right," protested Plum Leaf. "I only stopped to rest a moment." But her skin was clammy, and her breath came in hoarse, rasping gasps.

Traveler came running up. "I am sorry!" he blurted, dropping to his knees beside her. "I did not know . . ."

"It is nothing, Woodpecker. I will rest a little . . . it will be better."

He and Star looked at each other across the limp form. "It is good," he said, his voice tight. "We will camp near here. We all need rest."

He picked her up and carried her to the place they had left the packs. Pale Star picked up the bundle the sick woman had just dropped and followed. They made her as comfortable as possible on a thick sleeping robe and drew aside.

"She is very sick, Traveler," Star whispered.

"I know. What can we do?"

He felt lost, helpless, like a child. He could not think. There had been no time in his life so devastating. Even when their child was stillborn, he and Plum Leaf had had each other. Now he was without support. The threat was overwhelming. He was dimly aware that Star was speaking.

"Oh . . . what?" he mumbled.

"I said, do you know any plants that could be used?"

"I . . . no, I do not know."

Star seemed quite concerned. "Traveler, this is not my country . . . I do not know what grows here. *Aiee,* if only we had my uncle, Looks Far. He is a great holy man."

"It is too far," he said sadly. "Do you know what he might have done?"

"Aiee, I am not a holy person!"

She was silent for a little while, lost in thought. "I can make her something," she murmured, half to herself. "There were dried rose fruits near the trail." She turned to him. "Can you find some fresh meat?"

"I will try."

"It is good. I will start the fire and look for some other things."

Traveler picked up his bow and headed aimlessly into the woods. He did not even realize that he was letting Pale Star take charge.

It was perhaps sheer chance that led the yearling buck into the clearing ahead of him—that, or providence. The creature stood there staring at him, frozen still as stone. It took his confused brain a few moments to realize what he was supposed to do. Then he slowly raised the weapon and drew the arrow to its head. The string twanged, and the animal gave three convulsive jumps and fell, kicking its last.

Now, with something to do, he was functioning better. He cut the throat to let the animal bleed and slit the belly to begin the butchering. He wondered if Star needed any special parts. He knew that the plains people sometimes used raw liver as a tonic. He gutted the creature, made a hasty formal apology, and then began to drag it back toward the camp.

The fire was burning, and Pale Star had dug a little pit near it, in the custom of the plains people. She was preparing to cut one of the packs apart to use the rawhide in the cooking pit. Several stones were already heating in the fire.

"Ah, you have a deer!" Star exclaimed. "It is good! A fresh skin is more nourishing."

She took the deer skin and spread it as a lining in the hollow, fleshside up. Traveler carried water to fill the pit, and Star began to take the heated stones, as big as her fist, and drop them into the cooking pit with willow tongs. Each produced a sharp hiss and a burst of steam. Soon the water was bubbling.

"Use stones from the hillside," Plum Leaf called weakly. "Those from near the spring contain water spirits."

"Yes, Mother," Star answered. "I know."

Of course she would know, Traveler thought to himself. A woman of the prairie would learn quite early that a stone from the stream placed in a fire explodes violently as the spirits escape.

Star was busily adding ingredients to her stew—strips of meat, a handful of onions that she had found growing near the spring. The smells of cooking began to waft around the clearing.

Plum Leaf, who had been dozing, awoke and began to show some interest. Star took a wooden noggin and dipped a cupful of the simmering broth. She allowed it to cool a little, then carried it to Plum Leaf. Carefully she lifted the sick woman, an arm around her shoulders, and fed her sips of the broth.

"It is good, Star," Plum Leaf said.

"It will make you strong, Mother."

Plum Leaf soon tired and fell asleep as soon as they eased her down. But her color was better, her breathing regular.

Her fever rose that evening, and she seemed unresponsive. Pale Star stayed up all night, cooling the fevered face with water and stroking the hands, talking softly.

For three days, the ordeal continued. Star concocted a mixture of cooked liver and pounded roseberries, held together with melted fat. "Buffalo fat would be much better," the girl observed, "but this may do."

She also fed the sick woman bites of fresh raw liver. It was a custom of her people, she explained to Traveler. "The sun makes the grass to grow, and the buffalo eat it. In this way, the spirit of the sun is captured and stored in the buffalo's liver. My people crave it in springtime after a winter of dry meat."

"Do you think it is the same with deer liver?" asked Traveler anxiously.

"I do not know, Uncle. Maybe so."

The third night, Traveler insisted that Star get some rest. She had hardly closed her eyes through the long vigil. Reluctantly, the girl consented. "Maybe a little while . . ."

But day was breaking when Traveler woke her gently. "Wake up, little one," he said, smiling. "Your medicine has worked. The fever is gone, and she is better."

23

» » »

True, Plum Leaf seemed to have passed the threatening narrow point in the trail of her illness, but she was still very weak. It was three more days before she began to gain enough strength to consider traveling.

Traveler was encouraged by her improvement, perhaps too much so, because he began to make plans to go on. Pale Star warned of the weakness of the recovering Plum Leaf, but he brushed her objections aside. "She is strong. She will do better in the north country."

It was a day or two before Traveler realized what was happening. The roles of the two women had reversed, and their traveling positions as well. Plum Leaf had taken the middle position on the trail, and Pale Star brought up the rear. It was now Star who called ahead to him that the older woman must rest. Star chose the campsite, the most comfortable spot for Plum Leaf, hovering, comforting, bringing water.

And Traveler allowed Star to assume this role. Probably it was part of his denial of the reality. He was unable to admit that the patient was not really gaining much. Any progress was quite slow. Once, Star announced with finality that Plum Leaf would be unable to travel. Traveler accepted this without question, and they spent a day of rest. It was a great relief to have someone else making the decisions about a situation that he found so unacceptable.

He had completely forgotten his fears about Star's leaving. He had absolute confidence that she would not do such a thing. Plum Leaf needed her, and without a second thought, Traveler knew that Star would be there when she was needed.

His main concern was for Plum Leaf's recovery, and he found that he had no real judgment about that, so the help and support of Star was doubly comforting. He knew that it would be easier traveling when they reached the river, which should be only a day or two. His friend Hunts-in-the-Rain would help them find a canoe.

When they rounded the last turn of the trail and the river stretched before them, it was with a great sense of accomplishment. He stopped and gazed across the expanse of water at the fringe of willows on the far side. The women came up beside him.

"Aiee!" exclaimed Star. "How do we cross?"

Traveler laughed. "We do not, little one! This *is* the trail."

"The *trail*? But Uncle, I . . ."

"Yes, the Big River, the Missi-ssippi. We follow it north. We will trade for a canoe."

Now came the problem that occurred occasionally. Star was unfamiliar with the word *canoe*. He tried several tongues without success and finally resorted to hand-signs.

"Boat?" the girl asked incredulously.

"Of course!" Then he laughed again, realizing the reason for her consternation. To this girl from the prairie, a "boat" was the round unmaneuverable "bull boat" of the Mandans, also used by a few others, primarily for crossing streams or small bodies of water.

"This is a different sort of boat," he explained. "Long and narrow . . . made of bark . . . you will see."

"Where do we get this boat?"

He could see that she only half believed him, and reluctantly at that. He saw the dread in her eyes as she watched the swift muddy current sweep past. It reminded him of the reaction of Plum Leaf when she had been introduced to the river.

"We will travel upstream to the village we spoke of," he explained. "It is maybe two or three sleeps."

They rested, then moved on, following a well-used trail along the river. Pale Star continued to watch the stream at every opportunity. She seemed fascinated, yet repulsed. He could imagine the dread that the water's depths must hold for her. Her people were good swimmers, but their streams were clear and sparkling for the most part, certainly nothing like this. She probably imagined it peopled with monsters.

Star was amazed to see two men in a canoe well out in the stream. He called her attention to the men, who appeared to be fishing but waved to them. This was good. The village must be less than a day's travel away.

As he had expected, they were welcomed warmly. This was one of the villages that he especially enjoyed. They had been here many times, and both the stories and the trading were always profitable. People recognized him as they entered the town, calling out greetings or making hand-signs.

"Will there be stories tonight?" a man signed.

"Of course! Bring your friends!"

A young man ushered them to a longhouse and invited them to stay there. "My father sends his welcome," he explained.

"Your father is Hunts-in-the-Rain? Ah, you have grown up since I saw you! Tell him I will visit his lodge in a little while."

He must make the mandatory courtesy visit as soon as Plum Leaf was settled. She looked tired, but now she could rest. It was easy, in this friendly place, to forget what he suspected, that Plum Leaf was much sicker than she pretended.

* * *

The story-fires burned bright, and the crowd gathered that night to hear this most favorite of storytellers. He was appreciated here, and nothing inspires a teller of stories like a good audience. He warmed to the occasion. He used hand-signs as well as the tongue of their hosts for the benefit of any outsiders.

He first told of things that would interest the children, ending that portion with the perennial favorite, how Bobcat lost his tail. It was originally long, he related, and dragged on the ground. In that way, it was frozen in the ice of a stream when Cat paused to drink and there was a sudden change in the weather. Cat tried long and hard, but finally elected to sacrifice his tail to free himself.

The crowd rocked with laughter. Then their chief rose. "It is good, Traveler," said Hunts-in-the-Rain, chuckling, wiping tears of laughter from his eyes. "Here is our story."

The chief then related how Spotted Cat was instructed at Creation to be a night hunter and never, ever, to show himself by day. He did so but one night stayed too late and failed to reach his den before the sun rose. An eagle, wakening for the day's hunt, mistook the long tail for a small furry creature and swooped down, snatching the tail off short. Bobcat is still a night hunter, careful to avoid being seen in daylight.

The crowd responded with approval. Traveler was interested to note that Pale Star seemed quite absorbed in the stories.

As the crowd quieted, Hunts-in-the-Rain spoke to Traveler. "Is the Bobcat story of the girl here the same as yours?"

Traveler turned to Pale Star. "The chief wishes to know if your story of Bobcat is the same as mine."

"No. Tell him it is different."

Traveler relayed the message and turned back to the girl. "He wishes to hear your story."

"But I do not speak his tongue!"

"Use sign-talk."

The listeners were becoming restless as the girl rose to face their host.

"My chief," she began in hand-signs, "I speak none of your tongue, but I will try."

The chief nodded and relaxed to listen.

"In long-ago times, as has been said," she began, "Spotted Cat had a long tail."

The crowd nodded.

"In my country, among my people, there is a legend of the Old Man of the Shadows. He is a trickster, who can help or hurt. You have such a trickster?" she asked the chief.

"Not quite. We have heard of him."

"Yes. Well, Old Man had changed himself into a hollow tree, and Spotted Cat hid inside. But, Old Man played a trick. He made a knothole behind, and Cat's tail hung out."

She made a ring, like a knothole, with the thumb and forefinger of her left hand. Then she waggled her right forefinger through the hole to represent the tail. The crowd was chuckling, but her face remained quite serious.

Ah, this child is good with a story! thought Traveler in surprise. The crowd hung on her every hand-sign.

"A hunter passed by, and saw the fine fur of the tail," she continued. "He chopped it off to decorate his bow case."

She paused for effect—*just the right pause,* Traveler thought—and then continued quite seriously. "You can see that this story is true. Even now, there is still fur on bow cases."

The girl sat down, still somewhat embarrassed, while the listeners rocked with laughter.

How clever, thought Traveler. *A double twist . . . Bobcat's short tail and the bow case.* And she had managed it all with only sign-talk!

"Who is this girl?" Hunts-in-the-Rain whispered. "You did not have her before!"

"No, we bought her, last season."

"She is good with the stories. May we have more?"

"I will see."

He turned to the girl. "Stand up," he motioned. "The chief wishes to talk to you."

Hunts-in-the-Rain smiled and nodded. "Where are your people?" he questioned.

"Far to the west, my chief, in the Sacred Hills."

"How are they called?"

"We call ourselves the People, as most do. Some call us Elk-dog People."

Hunts-in-the-Rain nodded.

Now a new idea struck Traveler. Here was something quite useful that he had only begun to suspect. "Star," he suggested, "would you tell us of your people's beginnings?"

He did not know her Creation story and had no idea what she might tell, but he recognized a natural storyteller. She had already captivated her audience. And in sign-talk!

Star shrugged, still embarrassed by all the attention. "This story too tells of Old Man," she began. "He brought my people from inside the earth. It was soon after Creation . . ."

She went on, describing the cold, the darkness, and the hunger in the depths of the cavernous nether world. Her audience was completely absorbed.

"Then Old Man sat on a hollow cottonwood log and tapped it with a stick. First Man and First Woman crawled through to the outside." She paused and seemed to be waiting for something.

The crowd sat quietly, and finally a young man rose. "Are they still coming through?" he asked.

Ah, Traveler understood now. This was part of the game. The listeners try to catch the storyteller in a contradiction. Why is not the whole world filled with Star's people? This must be a trap, to let the storyteller catch the listener.

He watched as the girl turned an indignant frown on the innocent questioner. "Of course not," she signed. "The third person was a fat woman. She got stuck in the log, and no one has been through since!"

The listeners were delighted. They laughed and hooted at the young man who had been the innocent victim of the joke. He was embarrassed, but it was part of the evening's entertainment. Star thanked him with a smile, which seemed to help his embarrassment considerably.

The stories went on far into the night. Traveler was seeing Star in an entirely different light. She could be very valuable in the trading as well. In one evening, she had completely charmed this village. She was bright, attractive, and intelligent, and could help with the bartering. Yes, he would teach her. She could learn quickly—a sympathetic smile, a friendly glance, a suggestion perhaps of a more lenient trade. Judging from this evening, he felt that she would enjoy it.

He watched her—laughing, excited, eyes dancing, she was enjoying the attention, the laughter at her jokes. Well, enough for now; keep them a little hungry. Besides, he wished to go and see how Plum Leaf was doing. She had chosen to rest rather than attend the stories. Ah, she would be pleased with Pale Star's success.

He stood to speak to the crowd. "Now we must rest, my friends," he called jovially. "We have traveled far. Tomorrow we trade. I have many fine things—knives, arrow points, tobacco. And we will need a canoe!"

The crowd was beginning to break up.

"Ah, my friend"—Hunts-in-the-Rain was chuckling—"that one, how is she called, Pale Star? She is good, Traveler! A good addition to your trading."

"Yes, that is true," Traveler admitted. He was not quite ready to admit that until tonight, he had not fully realized her potential.

"Is she your wife, a second wife?"

Anger rose, and Traveler fought it down. It was a logical and reasonable question, and he was not quite certain why it bothered him so much. It was much like the feeling he had had when the lecherous old man had tried to buy her.

"No, my chief," he managed to say quite calmly, "she is more like a daughter. She is the child that Plum Leaf and I have never had."

The chief nodded. "I see. You bought her for this purpose?"

Traveler realized that his friend was merely making conversation. How could the man understand the change that had come into their lives since this proud girl had joined them? Traveler was not sure himself. Sometimes . . .

"Sometimes, my chief, there does not seem to be a purpose. Things just happen, and the purpose becomes clear later."

Hunts-in-the-Rain nodded. "It is so. But this has certainly happened well for you!"

24

Traveler watched the young man suspiciously as the trading progressed. That one had first caught his attention as the storytelling broke up.

There had been a number of young men casting admiring glances at Pale Star. Well, that much was as it should be. But this was different, a dark predatory gaze. It was like that of a hunting wolf as it creeps upon a sleeping buffalo calf. Or a snake, yes a snake, approaching a nest of hatchling birds. There was something even worse, maybe, a malevolence that reached out to disturb the easygoing quietude of the pleasant evening.

And here was the same man this morning, hanging around, watching the trading. Star was bothered by the man's presence, he knew. His bold stare was making her quite uneasy.

The trading had actually gone quite well. Traveler had explained to Pale Star how she might be of help, and she responded almost eagerly, taking over many of the functions of Plum Leaf, who was still quite weak. They could converse a little in the tongue of Plum Leaf's people, not understood by those who came to bargain. Then, if it seemed good, hand-signs were added.

"Smile at this one. Wait until we bargain a bit, then start to sign," Traveler suggested.

"Sign what, Uncle?"

"Ah! When I nod, you sign something like 'oh, let him have it, Uncle.' Or suggest something else he might want."

The girl understood immediately and gave every indication of becoming quite skillful. She was quite adept at communication, and people related to her with trust. She would be quite useful.

And then came the arrogant staring young man whose presence was becoming so disruptive. Star virtually ceased to function, so threatening was the man's presence. Traveler could not fault her for that because he felt much the same. It was disrupting the trade to have the aggressive intruder hanging over the bartering. He would have sent the man on his way except that it was poor custom to send potential trade away. In truth, Traveler too felt a little fear of the intruder.

The man and his companion seemed to be outsiders, probably visitors from another tribe. In fact, yes—the pattern of their moccasins, the cut of their garments, marked the two as men from the northeast. Unless Traveler was mistaken, they were of a tribe that was an enemy of his own, at least when he was last home . . . ah, how many years?

Maybe it would be best simply to send the men away. They were not only making Star quite uneasy but driving away trade. It appeared that the two were unpopular visitors. An interesting situation. If one is not welcome, why would he stay? He studied the men, trying not to be too obvious. One was large and heavyset, with a broad face and massive jaws. He appeared glum and irritable, probably not too intelligent.

The other man, whose arrogant stare was so unnerving, appeared to be the leader, the bearlike one the follower. The slender one moved with a sinuous gliding motion, like a hunting cat, alert to fly in any direction if the occasion arose. This man, though the smaller of the two, was certainly the more dangerous.

The crowd had thinned out now, and no one was waiting to trade, largely, Traveler thought irritably, because of the interference of the intruders, who were still loitering nearby, ogling Pale Star and making remarks to each other in their own tongue. Then the smaller, the evil-looking one, approached the trader.

Hunts-in-the-Rain, who happened to be nearby, watched closely. *He feels it too,* thought Traveler. *Something is wrong!*

"I am Three Owls," the newcomer began, using hand-signs.

"What is your nation?" Traveler inquired. "You are not of these people."

"No. I am a visitor here." He paused, shifting his weight from one foot to the other. "I would trade," he continued, ignoring the inquiry about his tribe. "You want a canoe. I have one."

Traveler was still suspicious. "What is your tribe?"

"It does not matter. Do you wish to trade?"

Traveler thought for only a moment. That was his purpose, after all. He swept a hand over the goods spread on a robe before him. "What do you want for your canoe?"

Three Owls smiled thinly, a smile that was humorless, oily, more like a leer. "A small thing . . . the girl, there."

Traveler managed to control his anger. He even managed a smile. "No, she is not for sale."

"Everything has a price . . . she is not your wife?"

"She is my daughter."

The exchange was getting out of hand. Traveler was tense and angry, as a trader must never be.

"No," insisted Three Owls. "She is of another nation. I know that. You bought her, so there is no reason you could not sell her."

"But I will not!"

His anger was rising, and Three Owls pushed on. "I only want to help you. We have a canoe and offer a good trade. This girl can tell us stories and warm our beds."

Traveler sprang to his feet, reaching for his knife.

Three Owls dropped to a fighting crouch, knife ready, and smiled at the approach of the older man. People scattered.

"Stop!" came the ringing voice of Hunts-in-the-Rain. He stepped between the two and continued in sign-talk, slowly and deliberately. "You should both be ashamed. You dishonor me by fighting when you are guests in my village!"

The combatants relaxed the fighting stance a little.

"Put away your weapons!"

They did so, still cautiously.

"Traveler, your tribes are enemies, back in your north country?"

Traveler nodded, still not taking his eye off Three Owls.

"I am sorry, Traveler," the chief continued, now using his own tongue. "I suspected, last night. They have been here nearly a moon. Troublemakers. I knew they were from your country, but . . ."

"It is nothing," Traveler signed. "I will not dishonor your hospitality, my chief. But I will trade nothing to him."

"Of course."

Hunts-in-the-Rain then turned to Three Owls. "It is best," he signed, "if you and your friend leave. You have insulted the family of my guest."

For a moment, Traveler was not certain that Three Owls would go. After a long pause, the man sneered contemptuously at the chief, made an obscene gesture at Traveler, and stalked away. He turned for a moment to cast a covetous leer at Pale Star.

Traveler had an uncomfortable feeling that they had not seen the last of this man. He turned to the chief. "Who are they? He is very strange."

"Ah, my friend, they are nothing but trouble. Three Owls, the small one is called. The other, Winter Bear. They are relatives, it is said. I am glad to be rid of them. But you must be careful!"

Traveler nodded. "May we stay a few days, to let Star learn to use the canoe? That will put them farther ahead of us."

"A good plan! Of course, be welcome."

They watched as the angry Three Owls threw his possessions into a canoe moored at the river's edge. He and Winter Bear (*What an appropriate name*, thought Traveler. *Big, grumpy, and dangerous*) climbed into their canoe and pushed off, moving rapidly upstream. Traveler devoutly hoped that they had seen the last of these two.

"What was the nature of their troublemaking?" he asked thoughtfully.

"The one, Three Owls, is a bully," Hunts-in-the-Rain explained. "The other mostly follows along, maybe. They try to start fights. No one here has had courage to fight them. It is said that they nearly killed a man downriver before they came here. They tried to take his wife. . . ."

Traveler shook his head, and then changed the conversation. "Now, my friend," he said more jovially, "about the canoe. Do you know of someone? . . ."

"Maybe so. Let me ask, while you continue trading. I assume you did not wish to trade the girl there?"

Traveler smiled ruefully. How different, a joke by a friend. "I think not today."

Hunts-in-the-Rain walked off, chuckling.

"I have found your canoe!" the chief announced. He was smiling broadly. "Small Fox has one. I know this canoe . . . a good one!"

It was late in the day, and the trading had tapered off. Plum Leaf, feeling a little better after her rest, was sitting outside now and had been taking an interest in the bartering. "Go ahead," she said. "Star and I will handle this. For anything big, we will ask them to wait for you."

Traveler hesitated only a moment. "It is good," he decided. "I will not be long."

The two men walked to the edge of the village, and Hunts-in-the-Rain pointed to a canoe that rested upside down on a rack of poles. "There!" he said proudly. "One of the best!"

"Ah, you sound as if *you* own it!" accused Traveler.

Both men laughed.

"No, no, Traveler, but I do know the craft."

"Why does Fox want to sell it?"

"Oh, he married a widow who owned one. They have no use for two."

Traveler nodded, thinking to himself that this would make trading more favorable for him. He looked at the canoe. It was nearly four paces long, slightly upturned at the ends. Good craftsmanship. Its lacing was tight, and the seam well pitched. A trifle wide, yet that might be an advantage. It would be slower, but there was no need for a fast craft. The wide flat bottom would make it more stable, a good quality for a trader's craft, especially for a trader with an inexperienced paddler. Plum Leaf was an expert with the canoe, but he wanted Star to assume much of the responsibility until his wife was better.

And now he must teach the girl in a very short time. No matter, she was quick to learn, strong and well coordinated. But she had never been in a canoe. The width— yes, this one would be much harder to upset than most. And the narrower type, though better in white water, would not be practical for the amount of baggage they must carry.

He thumped the canoe near the prow, noting that the ring was true. The craft was solid, the birchbark sound and in good condition. "A bit shoddy," he mumbled as if to himself. "How many seasons old?"

Hunts-in-the-Rain laughed. "You are not trading with me, Traveler," he said. "Save it for Fox."

"Yes, of course! Where do I find this fortunate man who has a new wife and two canoes?" Traveler chuckled.

The chief turned, looking toward the village. "Ah, here he comes now!"

25

» » »

The flimsy-looking birchbark shell trembled on the surface, wobbling dangerously. Star, in near panic, tensed every muscle and tried to balance her weight.

"The middle! Stay in the middle!" cried Traveler.

There were times when he doubted that the girl would be able to learn the use of the canoe at all. It seemed foreign to her culture.

"Keep your weight low!"

The girl crouched, gripping the sides of the craft. Gradually, the trembling subsided.

"You have really never seen a canoe before?" he asked, knowing the answer. "Your people do not use them?"

"Of course not!" she snapped. "What use would we have for such a thing?"

It was true, he realized. Star's people traveled with horses. A stream was only an obstacle to be crossed, and for that, a canoe was not needed. The girl simply could not conceive of the stream itself as a trail, a means of travel. Well, she would learn. She was quick, mentally and physically.

The quivering of the canoe, which seemed to give it a life of its own, was quieting now. Strange, he thought, how a canoe knows when a beginner steps into it. A canoe does have a spirit of its own, he reflected. The spirit of this one was good, though a trifle mischievous. He had never seen such a delicate trembling as when the girl first stepped in. It was as if the craft recognized a stranger, one from another culture who knew nothing of canoes.

He had tried the canoe himself before consumating the trade, and found it to be well balanced, stable, and quick to respond. There would be much difference, however, with a loaded canoe. The weight of the baggage would place the balance farther forward, another paddler in the prow. But this canoe would be good for their purpose.

After the custom of his people, he had painted eyes on the prow.

"Why is this, Uncle?" the girl had asked.

"So it can see its way . . . avoid danger to us."

Star had shrugged noncommittally. There were many things of each other's customs that she would never fully understand, but she dealt with it well, he thought. She had the ability to accept, even without understanding. This quality was invaluable to one who would trade in different areas among those whose customs are different.

"Now move to the front and sit down . . . in the *middle*," he told the girl.

Star looked forward and sighed. "That looks so far," she protested. "Could I not sit in the back until I learn?"

"No, no, little one," he laughed. "The experienced paddler sits in the back. It is he who guides the canoe. Now go ahead."

She took a step, still holding tightly to the sides. The canoe rocked alarmingly but then steadied.

"Good!" he encouraged. "Now another step."

Cautiously, the girl moved forward, a step at a time. By the time she had taken the few cautious steps, she was gaining confidence. Each quivering of the craft was shorter than the previous one. Traveler was pleased, though not surprised. The girl adjusted quickly to all things. Very soon, her spirit would be one with that of the unfamiliar craft.

He pushed off from the shore, stepping over the end into the canoe. They slid smoothly over the surface, still moving from the force of his push. Yes, this would be a good canoe, he thought. He lifted his paddle and took a stroke or two. The craft was quick and responsive. Good.

"Now," he called, "take your paddle and try it. You must sit up straight. Use your arms, not your back."

At the first try, the canoe tipped sharply. Before he could speak, however, the girl had made the necessary adjustment, and the craft became steady again. They maneuvered back and forth, upstream, down, and across the current. He taught her how she could assist in the steering by bracing her paddle motionlessly against the canoe.

"Uncle, I have seen one man handling a canoe alone," Star said. "How is this done? How can he steer without changing sides?"

"Ah, that will come later, little one, when you have more skill," he assured her. Yes, she was learning quickly.

Even so, it was several days before they had practiced enough to challenge the river. They had placed objects in the canoe; stones at first, to give a low center of weight. Later, their packs were substituted, and it remained only to add the slight weight of Plum Leaf. She would ride in the middle, with Pale Star in the front and him behind.

He was startled when he assisted Plum Leaf into the canoe on the morning of their departure. Her body seemed so frail. He practically lifted her into the canoe where she sank back against the packs, breathing heavily from even that slight exertion. Star arranged the packs around her, attempting to make her comfortable. The girl had learned much about the canoe in the past few days!

Plum Leaf seemed to enjoy the smooth travel on the river. She slept often and woke to spend much time watching the trees slide quietly past.

They stopped well before dark, and she managed to stroll along the sandy bar for a little while. It was not long before she tired, however. Pale Star had prepared the sleeping robes and now helped Plum Leaf to lie down.

Traveler was shocked by her weakness. *Well, she will be stronger tomorrow,* he told himself.

But she was not. Day by day, he could see her failing. It was a situation totally unacceptable to him, and he refused to think of it. Instead, he focused on another worry. They had progressed far enough north now that it would be time for Pale Star to take back her vow. The girl had given no indication that she knew, but he was certain that she did. They were past the nearest route to her home country, but she had said nothing. Surely, soon she would do as he feared and announce that the bargain was at an end.

Star had become skilled at helping Plum Leaf and looking after her needs. Besides, the girl was becoming an excellent help with the canoe and the stories and trading. With the present condition of Plum Leaf, Traveler did not know how he could manage without Star. If Star made her break, he did not see a way . . .

Traveler found occasion to talk with her about it. "Little one, I would speak with you." His voice was tight with emotion.

"Yes?"

"Long ago," he began, trying not to let his voice quaver, "you gave me a promise that you would not try to escape."

She nodded, and waited a moment for him to continue. "Yes, Uncle?" she prompted.

"But . . . you have never—taken back that promise," he said haltingly. "Why?"

"Well, I—"

"Do you wish to do so now?" He pushed on, afraid of the answer. "I said nothing when we were passing the place where your trail pointed west. I wondered if you knew."

"Yes," she said softly, "I knew. But Plum Leaf was sick and needed me."

"But she is better now," he insisted. "If you wished, you could take back your pledge and escape."

Now he really feared her answer. Star took a deep breath, and began, speaking very slowly. "Uncle . . . someday I will return to my people. When I am ready, I will tell you."

The answer pleased him, and he knew he could trust her once more. He chuckled. "Fair warning?"

"Of course, Uncle."

"It is good."

She went on, as if she needed to explain. "I have not yet learned enough about the use of the canoe. You must teach me more."

It was a deception, he suspected, to conceal her real reason for staying. He appreciated it and chuckled. "I will teach you, little one. You will tell me when you have learned enough?"

Star laughed, the strong laugh that he and Plum Leaf had come to love. "You will know! But yes, Uncle, I will tell you before I leave."

In the dim twilight, Traveler felt a tear of relief creep out of the corner of his eye and trickle down his cheek. He brushed it aside, hoping that the girl had not seen. She had told him what he desperately needed to know, even without saying so in words. She would not leave as long as Plum Leaf needed her.

He started to speak but found his throat dry and husky. He swallowed hard and spoke again, firmly. At least, he tried to sound firm, but his tight voice seemed only gruff as he spoke. "We must sleep. Tomorrow will be hard work."

He was glad for the deepening darkness, which concealed the emotion that he was sure would show on his face otherwise.

The next day, Plum Leaf seemed to enjoy the journey somewhat more. They glided smoothly, making good time. She watched the scenery and the occasional creatures along the river.

Once they rounded a curve of the river to see a doe

drinking daintily at the water's edge. Star, in the prow, saw it first as the animal lifted her head to stare, her large ears spread wide. The girl pointed silently with her paddle. Traveler too stopped paddling and watched. The canoe drifted forward under its own momentum. The doe stared, completely motionless. The paddlers also were frozen in the beauty of the moment.

Then there was a movement behind the animal, and a tiny fawn tottered out into the open, then another.

"Twins!" said Plum Leaf softly. "It is good. In a year when the deer suckle two, there is food in plenty."

Traveler had thought that she was asleep, but he was glad that she had been awake to relish the scene. With her gentle and sensitive nature, she had always enjoyed such things.

"Yes," he agreed. "Maybe this is a good sign."

Plum Leaf did not answer, but her silence spoke powerfully. Traveler wished that he had not spoken of good signs. He was afraid that Plum Leaf was concealing the severity of her illness and was suffering more than she would admit. It was not good.

He saw very little that day that was good. Here they were, many sleeps from any of their own people, alone and friendless. Their closest contact, other than slight acquaintances, was the village of White Squirrel, and that was still many days' travel upriver. Plum Leaf was sick and helpless. For perhaps the first time since he was a child, he felt alone and helpless. He longed for simpler times when small hurts could be comforted by his mother, softly crooning as she rocked him in her arms.

Tears came, and he quickly brushed them away again, hoping that Pale Star did not see. Pale Star. What a strange thing, how important she had become. A short few moons ago, she had been a defiant prisoner, tied to prevent escape, and possibly dangerous. He had not doubted her ability to cut someone's throat in his sleep if necessary to make her escape.

Now, of course, she was no danger to him or Plum

Leaf. She had become a daughter, and not merely a daughter, but a special daughter on whom they could rely. Pale Star was perhaps the only solid and trustworthy factor in the world that seemed to be crumbling beneath him. In this strange world of contradictions, his greatest help was this girl who had openly vowed to escape and was now held only by a temporary promise. It was a promise, however, that he knew was as reliable as the rising of Sun Boy's torch tomorrow.

26

It was perhaps ten sleeps later that it happened. In truth, Traveler had nearly forgotten their clash with the two strangers at the village of Hunts-in-the-Rain. His mind had been preoccupied with the ailing Plum Leaf, who seemed no better, perhaps a little weaker.

They had stopped early because the day was hot and the work of paddling was hard. A wide stretch of sandy beach lay before them, inviting a weary traveler to stop and rest. Star, in the prow, pointed with her paddle, and Traveler, with little more than a grunt of agreement, turned the canoe ashore. They were within a stone's throw when Star suddenly gave a shout of warning and backpaddled frantically. The canoe swung from its course and pivoted sharply, but the momentum carried it forward. He barely caught a glimpse of the dead snag in the water as the canoe slid gently alongside with a slight scraping noise. Then it was behind them. He turned the canoe back toward deeper water. Where there was one such limb lurking beneath the surface there might be another. It was one of the dangers of river travel. Some great oak, a fallen giant, might lie beneath the river's surface for a generation or more before the shifting sands of floodtime freed it to continue downstream. This had been a very dangerous obstacle. It pointed its broken tip nearly downstream, like a giant spear just below the surface, ready to pierce the belly of any canoe that chanced on it. Star had done well.

"Good, little one," he called to her.

It had been a skillful maneuver, one worthy of an experienced paddler, and she had saved them from destruction.

"Another place, ahead there," he called. "Does it look safe?"

"Maybe so, Uncle. Let us go slow."

They beached the canoe, perhaps two bow shots below their original choice. Star leaped out and pulled the prow on shore, then stepped back to help with the packs. Traveler assisted Plum Leaf to a comfortable resting place and tossed a few sticks toward the place where their fire would be.

"I go to bathe," Star announced. "I will bring more wood." She slipped into the trees and made her way back downstream.

"Be careful!" he called.

She was probably going back to that smooth sandy beach where they had nearly impaled the canoe. He smiled in appreciation of her quick thinking and skill, then turned to start the fire—a handful of dry bark from a dead cottonwood, a tiny cone of small twigs, then some sticks as thick as his finger.

He was taking out his fire-sticks, wondering whether he should learn to use the metal fire-striker . . . Maybe while at his own home village he could trade for one. The French supplied many of them for trade, he had heard. It was an object to be used with a stone of flint. Would the fire be the same, he wondered, as a fire made with the sticks? Probably, he thought. Fire is fire, is it not?

His pondering was interrupted by Pale Star's scream from downriver. "Traveler!" she yelled, her cry sharp and urgent, "load the canoe! Hurry! We must leave!"

Without a moment's hesitation, he began to throw things into the canoe. It would be foolish to do otherwise, and he must trust the girl.

"Traveler!" she screamed again. "Can you hear me?"

"Yes, yes," he called without pausing in his hurried tasks. "Come on!"

"Load the canoe! There is trouble!" came her answer.

He lifted Plum Leaf and placed her tenderly in the canoe, then turned to see Star, panting from exertion, slipping into her buckskin dress.

"Get the packs," he called.

Only two remained, and she grabbed them as she ran past. She dropped the packs into the canoe and scrambled to her position. Traveler pushed off and leaped into the stern.

Neither spoke until they were well into the current. Finally he rested his paddle. "Little sister," he asked in bewilderment, "will you tell me what is happening?"

She poured forth her story. "Those men . . . Three Owls, the one you quarreled with . . . they tried to catch me!"

That could certainly be, he thought. "Where are they?"

"I am trying to tell you! Their canoe . . . they came toward me where I was swimming . . . you know that tree? I got it between them and me—" she paused for breath, "and it speared their canoe!"

"It *did*? The log speared their canoe?" He laughed aloud.

"Yes, Uncle. But I am afraid they will repair it and come after us."

Traveler sobered. "Yes, they will. But it will take several days, and we will be traveling those days."

"What does it mean, Uncle? They left first. They should have been ahead of us."

"Yes, little one. It is not good. These men mean us harm. They have waited for us to pass and then followed us. But it is good that now we know."

"But what will we do?"

"Nothing, except watch and be prepared to protect ourselves. We will travel well, of course." He wished that he had as much confidence as he had tried to suggest. He knew that this was indeed a desperate situation.

"You know these men, Uncle?" the girl asked.

"No, but I know their tribe. They are enemies of my people."

"But that is far away!"

"Yes," he agreed, "it should not be so. Even enemies should be friends in strange country."

"I do not understand."

"Nor do I." He had thoughts that he could not share with her. *But I do understand. They hate me, but not because I am the enemy. It is because they want you, little one.* "They are very dangerous," he said. "We must take great care."

They paddled awhile, and it was Pale Star who finally broke the silence. "What will we do now, Uncle? It will soon be dark."

"Yes. I think we cannot stop now. At least, not on this side of the river."

"There will soon be a moon," Plum Leaf said. "We could travel."

Her voice sounded weak and old, and Traveler's heart was heavy. "But you are tired!"

"Yes, but afraid too," she answered. "We must move. I will be all right." She lay back and curled up in the center of the canoe like a little child.

There was little choice. The tired paddlers resumed their task while the sky darkened and stars began to appear. Nightbirds called in the darkening timber along the shore, and a coyote on a distant hill gave his eerie chuckle, answered by his mate.

It was nearly dark when the moon rose, red and full, over the trees along the far shore. They were traveling nearly northwest, and in some stretches of the stream, a long stripe of golden light would be reflected for a few moments. He heard Pale Star in the prow exclaim softly at the beauty of the scene. He wished to share it with Plum Leaf, but she seemed to be sleeping soundly.

The moonlight was a great help in their travel, and they moved on. The excitement of their escape had overcome the tiredness of their bodies. But now the quiet of the night gradually calmed their anxieties, and the dead weight of exhaustion began to affect tired muscles again. They had placed a considerable distance between them and their pursuers. Maybe when an opportunity presented, they could stop.

He looked down at Plum Leaf. A bright shaft of moonlight fell across her face. Her eyes were closed, and she was smiling. It was a calm, comfortable smile, free from worry and pain, an expression he had not seen for many days now. Tears came to his eyes, but they were tears for himself, for he was happy for her.

He continued to paddle, but now he was tired, his muscles protesting each stroke. He saw a sandbar ahead with a fringe of willows.

"We will stop there," he told Star, pointing.

The girl nodded without speaking, and the canoe turned toward the bar. Star jumped out as the prow grounded, pulled the prow farther ashore, and turned to carry some small items ashore. Traveler gathered the frail form in his arms and was just stepping to the sand when the girl returned.

"Is she all right, Uncle?" Star asked with concern.

"Yes," he murmured. His voice sounded hollow and wooden, even to himself. "She has crossed over," he explained. "She is dead."

He stood there, numbly, holding her in his arms, not knowing quite what to do. He was dimly aware that the canoe was swinging behind him in the current and that Star stepped past him to retrieve it and drag it ashore. Then she approached him again.

"I am sorry, Uncle. You knew?" Her voice was husky.

He nodded. "Yes," he said. "I have known all along."

"I too," Star almost whispered. "Here, Uncle, let me help you. Bring her here." She led the way to a level spot and spread a robe. "There. Now, put her there. We will care for her."

They built a little fire, and together they wrapped the frail remains in the robe, tying it securely.

"In the morning," said Star, "we will take her up that hill."

Traveler hardly noticed that the girl was making the decisions. He did not care. His mind was numb, his world undergoing changes that he could not fully accept.

"Would it be all right if I sing my people's Mourning Song?" Star asked.

Tears filled his eyes. "She would like that."

The clear keening wail of the Song of Mourning floated across the river, and sadness echoed from the brushy hillside behind them. Traveler knew that it was good, that Plum Leaf would understand the affection of this young woman from far away, mourning her loss.

When morning came, they carried Plum Leaf to a rocky glen on the hillside and scooped out a pocket beneath the ledge. Gently, they tucked the slight form away. They carried stones to cover the grave and then sat down for a few moments, looking at the peaceful scene.

"This looks much like the woodlands of her home, Uncle."

"Yes, I saw that too," he said.

27

They loaded the canoe and pushed off. Traveler looked downstream for any signs of pursuit while Star waited. He pointed upstream and dipped his paddle. The girl looked at him for a moment and seemed to shrug, but he did not notice. They moved out into the stream. He paddled slowly, reluctant to leave somehow. He felt incomplete, as if he had left a part of him behind in the rocky glen on the hill. It had been a long time, many winters, since he and Plum Leaf had started life together. Now he was alone.

He had not stopped to think about what he would do now or why they continued upstream. They had been going in that direction, so they continued. But he was thinking of her and the manner of her crossing over. "It is good," he said to himself.

"What?" asked Pale Star.

He must have spoken aloud without realizing it. He was embarrassed but went on to explain. "It is good, that she crossed over on the river. She loved to travel on the river. Did I tell you how good Plum Leaf was with the paddle?"

"No, Uncle. I never saw her use the canoe, you know."

"That is true."

He had forgotten that. He was so used to thinking of Plum Leaf as she had always been. And Pale Star had become so adept with the canoe, he had not had to think of it. Now it was coming back, the first time Plum Leaf had tried the canoe. She had been off balance, and the canoe had upset, throwing them both into the river. They had laughed together, laboriously emptied the swamped canoe, and tried again. They were young then, and everything they did was wonderful as long as they were together. Plum Leaf had tried hard and learned rapidly. She had become one of the best, so skilled with the handling of a canoe that it seemed she must have done it all her life. Now her supple limbs were stilled in death.

Star was speaking.

"What?" he said, returning to the present. "What did you say?"

"I said, what will we do now?"

"Oh."

"Traveler, we must plan. Where are we going? You have not told me. . . ."

He was tired and did not want to think, but he could see that the girl was irritated at his indecision. "You wish to return to your people now?"

"Of course!" she snapped, but then her face softened. "I am sorry, Uncle," she said sympathetically, "but we must plan. We cannot just keep traveling on the river. I do not know where we are going, or why. Please tell me your plans."

She was right, of course. He really had no plans, and she was forcing him to face reality. That was probably good. He was still floundering aimlessly, not knowing or really caring what his next move would be. Maybe talking with the girl about it . . .

"Of course, little one." He tried to sound more confident than he was. He had agreed to tell her his plans, but he had none. "Look," he continued, "let us stop on the sandbar ahead. We will talk."

The canoe slid gently to rest, and they disembarked, dragging it to a safer spot. Both turned to gather small sticks for a fire. No council of any importance could be held without the ritual fire, and both recognized this as an important discussion. They started the tinder, and as the flames began to embrace the larger sticks, both sat down on the sand, facing each other across the fire.

"Now," Traveler began, "what must we do?"

Astonishment showed in the face of the girl. He realized numbly that she had never seen him in such a role—tired, old, indecisive. She paused a little and seemed to gather her words carefully. "Uncle, you have been good to me, but you know that I would wish to return to my people."

He nodded, only half listening.

"Would you come with me, to the country of my people?" she went on quickly. "You have never been there. You could trade. My father would be proud to thank the man who has helped me."

Traveler had not even considered such an idea. Of course she would want to go home, but—a glimmer of interest penetrated his numb thinking. Maybe this . . . new country, trade, away from the familiar trails that he and Plum Leaf had traveled. "I am made to think that this is good," he said, still half lost in thought. "But there are many problems. It is far, and the season is passing."

"But we would go faster, traveling downstream, with the current."

"That is true. But we would have to slip past our enemies and then wonder if they followed us. Their canoe may be repaired soon."

He realized that it was still foreign to her thinking to consider the river as a trail. One could not easily take a shortcut or go around a danger. The trail led only upstream or down. But a plan was developing in his mind. Yes, it would work! "Look, little sister," he went on, "here is a plan: Let us go to my people. We can winter there and then, in the spring, travel to your country."

Star thought for a moment. "How far to your tribe?" she asked a little suspiciously.

"Nearly a moon, but closer than yours. We can get

supplies, goods to trade . . . pipestone, arrowpoints, to-bacco, and have better trading with your people next sea-son."

He did not even notice that he had been using the term "we" in talking of next season's trade. If Star noticed, she said nothing about it.

"It is good!" she agreed.

"Good. Then we go."

"Tell me first, Uncle, about our journey. You said we go overland?"

"Yes. Then we come to the lakes, the Big Waters where my people live."

"You mean, *this* is not the Big Water?"

There followed a discussion confused by language dif-ferences and Pale Star's unfamiliarity with any body of water too big to see across. Ah well, she would under-stand when she saw the Big Water.

"But I promise you now, little one, I will take you home to your people," he concluded.

"It is good!" she cried as they rose. "How long now until we leave the river to go overland?"

"Not far . . . three, four sleeps."

They scattered the fire, tossing the larger sticks into the water. Both felt much better as they launched the canoe and moved on.

As they made camp that evening on an especially beau-tiful stretch of the river, Star stood for a moment in ap-preciation of the bright evening sky.

Traveler too watched the changing hues of red, yellow, pink, and purple, shifting, ever changing. How many sun-sets he and Plum Leaf had enjoyed together! He had al-most turned, just now, to call her attention to it before realizing that she was not here. He must remember to tell her—no, he could not do that, either.

"She would have loved it," he said to himself, not real-izing that he had spoken aloud.

Star turned to face him. "Uncle," she said gently, "I am made to think that she still does."

* * *

They moved on upriver, and Traveler began to recover. It was not easy, and some days were worse than others, but at least he now had plans, goals, something to look forward to. Star had proved herself a capable canoeist, storyteller, and trader. Yes, they would make a good team. He looked forward to their arrival at the village of White Squirrel. There they would leave the canoe and travel eastward, overland. Squirrel was one of his best friends, and trading was always good there. Star could try her stories on a new audience, and he could bask in the pride of such a daughter.

He began to plan, to look ahead. Only a few more sleeps, and they would be at White Squirrel's. There they would trade, but first the stories. Yes, he would ask Star to tell her Creation story, with its joke, and her people's version of Bobcat's tail and the bow case. He thought of the stories he would tell, the gestures he would use for effect. This could be the best trading day ever, after the evening of stories he was planning. They would be a fine team, he and Star. He must tell Plum Leaf, but no! His pleasant thoughts dissolved again, like fog blown from the surface of the river when the wind quickens. She was gone, and he could tell her nothing.

Tears came again, as they had frequently the past days. There had been no chance for the customary three days of mourning. He and Star had pushed on to stay ahead of their pursuers. Plum Leaf would understand, he knew, but he was not sure he did. Would it hurt less, he wondered, if there had been time to spend in mourning? Would that have prevented these times of sorrow that kept striking him now? And how long would it go on?

"What is it, Uncle?" Star asked him.

"What?"

"I said, what is it? You stopped paddling."

"Oh . . . it is nothing. . . ."

He lifted the paddle and dipped it into the water. The

canoe moved forward again, its course straightening. Star resumed her own stroke.

Well, someday, he thought, *someday, when the mourning is finished, it will not hurt so much, maybe. If that time ever comes.*

Until then, maybe he could spend some time in private mourning and still manage to do the necessary things, like guiding the canoe. He smiled to himself. Plum Leaf would have laughed at him, the way he was behaving.

Now what had he been thinking of before? It had made him excited and pleased, and—oh, yes, the stories, the trading. He would think about that. And then, when he was alone, he would think of her and mourn, a little at a time, until his mourning was finished.

If that time ever came.

28

» » »

White Squirrel welcomed them to his village. "Come, you will stay with us!"

He looked behind them, toward the canoe moored below, its eyespots looking up the slope. "Where is Plum Leaf?"

Traveler swallowed hard. "She is dead," he said simply.

"Dead? That was a strong one, a great woman, my friend. I am sorry to hear this."

Behind him, his wives began to wail a song of mourning. Plum Leaf had been well liked here.

"Yes, it was hard to let her go," Traveler agreed. He tried hard not to show the tears that still came easily.

"Is this your new wife? asked White Squirrel, indicating Pale Star.

Traveler felt the flash of indignant anger but tried to throttle it. "No!" he snapped irritably. "This is my daughter."

"Oh," said Squirrel, pretending to understand.

Traveler was not quite certain why this reaction came so quickly. The very thought that Star could be anything but a daughter to him was offensive. He was twice her age.

There was an uncomfortable moment. Pale Star stood watching, not understanding this moment of friction between old friends. She did not know the language of this village, and no one was using hand-signs, so she had no idea what was causing the conflict. She knew it must concern her because their host and his two wives were all looking at her. However, their looks were of friendly curiosity, nothing else.

White Squirrel was caught completely off guard. He had asked a legitimate friendly question of his old friend and received a hostile answer. This was hard to grasp. In the many years he had known Traveler and Plum Leaf, he had been certain that they had no children. Yet here, after the news of the death of Plum Leaf, Traveler had introduced this remarkably beautiful young woman as his daughter. Squirrel had been ready to congratulate him for his good taste and good fortune in wives, but—well, it was no concern of theirs, whatever arrangement the two might have. Traveler had always been a strange one.

White Squirrel beckoned them inside and assisted with their packs. "My lodge is yours," he said. "You have much for trade?"

"Of course. Many things. And we have no use now for the canoe. I will trade it or leave it here until next season if you will allow."

"As you wish." White Squirrel nodded.

"We will see how the trading goes," Traveler suggested. "Maybe we will keep it . . . store it here."

There was a gasp from Star, and Traveler turned. A young woman was strolling past, wearing a bright-colored blanket of the sort used in trade by the Yen-glees. These had only begun to come in during his last trip to the area. He had considered their value for trade, but they were bulky to carry.

But Star, he realized now, would never have seen a wool blanket. He was amused at her reaction to the flaming colors, bright reds and yellows. The woman paused to speak to one of Squirrel's wives, and Star studied the fabric. "How is this?" she asked. "The paint is on the *fur* side of the robe? Not on the skin side?"

Traveler laughed and interpreted for the others. Pale Star was embarrassed at their amusement, and Traveler hastened to explain. "There is no skin side, little one. They use only the fur."

He asked the woman with the blanket to show the girl. She was pleased to do so, turning a corner over and back to demonstrate how it was made.

"*Aiee!*" exclaimed Star. "Fur on *both* sides? What sort of animal grows fur on both sides of its skin?"

He saw that the girl partially understood and was now amused at her own error. She would probably make a story of this.

"Star," he explained, "you remember some tribes who weave plant fibers into mats or cloaks? This is much the same, with the fur of animals."

"But, the colors . . ."

"Yes . . . I have been told that the animal whose fur is used is white. They color the fur before they weave it."

Star felt the soft wool of the blanket between her thumb and forefinger, relishing its luxury. "Why do you not have one, Uncle?"

"I had one, but I traded it. They are much prized."

"There are many blankets now," White Squirrel said to Traveler. "The Yen-glees like them for trade."

Traveler turned to Star. "He says there are more now. Someday we will get one for you."

"Really? What sort of people are these Yen-glees, Uncle?"

"They come from far away, across the Big Water . . . no, how can I . . ." There was the problem again— words not in the girl's culture. ". . . the Big Salty Water," he finished. "They have many things of strong medicine."

"They are hair-faced?"

Traveler remembered that Star had once mentioned a legend among her people, a story of a hair-faced outsider. The stranger had joined her people and become a prominent man. A sub-chief of some sort, it seemed. Was it not . . . yes, Star herself claimed to be a descendant of the man. This would account for her question, though he could see no connection. Star's people were much too far west.

"Some of them are," he answered. "Mostly, they cut their face hair with knives instead of plucking it."

"Medicine-knives?"

"What?"

"Medicine-knives, like the one you traded for me?"

He was constantly amazed at Pale Star's powers of observation. So long ago, when she was a prisoner, and she still remembered that trade.

"What? No, no! That was a knife for eating or skinning, even fighting. They use a special knife for face hair. It is used for nothing else."

She thought a moment. "Is the knife for cutting face hair made of the same shiny rock?"

"Iron? Yes, they make many things of iron."

"Where does it come from?"

"They dig it from the ground, I am told. How do I know, little one? You ask too many questions."

White Squirrel interrupted. "My friend, how long will you stay with us?"

Traveler shrugged. "Three, four sleeps. Until the trading is finished."

"You go to your people?"

"Yes."

"It is good! I will take a party that way soon. You can travel with us for safety."

It was not until later that the significance of that remark sank home. The stories were over for the night, and he and Star had spread their robes for sleep. They were outside, at their own fire. When the weather was good, most people slept outside.

He thought that Star was asleep. She had been magnificent in the storytelling, and had completely charmed her audience. It was good to have such a companion to help with the stories and the trading. But she must be tired now. It had been a long hard day. He was surprised, then, when she spoke.

"Uncle, what is the danger?"

"What danger?"

"White Squirrel has said we would travel with them for safety. If we must seek safety, there must be danger. From what? The Yen-glees?"

He lay quiet. How could he tell her of the strange situation, where men skin the heads of other men for a few items of trade?

"Uncle?" she asked. "Are you asleep?"

"No, no, I was thinking, little one. It is a very confusing story. We do not want to start it tonight. Now sleep! There is much trading tomorrow."

"Will many know the hand-signs?"

"Some. Not all. The stories went well. It will be the same."

She had used hand-signs, and Traveler had interpreted. But they were nearing the region where hand-signs were less frequently used. It was fortunate that Star learned languages well. But no matter, he thought. He would be with her, and in the spring they would move back west where hand-signs were commonly used.

It gave him a good feeling too, somehow, to think that Star would be going home and that he would be of assistance in her homecoming. He thought back to the first time he had seen her—a captive child, miserable but proud. It was a good thing he had done, to buy her. At the time, he had not done so as a generous act. He could not have said why he had done it.

But the presence of the girl had been a big change in their lives, his and Plum Leaf's. Star had grown to a woman, a very beautiful woman, though he still thought of her as a child. He did not know what the future held for her, did not want to think beyond a season or two when she would be helping with the trading. She was a help in many ways. He thought of the last days of Plum Leaf and realized that without Star's help—he did not know how he could have survived. The tears that came so easily welled up in his eyes again. But he thought that it was becoming easier.

He shifted his thinking back to next season's trading on the prairie. He enjoyed the open skies and far horizons of the region, the country of his stepfather's people. Star's country must be much like that. He wondered if they hunted buffalo in the same way, with lance or bow. His memory drifted back to his first buffalo hunt with Gray Otter. The thrill returned—the excitement of the chase, the thunder of hooves in pursuit through tallgrass prairie, the rush of the wind past his ears, and the smells of autumn. It would be good to be there again, to renew the sights and sounds of his youth.

And he looked forward to meeting Star's people, the holy man, Looks Far, of whom she spoke so highly. He was a relative of some sort, a wise man from whom one could learn much perhaps. Running Eagle, grandmother of Star, who had been a warrior, Star said, and was still an important person in their nation. It would be good to meet them.

Sleep was long in coming, but eventually Traveler dozed off. He slept well, better than for many nights recently. His sleep was untroubled now because his concern for Plum Leaf was behind him, and he was among friends.

He did dream, but the dreams were pleasant. He was young again, riding a fine buffalo-horse across open prairie with the wind in his ears while his beautiful young wife, Plum Leaf, watched with pride from the hilltop.

29

» » »

The trading was excellent; the renewal of acquaintances and friendships rewarding. Traveler elected to keep the canoe. It was stored on a rack of poles, and White Squirrel promised to look after it. They would need it for the trip downriver next season.

"Use it if you wish," Traveler urged. "Its spirit appreciates the contact."

"Yes, that is true. A canoe becomes lonely."

"Or, if a good trade comes along . . ."

White Squirrel laughed. "Traveler, I would not presume to enter your area of skill!"

Traveler laughed too. "It is good, my friend. Do as it seems best to you."

Squirrel nodded. "Now," he went on, "about this journey. Can you and the girl be ready?"

"When do you leave?"

"Two days. We are to meet at a council of one of our allies."

"We will be ready . . . two mornings from now?"

"Yes." White Squirrel paused, then added an apparently unconnected thought. "It has become dangerous to travel alone, or with a small party, Traveler."

Traveler shook his head. "More than the last time I saw you?"

"Oh, yes. Much worse!"

"How many men will you take?"

"Maybe ten . . ."

Traveler was startled. "That many? Fewer would be unsafe?"

"Maybe not, but . . . times change, my friend. It is not like the old days. And in strength there is safety."

Traveler was astonished, and depressed. Time was when he and Plum Leaf had traveled without fear almost anywhere. The only time he had been really afraid was the experience as a youngster, with Turtle, when he had seen the sightless eyes of the dead man staring at the sun while the skin was ripped from his head. That was bad. But that was long ago, ah, maybe twenty seasons. That too seemed impossible, but . . .

"Squirrel, is this sickness, the killing of men to skin their heads . . . is it spreading westward?"

White Squirrel thought a moment. "Yes, maybe so. The Yen-glees and the Fran-cois, you know. Each wants to go west before the other."

"But why?"

The other shrugged. "Who knows what goes on in the minds of these people? But one thing I know: If they will pay for the fur of men, other men will skin it!"

He must explain this situation to Star, Traveler knew. But it was so complicated. Where to begin? Well, there would be time. He would tell her later.

There were nine in the party besides Traveler and Star. At first, some of the other men had seemed concerned that an old man and a young woman could not keep up, carrying their heavy trade packs. It was amusing to see their increasing respect as the days of travel fell behind them. Such travel, of course, was a way of life for the Trader and his companion.

Their course was basically an eastward one, following an age-old trail that wandered along the grassland and into more heavily timbered country. The warriors of White Squirrel had become more alert and attentive after only a day or two of travel. The main body stayed closer together, with scouts in front and on the flanks.

It was enough to attract Star's attention. "What is it, Uncle? Is there danger?"

He tried to smile reassuringly. "Maybe, maybe not. But keep your bow ready."

The girl was carrying a bow that they had obtained in trade at Squirrel's village. It seemed to give her confidence, and he had learned that she had great skill with it. Among her people, she had explained, both boys and girls were taught the use of weapons in their learning process—the Rabbit Society, she called it.

"Some of our women have been great warriors," she boasted. "My grandmother, Running Eagle, killed over fifty of the enemy."

Even allowing for the usual exaggeration, Traveler thought, this grandmother of Star's must have been quite a woman. "Somehow, this does not surprise me, little one," he teased.

During a halt on the second afternoon, one of the scouts returned to report suspicious activity ahead. It might be nothing, but it would be well to remain alert.

"What is it, Traveler? I do not understand. What did the Wolf say?"

"There is sign of the enemy," he told her. "We must be ready."

The warriors around them were checking weapons, touching the knives at their waists, fitting arrows to bowstrings.

"Will there be a fight?" Star asked.

"Maybe. We must be ready. Have you killed, little one?"

"Of course!" she snapped, but then softened. "Only small game, and one deer, Uncle. Not men."

They remained alert, but nothing happened that day or the next. But there came a morning when the calm of the dawning day was shattered by a yell of alarm. Traveler leaped from his robe and looked to Star's position. The girl was already up, shuffling into her moccasins, her bow ready beside her.

Around the clearing, men were running, dodging, and there was a buzz of arrows searching through the gray light of dawn like angry hornets. An attacker charged into the clearing, heading toward Star. It was like a dream as Traveler moved to help her. One moves so slowly and ineffectively in such a dream.

The girl dropped calmly to one knee and fitted an arrow to her bowstring, but before she could loose it, the warrior fell heavily. One of White Squirrel's men stooped to retrieve his ax.

In a few heartbeats, it was over. Two of the attackers were dead, and two of Squirrel's party had been wounded. One sustained a long knife slash, the other an arrow through the fleshy part of his upper arm. There was much excitement, laughter, and the retelling of individual experiences.

The man who had retrieved his ax now drew his knife. He squatted, circled the crown of the dead man's head with one deft slash, and jerked the scalp free. There was a gasp from Pale Star.

"What is it?" he asked. "Are you all right?"

"What? Oh, yes, Uncle. And you?"

"Of course."

The girl was pointing. The bone of the dead man's skull gleamed white in the growing light. "He skinned the hair."

"Yes. He took the scalp of the man he killed."

"But why?"

"Ah yes," he said sympathetically. "Your people do not take scalps."

"Of course not. Why would we do such a thing?"

"Ah, little one, you have much to learn."

All the pent-up emotion seemed to boil to the surface, and she turned on him, furious. "How am I to learn," she yelled at him, "when you tell me nothing? And stop calling me 'little one'!"

He stared at her a moment, started to laugh, and then became serious. "You are right," he admitted. He had almost called her little one again, but caught himself. "Come, sit," he continued. "You are right. You are a grown woman, and there are things here that you need to know, for your own protection."

During the next few days, as they stopped for water, rest, or the night's camp, he attempted to explain the complicated politics of the region. She already knew of the hair-faced outsiders but had trouble understanding that there were two tribes of them.

"The Yen-glees and Fran-cois," he explained, "are enemies in their own land. They come here and are still enemies. There are not enough to kill each other well, so they ask our tribes to help."

"But why?"

"Each tribe has its own enemies. Is it not so in your country?"

"Yes, but—"

He waved her to silence again. "So, our people kill each other as they always have, but are given gifts by one side or the other, Yen-glees or Fran-cois."

"Gifts?"

"Yes . . . knives of iron, blankets, other things."

"But I still do not understand. What has that to do with this morning?"

"Oh, yes, the scalps. Well, if someone is to be rewarded for killing enemies, he must have proof, yes? The scalp is proof of a dead enemy."

He could see the revulsion in the girl's eyes. "They are rewarded by the number of scalps they bring? That is no proof. They could be anyone's hair!"

He was not surprised that a woman as intelligent as Star would see the heart of the problem immediately. "Yes," he agreed, "some sell scalps to both sides."

"Which side started this, Uncle?"

"No one knows now. People take scalps more to show their manhood now, anyway."

"Which side are your friends?"

"I would like to trade with both," Traveler said earnestly. "There is more trade that way. So I try to stay friends with both by killing neither. Sometimes it is hard."

"Which side do White Squirrel's people fight for?" she asked.

"I am not sure. Neither Fran-cois nor Yen-glees have come this far west yet. They probably have not decided."

"But, Uncle, they take scalps!"

"Yes, but that is something else, now. It does not matter which side, to many. Scalps are a thing of value, like furs, or to prove manhood. Some who take scalps here do not even know how it started."

He could see that she did not understand at all. In truth, he did not himself. How could he explain a region gone completely mad, skinning each other's heads for money or glory? Both groups of outsiders pushing west; the Fran-cois to the north, the Yen-glees on the south, each trying to push faster than the other. And *why*? No one was certain. At least, no one he had encountered knew why it was so important to push to the west. The customs of the hair-faces were very strange, and he doubted that he would ever understand their ways of thinking.

How much more confusing it must be for Pale Star. He had grown up with the knowledge of the outsiders and their strange ways, and he did not understand. What chance that this child of the prairie people could grasp the meaning of the whole confused conflict? He felt more sympathy for her than ever before. It would be good to forget the danger and horror of what this region had become. Next spring, when he and Star went west—he almost wished now that he had agreed to Star's request and tried it this autumn; the weather was holding well. No, that had not been a reasonable choice then and was not now.

They would soon reach his people and would winter

there. Then, as soon as the spring began to awaken, they would travel. This region had become so threatening, so dreadful, that he could hardly wait to shake its dust from his moccasins. They would start west. There would be risks, but new sights and sounds, new tongues to learn, new stories to tell. He would do as he had promised Pale Star—return her to her people.

30

It was good to travel in the safety of numbers, but it was a mixed blessing. The very presence of Squirrel's warriors seemed to remind them of the madness that had overtaken the land. But those same warriors had gradually become more relaxed in the ensuing days.

Star did not understand. Traveler did not, either, and was at a loss when she asked him, "Is the danger over?"

"What? How do you mean?"

"The warriors are not so watchful as they were. Is there no danger here?"

Traveler pondered a moment. He had not noticed, but now that the girl had called his attention to it, the change was apparent. Was there something different about the region where they now traveled? "I do not know, lit—Star. But it is as you say. Come, we will ask Squirrel."

The young chief was quite matter-of-fact in his answer. "Yes, we are nearer the town of the Fran-cois."

Traveler was puzzled. "And they protect . . ."

"No, my friend, not exactly." White Squirrel chuckled. "But those who scalp anyone for the value of their hair are more reluctant to do so here."

Traveler was still not certain how this worked as he tried to translate for Pale Star. "Maybe," he ventured, "those whose hearts are bad do not show their bad intent too close to those whose hearts are good."

The girl nodded. "Maybe." She seemed thoughtful and finally spoke again. "Uncle, there is a story among my people. It was a bad season for hunting, and the council decided that if the buffalo came, no one would hunt for himself, only in the planned hunt. That way, there would be more meat for all."

"What has that to do with this?"

"Let me finish, Uncle! One man went out to hunt by himself and made a kill, far from camp. He was found out when *his* family had meat and others were hungry."

"But, what—"

"I am trying to tell you! He could not have hunted near the camp because he was breaking the order of the council."

"But he was found out anyway," argued the puzzled Traveler.

"Yes," Star agreed impatiently, "or there would be no story. But he was *less* likely to be found if he was far from the camp.

"Maybe . . ." Traveler was still not quite certain what she was implying.

"Never mind, Uncle."

"No, wait, I see your thought. It is as I said. Those whose hearts are bad . . ." He turned to Squirrel. "Do the Fran-cois, or the Yen-glees, know about the trade in scalps?"

"Of course! They pay—"

"No, no. That there are some who buy and sell scalps like beaver pelts?"

"Oh. No, probably not. They suspect, maybe. But one person's hair looks much like another's when it is off the head. Some may suspect, but who is to say? A scalp could be from an enemy or from a stranger. They were killed far away, maybe. We try to prevent our young men from this."

Traveler nodded. It was much as he and Star had surmised. He turned back to the girl. "Yes," he translated, "that is it. There would be more danger to those whose hearts are bad nearer to the town of the Fran-cois."

"So, this removes the danger to us?"

"Sometimes. It is like when we were with Hunts-in-the-Rain. Enemies who are guests in another's territory do not fight. There is a truce."

Pale Star nodded, half lost in thought. He could sympathize with her confusion, for he was confused himself. And in the back of his mind was also the vague idea that even such a truce does not protect against someone who is without reason. Ah, well, each day starts anew. An unfinished thought came to mind. "What happened to him?" he asked.

"Who?"

"The man in your story. The hunter who broke the order of the council."

"Oh. They sent him away."

"Banished him? Put him out of your tribe?"

"Yes. And his family. His wife was quite angry with him. There were those who wanted to let her stay, and she could have, maybe. But she chose to go with him."

"What happened to them?"

She shrugged. "I am not sure. Maybe they joined the Head Splitters."

"Ah, I have heard of the Head Splitters. They are your enemies?"

"No. They once were, it is said. We are allies now."

"What made the change?" he asked curiously.

"A greater danger . . . an invader, from the north. It is before I was born. You have heard me speak of Looks Far, the holy man?"

Traveler nodded. "Yes. He is your kinsman?"

"That is the one . . . he helped to bring the two tribes together. He and another holy man, of the Head Splitters."

Traveler remembered vaguely having heard the story of this war and how the invasion had been stopped. Yes, Turtle's people had known of it—a buffalo stampede, created by the two holy men, by combining their medicines. Could one of these men still be alive?

"Star," he asked, "you mentioned Looks Far before . . . He is still living?"

"Of course! At least, when I was stolen, he was. You will meet him, next season, when we join my people."

Several times the party encountered travelers who were apparently friendly. They paused to visit with White Squirrel, usually in vaguely familiar tongues, sometimes with hand-signs. The conversations were about the weather, the trail, and scarcity of game. On a more cautious note, they spoke of the power struggle between the two groups of outsiders.

"Things are quiet now," one party told them. "The value of scalps is low this season. Maybe it will be better next year."

Traveler was revulsed. How could they calmly discuss the price of such a commodity as men's scalps?

Then came the evening when, as they camped, White Squirrel approached. "Tomorrow we part." Squirrel used hand-signs so that Star could understand.

Traveler nodded. "We thank you for your kindness. It has been good to be with your people, my friend."

"You are welcome in my lodge," Squirrel said, smiling. "Your canoe will be safe until you return."

"We will come in the spring."

White Squirrel then turned to Pale Star, smiling. "It is good to know you, also, little sister. Take good care of my friend Traveler."

Since their first day with Squirrel, he had not questioned, or even mentioned, the relationship between Traveler and the girl. If there was a question in his mind now, White Squirrel kept it to himself.

The next morning, where the trail divided, White Squirrel led his party on the fork that led northeast. Traveler and Star watched as the last man turned to wave and was quickly swallowed up in the forest. They lifted their packs and moved onto the other path, nearly due east.

It was a relief, actually, to be separated from the main party. They could talk more freely, could set their own pace, and had a freedom of decision that did not depend on someone else's whims. Traveler had to admit the presence of the warriors had bothered him. It served as a reminder of danger and bad times. Yes, this was better. And in a few sleeps, they would be in his home village. The excitement of homecoming was beginning to mount.

Apparently Star noticed it too. "How far to your people?" she asked during a rest stop.

He smiled. "Three, four sleeps." He felt confident, relaxed. He was going home. This was his country. He had not expected to feel like this. Maybe the day would come when he would not mourn in his heart quite so continuously. Maybe.

"You will find it good to see your people," Star suggested. "You have parents?"

"No. They are dead. A sister . . . We will stay with her."

"She has a husband and children?"

"Yes . . . you will like her family."

"Tell me more about your people."

"There is not much that you do not know. You know enough of our tongue to speak to them."

"How did you begin to travel and trade, Uncle?"

He smiled. That seemed so long ago. He lighted his pipe with a stick from the fire and settled back against a tree trunk to relax and tell his story. Star listened, attentively.

"When I was little more than a child, younger than you, Star, there came to our village a traveling trader. He was very good to me. My father had been killed, and my mother married the trader." He paused and chuckled. "He courted her with a courting flute. Do your people use the flute?"

"No, but we know of them." Star smiled. "That would be very romantic."

"Yes . . . I courted Plum Leaf with the flute. Turtle . . . my stepfather taught me."

Suddenly he realized something. He had talked of Plum Leaf with no tears. In fact, there had been pleasure in the remembering. Those glorious days with the world ahead of them . . . "It was wonderful, Star," he said simply.

She smiled, understanding. "Plum Leaf was a special woman, Traveler. She helped me, more than she knew."

"I am made to think she knew, little one," he said with a smile.

The girl smiled back, and he realized that she had not even complained at his calling her little one. And it was good.

31

It was a pleasant place, where they camped that evening. They had decided to stop early. The fine weather was holding, and there was no urgency.

After the parting with White Squirrel, the two had begun to talk. They found great pleasure in sharing this companionable activity. Perhaps it was that both were now alone and that the companionship was needed. Of course, there was the fact that Traveler, in his bereavement, was purging his grief. He had passed the initial period of mourning that had been so difficult for him. He had survived his loss. Now his stories of Plum Leaf were of the happy times. Pale Star, in the flower of young womanhood, was an avid listener to his tales of romance. She shared her memories of Plum Leaf.

"She hated me at first, Uncle," Star recalled.

Traveler laughed. "She was angry at *me* because of you!" he admitted.

"How can this be?" the girl asked in wonder.

"Well, I . . . Plum Leaf thought I had made a bad trade. My best metal knife . . . my *only* metal knife! It *was* a bad trade."

"*Aiee!* That does not speak well of me! Am I no use to you?"

Both were teasing, and both knew it. Then Traveler became serious. "I do not know why I bought you. I felt sorrow for you, but for the others too. It was meant to be, maybe." There was a slightly uncomfortable moment, and he continued. "Some have thought that I wanted you for a wife."

"I know . . ."

Now he was embarrassed. "That was not in my thinking, Star."

"I know. You would not have kept calling me little one."

He smiled ruefully. "I thought at first that was the reason for Plum Leaf's anger. She thought I wanted you."

"Oh," Star said thoughtfully. "I did not think that."

"I came to think not," Traveler went on. "I never spoke of it with her. Very soon, she came to think of you as a daughter . . . as I did."

"Tell me of your daughter, Traveler. You have mentioned her. . . . She is dead?"

"Born dead," he said sadly. "Her spirit was unable to enter her body. A beautiful child. We were never able to conceive, after that. It was not meant to be." He paused and chuckled. "Plum Leaf once asked if I wanted another wife, to have children."

"She did?"

"Yes . . . I did not want another. Any child would not have been hers . . . Plum Leaf's and mine."

"Then if she once offered to take another woman, Traveler, that was *not* why she disliked me at first."

He nodded, smiling. "I thought of that. No, Plum Leaf just saw it as a bad trade. But she came to love you, Star."

Now it was time for Star's eyes to fill with tears. "Yes, I know. And she was like a mother to me. Traveler, I will be pleased for you to meet my parents. We will be your family."

Traveler smiled. "The trail is my family, Star. I have friends everywhere. But *you* are my daughter."

"It is good," she signed, as if to avoid speaking. She rose to add some sticks to the fire.

They would have to gather more before dark, Traveler thought. This was a place he had camped before, a pretty glade with a good spring. It was one of those campsites that had been used for many generations because of availability of water and the favorable lay of the land. This generation favored the spot for the same reasons the previous generation had, and the ones before that and before, all the way back to Creation, maybe.

There was, however, one major disadvantage. Frequent visitors meant frequent fires. Blackened spots and unburned fragments of charcoal could be seen all over the clearing. They too might go all the way back to Creation, at least back to the time the red fox stole fire from Sun Boy and gave it to Man. But fires need wood. In such a campsite, all dead wood is quickly gathered by travelers and used for their fires. This makes it necessary to search farther from camp for enough fuel to last the night.

"I will get some wood," he said, rising to his feet.

"It is good. Be careful."

An odd remark, he thought. But maybe not. He knew that Star was still concerned about the scalping and unrest, though they had seen no other travelers since leaving White Squirrel.

He was also aware that Pale Star disliked the woodlands intensely. A child of the prairie, she always spoke of a trapped feeling when she could not see very far. He could understand that. There was a feeling to the wide horizons of the prairie that was awe-inspiring. One could see the smoke of a campfire a day's travel away. There was such a feeling of bigness, of sky and earth. It made a person feel big yet at the same time small, tiny even, as part of the prairie. He had spent enough time there to understand what Star meant when she talked of a need to "stretch her eyes."

He found a dead cottonwood and was busily breaking limbs from it, tossing the sticks in a pile. Maybe he would come back for another load. It was a giant of a tree, its base rooted far below the rim of the bluff on which he stood, overlooking the river. Below its top was a tangle of smaller trees and brush. The uppermost branches of the dying giant projected conveniently for him to break from his position above. It was odd that other travelers had not yet discovered this source of fuel. But it appeared to have been dead for only a season and was some distance from the campsite. He had had difficulty finding any dry sticks nearer at hand.

As he turned to toss a stick aside, he caught a glimpse of motion and turned quickly. A man stood among the trees, watching him, only a few steps away. There was something familiar about the heavyset bearlike figure. That was it—bear . . . *Winter Bear,* companion of the irrational Three Owls. This could not lead to any good. Traveler tossed his sticks aside and stood to face the danger. He glanced quickly around for the man's companion but did not see him.

Winter Bear smiled thinly, but with his mouth only, not with his eyes. It was not a friendly smile but a cruel one, a leering mockery that saw humor in this situation, desperate for his opponent.

Traveler licked his dry lips, realizing just how hopeless his predicament was. He was virtually unarmed, only the small knife at his waist. He was confronted by a much younger man, perhaps half his age, twice his size. Horrified, he watched the big man reach methodically for the ax at his waist. There was nowhere to run with the cliff behind him.

Then, as he drew his knife for a last effort at defense, an even more horrible thought occurred to him. Three Owls was not here, but he must be somewhere nearby. Pale Star was alone at the fire . . . "Star!" he shouted at the top of his lungs.

His voice was drowned in the bearlike roar of his assailant as he rushed. Traveler dodged aside, still more agile than the heavyset Bear. He hoped for an instant that the rush would carry the big man over the edge, but it did not.

There was a halfhearted swing of the ax, but it missed, and Traveler circled warily. He longed to run, but it was several steps to the trees, and he dared not turn his back. He had seen men use the small throwing axes, and the way this one held his ax, high and balanced. . .

Traveler backed away, ready to dodge a blow. He circled back toward the edge. Maybe that was worth another try if he could entice Bear into another rush.

But stupid though he might appear, there was a certain cunning in the big man. He smiled the cruel smile again, and readied his ax. It seemed to move slowly, so slowly— back over Winter Bear's shoulder, and then forward . . .

Traveler watched the weapon, the handle rotating around the heavier blade. One revolution, two . . .

He was starting to turn when the blow struck. Then everything accelerated to a frantic rush, and in only a couple of heartbeats, it was over. It was a slanting blow because his head was turning, and it struck just above his right eye with a sickening thud. But Traveler did not hear. By pure reflex, his right hand jerked upward, wrenching the ax free.

Then the pain struck—searing, blinding pain, causing him to cover his face with both hands while blood gushed into his eyes. He staggered backward, off balance, toppling over the edge, consciousness fading fast.

Long before his limp form struck the rocks below, Traveler's world had plunged into complete blackness.

Winter Bear lumbered to the edge and peered over at the crumpled body below. He grunted, stooped to pick up his ax, and wiped it clean on the grass before tucking it back in the thong around his waist. He looked over the edge again and seemed to think a little while. Then he turned away with another bearish grunt of disgust. The scalp below was not worth the tough climb to the river and back.

Besides, he wanted to see how his cousin was doing with the girl. Maybe Three Owls would share his good fortune. Winter Bear moved toward the campsite by the spring at a lumbering trot.

Part III

The Watcher

32

» » »

The old woman shuffled along the narrow path at the edge of the water, carrying her fish. It was a good fish, one that would last her for several days. Or maybe she could dry some of it for the coming winter. She had few supplies. Maybe she could kill a deer before Cold Maker swooped in from the north. It was hard, the life she had. Sometimes she wondered how she had managed to live all these winters. How many now? She had lost track. No matter, it was too many.

More to the point, *why* had she struggled to survive? Many times she had been near death. She had been condemned to death once, by her own people. It had been in her foolish youth, and her actions had indeed been stupid. She had had a good husband, her own lodge, but no children yet—the whole world before her, and she had thrown it away. A young man from the neighboring tribe, one of their allies, had encountered her at the stream as she bathed. Her husband was gone on a hunt, and the man was friendly. Strange, she had forgotten his name now. He had stayed near the camp of her people, and the romance developed quickly.

Short Horse had returned to find his wife in the robes with a stranger. The man was blameless. She had not told him she was married. Her husband could have killed her outright but instead took her before the council.

Judgment was swift. As she had thrown away her marriage, so she was to be thrown away—"left on the prairie." It was a death sentence, to be carried out by the Warrior Society. Very seldom used, it had been a generation since such a sentence was pronounced. There was no harsher punishment for a woman of the northern plains, and it was usually reserved for such crimes as treason against her people. Or infidelity.

She remembered little of that day. She had been taken on foot some distance into the prairie, accompanied by about thirty men of the Warrior Society. She remembered the first six or eight who assaulted her before it became painful. Then the whole sequence became a tortured memory, half forgotten in the agony. Sometime after a dozen, fifteen, or twenty had performed the rape, she had lost consciousness, and perhaps that saved her.

She awoke. It was night, a full moon shining. She was alone. She had been wakened by a pair of coyotes, apparently attracted by the scent of blood. Her feeble movements frightened the animals away.

Surely she was dead. She had never heard of one who had survived the throwing-away ceremony. But if she was dead, why did it hurt so much? It was the next day before she was able to drag herself to the stream to drink, another two before she could half crawl back to the camp.

It was deserted. The band had moved on. Of course— They would have moved away from the site of the throwing away, the area taboo now. With something like panic, she had realized that she too would be taboo. No man would lie with her, for in the way of her people, she was dead. She could not marry. No one would help her.

She had stayed there for several days, scavenging the refuse left behind. If she was to survive, it must be on her own. Her pitiful plunder was not much—a worn-out robe, a pair of discarded moccasins. She had lost her own footwear. She covered the holes in these moccasins with scrap leather from another cast-off garment. Her most important find was a knife, a real prize. It was not a discard, but an implement someone had lost. Slender, sharp, a fine gray-blue stone blade. She still had it, after all these years.

Her most urgent need had been for food. She found some sand plums and was fortunate enough to kill a rabbit with a throwing stick but was soon hungry again. She found her way to a village of Growers who had traded with her people. They had heard. They were amazed that she was alive and seemed afraid of her. Out of kindness, they gave her a pouch of corn and a few strips of dried meat. It was plain, however, that she was unwelcome. They considered her dead.

Somehow, she had survived that first winter, living in a tiny cave in a cutbank of shale and clay. She had grown thin, near the edge of starvation, but each time she was about to give up, something would prevent her demise. Once an aging buffalo bull was pulled down by wolves within sight of her cave. After they had gorged themselves on the carcass, she approached boldly, drove the animals off with a club, and quickly stripped as much meat as she could carry. That supply, dried and hoarded carefully, lasted her a long time.

Another time, she startled a hawk as it made a rabbit kill. The bird attempted to lift its still-warm prey as it rose to avoid the rush of the half-starved woman. At the last moment, the hawk released its burden to facilitate its own escape. It circled above, screaming in indignation while she rushed forward to pick up her prize.

By that first springtime, however, she had become so filled with self-pity that she wanted to die. In the Moon of Greening she sought out one of the other clans of her people. Not her own—she did not wish to see them, ever again. She demanded of the band chief that she be allowed to die.

"I am already dead," she had told him. "Someone must kill me, so that my spirit may cross over."

The matter was discussed that evening by the council.

Her story was already known throughout the tribe. But she found no comfort in their decision.

"Since you are already dead," the band chief announced solemnly, "we cannot help you."

They gave her a little food but made it plain that she could not stay. Furious, she left the camp.

After that, years of wandering. When she found herself far enough from her tribe's region, the people she encountered were not aware of her sordid past. Still she was received strangely. It was many years before she realized why. She was a trifle mad. Her disheveled appearance, her garments a mixture of castoffs from all the tribes she had encountered, her actions a trifle irrational, originally from hunger, then from habit.

The madness itself had become some degree of protection. Any tribe, anywhere, is reluctant to kill a person afflicted with madness. The release of a deranged spirit might be dangerous to anyone in the immediate area.

She had not realized this. She wandered from one people to another, unwelcome anywhere. But she began to notice their ways and to adopt the use of new food plants by watching local customs. She stole from crop-fields of the Growers and collected scraps and leavings after the hunters. When she found herself in the area where men trapped beaver for their pelts, she followed the trappers, salvaging the discarded carcasses for food.

Gradually she migrated to the east. In that area, she had learned that men skinned the hair of other men for its value. She still wanted to die—occasionally, anyway, though less often through the years. Her scalp would have had some value at that time, though it was old and ratty now. But an impossible dilemma had developed. If she requested that anyone honor her wish for death, that in itself was proof of her madness. She had become known as mad and thus protected from scalphunters by their fear for their own safety. A spirit this deranged? Ah, it should not be released!

Her hate for all humans had grown through the years

while her pattern of living had stabilized, that of a recluse. She had found a cave near the foot of this bluff overlooking the stream. It was sheltered, had access to water, and was near enough to the trails of trade that she could take advantage of any chance she might have. Travelers on the trail seldom noticed her cave because its entrance was hidden, and the river was too small and meandering at this point to support canoe travel.

She fished in summer. She had learned the technique, and how to make the barbed hook of thorns, from a tribe she stayed with for a while. In winter, she followed the beaver trappers. At any time, she might scavenge after travelers on the trail above who camped for the night at the spring. She had occasionally stolen small items—not too often because she did not wish to attract attention.

She had given up the idea of dying now. There had been many chances, and she was still alive, for what purpose she had no idea, but she had come to accept that her time had not come.

She had fished all night at the deep hole where the river swirled under an overhanging willow. It was an ideal spot, productive from season to season. This night, however, there had been no action until near dawn. Then she had felt the tug on the line, tied loosely around her wrist in case she fell asleep. She knew it was large by the way it had struggled, but she managed to keep her rawhide line taut and draw the fish to shore.

It was good. She whacked the creature's head a time or two with the club she always carried and sat down to catch her breath after the struggle. There was a great sense of satisfaction. She watched the yellow light of the false dawn brighten into sunrise and finally rose to make her way back to the cave.

She stopped to rest occasionally because the fish was heavy. The stick that she had inserted through the gills to carry it was slippery, and her grasp grew tired. But now, as the sun was rising, she neared her cave. But something did not look right ahead, something lying in front of the opening. Could there have been an intruder?

The old woman hurried forward, still clutching her fish. There, lying practically in the doorway of her lodge, lay a crumpled body. There was a pool of blood under the head, and a gaping wound above the right eye, splinters of bone showing white against the black of dried blood. She cursed under her breath. Someone had killed a traveler for his scalp on the trail above and tossed the body over the edge. It had happened before but not right in her doorway. Well, she could dump it in the river, let it float downstream so that it would not attract flies.

First, however, she would salvage anything of value. She removed the moccasins and shirt, and considered the leggings . . . no, she could not use them. Then she noticed a thing that was puzzling. The man had not been scalped! A sense of alarm ran through her mind. Why not? There was something odd here. She looked the body over again very carefully. There was no other wound, only the ax cleft above the eye. A single blow. If the enemy had struck him once, knocking him over the edge —ah, that was it! The scalp was not worth the climb. Or perhaps the killer was frightened away by the man's companions. No matter . . . there was no use wasting a good scalp.

She drew her gray flint knife and grasped the man's hair. A single slash, and she gasped in surprise. The knife wound was bleeding! He must still be alive! She looked again in the brightening daylight. Yes, it was true. Not the dark sluggish blood of a corpse, but bright red blood, the fluid of *life*.

She thought about it for a little while. It would be simple enough to wait until life ceased, but inconvenient. She would have to step over the bloody form, maybe for most of a day. It would be easy to cut the throat and have it done. Or, go ahead and remove the scalp now. The man had not moved when she made her first slash. He was as good as dead anyway. She lifted the knife, but paused, and the situation struck her as humorous. Here was one person, already dead, preparing to scalp another already dead, but both still lived.

She threw back her head and laughed long and loud. Well, no matter, she decided. She could watch him for a while until he crossed over. She had nothing better to do.

Without understanding why she did so, the old woman straightened the broken limbs and prepared the body as if for the burial scaffold. She really had no intention of carrying out the ceremony. As soon as he was dead, she would take the scalp and roll the corpse into the river, and that would be the end of it.

It did bother her, though, the way the flies were gathering as they became active with the warming of the day. The wound that her knife had made had now stopped oozing, and she thought maybe—but no, there was a pulse. It was weak and thready, but she could feel it, there in his neck. She shooed the flies from his wounds and from the clotted blood in his eyes. Finally she covered the head with a scrap of blanket to keep the flies off and, she finally admitted to herself, because she did not like to look at his face.

She studied his unconscious form as he lay there. He was a man of middle age, she judged, lean and wiry. His garments were a mixture. The breechclout and leggings were of the plains, the shirt of the woodlands. His moccasins, which she had already removed, were hard-soled with rawhide, much like those of her own people. This was completely different from the soft puckered-toe style that was almost universal here.

His hairstyle—it was hard to tell, it was so filled with

dried blood. The head was not shaved, however, and there was no elaborate plaiting, merely a simple braid on either side. There may have been a headband or a cap, now lost. It was no matter now.

She cleaned her fish, filleted it in strips, and built a small fire just under the overhang of the bluff to start the smoke-drying process. She tossed the entrails into the stream and paused to watch a few moments. It was important to see what sort of scavengers came to the feeding. She had been baiting this section of the stream for years, and it had been very productive at times.

She returned to the fire, ate a chunk of fish, and checked the pulse of the dying man again. No, still alive. She shrugged, mumbling to herself. Was this inconvenience worth the price of the scalp? Maybe she should just forget the scalp and roll him into the river. He would never know. No one would ever know, or care. Well, she would wait a little longer.

By midday, the sky was becoming overcast. A gray cloudbank moved in from the west. She had been here long enough to know what sort of change to expect. Not a hard rain, probably, at this time of year, but a cold drizzle. And colder tonight. She moved up and down the path for a while, bringing a store of firewood that she piled just inside the cave.

The still form in front of the entrance showed no sign of life, and she felt the neck again. No, still pulsing. She could just tighten her fingers there for a little while . . . no, it was better to wait.

The first tiny drops of rain began to spatter down, spotting the gray of the rocks to a mottled appearance for a few moments. Then everything became wet and shiny as the rain increased. She retreated inside. Through the door of the cave she could see droplets of rain dancing on the naked chest of the man outside or plopping soddenly on the scrap of blanket over his face. There was a chill in the air now. That would probably push his spirit on over, she thought.

Then, for the first time in years, a spark of something glowed for a moment amid the bitterness of her life. No one, she thought, should cross over this way, in a cold rain with no one to care. There had been a time in her life when she was virtually dying, and there had been no one. What if someone, anyone, had been there to comfort her, to show concern? Would it have changed her life? She wiped a tear from her leathery old cheek, the first time in years she had felt any self-pity. For a while she sat and watched the rain patter on the still form outside.

Finally she rose, cursing to herself, and shuffled out into the drizzle. It would do no harm to drag him inside. Let him die there, in shelter and relative comfort, and with a companion. She could drag the corpse back out later, after he crossed over.

He was heavier than he looked. She took his feet under her arms and backed toward the entrance. When she got the body moving, it was easier, sliding it on the muddy path. She pulled him inside and stopped, panting a little from the exertion. Then she rolled him over to spread a blanket, rolling him back onto it. Well, nothing now but to wait. She cursed to herself at the inconvenience. She often cursed to herself, a long-standing habit.

She smoked her pipe, using only a little tobacco, for her supply was scant. She had extended it some with shavings of red willow twigs toasted brown over the fire. She needed to find more. This man had none on his person, but maybe in his possessions. No, his killer would have plundered the possessions of the victim. Well, she would go up, after the rain stopped. Maybe something would be left. But not in the rain.

She drew the blanket around her against the chill. If the dying man were awake, she noted, he too would be cold. That thought bothered her. She sat there, finally cursed again, and threw a tattered scrap of an old robe over him.

Through the afternoon she sat there, rising to tend her fire or turn the fillets of fish occasionally. The unconscious man in the cave remained unchanged, but when she felt his throat toward evening, the pulse seemed stronger. She cursed again. Surely, he could not last much longer—the ax wound, the splintered bone. . . .

It was nearing dark, and the cold drizzle was falling steadily when she was startled by a groan. She turned quickly. The man's left hand was twitching convulsively. As she watched, the odd jerking motion spread, involving the arm, the leg, the entire left side of the body. It was severe; the pull of the muscles was enough to distort the left leg above the knee where it had appeared to be broken. The whole effect was frightening, and she watched, fascinated, holding her breath while the jerking movements continued. Then they became quieter and subsided.

The old woman exhaled audibly. She realized that she had been holding her breath through the entire episode. What did it mean? There was something more here than she had thought at first, and she was a little frightened. This man must have a powerful spirit, a spirit of a different kind. For a moment, she thought that it might have been better to roll him off the path into the river as she had thought at first. Then she recoiled from the thought. No, she must not think this way. Maybe the frightening demonstration she had just witnessed was a threat, a reminder, maybe, that the spirit lived and had no intention of crossing over. She might even be considered responsible for his well-being. Maybe this was some sort of holy man whose medicine was so powerful that he could not be killed, even by the blow of an ax to the head.

It was an awesome responsibility that had been thrust on her. Had she known, perhaps she might have evaded it, but it was too late now. The man was here, in her cave. If she thrust him back out, his spirit might seek revenge when he died. Of course, if he died *in* the cave, the bizarre spirit that had caused the convulsion would be released *right here,* with her.

She could see only one course of action open to her

now. It was too late to avoid whatever consequences there might be. She must give this man the best care possible to gain favor with his spirit when, and if, it crossed over. She was beginning to doubt that now. What strange and powerful medicine had kept the man alive this long?

Darkness was falling. She built up the little fire for light and rummaged in the cave for anything that might be of help. First, his head. Very gently, she removed the rag that she had thrown over his face so that she would not have to watch him. She laid it aside, brought water, and cleaned the clotted blood away. The head wound itself she did not touch. Not yet.

In the back of the cave was an assortment of small packets, things she had saved—herbs, seeds, plant medicines. She had been in contact with many tribes and had learned from them all. She assembled her various items and began her tasks.

One plant she burned in a little pile beside the fire. Its ashes were scraped together and carefully placed in a bowl. Meanwhile, she ground the dried leaves from another packet with some dark dried berrylike fruit from yet another. A root from still another, pounded and ground—she could not remember exactly the source or uses of some of these things. There was surely a song or chant connected with the use of each, but most of these she did not know or had forgotten. She formulated her own song as she formulated the salve in her bowl, mixing the medicinal powders with carefully hoarded buffalo fat from a gourd.

"Oh, Unknown Spirits," she sang, "look with kindness on these efforts; let this holy man be cleansed and helped. . . ."

Very gently, she spread the salve over the edges of the wound. A splinter or two of bone she picked out as she did so, consigning these to the fire. "Let no bad spirits enter this door," she sang, "the door of this man's life, or even the door of this lodge."

She finished covering the open wound with her salve and brought out a scrap of white linen. It had once been part of a French soldier's shirt and was one of her prized possessions. It now became a bandage.

"I close this door," she announced in song, covering the wound. "The holy man's spirit will not come out through this cleft, nor will evil enter in. . . ."

She finished her task and sank back, exhausted. She was tired, from the physical effort of the grinding and pounding but also from the tremendous energy required of the spirit. It seemed as if she had been wrestling with spirits all night.

For a little while she slept, then woke to replenish the fire. The unconscious man seemed unchanged as she felt his pulse and laid her hand on his cheek, looking for fever. He was warm but not hot. There was only a little bright red blood on her bandage, and that was good—clean blood from where she had started to lift his scalp. Ah, how stupid that had been!

He groaned, and she remembered the broken leg. She should fix that. She split the legging to remove it and carefully felt the thigh. Fortunately, there was no protrusion of bone through the skin. The limb was relatively straight, but she remembered its sharp angulation before she had rearranged him. Then she had dragged him by the legs. Well, it appeared in a good enough position, but she would need splints. And it was dark and raining outside. The splints would have to wait until morning.

She settled down with her back against the cave's wall, drawing her blanket around her against the chill. "I will take care of you," she said to the quiet form.

Outside, the drizzle fell steadily.

34

» » »

When daylight came, the woman tried to evaluate how the wounded man looked. There was not much change. His pulse was steady, his color still pale, but he was deeply unresponsive. At least, he did look better with the bandage covering his gaping head wound.

Twice during the night he had convulsed again. Each time, it had started with that writhing, grasping tremor in his left hand. It had been frightening to watch. At least, she told herself, these had been no worse than the first.

The storm had passed, and she stepped outside to greet the sun. The world, still sodden from the drizzling rain, now dripped from every rock, bush, and tree. There was the smell of warm leaf-mold, the earthy smell that was unfamiliar to her people of the prairie.

She chopped three splints for the broken leg, laid them inside the cave, and took a large bottle-gourd to bring water. The river itself appeared roiled and muddy, but she knew a place. Some fifty steps upstream, a wet-weather spring trickled clean clear water from the shale of the bluff. It flowed across a rocky shelf that formed that portion of her path and fell gently to the river an arm's length below. She held the gourd under the trickle at the point where it emerged from the bluff, waiting until it was full. She drank, sucking noisily, directly from the same trickle, then made her way back to the cave.

The woman had created a problem for herself. She had elected to take care of the unconscious man but was not certain how to do it. Well, she could at least splint the leg. While she cut strips of buckskin from his leggings and padding from the scraps of an old robe, she thought about it. She estimated that he had been wounded just before dark the night before last, the night she was fishing. Then it would be two days ago tonight, two days since he had eaten, probably. That was no problem yet. It was possible to fast for many days. But not without water. Three or four days, at most, was as much as one could live without water. His lips already looked dry, his cheeks hollow. She wet the tips of her fingers from the water-gourd, and gently moistened his lips. There was no response. She tried another dip of water. Maybe she could spoon a little water into his mouth. She would try that later, if she found courage. She must be certain that he could swallow. If not, the water would run down the wrong tube, and she could drown him with a single mouthful.

She turned her attention to the leg, which still seemed relatively straight despite the seizures. The pad that she had made from the buffalo robe fit nicely around the thigh, tied loosely with thongs. She propped the foot upright with a couple of large stones; the toe continually wanted to sag and point outward. She could hear and feel the grating of the broken bone, and the man moaned softly. It was good that he was unconscious, she thought.

When she had the foot adjusted appropriately, the splints were positioned. One with a fork, a broad open fork, was placed in his groin, well padded and tied at several places, ending below the knee. The other splints completed the procedure. There. She was proud of the result. It should hold the leg until healing began. It would be a long time, she knew, before that leg would bear any weight, however.

"But you cannot use it now, while you sleep, anyway," she told the still form. "Now we have to try some water."

She talked cheerfully, as if he could hear her. It was not for him but for herself. She dreaded this next step. If he had no way to cough, how could she tell if he was drowning? Just a little at first. She must be sure that he was swallowing the water, not letting it trickle into his lungs. Her hand trembled as she poured a bit of water from the gourd into the horn spoon. Very carefully, she brought the spoon close to his lips. Her shaking hand spilled a little, and she cursed softly to herself as she paused to steady her hand. Only a little at first. The water trickled between his lips and across his teeth to disappear somewhere. He showed no reaction.

She had a moment of panic. Was he drowning? She could see no motions of breathing. What could she do? "Come on, *breathe*!" she muttered irritably. "Swallow!"

Desperately, she massaged his throat, then paused and waited. There was no reaction, no sign of life. But wait— though she could see no deep breathing, his color was still good, well, *fairly* good. She realized that the previous day his breathing had often not been perceptible for a time. She watched his chest. *Yes!* He was breathing! She wondered, then—the water? Her ear to his chest, she listened, and there was no gurgling sound. Just then, came the best sign of all. The lump on the front of his neck, that curious hard knot that men have but women do not *moved*. Slowly and deliberately, it bobbed upward toward his jawbone, then downward.

The old woman gave a little squeal of joy. "You swallowed!" She chortled. "It is good! Let us try another sip. . . ."

This time, her hand was steadier, and she did not spill quite so much. Even better, the swallowing sequence seemed to come more easily. She found that if she lifted his head and shoulders, it seemed to help the swallowing. In this way, she managed to feed him several spoonfuls of water.

"There!" she declared triumphantly. "We will try again, later. It is good!"

It seemed not to matter to her that it had taken most of the day to fix the leg and experiment with the water. There was a thrill of accomplishment, a pride and a spark of interest that she had not had for a long time. *Aiee,* she had forgotten to eat! She laughed at herself, and ate a few bites of her fish.

"Now," she told the silent form, as if he could hear, "if you can take water, you can take soup. I will make some!"

She still liked to boil soup in a cooking pit, after the custom of her people. The pit was already there, just outside the cave's entrance. She kindled the fire, placed several of her cooking stones to heat, and turned to prepare the pit. Some of her precious supply of dried meat went into the skin-lined pit with some chunks of the half-smoked fish, dried beans, water from the gourd, and a tiny lump of buffalo fat. She would add some fresh onions maybe, later, but they grew some distance downstream. She lifted the heated stones with her willow tongs and began to drop them into the cooking pit.

"There!" she said finally. "We will let it stew for a while."

She looked at the unresponsive form in the cave and smiled. She did not smile often. She did not talk often, either, beyond mumbling to herself. Sometimes she even answered. But there was seldom anyone to talk to, really talk. Her usual habit was a mumbling word or two combined with idle thoughts. This was new, rather enjoyable, to have an uncomplaining listener.

She did not know how much he could hear. It was much like the time she had found a fledgling crow that had fallen from the nest, except of course that it had squawked, pecked her fingers, and eaten ravenously. She had originally intended to eat the bird after it grew a little. But she had come to enjoy its company and had kept it. It would ride on her shoulder and was a great amusement to her. Then, one day, it flew away with some other crows and never returned. One thing about this man—he would not leave, for he *could* not, at least not for a long while.

Now she found herself talking to him, and it was good to think that maybe he could hear a part of it. "I do not know who you are, traveler," she told the quiet form, "or why you traveled this trail. How are you called?" She paused as if she expected an answer, but then continued. "Well, since I have no name for you, I will call you the Traveler. What is your tongue, Traveler? You are not likely to understand mine, but I do not know if you understand anything anyway. But we will talk."

She was only dimly aware that she was saying "we" as she spoke to him. He was rapidly becoming a part of her life, though he had done virtually nothing to reciprocate beyond a moan or two. But he was alive, at least so far. Through all the years, there had never been another person who had consented to be with her like this.

The days passed, and she fell into a pattern of daily activity. She cooked, fed him the broth, ate the solids herself, gave him water, and cleaned him when his bladder leaked. His bowel, of course, was empty since he had taken no solid food.

She talked to him often, almost continuously now. "This is a fine day, Traveler, is it not? The good weather holds. I have brought us onions today. You should enjoy these. Here, have some soup. Come on, swallow."

"It looks stormy today, Traveler. Do not worry. I have kept warm for many winters. I will take care of us."

"I have to leave you a little while now. I have to hunt. A rabbit maybe? We need a deer before Cold Maker comes. I will take the bow."

The woman was hoarse at first from the unaccustomed talking, but that soon subsided. She still knew nothing about the unconscious man. She had climbed to the top of the bluff during his first few days with her, trying to learn something about him. There was a trail up the face of the rock, which she hated to use. It was a difficult climb, but she felt a driving curiosity about this man that drove her to investigate.

Her effort brought little reward. The rain had washed away most of the sign. At the top, where the big dead cottonwood outside her cave overhung the rim, someone had been breaking away branches. Strangely, he had not carried the fuel away. *Ah,* she thought, *it was probably my traveler.* Yes, there was a pile of sticks, ready to carry, but he had been interrupted by the attacker with the ax. She could find no tracks, but then the rain would have destroyed them.

She tossed the pile of firewood over the edge to the path below. She seldom wasted anything. Then she made her way very cautiously to the campsite by the spring. The last part of the distance she covered very quietly, peering around the trees as she advanced. She did not know why she needed to use caution, but after all, someone had had cause to murder here, and quite recently.

The glade was abandoned. She poked around but found very little. There was sign that two or three people might have camped here recently, probably on the night that the stranger was struck down. They had departed before the rain, however. No one had used the trail since.

"Well, Traveler," she said aloud, "I have found nothing. You will have to tell me when you wake up."

But that had been many days ago. There were times now when she wondered if he would ever change. What would happen if he never wakened but still lived?

There had been a time in her life when it would have been easy for her to avoid this responsibility. She would simply have rolled him into the river. Her hate for the world and everything in it, especially humans, would have driven her to it. But the past days had changed her. True, the days were alike, following one after another like beads on a string. But she had a certain purpose to her existence now. Since her throwing away, no one had depended on her for anything—no one or no thing, except the crow, ungrateful wretch that he was.

"Ah, Traveler, will you leave me when you are able?" she asked him. "Will you be like the crow?"

It was not a serious question, she was only talking. But she could not remember anything that had given her more pleasure than simply being needed. Without her, the man would die. Therefore, she was responsible for his life. It felt good when she half lifted him to feed him, cradling him against her as she crooned words of comfort. Somehow, she felt that he knew, though his only response so far was to swallow, moan occasionally, and wet himself. She moved his limbs, except for the broken leg, feeling that he might begin such movement on his own if she initiated it. Her maternal instincts were awakening after sleeping a long time. She had never had a child, and this helpless creature was filling the empty spot in her heart. She would rock him gently in her arms after feeding him, crooning fragments of a half-forgotten lullaby from her childhood.

It was after one of those episodes that she saw the first signs that he might really hear some of what she said. She had fed him as usual, talked of the weather as she did so, and then held him cradled in her arms, rocking him gently while she sang. Finally she eased him back onto the pallet, gently arranging his limbs into what appeared to be a comfortable position.

"You stay here," she instructed, though it was plain he could not do otherwise. "I will be back soon."

She was halfway out the door of the cave when she heard a rattling sound in his throat. She turned anxiously. Could he be choking? She knelt at his side, watching his blank facial expression change to a frown. The eyes remained closed, but the lips quivered and finally parted. Fascinated, she watched, holding her breath.

"M-m . . . Mama!" he whispered.

Then he sank back, exhausted from the effort.

35

» » »

He drifted in and out of consciousness in a dreamlike state. At first as his senses returned, he was aware of nothing but the blinding pain in his head. There was no sense of time, place, or identity. Gradually, he realized that it was sometimes dark but sometimes light. He would awaken, though not completely, realize that it was dark, then waken again to find it light. There was no sense of time, but a dreamy drift that had no beginning or end.

He could not see. The light and the dark were as much as he could distinguish. It hurt to try to see, and he would close his eyes again.

There was another person . . . yes, his mother. She was not always there, for sometimes he would rouse and find himself alone. He would feel a moment of panic, then drift off again, exhausted. But she always came back. The panic that he had felt at first eventually gave way to sadness, loneliness. He did not like to waken without his mother. No child should have to do that. When *he* was grown, with a child to care for . . . he drifted off again.

It was good when his mother cradled him in her arms and spooned soup into his mouth. He felt warm and protected. Sometimes he felt that he was about to choke, and she would gently rub his throat to help him swallow.

He could not talk. It was too much of an effort. Even the strength to *think* related thoughts was beyond him. The light hurt his eyes, so he opened them mostly by dark. That seemed to prevent the blistering throb in his head to some extent. Of course, he did not reason it out. That was beyond his ability. He simply learned by experience that light hurt his eyes and made his head pound, so he kept them closed.

He could not move either. That seemed a goal beyond reach, an unattainable thing. Well, that was to be expected. An infant does not walk at first. In some strange way, he had become an infant, unable to do the things that even children do. He must rely on his mother. She fed him, cleaned him, cradled and crooned to him, and it was good. She talked to him too, and he wondered how long it would be before he would understand the babble of syllables that made no sense.

All of this was quite gradual. Some days were better than others. There came a day when he made a startling discovery. There were two kinds of light. One was bright and glaring, and came in through the place where his mother came and went. When that light was there, he kept his eyes tightly closed. The other was soft and yellow and flickering, and gave a good feeling that was warm and safe. Sometimes, after the flickering light, Mama would feed him and rock him, and it was good.

Very slowly, his thoughts began to take form. He could consider simple ideas for more than the space of a few heartbeats. He wondered whether his mother knew this. It was a great achievement when he managed to make a sound. He tried again and again, making only gurgling noises. Even then, he was able to accomplish it only in his mother's absence at first. When finally he was able to mumble to her, she was as pleased as he.

She had fed him, rocked him, and talked to him in the strange syllables that meant nothing to him. Maybe that was supposed to come later. She prepared to leave again.

He did not want her to do so, and he rallied all his strength to call out to her.

"M-m . . . Mama!"

She turned in astonishment and hurried back, taking him in her arms again, talking rapidly in sounds completely unfamiliar. He wanted to respond but did not know how. With great effort, he managed to speak again.

"Mama . . ."

She hugged him and rocked him, and warm tears ran down her face and splashed upon his. He was unable to speak again but succeeded in blinking his eyes a few times before the glare forced him to keep them closed.

"It is good!" She chortled. "You are growing stronger, my little one. Soon you can tell me who you are."

He understood not one word, but he knew that his mother was happy with his accomplishment. He would try again to please her. But not now. He was tired, so tired.

When he awoke again, it was dark except for the light of the flickering fire. Yes, *fire*. That was the name of the flickering yellow! Other things must have names too. He would have to learn them. *Learn.* Yes, he would come to know, to understand. He could not say the words that now came crowding into his memory, but he must keep trying. There was something urgent. What was it? A dreadful danger. But how could an infant know? . . .

The stress and excitement of returning knowledge was too great. He watched with fascination as his left hand began to twitch, then undulate. He had no control, and it was a horrible thing to watch. Something alive, a part of him, yet not. The tremor spread, involving his entire arm and leg on that side, and he cried out in terror. His mother was at his side in an instant, but he was barely aware of her approach before the full force of the seizure descended upon him, forcing him back into black oblivion.

He awoke to find her holding and rocking him, crooning soft words of comfort. He was completely exhausted and wanted to sleep. As soon as she realized that he was awake, the rhythm of her song changed. Her lullaby quieted him. She eased him back onto the pallet, and he slept.

He was spending an increasing time awake now. He was discovering things about his body. His left side remained useless. His mother moved the left arm and leg through their range of motion at least once every day and rubbed the wasted muscles. He could, with great effort, move the right arm, but the leg was tied, somehow, with sticks. It hurt to move it. She indicated that he was to wiggle his toes as much as he could.

He was beginning to understand more each day. The leg had been injured and would heal. The pain in his head too was from some sort of injury. There had been a bandage on it at first, but now it was open to the air. He managed to feel the area over his right eye with his fingers—an irregular crust, in the process of healing. That was odd. How does an infant become injured?

He also found that when his eyes were open, he saw two of everything. The doorway to their lodge, the fire, even his hand before his face appeared twice. With great effort, he could induce the muscles to coordinate and bring the two images together. When he was tired or drowsy, it was impossible.

There were many puzzling things too. He studied the lodge where they lived, a strange lodge. But why did he think, how could he know it was strange unless he had seen other lodges? For that matter, how had he known about light and dark, and how to close his eyes? And why could he not understand his mother when she talked to him? He was beginning to recognize some of her words by repetition and their use: *food, eat, sleep* . . .

These were not the same words he knew. And this raised the great question. How did he know *other* words for these things? He could not *say* them yet, but he knew that his mother's words were different from his, and how could this be? How could he have learned different words? And how, after all, could he know that different words *existed*? He had never seen anyone since his birth except his mother. Then how did he know that there *were* other people and different tongues?

This hit him with a tremendous impact. There must have been other things that had happened to him—before . . . before *what*? Before his birth? No, no, something . . . the injury? He did not know what had happened to him, but if this incident was not his birth, then *what was it*? And his mother . . . He tried to remember.

His mother was young and beautiful, and when she crooned lullabies, he had understood the words, at least part of them. Now he did not. His mother had grown old too, while he . . . how had he remained an infant? But wait—his mother . . . his mother was dead! He clearly remembered mourning for her. And how had he . . . He held his hand before him and stared at it, confused. This was clearly not the hand of an infant but of a man of middle age. How . . . how did he even *know* that? He was not an infant, and this woman . . . This was not his mother!

He longed to talk to her, to ask. But he could not speak beyond a few mumbling syllables, and he could not understand her tongue. Who was she, and how did he happen to be in her care?

And who was *he*? At first, it had not seemed important. He was himself, and it had not been necessary even to ponder his own existence. But now it had begun to be important, this thing of his identity.

There was very little about this world that was familiar. Had he crossed over? Was this some sort of transition into the world of the spirit? Was the old woman a guide to show the way? Surely not. This was a world with food and water and pain, heat and cold, but who is to say that the spirit-world does not have these things? If he were able to talk, he would ask the woman. If of course he knew her tongue.

In addition to these troubling questions, there were the dreams. He dreamed of traveling, by canoe, on foot, or horseback. There was someone with him . . . a woman? His mother perhaps. No, his wife. Had he had a wife? Yes, he thought so. Was this old woman his wife? No, no. Sometimes there were two women in his dreams. Stories . . . They told stories!

Then, unexpectedly, would come the terror of the dream. Repeatedly, he would see a threatening figure—a man, a big man, with an ax. The ax flew through the air toward him, and he would try to escape, but in vain.

He would awake, terrified, in a cold sweat, and the woman would come to hold him and comfort him. He would cling to her, his one link with reality, and she would croon to him again the strange words whose tone he understood without understanding their meaning.

There was something else too, the gnawing question that had begun to bother him since he had awakened. It was a sense of something not completed, a necessity or responsibility. And it was urgent. There was great danger to someone. Someone close to him, a woman? This woman, in the cave? Cave, yes, that was this strange lodge! But the woman? No, someone else. The woman in his dream? There were more than one. Who were they?

The entire puzzle bothered him more and more as the days passed. He must find a way to ask. He did not know how to identify the people in his dreams, but maybe this old woman would know. If he could only understand her. But how could he ask? He could not ask because he could not speak and did not even know who he might be.

The woman continued to talk to him, cheerful and encouraging, seemingly not bothered by his lack of understanding.

When the breakthrough came, both were amazed that this mode of communication had not occurred to them before. The woman had been gone for some time. When she returned with a pair of fat rabbits, he was beginning to be concerned. The day was warm, and he was thirsty. The thought had occurred to him that if she was unable to return, he would die here, alone, with no food or water. That of course made him thirstier, and by the time she returned, he had become quite anxious.

She dropped the rabbits just outside the entrance to the cave and stepped in to speak to him. She talked as she always did, as if he could understand, and it irritated him slightly. He must find a way . . .

"Mama . . . ," he said. It was the only sound with any meaning that they shared.

"Yes, Mama is here," she crooned in her own tongue. "I have brought rabbits, and we will eat. Let me fix them."

He understood not one word, and his frustration overcame him. Without realizing what he did, "I want water!" he signed with his one good hand, giving the flowing-water ripple of the fingers.

The woman stared at him. *"Aiee!"* she cried. "You know hand-signs?"

He stared, confused. Slowly and carefully, she repeated, using the signs only. "You have hand-signs? You asked for water!"

It was his turn to stare. "Yes!" he gestured excitedly. "Yes, we can *talk* with the signs!"

36

» » »

Even so, their communication was slow and halting. He did not have the use of his left hand, and many signs require both. In addition, he tired easily, and there was still the possibility of the seizures.

"How are you called?" he asked.

The woman smiled and shrugged. "I was called Pretty Flower," she signed. "That was long ago. Now, no one calls me anything."

"I have called you Mother."

"That is true. To most, I am a crazy old woman. How are you called?"

"I do not know. How is it I am here?"

She shrugged again. "Who knows? Someone tried to kill you, and you fell at my door."

"My leg is broken?"

"Yes. It has been two moons now. It is partly healed."

"My head?" He touched the wound, now well healed.

"An ax maybe. You have enemies?"

"I do not know. An ax?"

"Yes."

He was thinking. The dream . . . an ax, whirling, spinning. It was a frightening thought. "But who am I? How am I called?"

"I call you the Traveler," she stated.

"Traveler? I have been called that. How did you know?"

"I did not know. You were traveling on the trail above when someone tried to kill you."

"But I have been called so. I have been called other names too. I cannot remember." He pondered a moment, then continued. "It is strange, Mother, that you chose my name to call me by. Am I dead?"

The old woman threw back her head and cackled with laughter. "Maybe so. *I* am dead! We make a good pair, then."

"Was anyone with me?" he persisted.

"Before? I do not know. Two, maybe three people camped above the night you died. I could tell little . . . the rain . . ."

He nodded absently. This was gleaning little information. "What moon is it?" he asked.

"The Moon of Madness," she signed, and laughed again. "Is that not right?"

"I have been here two moons?"

"Yes, almost. It is almost winter."

He tried to think. There had been plans for the winter. Where had they been going? Where had *who* been going? He did not even know who had been with him. Why had they not stayed to help him?

He tried another question.

"What is your people, Mother?"

She touched the back of her left hand with her right fingertips to indicate *tribe* and made another sign that was familiar to him. It was that of a tribe from far to the west, the northern plains. Strange, that he knew such things but not his own name.

"What is yours?" Pretty Flower was asking.

"I do not know, Mother. I seem to know more than one . . . Could that be?"

"Maybe. Your mother's, your father's people—are they different?"

"Yes . . . maybe so. Traders . . ." He looked at her in amazement. "I am a trader!"

"Your people?"

"No, myself. *I* am a trader, but that was not my tribe. It was the tribe of my almost-father, my mother's husband."

The confusion revolved around the fact that the tribe of his stepfather had two signs in common use. They were designated both as the Traders and as the Mother-Tribe. Both understood this, but the conversation in hand-signs became confusing.

"So, who are your mother's people?" Flower asked.

"I cannot remember. One of the forest-peoples, maybe."

"Traveler, you are tiring. . . . It is best that you rest now. Sleep. I will wake you to eat."

He thought that he would be unable to rest, but he fell asleep, exhausted. When he awoke, there was a thrill of excitement. They could talk more, and maybe he could remember.

But it was slow, so slow. He could not sign and eat at the same time, and either was difficult with one hand. This provided some incentive to recover the use of his left hand. Already it was possible to move his fingers a little.

"Try your toes too, your leg," the woman advised as she moved the flaccid limbs for him. "Come on, you help too. You are no deader than I!"

She goaded him into motion, making him angry sometimes. At other times, she was very gentle.

"You have had children, Mother?" he asked.

"No. What would I do with children? You are enough nuisance to me! Have *you*?"

"No . . . no, I think not. But I cannot remember. . . ."

There it was, that urgent threatening thing that seemed to hang over him. Something he could not remember, could not quite grasp. Other things were coming back—his childhood, his travels . . .

"I was married!" he remembered suddenly. "Plum Leaf! Yes. She is of one of the southern forest people."

"She was with you?"

"Maybe. Someone . . . no, Plum Leaf . . ."

Again the questions came sweeping back over him. Why had his companions, whoever they might have been, abandoned him? Even if they thought him dead, they should have cared for his body. Unless of course they had been the ones who tried to kill him. There was something missing here.

But his memory was returning, little by little, usually his earlier memories first. He awoke one morning to an insistent drumming on the trunk of the dead cottonwood. *Woodpecker!* he thought.

He looked over to Pretty Flower, stirring sleepily. "Woodpecker!" he said in his own tongue, thickly and with great effort.

"What?" she signed.

"Woodpecker," he answered with the sign.

"Of course. The dead tree is full of bugs."

"No . . . yes, that is true, but that is my name!"

"Woodpecker?"

"Yes . . . my child-name. My mother was Owl Woman!"

"It is good, Woodpecker! You remember more and more."

Physically, it was very discouraging. They were now well into the Moon of Long Nights. Pretty Flower had spent long days carrying firewood and piling it near the cave. She had also killed a deer, and they should have ample supplies for winter. But the recovery of Traveler's physical abilities was hindered in many ways. By this time, it should be possible for him to stand and use his healing leg for partial weight bearing. This was not possible because of the paralysis. His unbroken left leg still had severe muscle loss. It would not stiffen in the extended position to hold his weight. The left hand and arm too were weak. And he dared not place his full weight on the newly healed right leg.

Worse, perhaps, were the problems with his eyes. When he was tired, he was still troubled with double vision. Even when his eyes were functioning well, the glare of daylight was still torture. The woman humored him, trying to adjust their waking hours to avoid the brightest part of the day.

Gradually, the double vision improved, but the sensitivity remained. Like Kookooskoos, the great owl, he had become a creature of the night.

There were other discouragements. He had been aware that his lips did not work quite properly. Especially on the right side, his mouth refused to close properly. He drooled constantly, oblivious to the draining saliva. When Pretty Flower was around, she would wipe his face, but when he was alone, he would forget. Spittle would drain from the corner of his mouth, soaking the front of his shirt. He had seen people with such an affliction and had pitied them. Now it was an embarrassment to him. There had never been much that he could not control until now.

There was one other shock before the river froze and Cold Maker settled in to stay for the winter. He had dragged himself out to the water's edge just before dusk, hoping to bathe without the help of the woman. The air was still, and in the calm back-eddy of the pool below the cave, he looked over and saw his reflection in the surface of the water.

He recoiled in shock. If he had been asked before that experience about his appearance, he could not have answered, for he did not know what he looked like. But whatever he imagined, it was not this. There was a livid scar from his hairline to his right brow, a crimson slash that glared against the normal color of his skin. The right side of his face drooped as if it were melting and running off. The skin of his cheek, his mouth, the corner of his eye

—all sagged downward, lending a grotesque appearance to his facial expression.

At first, he did not even recognize the face but then looked more closely. He was still staring in consternation when he saw the form of Pretty Flower standing over him, looking at his reflection with him, over his shoulder.

"What is it?" she asked.

He did not answer for a moment. "My . . . my hair!" he blurted. "It is white!"

It was true. Somehow, he had expected it to be as black as a crow's wing. Was it not like that when last he had seen it? Or was it white then? As white as driven snow.

"Come," Flower signed, "I will help you back to the cave."

Numb from the experience, he half crawled back, assisted by the woman. He was quiet and thoughtful that evening, and awake, listening to Pretty Flower's soft snores through the night. He was older than he thought, much older. When day began to lighten the eastern sky, he had new memories to share.

"Mother, I remember, now. My wife, Plum Leaf . . ."

"Yes?"

"She is dead. We mourned her, on the river."

"Ah, I am sorry, Traveler. And you had no children?"

"No. Only Star."

"Star?"

"Yes, my daughter, Pale Star."

"But you said . . ."

They stared at each other for a moment, the woman puzzled, Traveler horrified. The color drained from his face. Pale Star . . . the men who had followed them . . . the man with the ax—Winter Bear! That was the reason for the dream, the threatening danger that he had been unable to remember. The danger was not to himself but to the girl, who had become closer than kin.

"I must go to Star!" he signed frantically.

"Lie down!" Flower signed. "You cannot go anywhere.

You will only bring on another seizure. Now, tell me about this Pale Star."

The story poured out, with tears and anguish. There were a few things that he could not recall, but his memory of the threat to the girl was strong. With it came the anguish, the guilt and remorse. He had failed her. After buying her from her captors, he had betrayed her, allowed her to be caught by the sadistic Three Owls and his companion. At least, it was probable. It was possible that Star had escaped capture, but it seemed unlikely. And that had been three moons ago! Waves of guilt struck him again. By now, she could be dead! No, he could not accept that.

Pretty Flower absorbed the story and nodded thoughtfully. "Yes, but you cannot blame yourself, Traveler. You nearly died, defending Star."

"But I failed! Now I must find her!"

"Be sensible," she signed impatiently. "You cannot travel from here to the stream's edge there. I will have to go."

"But, Mother, it is too dangerous."

"Nonsense!" She flipped at her hair carelessly. "This old scalp is worth nothing. Everyone here knows me—a crazy old woman, harmless. I can find out more than you anyway."

He argued some more but had to admit that it was the best plan—the only plan unless he could speed his recovery. There was really no choice.

37
» » »

Pretty Flower started that very day. She gathered a few supplies and left plenty within his reach.

"I do not like to leave you," she told him, "but you will do well. Move your leg!"

He nodded impatiently. "Remember," he signed, "two men, a tall girl, very beautiful."

"Yes, yes, I remember."

She shouldered her pack. "I will be back . . . three, four sleeps. Maybe more. You wait"—she paused and laughed, "you can do nothing else!"

She turned away, then back for one last bit of advice. "No one will come here," she stated, "but if they do, you act a little crazy. No one harms a person with a crazy spirit."

And then she was gone. The next few days were the most difficult of his life. He had never been alone for any length of time. True, he had enjoyed periods of solitude, alone with his own private thoughts. But that was by choice. Now his private thoughts were not pleasant. They were confused, often threatening, and he had no choice. He could do nothing but wait.

Since his entire life had been spent in active communication with a wide variety of people, he was now doubly at a loss. Not only was he unable to speak, beyond slurred monosyllables, but there was no one to speak to.

It was two days before he settled down to a resigned waiting. He tried constantly to talk, speaking to himself aloud, answering himself, working hard to improve the sounds that spilled from his distorted lips. He became hoarse from using neglected vocal structures, waited a day, and tried again.

His frustration was actually beneficial. It forced him to move, to drag himself around the cave and to the water's edge. His strength was growing, day by day. He did not dare yet to place his full weight on his injured leg. He was able, however, to draw himself to a standing position, leaning against the rock of the cliff. It took all his will-power and most of his strength to do so. When he stood, half sitting on a protrusion of the stony surface, it was a magnificent accomplishment. The night breeze ruffled his hair, and though he shivered from its chill, it was good. Yes, he *would* walk again. He would somehow find a way to help Pale Star. He had promised, had assured her that he would take her home to her people on the plains. This memory was becoming a singleness of purpose, a driving force that was all-important.

Most of his activity was at night because the light still hurt his eyes. He was beginning to see himself as a night creature, brother to the owl and the bobcat. He could understand their preference for the night. It was pleasant, the concealing darkness. It was also pleasant to curl up in the warm robes during the painfully bright time of the day. Again, the thought of the bobcat in its lodge in a cleft of the rock, or Kookooskoos in his hollow tree. Yes, he was like them, by day and by night, in his own cleft of the rock.

His thoughts became more strange as his solitude extended day by day. It was easy to believe sometimes that he was the only human on earth. Or, more likely, that he was for some reason or other suspended between worlds, between Earth and the spirit-world. Surely, he had not crossed over yet. No, of course not. He still ate and drank. And yes, there had been the old woman. Unless she too was caught between.

He thought more about that. Since his injury, he had seen or heard no one. It was a frightening thought. If true, though, why was he not allowed to cross over? He must be dead from the ax wound but kept here for some purpose. What purpose could it be? He pondered that at length before the answer came to him. Of course! He must help Pale Star. That was his reason for being. And the crazy old woman, who was also dead, was kept between with him to help him!

He felt better having come to that solution. He was still restless and impatient but felt that he understood. It made the waiting a little easier.

On the third evening—or maybe the fourth, he was not sure—he awoke to find a new chill in the air. It was overcast and growing dark earlier than usual. The odd blue-gray color of the low-hanging clouds appeared ominous and told of coming snow. He built up his fire. It was good that it had not gone out entirely. He wondered if he could rekindle a fire, his left hand virtually useless.

By dark, plump flakes of snow were falling from the blackness of the sky. Traveler was concerned, both for himself and for the old woman. Would she be able to find shelter? And did it matter if, as she had said, she was already dead anyway?

That brought him back to the puzzle of his own status. But he was beginning to have more confidence, a sense of purpose. There *was* a purpose to all this. He was still alive, or perhaps caught in between worlds, for a reason. His purpose for being was to save Star. He had promised, and he had failed her. Now he must redeem that failure by helping her. That was the reason for his continued existence.

Idly, he wondered . . . if he and the old woman were dead and caught between worlds, could they be seen by ordinary mortals? They could of course see each other, but would they be invisible to others? Maybe they had the power to *become* invisible, like the Old Man of the Shadows in Pale Star's stories. He tried it, concentrating as hard as he could to achieve invisibility, but nothing happened except that it made his head ache. But, he wondered, if one is invisible, can he see himself? He held up his good hand and studied it. No, there was no suggestion of transparency. Well, he might already be invisible to mortals but seen by himself and Pretty Flower. They seemed to have a similar existence. He would not know for sure until he encountered other persons and was able to watch their reactions.

He watched the snow fall, the flakes illuminated briefly for an instant as they sifted past the doorway and the light from the fire. Then they fell soundlessly, to add to the growing depth on the path outside. Well, that would make the cave easier to warm.

Another thought occurred to him. The old woman had instructed him how to behave if anyone came. Ah, he *could* be seen, then, at least part of the time. It would be interesting. . . .

His thoughts returned to Star and her stories. She was good, maybe the best storyteller he had ever known. He knew that he was good, taught by his almost-father, Turtle. Would he be able to tell stories again, he wondered? If he could regain his ability to speak, what tales he could tell. And if in addition he could make himself invisible— ah, what a show that would be! He would do it only after dark. That would lend to the mystery. Maybe . . . was that why the Old Man had forbidden stories of himself until after dark? He slipped off into fantasy again.

After a while he decided to try to tell stories. It was a long time until daylight when it would be time to roll in the robes and sleep again, so he would try it. He tried to ignore the strange gurgling noises that came from his lips, saliva dribbling. He could see little progress but recalled that two moons ago he could make no sounds at all.

He became tired of speaking and turned to exercising

his flaccid arm and leg. He had neglected that since the woman had gone. She had pushed him to move the lifeless limbs, to keep them moving, and he had not continued to do so. Well, he would now. Maybe she would not scold him too much if he did well until she returned.

When dawn came, the snow had stopped. The brilliance of the sun on the sparkling world of snow and ice was torture to his eyes. The thin film of ice along the banks of the stream reflected Sun's rays. He retreated into the cave and covered his head against the brilliance.

He did not know how long he slept before he was awakened by the sound. It was a familiar sound, a squeak of footsteps in new snow. Anxiously, he watched the cave opening, his eyes slitted against the glare. The opening darkened, and he sighed with relief to see that the figure stooping to enter was Pretty Flower.

The old woman dropped her pack, nodded to him, and tossed sticks on the fire to warm her hands. Neither of them spoke or signed for a moment. He was anxiously awaiting her story, but beyond a grunt and a nod, she barely acknowledged his presence.

Finally, he could stand it no longer. *"Ah-koh!"* he said aloud, accompanying the exclamation with the hand-sign for question, *"what?"*

She roused herself from the fire and turned to him. "I have talked to some who have seen a young woman," Flower signed. "Tall, pretty . . . she was with two men, as you say. One big, like a bear . . ."

"Go on, go on," he urged impatiently. "She was all right?"

Pretty Flower shook her head sadly. "The woman was alive then . . . it was three moons ago, Traveler . . . much can happen."

"I know. But she *is* alive!"

"Yes. It was said this woman seemed to be a slave-wife to one of the men, maybe both. But she carried herself with pride."

"Ah, yes. That is Pale Star."

"But, Traveler, there is more. These men are known here . . . bad men. The one, Three Owls, is a crazy . . . not crazy like you and me, but dangerous. He would kill for a scalp, but worse! Just for the fun."

Traveler's heart sank. "I must go to her."

She gestured derisively. "You cannot go anywhere! Besides, winter comes. But look, there is more. The other man, Bear, is his kinsman. He is stupid, but safer to be with."

She paused, and then broke into a cackling laugh. "Bear is safer, but he is the one who killed you! Anyway, I learned more. They were going to *Mishi-ghan.* There is a town of the Fran-cois there, a new town, with warriors. It is maybe six sleeps from here."

"I have heard of it." He nodded. "Why do they go there?"

She shrugged. "Who knows? There is trade in scalps . . . many people to steal from. Maybe he will sell the woman there. There are many men . . ."

Traveler's heart cried out against the thought, denying what he must admit was quite likely. "Mother," he signed, "I will do as you say. I must stay for the winter. But then I will go to her."

She laughed contemptuously. "How? You cannot walk!"

"I *will* walk," he signed positively. "When spring comes, I go to Mishi-ghan!"

38

Sometimes it seemed that the winter would never end. Each time the sky would clear, it was briefly and in vain. The weak and watery yellow of Sun's torch would barely begin to warm the frozen world before Cold Maker came roaring back, howling in rage, to attack again. In the course of the battle, Sun had been pushed far to the south.

They moved around very little during the Moon of Snows and the Moon of Hunger. There was no reason to be outside when Cold Maker was abroad. Their food supply was in the cave. The Moon of Hunger, even, was not much of a threat. Pretty Flower, through many winters, had reached a conclusion. The Moon of Hunger was named so for people who did not plan for it. She had come close enough to death from starvation that she had become cautious and thrifty. It was not that she planned to eat well but that she planned for survival. A woman alone with less insight and less tenacity would have starved long ago.

Traveler still avoided the brightness of day. The glare of light on a world of snow was still a torment to his senses. It was uncomfortable to his eyes and caused his head to ache long afterward. Consequently, he had completely adopted the nocturnal habits of the night creatures.

He could feel his strength returning. During every waking moment, he was constantly flexing his muscles, moving fingers and toes. With his right hand he would lift the limp left arm, placing it in positions that would force him to attempt its use. There was little sensation in the hand but some motion, very slight at first. The left leg also was slow to obey his commands. It was discouraging. When he discovered how to use the weight of his crippled left leg to swing it into a locked position of extension, it was his greatest triumph. He could walk! It was a strange gait, of course. A step forward on his right leg, the bone newly healed and still weak, then swing the left leg by a toss of the hip, let the heel strike the ground to straighten the knee to a locked position, and stand on that leg to step forward again.

He fell often at first. The flaccid left leg did not want to become completely straight, and he could not always tell if it was solidly braced to bear his weight. Impatiently he would thrust the knee into alignment with his one good hand and shift his weight to it. The cave was so small that such exercise was difficult too, a step or two, turn and back. The old woman complained, at both his antics and his nocturnal habits.

"You will fall into the fire while I am gone!" she predicted. "You will lie there and burn!"

He laughed at her. "No, Mother, I could roll out of the fire. You are not gone much anyway."

"I have to get away from you sometimes," she fretted. "Moving around all night, grunting and making those noises. Why not sleep at night?"

"The light hurts my eyes. Maybe you should sleep by day!"

She threw up her hands in resignation. A sort of truce evolved in which there was compromise. Each refrained as much as possible from disturbing the other's sleeptime. Pretty Flower spent part of the day in sleep to adjust to his nocturnal ways, but not without complaint.

"You want me to become a bat or an owl!"

"Why not? *I* have!"

Her other complaint, about his "noises," was a worry for him too. He was trying to learn to speak again. It was very difficult. He would attempt a simple word, but what came out of his mouth was entirely different. The most frustrating thing about it was that the woman could be of no help. To her, nearly all of his sounds were gibberish. It would be necessary for him to learn her tongue so that she could tell if he spoke it correctly.

This led to long sessions in the cave during long winter nights when the snow fell softly outside. Very slowly, he began to have an understanding of Pretty Flower's language. It was quite helpful, though exhausting. He would struggle to make a sound, and she would smile at his success or sometimes laugh at his failure. But prior to that, he had had almost no way to tell whether the idea that came out of his mouth with the word was as he intended.

He began to tell stories to her, using hand-signs as well as spoken words. That was helpful too as the strength of his vocal cords returned and the sounds became more normal. The old woman was delighted with the stories. It had been most of a lifetime since she had heard stories. She cackled with laughter over the Creation story of Star's people and the fat woman who became stuck in the log. He told her of Bobcat and the many theories about his missing tail.

Sometimes he would have a bad night. "Your words make no sense, Traveler. Rest now, and you can tell me tomorrow."

That was always a frustration, but it too was helpful. He found that when he was tired or did not feel well, he made more mistakes. Rest and well-being improved his skills. That was good to know.

Eventually, Sun started a new thrust, a war party into Cold Maker's hunting ground. The days became longer, the breezes warmer. There came a day that marked a change. Traveler awoke as shadows lengthened to welcome the night to find a soft noise along the cliff face and in the woods above. It was the drip of melting snow and ice, falling gently from trees, bushes, and rocks to plop into the layers of snow on the ground. The buds on the maples were already swelling, and the twigs of the willows were becoming yellowish in the sunlight. It was the Moon of Awakening.

With the Moon of Awakening came the restlessness that he had always felt at this season. He watched the geese on their northward trek, envying their apparent ease of motion. This season, the urgency was infinitely stronger. He must go to help Pale Star. The snow had barely started to melt when he began to push for departure.

"You could not even climb the path to the top of the cliff!" Pretty Flower reminded him.

"I *could*!" he insisted. "Look, I stand and walk!" He took a step or two on the level strip in front of the cave. "See?"

"No, no, Traveler. Not only you. *I* would not attempt that climb. The path is slippery with melting snow. I have been here for many Awakenings, and I know. You have never climbed it before."

It was true, and when he thought about it, he had to admit it. But that seemed only to make the frustration worse. He fretted and brooded, and became intolerable to be with.

"Traveler, go out and walk up and down the path along the river," Flower said one night when he had become particularly unpleasant. "It is moonlight, so you can see a little. It will help your strength to walk."

Angrily, he lurched out into the night, dragging the left leg. For some time he walked up and down the snowy trail, perhaps a stone's throw in either direction. Once, he slipped and fell on an icy spot.

By the time the eastern sky began to pale with the gray of the false dawn, he was exhausted. He would sleep well that day as he sought his burrow with the other night creatures. It had been hard work, but it had allowed him to see what he could do. He began to see his infirmities more realistically. The old woman was right. It would be a slow, hard journey. Some six sleeps, Flower had said. But with the handicap that he faced, it would be at least twice that, maybe fifteen sleeps, half a moon or more.

For the first time, he began to wonder what he would do when he arrived at this Mishi-ghan. Always before, there had been no question. Once he had reached his destination, he could handle nearly any eventuality. But now, even as he drifted into an exhausted sleep, his muscles were twitching and crying out over the abuse they had suffered. He still had a long way to go toward recovery. At least, he told himself, the use of his voice was coming along well.

He awoke that evening, stiff and sore. It was sheer torture, but he knew that he must spend more time exercising on the trail along the stream. It was warmer tonight.

"I go to walk," he told the woman.

She nodded, noncommittally. "But eat first," she ordered.

Impatiently, he wolfed down the stew she had prepared and lurched out the doorway. Dusk had just descended, and the great hunting owl sounded his hollow cry from downriver.

"Good hunting to you, Kookooskoos," Traveler said aloud as he began his painful march up and down the trail.

In three or four nights, he could begin to see a more rapid change. His muscles no longer cried out in agony. If he pushed himself too hard, it still made his head throb, but he was learning his limits. Flower had been clever to goad him into anger and force him to be realistic. He smiled to himself at the realization. Someday, maybe, he would tell her that he knew.

In another few days, his strength was gaining rapidly. He still had a severe limitation of the left leg. It refused to lift properly, and the foot dragged at each step, but he no longer had to lock the knee consciously. It still required special effort, but it happened without the need to stop and think about it. It had become a normal pattern, though it would appear strange to those fortunate enough to walk normally.

This lopsided gait, swinging and dragging, would still be far slower than his old mode of travel, perhaps half the speed, but it would get him there, given time.

That was his concern now. Did Pale Star have time? He refused even to consider the possibility that she might not be alive. What had happened to her since he last saw her might be worse, however. It had been six moons now, nearly seven. Pretty Flower's information that the girl had been seen in the company of the two renegades and seemed to be a slave-wife—*aiee,* the hurt. He must go to her. He was certain that he could and *would* kill her tormentors with his one good hand if he must. Grimly, he struggled on, dragging himself along the dark stony trail.

There came a night, however, when he climbed to the top of the bluff. He had planned it for several days. The moon was past full but would be rising in time to give him some light—not the glare of sunlight, which would have made his head ache, but the soft light that would let him see. He knew where the path began. It followed a rift in the rock. He sat and rested a little while, then began the climb. Pretty Flower would be sleeping by now.

It was harder than he had thought. He must make every move with the right leg and drag the left to a secure position before tightening the knee to attempt the next step. Halfway up, he became exhausted and frightened, and paused to wait until he was calmer.

When he reached the top, he was disoriented at first but managed to find the campsite by the spring. The smell of smoke as he approached told him that someone camped there. He skirted around the area, uncertain why. Several heavily bundled figures lay on the ground near the smoldering fire. There was a man on watch, leaning against a tree. Traveler observed him a little while and melted into the forest again.

He was back at the cave before the sun rose. Pretty Flower was stirring sleepily.

"I am ready," he told her.

"Ready for what?" she grumbled.

"To go to Mishi-ghan. I have been to the top and back."

She looked at him in astonishment. "Up the cliff?"

"Yes."

"It is good. When shall we go?"

"You?"

"Of course!" she scolded. "Someone will have to look after you! You are not able to take care of yourself!"

39

» » »

They traveled at night and holed up in the brush during the day. Pretty Flower complained, but that had become her way. She complained about the trail, the weather, the slowness of their progress, and night travel.

It was slow, of course. Traveler, with his lifetime of experience on the trail, was constantly frustrated by their rate of travel. Dawn would come, and they had covered so little distance that he would fret.

"Then you must do better tomorrow," the old woman would say sarcastically.

It was some time before he realized that she was still goading him to keep him moving, to keep his anger and frustration working for him. It was doubtful that she fully realized it herself. They were developing a strange relationship, supportive to both, by constant complaint and criticism.

When they neared the French fort, she began to make plans. "You will stay behind," she said, "while I go to find out, to learn about your Star."

"No! I will go!" he insisted.

"Traveler, you must think about this. One does not crawl into a bear's den without knowing whether the bear is at home."

It was true. He had worried that his sudden appearance might become a danger to Pale Star. In addition, he had been constantly concerned about his appearance. It had been such a shock when he looked over the bank into the water. His distorted face, sagging left arm, the snow-white hair—he would never have recognized himself. He was quite self-conscious about it and dreaded the reactions of others. He may have been unaware that this was part of his reason for becoming a creature of the night. His eyes might adjust to the daylight in time, but time would not change his grotesque appearance. Time would make that only worse. He was increasingly reluctant to let anyone see him, and the protection of darkness helped to remove that threat. As for Star, there was no way, he decided, that she could be allowed to recognize him. His pride would not permit that this young woman who had been closer than a daughter would see him like this.

No, he had decided as they neared the region of the fort, he would remain unseen. Invisible, as it were. He had begun to think of himself as nearly immortal now, an avenging spirit. Yes, an invisible creature of the night, unseen but seeing all. When he had learned what was needed, with the help of Pretty Flower, he would wait until the proper moment and then strike down the renegades to free Pale Star.

An ax—yes, the silent flight of a thrown ax, whirling out of the darkness to complete the vengeance that was due. It was appropriate that the weapon that had been used to strike him down would be the instrument of revenge. One at a time, out of the darkness . . . He relived the scene in his mind many times and relished it.

After that—well, he did not know. A plan would develop, later. First, Star must be freed. He did want to carry out his promise to take her to her people, but he would not think about that yet. The thing of primary importance was the destruction of Star's tormentors. He was reluctant to approach the matter of how he could keep his promise, restore her to her home, and at the same time remain invisible. Later, he would plan.

Pretty Flower left him there, hidden in a brushy cleft

in the rocks, and continued on toward the fort. He managed to sleep some during that day but mostly in short spells separated by periods of anxiety and worry.

When evening came and the other night creatures began to stir, he became even more restless. He did not know when to expect the woman's return. What if something had happened to her and she *never* returned? Alarmed at the thought, he fed the little fire they had built after daylight, carefully choosing only dry sticks that would not produce much smoke. That was one good thing about the woodlands—a fire, or a person, could not be seen from very far. He thought again of Flower's advice in case of discovery. He could pretend to be crazy easily enough.

But if she never returned, what then? He had only a sketchy idea of the direction of the French emplacement. If he was forced to find it himself, would he be able to learn what he must? His speech was continuing to improve, and surely he could use the tongues of this region, near his own nation. He wondered whether Pretty Flower would have difficulty communicating here. Of course, she had rarely talked to anyone until he dropped into her life from the cliff. He now realized that this may have been part of their problem initially—Flower's long-disused speech skills. She was doing much better now. She must have used many tongues to survive alone all the way from the western plain.

Idly, he wondered about her story. She had been quite vague about it, mentioning only that she had lived alone since leaving her people many seasons before. In his own confused condition, it had not occurred to him until now to wonder why it had been so. Some people became reclusive by choice, some were outcasts. . . .

The night passed and most of the next day before he heard someone's approach. He quickly concealed himself in the bushes, watching the path that they had entered by, a path scarcely worthy of the name. The bushes parted, and he was relieved to see the familiar form of

Pretty Flower. Nothing had changed about her, although she looked tired. He rose to greet her by the fire.

"How is it?" he asked, half fearful of the answer.

She dropped her pack, and turned to him. "It is good," she stated. "The woman is alive. She is married."

"But that is *not* good! We heard that she was a slave-wife of—"

"No, no, Traveler," she said wearily. "Star is not with them."

"Then who . . . what . . . ?" he demanded impatiently.

"I am trying to tell you. Let me do so. Then I must rest. I have had little sleep."

"I am sorry, Mother. Go on." It was all he could do to remain calm and listen.

"I came near the Fran-cois town and began to ask," she began. "Everyone knew the name of Pale Star. She came, with the one man—"

"*One* man?" he interrupted.

"Yes. Let me tell. It is said that he killed his kinsman."

"But which—"

She held up a hand for silence. "Three Owls killed the other, before they arrived here. Scalped him. His own kinsman!"

She shook her head and clucked her tongue disapprovingly while Traveler waited impatiently.

"How is this known?" he blurted finally.

"She told it, after . . . Oh, *she* killed the other one!" Flower chuckled with delight. "The man, Three Owls, fought with another man who tried to help Star. A scout for the Fran-cois . . . half-breed, called Hunting Hawk."

"Wait, Mother, who was killed?"

"Three Owls, the man you seek. He was winning the fight, and Pale Star came up behind and killed him."

"But what of this other . . . Hunting Hawk?"

"Oh, she married him."

Traveler was having difficulty absorbing all of this. "But, so soon? . . ."

"It is not soon, Traveler," Flower said irritably. "This all happened last autumn . . . six, seven moons ago."

"But I . . ." He could not realize that Star would ignore him in her plans, in her life. He was sure that she too felt much like a daughter to him, as he felt like a father to her. And he had promised to take her home. She should not have . . .

"She heard of your death, Traveler," Flower was saying gently.

"You *talked* to her?" he asked anxiously.

"No, no, but I saw her. A beautiful woman, with the look of the eagle about her. Now, let me get some rest, and then we will go to see her. She will be pleased that you are alive."

"No!" he cried in alarm. "I am not . . . I cannot . . ."

"What? We come all this way, and you do not want to see her?" she almost shouted at him.

Pretty Flower was exhausted, and this was beyond her comprehension. "Why did you come?" she yelled in anger.

"I . . . I am sorry, Mother. I had to know, but I . . . She must not see me, like this."

"Good. Then let me rest, and we start home." She turned to seek her sleeping robe.

"But I want to see her," he protested.

Flower had started to lie down but almost bounded up to stand, furious, hands on hips. There was fury in her face. "You said—" she began.

"No! I want to see her. I do not want her to see me."

"Aiee!" she shouted. "You *are* crazy! I should have taken your scalp and pushed you into the river when I found you!"

She turned her back to him, wrapped herself in her robe, and lay down near the fire, her face away from him.

He stood, saying nothing. He realized that he was on thin ice and did not wish to exacerbate the situation further.

Then she rolled to her back and spoke again, more quietly. "Let me sleep now. We will talk, later."

"It is good," he answered eagerly. "Mother, one thing . . . Do you know how Star killed Three Owls?"

"I *told* you," she snapped irritably.

"No, I mean . . . what weapon?" He could not have told why that was important, but it was an answer that he needed.

"Oh," she said, chuckling. "I did not say? With an ax!" She turned away again.

Traveler smiled to himself. It was a lopsided smile, but he did not have much to smile about anyway. But now he understood why it had been important for him to know. An ax. He had spent all these moons planning how he would wreak vengeance for Pale Star. Now, in a strange and illogical way, *she* had carried out vengeance for *him*.

He wondered whether she knew.

40

That spring and summer, there came to be tales of a half-human creature who inhabited the area around the French fort of Mishi-ghan. It was an ethereal thing, standing on two legs, but moving with an odd gait, like no other creature anyone knew of. Some tried to track it but soon lost the trail. It seemed to drag something behind it, which some said was a deliberate attempt to brush out its tracks even as it lurched along. This seemed unlikely, though the half-breed scout Brulé, known to the natives as Hunting Hawk, had strong opinions about it.

Hawk had probably seen it more than anyone, for reasons even he did not understand. His wife had seen it too. They agreed that it appeared much like the figure of a man. Star had watched it in the moonlight once as it crossed a clearing. A lurch forward, like a long step, and then a dragging motion with the other foot or leg or whatever—a tail perhaps. Hawk, one of the finest trackers in the territory, was sure it was human, or nearly so. He had tracked it far enough on two occasions to convince himself that it wore moccasins, even though the moccasin tracks were always nearly obliterated by the dragging appendage.

It had never been seen except at night. Usually it was around the perimeter of a camp or a lodge, or near the fort itself. It would stand in the shadows and always appeared to be watching. It had loose flowing white hair and either a polyglot assortment of ill-fitting garments or a very unusual shape with fluttering projections and swinging appendages.

It appeared harmless, though several people had been quite frightened when they encountered it unexpectedly in the woods. It seemed uninterested in *doing* anything, beyond watching. It became known as the Watcher. No one ever tried to interfere with its movements because it seemed to have such strange medicine. Some said it was a ghost, but Hunting Hawk, who had tracked it, was inclined to think that most ghosts do not leave tracks. At first, since it seemed attracted to Hawk and his wife, there were those who thought that it might be the ghost of Three Owls, the man killed by Pale Star to save her husband. This helped to convince people to let it alone, for the evil in *that* ghost might be considerable.

In time, Hawk and Pale Star refrained from telling others that they still saw the Watcher frequently, and the stories quieted somewhat. But they both knew it was still there. It was attracted to them, but since it was not aggressive and seemed harmless, why not let it be? Pale Star was sure that her uncle back on the plains would have treated it in this way. And this uncle, Looks Far, was a famous holy man of her people, wise beyond all.

Consequently, though many had seen the Watcher and many more had heard the tales of its appearance, no one interfered with it. It was accepted in the area as something that defied explanation, but is that not true of many things?

There had been one odd encounter, which Pale Star often pondered in later days. She had been going to the shore for water. It was well after dark, but she wished to set some dried corn to soak. It was not really necessary, but she always felt that soaking made the grains more plump and tender, and improved the flavor of the stew.

The moon lacked a few nights before it would be full, but there was enough light to find her way. The path was familiar, and it was only a little way, less than a bow shot.

It was not that she *saw* anything at first but *felt* a presence. That in itself was odd because there were many people in the area. The lodge that she and Hawk shared was one of a hundred or more scattered between the walls of the fort and the lake shore. She knew most of these people. Since the death of Three Owls, there was no one she really feared. Everyone knew her, of course, after the spectacular fight in which she had been able to kill her tormentor and save the life of Hunting Hawk. He had since become her husband, and the community had approved. Everyone had been, and still was, friendly toward her.

But tonight there was a strange feeling, a sense that someone was out there in the darkness, someone, or some thing, whose spirit reached out to her. It was not a threatening spirit, and she felt no fear. This had been about the time of the first rumors of the night-creature who watched. It had not even been called the Watcher yet.

Star felt confident that there was no threat there on the familiar path to the lake shore. She moved ahead, rounding a giant old tree at a turn of the path when she saw it. It was hardly an arm's length away, face-to-face. She was unsure of the creature's nature, then or later, though she realized afterward that it must have been what others were calling the Watcher. She was startled but felt little fear, only curiosity. She was looking directly into the creature's eyes and felt that it was more alarmed than she. The thing was very nearly human in shape, although somewhat stooped and twisted. The eyes too were twisted somehow, one distorted in shape by the overhanging bulge of the brow. Most unsettling, however, was the haunting quality of the eyes, dark and deepset in the distorted half-human face. Their gaze reached out to her in a searching, yearning way. She could feel the spirit reach-

ing out to her, but the feeling was mingled with alarm—
and regret, regret at having disturbed her.

Then a shifting of the scattered clouds in the spring sky
hid the moon for a moment, and the thing was gone. She
continued on her way and later discussed the occurrence
with her husband.

"And you were not afraid?" he asked.

"No," Star answered, a bit puzzled. "There seemed no
need for fear. It means us no harm."

Hawk shrugged. "Maybe you imagined it. The moonlight and shadows—"

"No!" she snapped. "I know what I saw."

"Yes . . . I meant only . . . Star, you are different.
You see things that are not there. No, that is not it.
Things that are not seen by others. Maybe this is a thing
of the spirit, like the Old Man of your people in the
stories you tell."

Her anger calmed. "Maybe," she agreed. "But I *did*
see it, and I knew how it felt."

Traveler and Pretty Flower had argued over what
should be done next after they arrived at the fort. With
the somewhat bizarre sense of responsibility that he still
felt toward the girl, he insisted on remaining in the area.
Flower would have been happy to go home to her cave,
but a new dimension had been added to her life. It was
more than twenty years since anyone had relied on her,
since she had felt useful and needed. The crow had
needed her for a while, but when it learned to fly, she
had felt abandoned, useless.

The coming of the desperately injured man had
changed her life. Someone needed her, could not have
survived without her. It was easy for her to assume, then,
that this was meant to be, that for this purpose she had
been spared from death on the prairie. It gave her a warm
feeling, this mothering role. She had never been a mother,
did not know how it might feel, but her maternal instincts had come to the fore, and she had been pleased to

help the helpless one who had been thrust so rudely into her life.

So when Traveler had stated his intention to stay in the area and look after the well-being of Pale Star, she reacted appropriately.

"I must stay here," he said. "I must know that her husband treats her well and that she is happy."

Pretty Flower threw up her hands in mock consternation. "Ah, that I should be reduced to this," she complained. "Looking after a helpless madman who wants to look after someone else, but who must not know of it."

Traveler bristled. "I am not helpless, Mother. I came all this way. Go back to your cave! It is no matter to me."

"And let you die? You deserve it, and are probably dead already but too stupid to fall down. No, I will not be blamed for that!"

He continued to protest, she to complain, even while they made arrangements to stay. Pretty Flower found a hidden cleft in a rocky glen off the beaten paths that crisscrossed the area near the fort. By moving a few stones and piling poles and brush for a roof and one side, she created a rude shelter. A strategically located skin or two to shed the weather, and it would furnish shelter from the elements.

"It is a poor thing, compared to my cave," she complained.

"Then go on back to your cave," he retorted.

"And who would look after you?"

Gradually, the two misfits established a sort of routine. By day, Traveler slept while the old woman shuffled around the fort, listening and watching. She sometimes helped with someone's butchering or tanning, and would be given some meat, corn, or dried pumpkin in return. Sometimes someone would give her food or a castoff robe or garment, out of pity. She had long since lost the pride it would take to refuse. And she listened. People would gossip in the presence of a mumbling half-crazy old woman, saying things that they would ordinarily not share before a stranger. She was a nonperson, invisible almost.

She saw Pale Star often and once even helped the young woman dress an elk skin. Flower was uneasy about that and pretended to understand less than she actually did. Star was kind to her and gave her some elk meat and pemmican.

"Do you have a good man?" Flower ventured to ask in hand-signs so that she might answer Traveler's questions when she returned to the hut.

Star laughed, her voice like silvery water in a prairie stream. "Of course, Mother, but I will not share him!"

Both women laughed, and Flower shrugged in dejection as if that had been her intent. "It does no harm to try!" she signed.

She could have carried on a conversation aloud but had decided to avoid it. She might hear more if people thought she could not understand.

"I like your Star," she told Traveler that evening.

He would rise before dark, they would talk a little, and Flower would tell him anything she had learned. Then Traveler would go and prowl with the night-creatures while she slept. At dawn he would return.

In his identity as the Watcher, he was able to learn much. His hearing had always been acute, and it seemed not to have suffered from his dreadful injury. Or maybe he *was* supernatural, immortal, and possessed of acute senses. No matter. He learned to stand perfectly still for long periods of time, watching, listening. He found that if he remained motionless, as a rabbit freezes, he was seldom noticed. This strengthened his suspicion that he had the gift of invisibility.

Sometimes he saw Star but was careful not to approach too closely. There was the occasion, of course, when he had encountered her on the trail, face-to-face. They were quite close, and for a moment he thought Star had recognized him. Then a shifting cloud allowed him to melt into the darkness of the trees. He was more careful after that.

He loved to roam around the outskirts of the story-fires because he missed that world, now a part of his past. There were good storytellers here, and sometimes he was able to listen to Star's stories. He would shed tears in the darkness as she skillfully brought forth the stories he knew so well—her Creation story, Bobcat and his tail, why Fox is red. He remembered them all.

Once he saw her match wits with a medicine man of the Fran-cois. The man was a good storyteller, he had to admit. Traveler had begun to understand some of the French tongue, which was in common use by the natives also. He was able to follow the story fairly well. It was a Creation story about a beautiful place with First Man and First Woman when the animals still talked. At least, the real-snake did. The snake told the woman to eat something, Traveler was unsure what. But she did it and gave some to the man. This made a great father-spirit very angry. The man blamed the woman, and she blamed the real snake, so the father-spirit drove them all out into the world. It was very good, and the audience loved it.

Then Pale Star rose. She used both the previous story-teller's tongue (ah, she had learned that already) and hand-signs as he had taught her.

"It is good, Uncle," she began respectfully. "I especially liked the part about the real-snake."

The holy man smiled, pleased.

"I am glad, my child. You are blessed."

"Now, here is the story of my people," Star began. "In long-ago times, they lived inside the earth where everything was dark and cold. Then Old Man sat astride a hollow cottonwood log and tapped on it with a drumstick. First Man and First Woman crawled through, and then some others, and—"

The holy man sat staring at her in open-mouthed astonishment. "Stop! This is blasphemy! Heresy!"

He jumped around, so excited that the silver chain with its dangling emblem sparkled and reflected the fire-light.

Traveler was puzzled. He did not know what these words meant. It was apparent that the Fran-cois story-teller was quite angry at Pale Star. But why? He had finished his turn at the stories. Now it was time for Star to tell hers. To interrupt was very impolite.

Pale Star drew herself proudly to her full height, made taller by her queenly confidence. The dark eyes blazed, but her voice was strong and calm. "You are very rude," she said. "We have listened to your story, and now you refuse to listen to mine. I am going home."

She swept her blanket-robe around her in a sweeping gesture and turned on her heel. There was a murmur in the crowd, and people began to rise and follow her.

"Wait! Wait!" called the Fran-cois medicine man. "Come back! I will tell you more."

But the audience was leaving. From his place in the darkness of the trees, Traveler chuckled with pride. Pale Star had beaten the man at his own game. And in his own tongue.

41

》 》 》

Pretty Flower was first to encounter the information that something was about to happen. There were rumors about an exploration to the west. Each time the rumor was repeated, the direction, destination, and goals of the venture were different. A trek to the northwest, to explore more of the chain of giant lakes, like the one on which the fort was located. No, straight west, across the Missi-sippi, to see what lay beyond. Ridiculous, said another, it is a war party, to strike at the Yen-glees to the south.

There was even more disagreement among the rumormongers about the size of the upcoming mission. It would be full platoon strength. No, bigger. Troops were coming to join the garrison and move on together. No, only a handful of men. Maybe a scout or two.

When Hunting Hawk, called Brulé by the French, began to assemble supplies, it became apparent that the party was a small one, only a few people. By the next day, the identities of the entire party were known.

The leader would be Lieutenant André Du Pres, whom the natives called Sky-Eyes because of the strange light color of his eyes. It had been quite a surprise to find that Sky-Eyes could actually see quite well. Such light eyes had been seen before only in the blind. He was somewhat new to the area but appeared eager to learn and was well thought of by the natives.

The other Fran-cois was Sergeant Jean Cartier, a more experienced woodsman. He had long been known by the descriptive name of Woodchuck because of his full jowls and slightly protruding front teeth. The party would be guided by the scout Hunting Hawk.

An element of surprise was that the wife of Hunting Hawk would also accompany the expedition. But why? There were rumors about that too, some quite ribald and obscene. None of these were taken seriously. The respect that the community held for the proud and dignified woman from the plains simply did not permit it. The theories then boiled down to two. It might be that on a journey that was expected to be long, Hunting Hawk had simply requested permission to take his wife. On the other hand, maybe Pale Star's skill with languages and hand-signs might be needed. Either way, everything pointed to a long journey.

And how many warriors would go? Pretty Flower cautiously ventured to ask. *None.* None at all? Only the four people? It was unthinkable, but it seemed to be true. That set off another flurry of rumors, none of which seemed to have any basis in fact.

Traveler was devastated. Three years ago, he and Flower had come here. It did not seem so, but three winters had come and gone. He had gradually regained much of his strength, except that his left foot still dragged awkwardly and the left arm was still all but useless. But he had learned to use the abilities he still had. His balance was better. His speech had improved so that there was hardly any slurring. He had talked to no one except Pretty Flower, but this had given him the practice that he needed.

He had become even more of a recluse, however. After the novelty of his first appearances as the Watcher, people had a tendency to forget. True, there was a strange someone or something out there in the darkness, but its presence was uneventful. Soon, even the tales of the Watcher were used mainly to frighten recalcitrant children into proper behavior.

He continued to be concerned about the welfare of Pale Star. Her husband was well respected, a skilled tracker who seemed to act as a Wolf for the French. Hunting Hawk treated her well, but there was a slight doubt on the part of the Watcher. The spirit of the couple as they related to each other was good but not as he would have wished for Star. He could tell, as he observed them and felt the quality of their combined spirit, that their marriage was lacking something. There was commitment, yes, and loyalty. What was lacking, maybe, was the excitement that he and Plum Leaf had experienced so long ago as they started their life together. That had been a singleness of purpose that had been undeniable. He shed a tear at the memory. But even as he did so, he realized that few marriages are as meaningful as his and Plum Leaf's had been. Maybe he was expecting too much for Star. If she was happy . . .

But no! There was a quiet attitude that he felt, a communication with the girl's spirit that occurred when she was alone. He could almost read her thoughts. Sometimes the feeling was so strong that he would quietly leave, afraid that she would feel his presence. The thing that he could read in her thoughts was something unfinished, unfulfilled. That she and Hawk had no children yet? No, something else. Through the many nights that he kept watch over her, he tried to solve the riddle.

When the answer came to him, it was so obvious and such a part of *him,* he was amazed that he had not seen it before. It revolved around his own unfulfilled promise— to take her home.

He sensed the change in her spirit immediately when the rumors about an expedition began. Flower told him what she had heard, and that very night he sensed the change in Pale Star's spirit as soon as he drew near in the darkness. There was an excitement. At first he mistook it for the natural excitement of one who is about to begin a journey. Then it became more apparent—a sense of relief, of the accomplishment of something long awaited. He did not understand. Why was it so important to her, this journey to an unknown destination? Her spirit felt a different, more intense excitement than the others of the party. What was the difference? An unknown. But wait, he thought. Does Pale Star know something unknown to the others? *Yes,* that must be it! He thought some more and began to reason it out.

This appeared to be a journey of exploration into unknown country. No one in the party had been to the west, beyond the Big River, probably, *except Pale Star.* The Watcher almost laughed aloud when he realized what was happening. Regardless of the reasons for the journey, only one of the party knew the country to the west. She would be able to lead the others, overtly or in any number of subtle ways. The end result was inescapable. *Star was going home!*

He told Pretty Flower of his conclusion at dawn as she grumpily rolled out of the robes to begin her day. The old woman was always like a bear aroused from winter sleep when she awoke each morning. "It is many years since I woke with anyone," she had once told him apologetically.

He still did not know why and did not venture to ask. If one chooses the life of a recluse, what is that to anyone else?

On this occasion, she was growling, hawking, and spitting, as she did each morning to clear her nose and throat. Between the sickening noises, he explained his discovery.

"Good!" she croaked. "Now maybe we can go home too."

"Home?"

"To the cave! There is no need to stay here."

He thought about that for a time. He had promised . . . "No," he said finally. "I will go with them."

This loosed a tirade like none he had heard before. "You are mad!" she yelled at him. "Completely mad! I thought you were crazy to stay here to watch over your Pale Star, but *aiee!* You are crazier than I am, even. You cannot go with them!"

"Not *with* them, but I can follow, to see that it is well with her."

"Traveler, this is too much. You are strong now, but this—"

"I promised," he interrupted.

They argued until the sun was high, but she could not dissuade him. "Go, then," she finally snapped. "I can do no more for you, now that you have become completely mad. I will see if I can learn when they will leave." Angrily, she shuffled out of the shelter.

She was calmer when she returned, late in the day. "They leave at daylight tomorrow," she reported. "I will fix a pack for you."

She busied herself with packing dried meat, pemmican, and an extra pair of moccasins into a rawhide bag, stuffing each item almost angrily. "You will need a weapon," she told him. "You can take the small ax. I do not know what else you could use with one arm."

"You . . . you are not coming?"

For a moment, he thought that she would begin to shout again, but she calmed quickly. "Traveler," she said quietly, "I could not stand the journey. My bones ache with the changing weather. You are younger—" she paused, and a little bit of remaining pride came to the surface as she continued, "not *much,* but younger. But you are strong, except for your arm and leg. Your spirit is willing, and you can follow them, maybe. I will go back to my cave—if a bear or somebody hasn't taken it over."

He was quiet.

"After you take Star home," she went on a trifle sarcastically, "you can come back if you are still alive. If you want, of course."

He was quiet for a moment before he spoke, his voice a little husky. "Thank you, Mother."

It had not seemed to occur to him that there might come a time when he would be alone. He had slipped easily into the routine of living with old Pretty Flower. An odd routine, to be sure, but an interpersonal exchange anyway. And he still had never experienced a period of aloneness such as that he now faced.

"Here!" Pretty Flower said, tossing the rawhide pack in his direction. "I will probably be asleep when you leave."

She was not, of course. As the gray light of morning began to pale, he gathered the few items that he possessed and prepared to leave. He hesitated, unable to express the things that he felt. This reclusive old outcast, whose full story he would never know, had brought him back from the very edge of death. He had spoken to no other living being since that time. He still had the feeling sometimes that he might actually be dead, crossing back and forth from the spirit world each night. How would one know? Could he not easily be a spirit, as some who had seen him around the fort insisted?

"Go on, now," Pretty Flower fussed at him. "They will start without you, and you will never catch up."

"Yes," he said flatly.

There was so much that he wanted to say. She had fed and changed him like a baby, had, in effect, raised him a second time. She had left her own lodge to help him in his resolve. He picked up the pack and swung it to his shoulders. It was clumsy and difficult because of his useless left arm. She made no effort to help him but busied herself with meaningless little tasks in the hut.

He tossed his robe across his back, looked at her for a moment, and blinked back a tear. Tears seemed to come so easily now. Was this a thing that spirits do easily? He cleared his throat.

"Goodbye, Mother. I thank you."

He waited, but she did not answer, and he turned away.

Pretty Flower straightened outside the hut and watched him vanish into the morning mist like—well, like a spirit. Now her eyes filled with tears. "Goodbye, my little one," she whispered. "May your trail be easier than I think it will."

She turned to gather her possessions, planning her own journey back to the cave that had been her home.

42

» » »

It was not easy, the task of following the party. The pace was being set by Hunting Hawk, who was young and agile.

After the first day, in which he fell far behind, Traveler decided on a different approach. He had overtaken the party long after dark when he was more comfortable anyway. The light had bothered his eyes considerably during the day. Twice he had been obliged to leave the trail to avoid being seen by other travelers. He must do something differently. Why not travel at night, *ahead* of the others? This would let him locate possible dangers and intervene as he was able. He could probably estimate where they would make camp and conceal himself to wait there. There were few branches to this well-traveled trail. If a questionable fork was encountered, he would wait there until the others passed and then follow.

This proved quite practical. Well into the night, he left the area where the little party had camped. He was familiar with this area and knew that there were few main crossings or divisions to the trail. He even estimated the place where they would camp and was delighted to find that he was correct.

He remained hidden, of course, and was able to watch while Pale Star began to instruct the two soldiers in hand-signs. That was good. He could respect men who wished to learn the ways of the people they would encounter. He had been pleased, too, that the two Francois had abandoned their impractical blue and white uniforms for the buckskins of the natives. That was Hunting Hawk's suggestion, most likely.

He was disturbed by one attitude that he saw on the part of the lieutenant, Sky-Eyes. Actually, it was nothing more than a sense of how the man *felt*. Traveler, since he had become the Watcher, had developed this ability to see into the thoughts of others. It was part of the sense of immortality he sometimes felt. It was as if his spirit could reach out and commune with those of others, without their knowledge. It had been uncomfortable at times to sense an evil scheme, half formed, in someone that he watched. Gradually, he had learned to deal with it.

But this was different, different in one respect—it concerned Star. He had felt the lust and envy on the part of men as they stared at her beauty. Sometimes it angered him. He had finally resolved his uneasy thoughts with the realization that Star or Hawk, or both, could handle the unwelcome attentions of any man with evil on his mind. That had made him feel more confident.

The thoughts of the lieutenant were slightly different. Not lust, but honest admiration. There was a difference, of course. Any man with normal feelings and needs would be attracted to such a woman. But appreciation of her beauty, with recognition that she was unavailable, was quite different from the scheming thoughts of how it might be possible to bed with her. The lieutenant actually seemed embarrassed by his thoughts, which were above reproach. The Watcher sensed respect for both Star and her husband, and for their union. It was plain, however, that if circumstances were different, Sky-Eyes would immediately have a romantic interest.

The Watcher was pleased with the way the lieutenant chose to deal with his feelings. He avoided contact with Pale Star—as much as he could in a party of four. It was good.

It was somewhat disconcerting to him, then, to sense a similar feeling on the part of Star. She seemed attracted to Sky-Eyes but chose the same method to put aside her feelings—avoidance. The Watcher had the strong impression that neither was aware of the other's feelings. Hunting Hawk too seemed completely oblivious to this interaction.

The Watcher wondered whether Hawk's mixed blood was a factor in his lack of recognition. The light-skinned outsiders certainly seemed less concerned with things of the spirit. Maybe they did not have the usual ability to see and feel such things. But no, it was probably not that, he decided. More likely, he, as the Watcher, had developed more sensitivity than most. Whatever, everyone concerned seemed to be handling the situation well, but it would bear watching.

An incident on the trail a few days later gave him more confidence in the abilities of this group to meet emergencies. In his travel that night, he came upon the camp of a party of seven heavily armed men. He spent some time scouting the camp. This was a dangerous area, with numerous scalphunters. He decided to stay near these men to see that they did no harm to the party of Star and the others. He found a hiding place where he could observe unseen.

It was past midday when he noted increased activity. One of their Wolves apparently reported the approach of another party. Two of the warriors ignited smoldering matches on their thunder-stick muskets. Then they all scattered to conceal themselves, except for the leader. That one stood casually in the clearing, waiting, a throwing-ax held casually in his left hand. That was worth noting. Was it so that he could give the peace sign with his right? Or because he was left-handed and the ax was ready in his throwing hand? Or *both*? The Watcher slipped his own ax from his belted waist and made ready. He would prefer not to show himself but would intervene if he must.

Hunting Hawk entered the clearing and paused to greet the waiting warrior. The others of his party spread out beside him, weapons ready. The Watcher stared, fascinated. He could not hear the conversation but gathered that the leader of the war party was delaying communication to give his allies time to get into position. He could smell the acrid smoke from the matches of the muskets. Hunting Hawk and the others must smell it too.

Hawk was speaking, apparently to the other leader, when the hidden warriors began to show themselves. Hawk had apparently demanded that they come out of concealment.

Then everything happened at once. The left-handed ax-thrower let fly at Sky-Eyes, and the Watcher was concerned that he would not be ready. He nearly broke from concealment to help, but the lieutenant was equal to the threat. He pointed a little hand-held thunderstick that must have been a special kind. It seemed to have no burning match but exploded anyway. The enemy leader was thrown backward, to land heavily on his back, apparently stone dead. His ax flew harmlessly.

There was another shot from one of the attackers, screams of pain, and the remaining enemies were gone. The Watcher noted with pride that Star herself had used the throwing-ax to good advantage. Her opponent lay dead, the ax jutting from his forehead. Still another warrior was transfixed by Woodchuck's arrow. One more of the fleeing scalphunters seemed badly wounded, swaying as he ran, an arm dangling helplessly.

The Watcher was pleased. This fighting team to which Pale Star belonged was certainly able to defend well. Star's skill with the ax was a pleasant surprise and gave him a feeling of confidence.

Hunting Hawk was methodically harvesting the scalps. It was pleasing to note that although Star had had no qualms over killing an attacker when necessary, she did not participate in the scalping. The Watcher was proud.

The party moved on. They did not camp at the spring

where Star had been abducted. His impression was that she had asked Hunting Hawk not to do so. They moved on, heading toward the village of White Squirrel.

Now they passed places where he and Star had camped, and he felt the tug of nostalgia, the mourning for Plum Leaf. He could tell that Star too was remembering better times. She was quiet and morose, withdrawn from conversation around the campfire each night. He longed to talk to her, to comfort her and assure her that he would still see her safely back to her people on the prairie.

At the village of White Squirrel, the party was welcomed. They would buy canoes here. This presented the Watcher a new dilemma. How could he follow the party on a river trip? Maybe his travels were at an end. He sat in the dark, tears coursing down his cheeks—why did tears come so easily now? Well, maybe it was over. He had done all he could. They would buy canoes and move on. He remembered the selection of the canoe in which he and Star had come upriver, the canoe in which his beloved Plum Leaf had crossed over. It had been a good one, the best craft they had ever owned.

He almost leaped to his feet as the thought struck him. That canoe had been left *here*! He had told White Squirrel to use it or sell it. Could it still be here? Usable?

He searched for some time before he found it, the small trees and bushes had grown so much in the intervening years. He ran his right hand over the craft, trying to evaluate in the darkness what could not be seen. Was it still sound? The bark was dry and peeling in some areas but was firm to the touch. The tiny cracks would quickly swell shut when placed in the water.

Before daylight, he concealed himself nearby and was able to watch as Star and White Squirrel came to evaluate the canoe. Star ran her fingers over the painted eyes on the prow, lost in thought. Finally they turned away. He could tell that Star had rejected this canoe. He was glad, for two reasons. They should select a new canoe for their purpose. But also, that would leave this one for his use, if he was able to launch it. And if so, could he handle it? He thought so. It would not be as difficult as traveling upstream. It was necessary only to drift with the current, guiding occasionally.

After dark that evening, he made his way back to the pole rack where his canoe rested. He would launch it, drift downriver for some distance, and conceal himself and the canoe until the explorers passed, so that he could follow. He placed his shoulder under the prow and heaved gently. It moved easily, and he eased it back onto the rack. Now, he could not lift, balance, and carry with one good arm. He looked at the gentle slope, uniformly stretching down toward the river. If he could lift the canoe down from the rack, he could slide it quietly to the water. But paddles. He thought for a moment, then reached up under the inverted canoe. Yes, they were still there, tucked behind the cross members.

He lifted the prow again and shifted sideways, straining to clear a young tree that limited the swing of the prow. That was accomplished, but now the stern was entrapped by the brush. He set the prow on the ground and stepped to the rear. Now the hard work would begin. He tugged at the stern of the canoe, cursing the handicap of his limp left arm. The canoe moved a little. Maybe he could use a pole to pry it over a little for a straighter pull. He searched for a suitable pole but could find nothing.

Maybe he could concentrate on the prow. He had moved that more easily. He moved there, lifted and pulled. The canoe slid forward a handspan. Now he had a new problem. If the stern dropped from the rack unsupported, it would crash to the ground and very likely shatter the fragile shell.

Anxiously, he cast an eye to the east where the sky was graying. The village would soon be stirring. He hurried to the stern again and tried to lift the canoe with his one good arm and shoulder, straining every muscle. Sweat poured from his body despite the chill of the night. At first there was only firm resistance, but suddenly the craft moved, smoothly and easily.

He looked up and was alarmed to see a man handling the prow, expertly lifting and drawing it forward. Without a word, the helper moved toward the river, moving slowly to give the other a chance to get under the stern and achieve balance on his shoulders. They reached the shore, inverted the canoe, and set the prow into the water. It was not until then that he recognized White Squirrel.

The two men straightened.

"Good day to you, Uncle," said White Squirrel conversationally. "May you have a successful journey."

The Watcher did not speak. How long had his old friend been watching? He was certain that he had not been recognized. He decided to pretend that he could not speak. In truth, he probably could not without breaking down in emotion.

"It is good," he stated in hand-signs in the growing light of dawn. He must hurry now. "Thank you for your help."

He lifted his pack from where he had placed it near the river and set it in the canoe. He stepped in, and White Squirrel gave the canoe a shove. In the space of a few heartbeats, the canoe and its ghostly occupant were swallowed in the morning fog of the river.

White Squirrel stood looking after it for a moment.

"Good-bye, old friend," he said softly.

43

» » »

He rode downstream, letting the current carry him, using an occasional stroke of the paddle to direct the canoe across the river. There was an urgency, a need to be out of sight before the fog lifted. He should be far enough downstream that when he concealed himself, there would be no chance of a stray fisherman accidentally discovering his hiding place.

It was good to be on the river, traveling with little effort. He did not think of the fact that he would not be able to travel back upriver. That would be hard work, paddling against the current, even for two canoeists. For a single one-armed man, return would be impossible.

His hiding place was behind a screen of overhanging willows on the west bank. The canoe slid comfortably into the shelter, and he tied the prow to a sturdy limb. He was certain that the exploring party was not prepared to start the journey today. They had not yet selected canoes. Such a journey would always begin on a morning, so he would merely watch for a while after daylight each day. From this vantage point, he would see them pass, would wait a reasonable time, and then follow them. Until then . . . he wrapped himself in his robe, stretched full length in the bottom of the canoe, and fell asleep, the lapping of water lulling him with its rocking motion.

It was two more days before the party passed, in two

canoes. He could plainly see them, out near the middle where the current was strong. Hunting Hawk guided one canoe, Sky-Eyes in the prow, while Pale Star was paired with the sergeant. That one, in the prow of Star's canoe, seemed to have handled a canoe before. The lieutenant was inexpert but trying hard. Yes, he would improve.

The Watcher observed them as they passed, then on down the river until they were out of sight. It took some courage to push the canoe out from under the willows into the open. Nervously, he chewed some dried meat while he waited a little longer, just to be sure. Finally, he eased out into the current. He kept close to shore, for quicker concealment in case it was needed and because the current was slower there. In that way, he would never quite overtake the other canoes in the main current unless they stopped. They would stop at night. He would pass them in the darkness, perhaps stopping to observe them if it seemed prudent. Then he would hide again as dawn approached and wait until they passed again.

He was pleased that his eyes seemed to be tolerating the daylight well. He wondered if Pretty Flower had been right, that he only wished to be active in darkness to avoid being seen. Well, no matter now. That had been as good a reason as any, anyway.

The day slipped past as smoothly as the water that carried the canoe. When shadows began to lengthen, he steered to shore. He did not yet know how early the others might want to make camp, and he certainly did not want to encounter them unexpectedly. He sat, listening to the murmur of the water, the soft sigh of the breeze in the trees above him, and the slap of a beaver's tail across the water. A loon called, and its mate answered.

He waited until it was nearly dark, then pushed away from shore. It was some time before he saw their fire, a tiny point of light in the darkness of the wooded shoreline. He steered into the quieter water next to shore and drifted as close as he dared.

The two canoes were pulled well up on the bank, the

fire on a flat area a few paces beyond. He could hear their voices as they discussed the day's travel and continued the hand-sign lessons. He had gathered through his previous observations that the mission of this party was to find a waterway of some sort, to the southwest. This puzzled him because it was well known that the Big River, the Missi-sippi, ran straight south. Some said it emptied into a huge salty Big Lake, a long, long way below. He had never been that far, but the stories of the southern tribes with whom he had traded seemed true enough.

And Pale Star should know this. She would not wish to explore the lower Big River since her people were far to the west. He was already certain that she meant this trip to take her home. If he was correct, the party would leave the Big River to head west, overland, when the time was right.

One other possibility occurred to him, though it seemed unlikely. Star and her husband might leave the others to head overland. But no, that did not fit. Hunting Hawk was known to be loyal and dependable. He would not abandon those for whom he scouted. But Pale Star had no such loyalties!

He thought back to the time, years ago, when Star had been his prisoner. She had agreed to the pact. She would not attempt to escape and return home without giving him warning that the bargain was at an end. Could it be that Star had such a bargain with her husband? It had been a marriage of convenience in the beginning. . . .

The more he thought about it, the more he was convinced that there was something of the sort. He must learn more. He drifted downstream a few hundred paces and beached his canoe. Then he made his way back toward the camp, to watch and listen. His skill as the night-dwelling Watcher came into its own as he approached quietly, searching for a spot where he might conceal himself.

He settled in, outside the circle of the firelight, and tried to attune himself to the spirits of those around the fire. Star's spirit was familiar to him, of course. He could feel the proud courage of her, but something else too. A sadness, maybe. It was a feeling that something was almost over, a thing that was nearly past. He pondered that a little while. She was surely preparing to go home. But this should give her a light and pleasant spirit. There was a hint of that, but of some sorrow too. Yes, she might regret a separation from her husband yet still carry it out.

He wondered whether Hunting Hawk knew. He had no definite feel for the spirit of the man and turned his attention back to Star. He saw her glance at the tall lieutenant and was startled to see a flash of genuine affection. But wait—surely Star would not be guilty of infidelity. *No,* he decided, *she is attracted to Sky-Eyes but will not be unfaithful.* Yes, that would fit what he knew of the girl. She might leave her husband to go home but would never be unfaithful to him. She would control her attraction.

He watched the lieutenant for a little while, reaching out to feel that spirit. *No,* he thought, *Sky-Eyes does not know how Star feels, and that is good.*

Just as he reached that conclusion, the lieutenant glanced up at Star. She was looking the other way at the moment, and the Watcher was startled again. Sky-Eyes had a strong attraction to Star. *And she does not know that, either,* he thought. It was somewhat overwhelming to watch these two, each with the burden of a forbidden emotion, unknown to the other.

He watched until the fire burned low and the party retired for the night. He became more strongly convinced as the evening wore on that he was right. These two, Pale Star and Sky-Eyes, were strongly attracted to each other, but neither knew of the other's feelings. The reaction to these disturbing feelings was quite similar for both. They avoided each other, avoided eye contact, any closeness at all, and did not even speak to the other unless it was necessary. To a casual observer, it might appear that these two carried an extreme *dislike* for each other.

He recalled that they were in different canoes for the

journey and wondered who had initiated the pairing.
Maybe it was merely coincidence. The two most experienced with the paddles should, after all, be the two
steersmen. That would be Hawk and Pale Star, of course.
One of the soldiers would be placed in the front of each
canoe. Maybe the fact that Sky-Eyes was assigned to
Hawk's canoe had been merely an accident. But maybe
not. Was it Hawk's choice, because he suspected his
wife's feelings for the lieutenant?

He watched Hunting Hawk carefully. The man was
relaxed, quiet but cheerful, and spoke easily to any of the
others. There seemed no suspicion on the scout's part.
Well, time would tell, the Watcher supposed. He backed
away carefully, avoiding the sergeant who was standing
watch, and moved back to his canoe to start downriver.

The pattern worked well, though sometimes it was difficult for him to match the pace set by the others. With
the help of the current, his experience, and skill as a night
creature, he managed to observe their camping place
each night. Sometimes it was well located for him to
watch and listen. On other nights, he was forced to
forego that activity because of unfavorable terrain and
lack of suitable cover.

Each night that he did watch, his impression of Star's
attraction to the lieutenant was strengthened, but also the
feeling that she would never do anything overtly to express it. For her, there was not only her strict upbringing
but a stronger goal: *home.* There was still no indication
how she expected to accomplish that. The party was far
enough south now that it would soon be time to move
westward into the plains and hills of the tallgrass prairie.
Pale Star must know that, but as far as the Watcher could
tell, she had made no move to alter the daily journey on
the river.

He began to wonder now not *whether* Star would make
the break, or even *when,* but *how.* Would she announce
her intention to leave? That would be like Star. But then

the others might prevent it. She must have lost much of her trust in others by this time. He tried to decide whether Hunting Hawk knew of the impending event.

He studied Hawk at great length, trying to decide whether Star would have told him any of her goals and plans. It was difficult to grasp a feel for the man's spirit. It was a bit morose, impenetrable. The Watcher perceived a little doubt and mistrust—no, not mistrust exactly, more like a knowledge, a resignation. Hawk knew that someday he would lose his wife, not to another man but to the freedom of the prairie. The Watcher knew that feeling well. Ever since he had become well acquainted with the girl-child he had bought, he had known that someday he would lose her.

One does not keep an eagle captive and expect it to remain when escape is possible. A fettered eagle will allow itself to be fed to keep its strength and fitness. But no matter how many years it may be, when the chance comes, the comfort of the padded perch and the sureness of the meat provided is forgotten. The eagle will spread her wings and soar, back into her own element, into freedom.

44

» » »

The weather change made river travel miserable, sometimes impossible. There were days of mist and rain, and occasional visits from Rain Maker himself, with the boom of his celestial drum and his spears of real-fire crashing down on Earth with a vengeance. The Watcher oould do nothing but take cover and wait. At least he knew that the other party was subject to the same limitations. They could not travel either but would be seeking shelter as he was.

The overturned canoe was ideal . protection. He dragged it up the bank a little way and lay beneath it while the rain drummed on the shell. He slept for a while and wakened to find it still raining. He was sure that the others were upstream and that they would wait until the downpour was over. The rain continued as darkness fell, and he knew that he need not watch. He slept, then woke, chewed a little of his dried meat, and drank from a rivulet of water that trickled from the overturned shell. Then he slept again.

Dawn was marked not by the rising of the sun but merely by the fading of the blackness to dull gray. The driving rain had stopped, but a slight mist continued to wet the earth. It formed in fat drops on the trees and bushes, and dripped to the sodden turf. He propped up the canoe so that he could sit under it and watch the river. There would be no travel today.

Pale Star was the only one of the party with experience on this part of the Big River, and she knew the treachery of the incoming streams after a rain. Any storm system sweeping across the plains could drop great amounts of water into the tributaries upstream. Those smaller streams could be quite dangerous, rushing down in a torrent to catch a traveler unexpectedly in an area that had been relatively free of rain.

Along the Big River, the problem was slightly different. Other large streams emptied into the main river at intervals. These rivers might be swollen, carrying flotsam that could become dangerous. An unwary canoeist passing by the mouth of such a river at flood stage could be threatened by an attack of floating logs, trees, and brush driven at a considerable speed, easily damaging a canoe—this, of course, in addition to the danger of being overturned by the sudden onslaught of an unexpected sideways current.

Star would know such things. She had gained much experience from their travels on the river. Besides, the girl had an intuition, a feel for such things. Yes, he had not realized it so much at the time, but it seemed quite likely that Pale Star possessed a gift, the gift of the spirit. She had spoken of her kinsman—what was his name? Looks-Ahead, or some such. *Looks Far,* that was it! A great holy man of her people. Yes, in the blood of Pale Star there must be much of this gift, this ability to relate to things of the spirit.

He shifted his position a little, settled comfortably, then shifted again to avoid a troublesome drip of water on his left elbow. He wondered when Star would make her break westward. She could go by canoe, up one of the tributaries they would pass, but he thought not. That would take her northwest, too far north to find her people. No, she would leave the river and go overland. It would remain to be seen whether she would take the others with her or abandon the party altogether.

He was staring dreamily at the river, wondering when the fog would lift, when he saw the canoe. He gasped in astonishment.

The craft held two people. It was quite near the shore, or he would never have seen it through the mist. In the space of a heartbeat, it was gone, swallowed in the gray fog of the morning. It had been within calling distance. If the paddlers had looked up, they could have seen him. Unless he was mistaken, the steersman had been Hunting Hawk, and the lieutenant, Sky-Eyes, had been in the prow. He peered through the fog and saw the other canoe slip past like a silent ghost. There were two people in it also, though he could not identify them.

This meant, then, that Star had not yet left the party. She was still guiding them, and she must have made the decision to travel. But *why*? She knew better, understood the dangers involved. It must be that this was part of her plan, this madness of traveling in a dangerous situation where one cannot see.

Another possibility struck him even as he struggled to drag his own canoe into the water—more chilling, more dangerous, than his other theory. Could it be that in her preoccupation with escape from the expedition, her judgment was clouded? That she was overlooking the danger because she was thinking of other things?

He stepped into the canoe, tossing his pack ahead of him. Fear gripped him. He had been nearly helpless before, having only his right arm to use the paddle and to steer. Now he felt completely at the mercy of the river. Before, it had been a calm friendly spirit. He had only to let the current carry him, with a stroke of the paddle occasionally to maintain direction. Now it was completely different. In his anxiety for Pale Star and her party, he had lost the kinship with the river. He was fighting it, unable to control his progress. The same current that had carried him gently now fought back, turning and twisting the canoe as it moved.

With great difficulty, he controlled his panic and spoke softly, trying to reestablish his contact with whatever spirits lay in the depths of the dark water. "I would travel on your surface, Mother," he whispered. "I will harm nothing, will leave no tracks, but I cannot do this alone."

There may have been an imperceptible change in the motion of the craft. He was not certain. "There are those who need me," he pleaded.

The canoe rode through a back-eddy, turning completely around once. As the craft emerged from the other side of the whirl, he gave a skillful stroke of the paddle, and the prow headed downstream. He began to relax now, riding with the flow instead of fighting it.

He stayed near the shore, not wishing to come too close to the others in the fog. Everything was still, the sounds of the creatures who made their homes here muffled by the fog, but he heard the croak of the small green heron. It could have been a bow shot away or just out of sight, concealed by the fog.

There was no warning when the crisis came. One moment, he was riding the current complacently, comfortable in spirit if not in his wet buckskins. Within a few heartbeats, he felt the tug of the river from the right and saw a tangle of floating sticks and brush bearing down on him. He managed to avoid the hazard, but as he did so, was aware of being shoved forward by a new current. He must be passing the mouth of another river, a large river, judging by its force. The other realization came quick on the heels of that. Floating debris would gather along the banks as the river receded, but the flotsam was apparently directly in the middle of the stream's mouth. This river was *rising,* was at flood stage.

The bloated carcass of a buffalo floated into his vision, bobbing gently in the swell where the two currents met. Beyond that was a cottonwood, torn loose by the roots in the powerful flood. He tried to steer around these obstacles and reach the west shore. He was now far more concerned with survival than with the other party. Even at the time this seemed ludicrous. If he was concerned about his own survival, he must *not* be dead, after all!

Somewhere ahead of him in the fog he heard excited shouts and a yell of alarm. His canoe was completely out of control now, being swept helplessly along on the torrent. The curtain of fog lifted, and tragedy loomed ahead of him. Rolling along in the current was an old giant of a tree, probably an oak from its shape. It may have spent decades in the river, its trunk so waterlogged, it barely floated. Now, pulled loose from its resting place by the flood, it was carried along. Jagged snags of broken branches caught at the muddy bottom and lifted again as it rolled. The dead giant seemed to live again. Great limbs rose, grasping like huge claws at anything that came within their grasp, disappearing beneath the water again as others reared to take their place.

To his horror, he saw the crushed and broken shell of a canoe caught in a back-eddy, circling slowly. He thought he saw a body in the water but could not be sure.

He was being carried by the current directly into the grasping horror of the rolling tree and could do nothing to avoid it. There was a grating sound as a massive limb rose under his canoe, raising the prow. The craft slid away and bobbed on.

Then, right beside him, scarcely an arm's length away, another branch rose above the surface, thrusting upward like a groping arm. Impaled upon it was a canoe, the other of the French expedition. In a moment, it was gone again, pulled under by the inexorable roll of the sodden monster. Both canoes, then, had been destroyed.

A cry of anguish escaped the Watcher. He dropped the paddle and raised his face to the sky. Why? Why had he been saved from death by the ax long ago, to come to this? And to be unable to help Pale Star in her final time of need—ah, this was worst of all.

He had no control over his canoe and did not care. He

had failed completely, after all, to help Star in any way. Even his pitiful attempt to follow the expedition, to assure himself that Star was with her people, that was a failure too. Surely no one had survived the destruction wrought by the trees. He sat waiting for his time to die. Surely the next thrust of the clawing arms would drag him too to his death. He clung to the sides of the canoe, eyes tightly closed, braced against the coming impact. He found himself mouthing the Death Song of one of the nations he knew. He could not remember which one.

> *The earth and the sky go on*
> *forever,*
> *But today is a good day to*
> *die.*

And then the water was calmer, and the clawing tree was behind him. Hesitantly, he opened his eyes and found that the river around him, though still swift, no longer seemed angry. Maybe . . . could he ride the current to safety?

It was not until then that he noticed the water rising *in* the canoe. It was pouring in through several cracks in the rotting old shell. The canoe was breaking up under him. *There will be no one left to tell the tale,* he thought.

45

"**W**ake up, Uncle!"

The voice was distant, and he had difficulty understanding at first.

"You must wake up now!"

He was tired, so very tired. He had not realized that it would be so exhausting to cross over. He remembered drowning, trying to cling to the pieces of the canoe as he went down. A strange sensation, looking up through the water at the dull gray light of day. He could not remember what had happened next.

The voice that kept calling to him was that of a woman. His mother? No, that had been after the ax wound. But it must be someone who had already crossed over, someone who had been waiting.

"Plum Leaf?" he managed to gasp.

The woman chuckled. "Ah, he *does* awake," she said to someone else.

Confused, he tried to think what tongue she spoke. It had never occurred to him to wonder what tongues were spoken on the Other Side. He understood the words, but it was not his own tongue. One of many he had used, maybe. But it was not the tongue of Plum Leaf's people either. And not that of Pale Star, or of old Pretty Flower. Something was wrong. . . . He opened his eyes.

A young woman was bending over him, speaking to

him and trying to rouse him. He had never seen her before. Behind her was a capable-looking young man. This must be some sort of welcome for new arrivals. He would be expected to make an acknowledgement, he supposed. He adjusted easily, through years of practice as a trader, and addressed them in the tongue they had spoken. "Good day to you," he said huskily, "I am pleased to be here on the Other Side."

The woman laughed. "Ah, you nearly were, Uncle. We thought you were dead when we dragged you from the water."

"It is nothing," he said. "I have been dead before."

The two chuckled again, a little nervously. He thought about that for a moment. Could he be still alive? "Who are you?" he asked. "Where is this place?"

He tried to sit up, but they persuaded him to lie back. It did feel better to lie back and rest. Slowly, the story came out. These two, who appeared to be young lovers, had found his body, as they thought, washed up on a sandbar amid pieces of a wrecked canoe. He moaned, and they dragged him ashore and tried to resuscitate him. They had a small fire going, which was helping to drive away the damp and fog. Its warmth was welcome after his chilling experience.

Then he remembered. *Aiee,* what of the others? "You saw no one else?" he asked.

"No, Uncle, only you. Was there someone with you?"

"No, no. Not *with* me. Another party—two canoes."

"They were chasing you?"

"No . . . friends of mine. I was following them."

"We saw no one, Uncle. Maybe they went on downstream."

No, he had clearly seen two wrecked canoes and at least one body in the water. He should sing the Song of Mourning for Star, as she had done for Plum Leaf, but he was not certain. If by chance she had survived, it would not be good to have mourned. It would invite trouble.

"You rest a little by the fire here," the woman was saying. "Then we will help you to our village."

"Could . . . will someone look for my friends?" he pleaded. "Their canoes were broken. It was near the junction of the two rivers."

"*Ah!* That is far *upstream!* Uncle, you must have floated a long way before your canoe went down!"

He did not remember. He had seen the water leaking into the canoe, and dimly remembered trying to reach a floating log, but—well, no matter now.

It was several days before there was any word. Yellow Birch, as the young woman was called, came to him, gently and seriously. "We have learned of your people, Uncle!" she announced. "Three of them—"

"But there were *four!*"

"Four? No, they found only three."

Fear clutched at his chest. *Which ones?* He tried to remain calm. He dreaded the answer that he sought, but he must know. Maybe the one who had escaped was Star. "Tell me of it," he asked sadly. "Where were the bodies found?"

"Bodies? No, no, Uncle. Three were *living.* The next village upstream found them. But then, one is dead?"

"Maybe so," he agreed, his mouth dry as ashes. "Tell me of the ones who were found."

"Of course. A woman . . . very beautiful, they said . . . her husband, and another man."

He heaved a deep sigh of relief. Star was alive! Tears of gladness streamed down his face.

"Is her husband blind?" Yellow Birch asked curiously.

"Blind? No, why do you ask that?"

"Oh—" the girl seemed puzzled, "they said his eyes were light-colored. Like the sky, someone told us. But he can see, you say?"

His brain whirled in confusion. The man they were describing as Star's husband was not Hunting Hawk but Sky-Eyes, the French lieutenant! He had observed their affinity for each other, though the two seemed not to know it. But now they did? And what of Hunting Hawk?

There was only one possibility, as far as he could reason. The man who was lost must have been the husband, and Star and the lieutenant . . .

"The one man wandered into the village, half dead," Birch was saying. "He told of the others, and some men went to look for them . . . or their bodies, of course. They found the woman and her husband . . . maybe three sleeps later. His head was hurt."

"He is badly hurt?"

"No, they said he is better now. The woman had cared for him. Their supplies were gone, but she had done well for them."

Yes, he thought, *she would do well.* The two must have discovered their feeling for each other during the time they were striving for survival. But to be accepted as man and wife? *Aiee!*

"I must go to them," he said.

Yellow Birch laughed. "No, Uncle. You are not strong enough to travel. Besides, they are gone!"

"Gone? How is this?"

"They bought some supplies and went on!"

"Down the river?"

"No, I think not. West, someone said."

Of course! Nothing could deter Pale Star from her goal for very long. She was headed home.

"Both men went with her?" he asked.

"Yes, I suppose so."

"When?"

"I do not know, Uncle! I will try to find out."

"It is good. I must follow them."

Yellow Birch sighed in exasperation. "You must be stronger first. You rest and eat, and we will learn all we can about your people and where they went. Spotted Bird will go and ask at the other village."

He knew that it was true. At this time, he would not have had the strength to travel very far. Impatiently, he settled into a routine of resting, eating, and walking to gain strength.

These were friendly, pleasant people who had taken him in, and he enjoyed the life in their village. It was much like that of his early childhood. As days passed, he wondered how he could repay them for their kindness. They seemed not only to pity him but to respect him for his age and wisdom. He thought himself not as old as he looked but was grateful that the people seemed to accept him easily, despite his distorted scarred face and paralyzed arm. Maybe he would not have had to fear returning to the life of normal people.

Some things he could not do, however. He could never be a trader. It would be impossible for him to lift and carry. He could not travel well. He now realized that it would take everything he could muster just to follow Star to her people. But he *must* do that. He had promised. He still could not bear to think of having her see him like this, but he felt that he had to make certain she was home.

It was on a cool quiet evening that he began to realize that there was one skill that remained to him. He was seated near a small fire that someone had lighted for warmth and for its spirit. Several children were playing near the edge of the circle of light when they suddenly stopped to listen. In the distance, there came the laughing, chuckling cry of a coyote. From another quarter came the answering call of another.

"Do you know why he laughs?" asked the old man.

They looked at him curiously. "Why, Uncle?"

"Well, it was in the long-ago times, when the world was young. All the animals could talk, and people too. All tribes spoke the same tongue, you know." The children gathered around him. It had been a long time, but the skill of the storyteller is never forgotten. He began to warm to a receptive audience.

"People had no fire yet, and they wished to cook their meat. But where could they get some fire? Real-fire was too dangerous. When Rain Maker throws his spears, who would be brave enough to catch them? Or who could hold them, or use them to cook with? They had to catch the fire from somewhere else."

"With a flint!" suggested a bright youngster.

"No, no," smiled the storyteller. "They had no metal to make the spark. No one had thought of rubbing-sticks yet, so they decided to steal it from Sun Boy."

There was a murmur around the circle.

"They could not decide how to do it," he continued. "They argued for a long time. Finally Coyote came and offered a bargain. He would steal the fire and bring it. 'I can run faster than you,' Coyote said, 'so I will not be burned.' The people thought about that. 'But what will you ask in return?' they wanted to know. Coyote chuckled. 'Only the leavings from your kills.' Ever since, the scraps and unused parts of every kill belong to Coyote. That is why he laughs. He made a good bargain."

"But, Uncle! How did Coyote get the fire?" a child asked, wide-eyed.

"Oh, yes! Coyote waited until Sun Boy slid beyond Earth's rim. Then he ran quickly, reached over, and grabbed a brand from Sun Boy's torch. He ran quickly, to keep from being burned. But the torch was cool and red, of course, because it was evening."

The listeners nodded.

"Now, Coyote forgot one thing. He ran so fast that the wind of his passing fanned the firebrand in his mouth. It became hotter, and flames swept back along his sides, scorching his fur."

"Really?" asked a fascinated listener.

"Of course! Next time you see a coyote, look at his fur. Since that time, all coyotes have a scorched stripe down each side, where the fire almost burned him!"

"Tell us another story, Uncle!"

He lay staring at the sky a long time that night before sleep came. He was beginning to understand something.

A part of his struggle after the ax nearly killed him was that he had lost his identity. He could no longer be the Trader or the Traveler because he no longer had the ability to do so. He had denied that fact and had become depressed and bitter, shunning human contact. He had become the Watcher because in that way he could, partly at least, fulfill his promise to look after Pale Star.

He must still do that. He could never rest until he saw her safely home. But meanwhile, he had rediscovered something.

He still had an identity that he had almost forgotten. In fact, he had come full circle. He was the Storyteller again.

46

» » »

He still considered himself supernatural, of course. How else had he survived death, not once but twice? Once by the ax, another by drowning. There was no question in his mind. He might be a little crazy too. Pretty Flower almost certainly was. He could account for his own madness by the head wound, but she had never told him how she had arrived in her present condition, and he had never asked. But he was grateful to her.

The purpose for his survival? It was obvious to him: to see Pale Star back to her people, he had always known that. But now that he had reestablished himself as the Storyteller, all the pieces seemed to fall into place. He felt good about himself now, felt that he was useful. It had been a thrill to watch the faces of his listeners as he retold the favorite stories he had gathered in his travels. Bobcat's tail, in all its versions. The story of why Woodpecker's head is red, and of Kookooskoos, who hunts at night.

The people of this river village were charmed by the Storyteller, especially the children. They could not do enough for him, and as he prepared to depart, they plied him with gifts of supplies, new buckskins, and robes. Finally he asked that he not be given any more.

When the time was set, he chose a buffalo robe, new leggings and shirt, and new moccasins. A rawhide pack was stuffed with jerked meat and pemmican, as much as he could carry, and he gave away everything else to those who had helped him.

"We would like to have you stay," Yellow Birch told him, "but we understand. You must look for your people."

It had been half a moon since the accident, and there was little chance that he could overtake them, even without his handicaps. He would merely head west, asking as he went. He knew that news travels fast on the prairie. And the Growers, who traded with everyone, would keep abreast of the happenings in all directions.

It was not difficult to follow the trail of the three.

"Oh, yes, we heard of them . . . a very beautiful woman and two men."

"Yes, they stopped with us. She is a teller of stories. . . ."

"Her husband has blind eyes, yet he sees. . . . We wondered at that."

"No, they did not come this way, but my nephew talked to a man who had seen them. Farther south . . ."

He traveled as fast as he could, hoarding his supplies carefully. He could stop for a day or two and tell stories in return for more, but he hoped to keep moving. He had a general idea of the area where Star's Elk-dog People might live, but it was unfamiliar to him. She had once mentioned the River of Swans, but no one he encountered had heard of such a place. He struggled on, westward.

He became aware that he was losing weight. The increased activity, the hard work of travel, was requiring more effort and therefore more food than he had used for a long time. He could not continue on the scant rations he was allowing himself. He began to use a little more food but saw his supplies dwindling and resumed his more meager fare. Somehow, though, he grew more tired, and traveled shorter distances. He had to stop for a little while at some camp or village to regain his strength. That, or find fresh meat. *Aiee,* how good that would be!

His mouth watered at the thought of browning hump-ribs over a fire of buffalo dung. But how could he kill any game, even if the opportunity arose? Frustrated and becoming depressed again, he pushed on, growing weaker.

It was perhaps the night of the driving rain that finally broke him. He was unable to start a fire because of an unexpected damp and gusty wind. He tried again and again, but sparks from his French fire-striker failed to live on the damp tinder. He spent the night wrapped in a robe, shivering against the rain that flapped the robe's edges and chilled him to the bone.

When the storm broke and blue sky appeared the next morning, reason told him that he could not go on. Yet his heart told him that he must.

He staggered on, defying the gnawing suspicion that he had already failed. There was gnawing of another sort too. Hunger pangs plagued him throughout the day, for his food was gone. Logically, he could have stopped to look for food, but he was beyond reason now. He struggled on. He somehow convinced himself that fasting would bring him closer to the purity of spirit that he sought. Of course! Why had he not seen that before? He had only to stop eating to become more supernatural than he already was! In time, he would become pure spirit, immortal. That would free him of the pains of hunger, the cramping muscles in his legs, and the throbbing in his head that had now returned.

He managed to build a fire that night and was a little more rational for a while. He thought of Star and that the man with whom she traveled was now assumed to be her husband. That had happened quickly! But he had known already of the feelings of the two for each other, though they had not. If Hunting Hawk had been lost in the river, they would have been drawn together, depending more on each other for survival. This would have allowed them to discover their inner thoughts.

There was no doubt that Star would have appropriately mourned her husband. The young woman had a strong sense of tradition. In the custom of her people, the three days of mourning would be followed by a return to the ways of the living. It was the way of things. And after those three days, well, one must look ahead. Star had taught *him* that when they lost Plum Leaf.

He slept fitfully and awoke toward morning with a fever. Intermittently, he woke and slept, confused and disoriented. He did not travel at all that day but lay in his robes, delirious at times. He was forced to rest by the demands of his sick body, against his will.

When the sun rose the next morning, his thoughts were bright and clear, his understanding keen. Colors were more intense, the most puzzling things simple. *Aiee,* he should have thought of fasting before! It was exhilarating, wonderful! He could do anything.

He had never undertaken a vision quest, as some do. His coming into manhood had been distracted by travels and trade. Now he wished that he had tried it before, the fasting and spiritual growth. What a wonderful feeling, to understand all the world and be able to do *anything*! He could go on now and follow—whom was he supposed to follow? Oh, yes, Pale Star. He must help her! No matter, he would fly. That would be easier than walking. He should have thought of it before. Now that he could do anything, and do it instantly, there was no hurry, of course. He could fly on later. He fell asleep, still enjoying the prospect.

This was an extremely dangerous situation. The delirium brought on by fever was hopelessly mixed with the uplifting clarity of spirit produced by his fast. To undertake the fast of the vision quest, one must be in top physical and mental condition. He had been in neither and in addition had suffered the stress of a wet night in the cold rain. The unfortunate combination gave him delusions that were potentially destructive. What if, for instance, he had been camped near the edge of a precipice, convinced as he was that he could fly?

But this was flat, rolling land, the beginning of the

great grassland. And he did not have the strength to attempt flight, though he would not have believed it. In his delirium, he was invincible, immortal. He would accomplish whatever he wished when he got around to it.

Then, as the fever raged, he began to hallucinate. Plum Leaf walked into his camp—not thin and pale, as she had been in the last days on the river, but strong, healthy, and young again. That was good, for with his achievement of immortality . . .

She smiled at him and came close but would not let him touch her. There was a sweet-sad, sympathetic expression on her dear face, and then she faded and was gone, though he called after her.

Much later, he realized that there must have been a time when he hovered once more on the edge, about to cross over to the Other Side. His hallucinations peopled the air with disembodied spirits and strange half-real, half-spirit beings. He watched, rather enjoying the experience.

Then another figure walked out of the mists of his delirium to accost him. "Uncle, you must do something! You cannot just stay here. Where are you going?"

The voice and the content of the words were both familiar. Had this happened before?

"Star?" he asked. "Is it you?"

"You must decide, Uncle. I cannot plan for you. Get up now!" she scolded.

He struggled to his feet. The day was just dawning. Now, what . . . yes, he was supposed to go west. . . . He turned so that the warm rays of the rising sun struck him across the shoulders and shuffled forward.

Pale Star sat up in the robes with a gasp of surprise. It was near dawn.

"What is it, Star?" her husband asked sleepily.

"It is nothing," she said. "A dream."

"You jumped," he observed. "Are you all right?"

"Yes . . . yes, I think so. A strange dream, Sky-Eyes. I was with Traveler again."

Sky-Eyes was fully awake now. "The dream of the bad one, Three Owls?" he asked sympathetically.

"No, no." She smiled at him in the dim light. "I do not have that dream often now. This one I have not felt before."

She paused, puzzled. "I have told you of Plum Leaf, who became like a mother? When she died, on the river, Traveler gave up. He could not decide what to do. This dream was about that . . . no, not that. *Aiee,* I am confused, Sky-Eyes. I was talking to him, but not on the river. It was on the prairie!"

"But what . . . I do not understand, Star. A dream of the river, the prairie . . . What difference does it make?"

She thought for a moment. "I do not understand either. But in the dream, he needed me, as he did on the river!"

"But what difference?"

"Sky-Eyes, I do not know, but this dream, on the prairie. Traveler did not . . . *I was never with them on the prairie!* How could I dream of it?"

"One may dream of anything," her husband said thoughtfully. "Who knows?"

She nodded, still thoughtful. "Maybe I will ask Looks Far about it."

She snuggled back into the robes beside him and drew him close. "It is early," she whispered. "Let us stay here a little while."

47

The Growers found him when they reached the corn-field to begin the day's work. He was lying between the rows of growing plants where he had fallen. Fortunately, his fall had not damaged many of the tender young stalks.

At first they thought he was dead, but he moaned when they touched him. They carried him out of the field and placed him in the shade of a sycamore a few paces away. A couple of the young women stayed to minister to him, and the others went back to work. It had been assumed that the old man was dying. With his snowy hair, he appeared to be very old. He was very thin and weak, and had a high fever. However, the girls decided that this was a challenge. They cooled his brow, brought sips of water and broth in a gourd dipper, and he began to show more signs of life.

The village was astounded at the old man's will to live. He grew rapidly stronger. He was from a tribe far to the east, he told them, using hand-signs. That in itself was a bit remarkable. It was well known that the eastern people did not readily use hand-signs.

They asked him questions as he gained strength. His memory improved as his lungs cleared and a more healthy color began to return to his cheeks. He had been dead twice before this, he told them, once from an ax wound to the head, once from drowning. He did not know why it seemed impossible for him to cross over.

There was much discussion whether the old man was lying. Those who believed him had the weight of evidence on their side, in the livid ax wound over his right eye, that and their own observations on the day they found him. Surely he had been as near to death as one comes without crossing over.

He, in turn, began to ask questions. He was following, he said, a party of three people—a man and wife, and another man. "Have you seen them? The woman's husband has blind eyes, yet he sees."

Such a description was hard to put into hand-signs, so he was pleasantly surprised when they were able to answer. "Yes, they were here. The man's eyes *are* strange. He is called Sky-Eyes."

"Yes, that is the one. It goes well with them? Where did they go?"

"They said they were searching for her people, the Elk-dog People."

"You know the Elk-dog People?"

"Of course! They camped here for the winter."

"Ah! You speak their tongue?"

"Yes, Uncle. They trade with us, for many generations."

Now the stranger became quite excited. Haltingly at first, he tried some words in the tongue of the Elk-dog People.

"How is it," someone asked, "that you speak in this tongue?"

"I was taught by the woman, Pale Star," he answered eagerly.

"Ah, yes . . . she is a storyteller. How do you know her?"

"She is my almost-daughter."

"It is good! You are a storyteller too?"

"Yes. I will—"

"Wait, Uncle," interrupted an older woman. "You rest

now, and eat, and when you are stronger, you can tell us your stories."

"Yes, but . . . where did they go? I must follow them!"

"Not now, Uncle. Later. The Elk-dog people who camped here are their Eastern band. They go to their Sun Dance. You can find them."

"But how?"

"Start southwest . . . ask Growers."

"Of course."

"But now, Uncle, wait until you are stronger."

It was an impatient time for the Storyteller. He wanted to be traveling but knew that he was too weak. He did have the gratification of telling his stories once more, to people who were interested and appreciative.

In his own thoughts, however, he was becoming unsure of his mission. He had been certain that he had been denied the opportunity to cross over, had been spared from death twice—no, three times now. He had also been certain of the *reason:* to help Pale Star return to her people. Now it appeared that she had already done so, and without him. He must make certain, of course, that Star had actually made the contact, but beyond that, what was he to do? The driving urge to do right by the child he had purchased had dominated his existence for so long. What now? In his preoccupation, he had never thought beyond that point.

His time of recovery with the Growers gave him time to consider. Star was now a woman, restored to her people, and with a husband who appeared devoted to her. What now would be his own role? It was quite puzzling to him that he would be spared from crossing over, repeatedly, driven by the mission of helping Star, only to find that he was not needed at all. Ah, well, some things are not meant to be understood.

As soon as he was strong enough, he insisted on leaving. The Growers were quite helpful, telling him as much as they knew about the area where the Elk-dog People were holding their Sun Dance this season. It would be somewhere in their Sacred Hills, he was told, west of the River of Swans.

"Come and stay with us again, Uncle! We would hear more of your stories!" they urged.

"Maybe so . . . ," he agreed tentatively.

He was still unsure. He would be unable to trade or travel as he once had. Yet he could see a pattern developing. Twice he had been taken in, almost dead, by people who seemed willing to have him around merely to hear his stories. Maybe he could travel a little. He had no desire to go back to the region of his childhood, now so unsettled and dangerous. The part that had been good was gone.

So he traveled more slowly now than he had when he wore a younger man's moccasins. He found that he was feeling a thrill, an exhilaration over the tallgrass country, the Sacred Hills of Star's people. There was a special spirit here. It was rather like that of the country of his stepfather, Turtle, and the Trader-people. Yet it was different. He could not say how, but it was like nothing he had ever felt before. It was a spirit that was exciting and at the same time calming. He felt that he could understand the spirit of Earth, of all Creation, better than he had, ever before.

The sunrises and sunsets were glorious, spectacular beyond belief, seen above far horizons. He began to realize how important it had been to Star to return home, and *why*. He was a child of the woodlands, yet he was feeling a closeness, an understanding, a oneness with the land, that was more awe-inspiring than anything he had ever felt. It was, somehow, as if he had come home, though it was an area he had never seen before.

He found too that the urgency was gone from his mission. He must still find Star and assure himself that all was well with her, but the worry and concern were no longer there.

It was ten sleeps, maybe more, before he encountered two Wolves on horseback. He assumed that they were outriders from a traveling band. He stopped and held up his open right hand in the hand-sign of nonaggression.

"Ah-koh, Uncle," one of the warriors greeted him, using both hand-signs and speech. "How are you called?"

It took a moment for him to realize that the man was speaking the tongue of Star's Elk-dog People. He must be careful now. There was a moment of panic. He still did not want Star to see him in his present condition. He had not stopped to consider. How could he find Star's people without the risk of revealing himself to her? Well, it was too late now. Maybe she would not recognize him. She had not, that time in Mishi-ghan, face-to-face, so long ago.

"I am called Storyteller," he said in voice and hand-sign. "Your tribe is Elk-dog?"

"It is, Uncle. You speak our tongue?"

"Only a little. I speak many tongues."

The other nodded. "What is your tribe?"

"Ah, I have no tribe. I travel and tell stories."

He could see the expressions change a little on their faces. They thought him a little crazy. Well, maybe they were right. "Who is your chief?" he asked. "I would pay my respects."

"Red Feather," answered one of the Wolves. "Come, the band is just over the ridge there."

"Is it not time for your Sun Dance?"

"Aiee, Uncle, the Sun Dance is over! We are moving to summer camp."

He thought about that for a moment. These people must be moving northeast. That would mean that they were the Eastern band of their nation. He tried to remember. Had not Star spoken of hers as the Southern band?

The two men turned their horses now, and he walked between them, back toward the ridge. Maybe he could seek information.

"Yours is the Northern band?" he asked innocently.

"No, no, the Eastern, Uncle."

"Ah, yes . . . How many bands in your nation?"

"Five."

"Named for four winds, and . . . what?"

"No, no . . . there is no Western band. On the west, there are two, the Mountain and Red Rocks. Then the Northern, our own, and the Southern band. Why do you ask, Uncle?"

"I only wondered. I once knew someone of the Elk-dog People."

"Ah! How was he called?"

"I . . . it was long ago . . . *Aiee,* I cannot remember."

The other nodded sympathetically.

"I am made to think," said Storyteller carefully, "that he said his was the Elk-dog band. Could that be true?"

"Maybe. Our Southern band is sometimes called that, as well as the nation."

"Where will the other bands summer?" he asked, still fishing for information.

"Who knows? The Red Rocks have their own place. The Mountain band northwest. It is no matter. We will meet next year for the Sun Dance."

The Storyteller was somewhat familiar with the Sun Dance, the most holy of religious celebrations for the nations of the plains. "Was your Sun Dance a good one this year?" he asked.

"Yes. Very good. One of our women who was stolen as a child was returned to us!"

"Returned?"

"Yes! She made her way back to us. Brought two men. One, she married, here in our band."

"She was of your band?"

"No, no. The Southern band. But the other man—Woodchuck, he is called—he married one of our women, Pink Cloud, the daughter of our band chief, Red Feather."

"Then they are here? With your band?"

"No, Uncle. After the Sun Dance, they went on west, with the Red Rocks, to see the mountains. The one man, the one with strange eyes—he makes pictures in a stack of thin skins, like—"

"Yes, I have seen such a thing," Storyteller mused. "Some people call them talking leaves."

It had happened well, he thought. He had wondered how he could find out about Star without asking, and now it had just happened. And he did not have to worry about Star recognizing him. Not yet, anyway.

48

» » »

The Storyteller had been quickly welcomed by the people of the Eastern band. He had found a place and was quickly accepted. Storytelling was an art that was greatly honored here, and his old skills quickly found approval. His language skills improved, and as he became more at home, he began to pay more attention to detail— the effect of light and shadow, the flickering patterns of firelight on a lodgeskin, the background the observers would see *behind* him in the darkness.

The People loved it and responded to it. The wandering Traveler, now the Storyteller, had found a home. They had welcomed him. He had been taken into their lodges and into their hearts. The Eastern band of the Elk-dogs had never enjoyed the prestige of the others, he was told. The Real-chief, elected over the whole nation, was usually from the Northern band. The Southern band had been the first to acquire horses, several generations ago. The greatest of holy men in the nation was Looks Far, of the Southern band. And so it went. True, the new chief of the Eastern band, Red Feather, had distinguished himself as a young man in the war with the Blue Paints. That was why he had been elected chief upon the death of Small Ears.

But overall the Eastern band had had little to make them proud. The other bands scoffed and made jokes about their foolish ways. Red Feather had given them pride, but there was much resentment, even now.

The alliance was a natural one. The Eastern band welcomed the Storyteller at first merely because they liked his stories. Through the long moons of winter, however, he had become more greatly honored and more greatly appreciated. The People began to realize that they now had something special to share and boast of when the Sun Dance brought all the bands together. No other band had such a skilled storyteller. There had been none, in fact, since the death of the legendary Eagle, of the Southern band, generations ago.

But this man . . . *aiee,* he knew the stories of *all* nations. His strange appearance, the odd manner of his behavior, and the vagueness with which he spoke of his past all combined to create an aura of mystery. He had simply walked in out of the prairie, where no one should have been. He had been alone and on foot, and had calmly greeted the Wolves who discovered him. Some said he was crazy, of course, but it was no matter. There were also those who were convinced that he was some supernatural being. Maybe the Old Man of the Shadows himself!

The Storyteller himself was unaware of most of this, realizing only that he was respected and honored. This was reassuring and gave him confidence, and it was good.

So the winter passed quickly for the Eastern band, and it was almost a surprise when the Moon of Awakening arrived and the buds began to swell on the trees. The People looked forward to the Sun Dance and the opportunity to boast a little to the other bands of the tribe, to show off their Storyteller.

The Storyteller was somewhat concerned over this. He had never envisioned such acceptance that these people would want to boast about it. He wanted to see Pale Star —yes, of course. But he was still reluctant to let her see *him.*

* * *

It was in the Moon of Growing that they prepared to move to the area where the Sun Dance would be held. The French sergeant, now known as Woodchuck, came to the Eastern band with tragic news. His wife, the daughter of the band chief, had been killed in an accident during the spring hunt, far to the west. A wounded bull—the bereaved husband broke down in tears as he told the story. She had left an infant son, who was now in the lodge of Pale Star and Sky-Eyes. They would bring him to the Sun Dance, to be given to his grandparents to raise if they wished.

Red Feather's lodge, relatives, and friends of the dead woman began the ritual of mourning, which would last three days. Then, as they resumed the ways of the living, Woodchuck prepared to leave the band, to return to his own people in a far place called Mishi-ghan. It was apparent that he was not mourning well, holding in his grief, and it was hurting him badly.

Storyteller felt sorry for the young man and felt an unusual closeness to him. He knew how it felt to lose a beloved wife. He would have liked to talk to Woodchuck, not only to comfort him but to ask him about Star. He did not dare to do so. However, the two men did come into close proximity a number of times, and Woodchuck showed no sign of recognition.

With Star, it would be different. Though it had been several years, they had been very close. Could he trust that she would not recognize him? In a moon or two, he would see her at the Sun Dance. He considered asking Woodchuck if he could travel with him, back to Mishighan or to rejoin Pretty Flower. But no, he would stay with the Eastern band. He had found a place here among the people of Pale Star, even though it was a different band of Elk-dog People.

Woodchuck moved on, headed eastward, still appearing depressed and morose. It was as if the People should have mourned for *him*, so pitiful he seemed over his loss. He had been very popular with the People, having a gift for carving wood. Several people in the band possessed fetishes that had been carved by the Woodchuck. They would take pride in his work for generations. But now it seemed that they could not help him.

"Someday, maybe he will return," said Red Feather.

But now they must turn their attention to their own journey. They would meet the rest of the tribe at Turkey Creek for the Sun Dance. The day of departure was selected, and the People began to stow their belongings in rawhide pack bags for travel. Young horses, not yet accustomed to pulling baggage on pole-drags, were quickly taught their function. Heavy logs or pack-carriers filled with stones were lashed to the drag, and the animal was led or driven around the meadow to accustom it to the load.

It was shortly after dawn on the day of departure that the first of the big lodges came down, and by noon, the winter camp of the Eastern band was empty. Only a few worn-out garments and discarded belongings marked the site of the village. A dog or two hung behind to forage through the refuse as the caravan headed southwest across the rolling prairie.

The Storyteller had been living with a middle-aged couple, relatives of Red Feather. He rode at the side of Lizard while She-Elk rode the horse that pulled the pole-drag. This had been a good relationship. Their lodge had had no children, and the company of one such as the Storyteller was both interesting and a matter of prestige.

Storyteller was enjoying the sense of belonging, of being part of a family again. He had found that he also enjoyed the travel of a horse under the vastness of a prairie sky. He remembered the thrill of the buffalo hunts long ago with Turtle's people and his friend Gray Otter. He could not have participated in such a hunt now. He was stiff and sore, even after a day's slow travel. But the thrill was still there.

He was apprehensive about the Sun Dance meeting. There was no question but that he would see Pale Star.

His doubts had faded somewhat now. He had a measure of self-respect, which had been missing for years. He had reestablished himself as an honored storyteller. Despite his handicaps, he had done well at that. His garments, sewn and decorated by She-Elk or some of the other women, were new and of good quality. His hair, once wild, dirty, and unkempt, was now clean, well-groomed, and plaited in the style of the People. If he must meet Star now, it would be with a degree of pride and dignity. It would not be with helplessness, crippled and unable to talk, drooling from distorted lips. True, there was still considerable disability, but it was well controlled. And many things, though not controllable, are made less through pride and confidence. He filled his lungs with clean prairie air. It was almost like being young again.

A disturbing thought struck him. Suppose Pale Star would not *want* to recognize him? After all, their contact, which began when she was little more than a child—she had been traded like a horse. Tears filled his eyes, and he brushed them away with his good hand as he rode. The entire part of her life that related to him had been one long and varied tragedy.

No, he decided, he would wait. If she recognized him, so be it. He would try to explain. If not, he would say nothing. But either way, he decided, he had found his place with the People. The Traveler had come home to stay.

49

The Sun Dance was a glorious annual event for the People, partly religious, partly recreation, and partly social with the renewing of friendships and greeting of relatives. Parents who had exchanged their children with relatives of another band joyfully reclaimed their own. Everyone remarked about how each had grown in the intervening year and how much maturity each child now exhibited. The children reveled in the opportunity to display new skills and relate their experiences while with the lodge of a favorite aunt and uncle.

There were horse races, foot races, shooting contests, and gambling—something for everyone. Meanwhile, the preparations for the ceremonial Sun Dance went on.

There was the usual news of each band, accompanied by political rumor and gossip. The tragic story of the death of Pink Cloud, daughter of the Eastern band's chieftain, was one of the major items of discussion. The two outsiders, brought back by the returning Pale Star last season, had been popular and well liked. Both marriages had seemed good, and to have one end in tragedy . . . *aiee!* But that is the way of the world.

Pale Star, now large with child, handed Cloud's child to his grandparents. "He will always be mine, a little bit," she admitted.

"Of course," Red Feather agreed. "We will always think it so."

One story of some interest to Pale Star was of a new storyteller, an old man who had wandered in out of the prairie, said to be living with the Eastern band. He seemed to have no tribe but had adapted well to the ways of the People and was greatly respected. Some in the Eastern band declared without reservation that he was a reincarnation of the Old Man himself.

"But you know how *they* are," someone was always sure to say.

"Do not say that," Pale Star retorted. "They have done well under Red Feather."

"Of course," the other apologized, "but Star, you know . . ."

Yes, of course. It was tradition to make jokes about the Eastern band. An inept person, or one who suffered an illogical bit of bad luck, was chided with remarks like "Well, his grandmother was of the Eastern band."

But now this band had something to boast about—the finest storyteller seen for generations. It was almost enough to make up for the loss of one of their favorite daughters.

"Sky-Eyes, we must go and see this storyteller," Star told her husband. "Tonight, we will see. . . ."

The Storyteller had chosen a location that offered the dark background of rocky bluff and trees behind him for the stories. He had planned well, Star noted. The stark snowy whiteness of his hair stood out against the darkness across the stream as he began to talk.

"In long-ago times," he began, "when Earth was young and all the animals could talk, Bobcat had a long tail. . . ."

Star listened intently as the Storyteller wove the storylines skillfully, intertwining them, relating one to another.

"That is odd," she whispered to her husband. "I have never heard anyone tell that story but Traveler."

"The man who bought you?"

"Yes. But he was much younger."

"So were you!" Sky-Eyes chuckled.

He received an elbow in the ribs. "No, really, Sky-Eyes. This man is very skillful. I have always wondered. Could Traveler be alive?"

"But you said he was killed by Three Owls!"

"No, Winter Bear. I said I was *told* that. Let me—"

Just then, the Storyteller finished his tale. There was a murmur of approval.

Pale Star jumped to her feet, and strode forward. "It is good, Uncle," she began very formally, with no hint of recognition. "As these others know, I have traveled much. There is another Bobcat story which I have heard, from far east of here. Bobcat, as you have said, had a long tail . . ."

If the People had happened to look at that moment, they would have seen just a hint of a tear in the eye of the old man. But they would also have seen that he was smiling.

It was a strange lopsided smile, but a smile. A smile of . . . well, of something like *pride*!

About the Author
>> >> >>

DON COLDSMITH was born in Iola, Kansas, in 1926. He served as a World War II combat medic in the South Pacific and returned to his native state where he graduated from Baker University in 1949 and received his M.D. from the University of Kansas in 1958. He worked at several jobs before entering medical school: he was a YMCA group counselor, a gunsmith, a taxidermist, and, for a short time, a Congregational preacher. In addition to his private medical practice, Dr. Coldsmith is a staff physician at Emporia State University's Health Center, teaches in the English Department, and is active as a free-lance writer, lecturer, and rancher. He and his wife of 26 years, Edna, have raised five daughters.

Dr. Coldsmith produced the first ten novels in "The Spanish Bit Saga" in a five-year period; he writes and revises the stories first in his head, then in longhand. From this manuscript he reads aloud to his wife, whom he calls his "chief editor." Finally the finished version is skillfully typed by his longtime office receptionist.

Of his decision to create, or re-create, the world of the Plains Indian in the 16th through 18th centuries, the author says: "There has been very little written about this time period. I wanted also to portray these Native Americans as human beings, rather than as stereotyped 'Indians.' That word does not appear anywhere in the series—for a reason. As I have researched the time and place, the indigenous cultures, it's been a truly inspiring experience for me."